La Belle Sauvage

SPED LIKE A DART OVER THE MAD RIVER,

TOWARDS WHATEVER LAY BEYOND.

THE BOOK OF DUST

VOLUME ONE
LA BELLE SAUVAGE

ALSO BY PHILIP PULLMAN

HIS DARK MATERIALS

The Golden Compass

The Subtle Knife

The Amber Spyglass

Lyra's Oxford

Once Upon a Time in the North

The Collectors (an e-story)

The Golden Compass Graphic Novel

❧

SALLY LOCKHART MYSTERIES

The Ruby in the Smoke

The Shadow in the North

The Tiger in the Well

The Tin Princess

❧

The Broken Bridge

The White Mercedes

Count Karlstein

I Was a Rat!

The Scarecrow and His Servant

Spring-Heeled Jack

Two Crafty Criminals

THE BOOK OF DUST

VOLUME ONE

LA BELLE SAUVAGE

PHILIP PULLMAN

ALFRED A. KNOPF · NEW YORK

THIS IS A BORZOI BOOK PUBLISHED BY ALFRED A. KNOPF

Visit us on the Web! GetUnderlined.com

Educators and librarians, for a variety of teaching tools, visit us at RHTeachersLibrarians.com

Library of Congress Cataloging-in-Publication Data is available upon request.
ISBN 978-0-375-81530-0 (trade) — ISBN 978-0-553-51072-0 (lib. bdg.) —
ISBN 978-0-553-51073-7 (ebook)

The text of this book is set in 11.5-point Goudy Old Style.

Printed in the United States of America
October 2017
10 9 8 7 6 5 4 3 2 1

First Edition

TO JUDE

World is crazier and more of it than we think,
Incorrigibly plural. . . .
                    —Louis MacNeice, "Snow"

CONTENTS

THE
BOOK
OF
DUST

VOLUME ONE
LA BELLE SAUVAGE

ONE

THE TERRACE ROOM

Three miles up the river Thames from the center of Oxford, some distance from where the great colleges of Jordan, Gabriel, Balliol, and two dozen others contended for mastery in the boat races, out where the city was only a collection of towers and spires in the distance over the misty levels of Port Meadow, there stood the Priory of Godstow, where the gentle nuns went about their holy business; and on the opposite bank from the priory there was an inn called the Trout.

The inn was an old stone-built rambling, comfortable sort of place. There was a terrace above the river, where peacocks (one called Norman and the other called Barry) stalked among the drinkers, helping themselves to snacks without the slightest hesitation and occasionally lifting their heads to utter ferocious and meaningless screams. There was a saloon bar where the gentry, if college scholars count as gentry, took their ale and smoked their pipes; there was a public bar where watermen and farm laborers sat by the fire or played darts, or stood at the bar gossiping, or arguing, or simply getting quietly drunk; there was a kitchen where the landlord's wife cooked a great joint every day, with a complicated arrangement of wheels and chains turning a spit over an open fire; and there was a potboy called Malcolm Polstead.

Malcolm was the landlord's son, an only child. He was eleven years old, with an inquisitive, kindly disposition, a stocky build, and ginger hair. He went to Ulvercote Elementary School a mile away, and he had friends enough, but he was happiest on his own, playing with his dæmon, Asta, in their canoe, on which Malcolm had painted the name LA BELLE SAUVAGE. A witty acquaintance thought it amusing to scrawl an S over the V, and Malcolm patiently painted it out three times before losing his temper and knocking the fool into the water, at which point they declared a truce.

Like every child of an innkeeper, Malcolm had to work around the tavern, washing dishes and glasses, carrying plates of food or tankards of beer, retrieving them when they were empty. He took the work for granted. The only annoyance in his life was a girl called Alice, who helped with washing the dishes. She was about sixteen, tall and skinny, with lank dark hair that she scraped back into an unflattering ponytail. Lines of self-discontent were already gathering on her forehead and around her mouth. She teased Malcolm from the day she arrived: "Who's your girlfriend, Malcolm? En't you got a girlfriend? Who was you out with last night? Did you kiss her? En't you ever been kissed?"

He ignored that for a long time, but finally rat-formed Asta leapt at Alice's scrawny jackdaw dæmon, knocking him into the washing-up water and then biting and biting the sodden creature till Alice screamed for pity. She complained bitterly to Malcolm's mother, who said, "Serves you right. I got no sympathy for you. Keep your nasty mind to yourself."

From then on she did. She and Malcolm took not the slightest notice of each other; he put the glasses on the draining board, she washed them, and he dried them and took them back to the bar without a word, without a glance, without a thought.

But he enjoyed the life of the inn. He especially enjoyed the conversations he overheard, whether they concerned the venal rascality of the River Board, the helpless idiocy of the government, or more philosophical matters, such as whether the stars were the same age as the earth.

Sometimes Malcolm became so interested in the latter sort of conversation that he'd rest his armful of empty glasses on the table and join in, but only after having listened intently. He was known to many of the scholars and other visitors, and was generously tipped, but becoming rich was never an aim of his; he took tips to be the generosity of providence, and came to think of himself as lucky, which did him no harm in later life. If he'd been the sort of boy who acquired a nickname, he would no doubt have been known as Professor, but he wasn't that sort of boy. He was liked when noticed, but not noticed much, and that did him no harm either.

Malcolm's other constituency lay just over the bridge outside the tavern, in the gray stone buildings set among green fields and neat orchards and kitchen gardens of the Priory of St. Rosamund. The nuns were largely self-sufficient, growing their vegetables and fruit, keeping their bees, sewing the elegant vestments they sold for keenly bargained gold, but from time to time there were errands a useful boy could run, or there was a ladder to be repaired under the supervision of Mr. Taphouse, the aged carpenter, or some fish to bring from Medley Pond a little way down the river. *La Belle Sauvage* was frequently employed in the service of the good nuns; more than once Malcolm had ferried Sister Benedicta to the Royal Mail zeppelin station with a precious parcel of stoles or copes or chasubles for the bishop of London, who seemed to wear his vestments very hard, for he got through them unusually quickly. Malcolm learned a lot on these leisurely voyages.

"How d'you make them parcels so neat, Sister Benedicta?" he said one day.

"*Those* parcels," said Sister Benedicta.

"Those parcels. How d'you make 'em so neat?"

"Neatly, Malcolm."

He didn't mind; this was a sort of game they had.

"I thought 'neat' was all right," he said.

"It depends on whether you want the idea of neatness to modify the act of tying the parcel, or the parcel itself, once tied."

"Don't mind, really," said Malcolm. "I just want to know how you do 'em. Them."

"Next time I have a parcel to tie, I promise I'll show you," said Sister Benedicta, and she did.

Malcolm admired the nuns for their neat ways in general, for the manner in which they laid their fruit trees in espaliers along the sunny wall of the orchard, for the charm with which their delicate voices combined in singing the offices of the Church, for their little kindnesses here and there to many people. He enjoyed the conversations he had with them about religious matters.

"In the Bible," he said one day as he was helping elderly Sister Fenella in the lofty kitchen, "you know it says God created the world in six days?"

"That's right," said Sister Fenella, rolling some pastry.

"Well, how is it that there's fossils and things that are millions of years old?"

"Ah, you see, days were much longer then," said the good sister. "Have you cut up that rhubarb yet? Look, I'll be finished before you will."

"Why do we use this knife for rhubarb but not the old ones? The old ones are sharper."

4

"Because of the oxalic acid," said Sister Fenella, pressing the pastry into a baking tin. "Stainless steel is better with rhubarb. Pass me the sugar now."

"Oxalic acid," said Malcolm, liking the words very much. "What's a chasuble, Sister?"

"It's a kind of vestment. Priests wear them over their albs."

"Why don't you do sewing like the other sisters?"

Sister Fenella's squirrel dæmon, sitting on the back of a nearby chair, uttered a meek "Tut-tut."

"We all do what we're good at," said the nun. "I was never very good at embroidery—look at my great fat fingers!—but the other sisters think my pastry's all right."

"I like your pastry," said Malcolm.

"Thank you, dear."

"It's almost as good as my mum's. My mum's is thicker than what yours is. I expect you roll it harder."

"I expect I do."

Nothing was wasted in the priory kitchen. The little pieces of pastry Sister Fenella had left after trimming her rhubarb pies were formed into clumsy crosses or fish shapes, or rolled around a few currants, then sprinkled with sugar and baked separately. They each had a religious meaning, but Sister Fenella ("My great fat fingers!") wasn't very good at making them look different from one another. Malcolm was better, but he had to wash his hands thoroughly first.

"Who eats these, Sister?" he said.

"Oh, they're all eaten in the end. Sometimes a visitor likes something to nibble with their tea."

The priory, situated as it was where the road crossed the river, was popular with travelers of all kinds, and the nuns often had visitors to stay. So did the Trout, of course, and there were usually two or three guests staying at the inn overnight whose breakfast

Malcolm had to serve, but they were generally fishermen or commercials, as his father called them: traders in smokeleaf or hardware or agricultural machinery.

The guests at the priory were people from a higher class altogether: great lords and ladies, sometimes, bishops and lesser clergy, people of quality who didn't have a connection with any of the colleges in the city and couldn't expect hospitality there. Once there was a princess who stayed for six weeks, but Malcolm only saw her twice. She'd been sent there as a punishment. Her dæmon was a weasel who snarled at everyone.

Malcolm helped with these guests too: looked after their horses, cleaned their boots, took messages for them, and was occasionally tipped. All his money went into a tin walrus in his bedroom. You pressed its tail and it opened its mouth and you put the coin in between its tusks, one of which had been broken off and glued back on. Malcolm didn't know how much money he had, but the walrus was heavy. He thought he might buy a gun once he had enough, but he didn't think his father would allow him to, so that was something to wait for. In the meantime, he got used to the ways of travelers, both common and rare.

There was probably nowhere, he thought, where anyone could learn so much about the world as this little bend of the river, with the inn on one side and the priory on the other. He supposed that when he was grown up he'd help his father in the bar, and then take over the place when his parents grew too old to continue. He was fairly happy about that. It would be much better running the Trout than many other inns, because the great world came through, and scholars and people of consequence were often there to talk to. But what he'd really have liked to do was nothing like that. He'd have liked to be a scholar himself, maybe an astronomer or an experimental theologian, making discoveries about the deepest nature of things. To be a philosopher's apprentice—now, that would be a fine thing. But there was little likelihood of that; Ulvercote Elementary School prepared its pupils for craftsmanship or clerking, at best, before passing them out into the world at fourteen, and as far as Malcolm knew, there were no openings in scholarship for a bright boy with a canoe.

One evening in the middle of winter, some visitors came to the Trout who were out of the usual kind. Three men arrived by anbaric car and went into the Terrace Room, which was the smallest of all the dining rooms in the inn and overlooked the terrace and the river and the priory beyond. It lay at the end of the corridor and wasn't much used either in winter or summer, having small windows and no door out to the terrace, despite its name.

Malcolm had finished his meager homework (geometry) and wolfed down some roast beef and Yorkshire pudding, followed by a baked apple and custard, when his father called him to the bar.

"Go and see what those gents in the Terrace Room want," he said. "Likely they're foreign and don't know about buying their drinks at the bar. Want to be waited on, I expect."

Pleased by this novelty, Malcolm went down to the little room and found three gentlemen (he could tell their quality at a glance) all standing at the window and stooping to look out.

"Can I help you, gentlemen?" he said.

They turned at once. Two of them ordered claret, and the third wanted rum. When Malcolm came back with their drinks, they asked if they could get a dinner here, and if so, what the place had to offer.

"Roast beef, sir, and it's very good. I know because I just had some."

"Oh, *le patron mange ici,* eh?" said the oldest of the gentlemen as they drew up their chairs to the little table. His dæmon, a handsome black-and-white lemur, sat calmly on his shoulder.

"I live here, sir. The landlord's my father," said Malcolm. "And my mother's the cook."

"What's your name?" asked the tallest and thinnest of the visitors, a scholarly-looking man with thick gray hair, whose dæmon was a greenfinch.

"Malcolm Polstead, sir."

"What's that place over the river, Malcolm?" said the third, a man with large dark eyes and a black mustache. His dæmon, whatever she was, lay curled up on the floor at his feet.

It was dark by then, of course, and all they could see on the other side of the river were the dimly lit stained-glass windows of the oratory and the light that always shone over the gatehouse.

"That's the priory, sir. The sisters of the Order of St. Rosamund."

"And who was St. Rosamund?"

"I never asked them about St. Rosamund. There's a picture of her in the stained glass, though, sort of standing in a great big rose. I 'spect she's named after it. I'll have to ask Sister Benedicta."

"Oh, you know them well, then?"

"I talk to 'em every day, sir, more or less. I do odd jobs around the priory, run errands, that sort of thing."

"And do these nuns ever have visitors?" said the oldest man.

"Yes, sir, quite often. All sorts of people. Sir, I don't want to interfere, but it's ever so cold in here. Would you like me to light the fire? Unless you'd like to come in the saloon. It's nice and warm in there."

"No, we'll stay here, thank you, Malcolm, but we'd certainly like a fire. Do light it."

Malcolm struck a match, and the fire caught at once. His father was good at laying fires; Malcolm had often watched him. There were enough logs to last the evening, if these men wanted to stay.

"Lot of people in tonight?" said the dark-eyed man.

"I suppose there'd be a dozen or so, sir. About normal."

"Good," said the oldest man. "Well, bring us some of that roast beef."

"Some soup to start with, sir? Spiced parsnip today."

"Yes, why not? Soup all round, followed by your famous roast beef. And another bottle of this claret."

Malcolm didn't think the beef was really famous; that was just a way of talking. He left to get some cutlery and to place the order with his mother in the kitchen.

In his ear, Asta, in the form of a goldfinch, whispered, "They already knew about the nuns."

"Then why were they asking?" Malcolm whispered back.

"They were testing us, to see if we told the truth."

"I wonder what they want."

"They don't look like scholars."

"They do, a bit."

"They look like politicians," she insisted.

"How d'you know what politicians look like?"

"I just got a feeling."

Malcolm didn't argue with her; there were other customers to attend to, so he was busy, and besides, he believed in Asta's feelings. He himself seldom had that sort of feeling about people—if they were nice to him, he liked them—but his dæmon's intuitions had proved reliable many times. Of course, he and Asta were one being, so the intuitions were his anyway, as much as his feelings were hers.

Malcolm's father carried the food in to the three guests and opened their wine. Malcolm hadn't learned to manage three hot plates at once. When Mr. Polstead came back to the main bar, he beckoned Malcolm with a finger and spoke quietly.

"What did those gentlemen say to you?" he said.

"They were asking about the priory."

9

"They want to talk to you again. They said you were a bright boy. Mind your manners, now. You know who they are?"

Malcolm, wide-eyed, shook his head.

"That's Lord Nugent, that is—the old boy. He used to be the lord chancellor of England."

"How d'you know that?"

"I recognized him from his picture in the paper. Go on now. Answer all their questions."

Malcolm set off down the corridor, with Asta whispering, "See? Who was right, then? The lord chancellor of England, no less!"

The men were tucking into their roast beef (Malcolm's mother had given them an extra slice each) and talking quietly, but they fell silent as soon as Malcolm came in.

"I came to see whether you'd like another light, gentlemen," he said. "I can bring a naphtha lamp for the table, if you like."

"In a minute, Malcolm, that would be a very good idea," said the man who was the lord chancellor. "But tell me, how old are you?"

"Eleven, sir."

Perhaps he should have said *my lord*, but the ex–lord chancellor of England had seemed quite content with *sir*. Perhaps he was traveling incognito, in which case he wouldn't like to be given his right form of address anyway.

"And where do you go to school?"

"Ulvercote Elementary, sir, just across Port Meadow."

"What are you going to do when you grow up, d'you think?"

"Most probably I'll be an innkeeper, like my father, sir."

"Jolly interesting occupation, I should think."

"I think it is too, sir."

"All sorts of people passing through, and so on."

"That's right, sir. There's scholars from the university come here, and watermen from all over."

"You see a lot of what's going on, eh?"

"Yes, we do, sir."

"Traffic up and down the river, and such."

"It's mostly on the canal that there's the interesting stuff, sir. There's gyptian boats going up and down, and the horse fair in July—the canal's full of boats and travelers then."

"The horse fair . . . Gyptians, eh?"

"They come from all over to buy and sell horses."

The scholarly man said, "The nuns in the priory. How do they earn a living? Do they make perfumes, anything like that?"

"They grow a lot of vegetables," Malcolm said. "My mum always buys her vegetables and fruit from the priory. And honey. Oh, and they sew and embroider things for clergymen to wear. Chasubles and that. I reckon they must get paid a lot for them. They must have a bit of money because they buy fish from Medley Pond, down the river."

"When the priory has visitors," said the ex–lord chancellor, "what sort of people would they be, Malcolm?"

"Well, ladies, sometimes . . . young ladies . . . Sometimes an old priest or bishop, maybe. I think they come here for a rest."

"For a rest?"

"That's what Sister Benedicta told me. She said in the old days, before there was inns like this, and hotels, and specially hospitals, people used to stay at monasteries and priories and suchlike, but nowadays it was mostly clergymen or maybe nuns from other places and they were convales—conva—"

"Convalescing," said Lord Nugent.

"Yes, sir, that's it. Getting better."

The last man to finish his roast beef put his knife and fork together decisively. "Anyone there at the moment?" he said.

"I don't think so, sir. Unless they're indoors a lot. Usually visitors like to walk about in the garden, but the weather en't been very nice, so . . . Would you like your pudding now, gentlemen?"

"What is it?"

"Baked apple and custard. Apples from the priory orchard."

"Well, we can't pass up a chance to try those," said the scholarly man. "Yes, bring us some baked apples and custard."

Malcolm began to gather their plates and cutlery.

"Have you lived here all your life, Malcolm?" said Lord Nugent.

"Yes, sir. I was born here."

"And in all your long experience of the priory, did you ever know them to look after an infant?"

"A very young child, sir?"

"Yes. A child too young to go to school. Even a baby. Ever known that?"

Malcolm thought carefully and said, "No, sir, never. Ladies and gentlemen, or clergymen anyway, but never a baby."

"I see. Thank you, Malcolm."

By gathering the wineglasses together, their stems between his fingers, he managed to take all three of them as well as the plates.

"A baby?" whispered Asta on the way to the kitchen.

"That's a mystery," said Malcolm with satisfaction. "Maybe an orphan."

"Or worse," said Asta darkly.

Malcolm put the plates on the draining board, ignoring Alice as usual, and gave the order for pudding.

"Your father," said Malcolm's mother, dishing up the apples, "thinks one of those guests used to be the lord chancellor."

"You better give him a nice big apple, then," said Malcolm.

"What did they want to know?" she said, ladling hot custard over the apples.

"Oh, all about the priory."

"Are you going to manage those? They're hot."

"Yeah, but they're not big. I can do 'em, honest."

"You better. If you drop the lord chancellor's apple, you'll go to prison."

He managed the bowls perfectly well, even though they were getting hotter and hotter. The gentlemen didn't ask any questions this time, just ordering coffee, and Malcolm brought them a naphtha lamp before going through to the kitchen to set the cups up.

"Mum, you know the priory has guests sometimes? Did you ever know them to look after a baby?"

"What d'you want to know that for?"

"They were asking. The lord chancellor and the others."

"What did you tell 'em?"

"I said I didn't think so."

"Well, that's the right answer. Now go on—get out and bring in some more glasses."

In the main bar, under cover of the noise and laughter, Asta whispered, "She was startled when you asked that. I saw Kerin wake up and prick his ears."

Kerin was Mrs. Polstead's dæmon, a gruff but tolerant badger.

"It's just 'cause it was surprising," said Malcolm. "I 'spect you looked surprised when they asked me."

"I never. I was inscrutable."

"Well, I 'spect they saw *me* being surprised."

"Shall we ask the nuns?"

"Could do," said Malcolm. "Tomorrow. They need to know if someone's been asking questions about 'em."

TWO

THE ACORN

Malcolm's father was right: Lord Nugent had been lord chancellor, but that had been under a previous government, a more liberal body than the present one, and ruling at a more liberal time. These days the prevailing fashion in politics was one of obsequious submissiveness to the religious authorities, and ultimately to Geneva. As a consequence, some organizations of the favored religious kind found their power and influence greatly enhanced, while officials and ministers who had supported the secular line that was now out of favor had either to find other things to do, or to work surreptitiously, and at continuous risk of discovery.

Such a man was Thomas Nugent. To the world, to the press, to the government, he was a retired lawyer of fading distinction, yesterday's man, of no interest. In fact, he was directing an organization that functioned very like a secret service, which not many years before had been part of the security and intelligence services of the Crown. Now, under Nugent, its activities were devoted to frustrating the work of the religious authorities, and to remaining obscure and apparently harmless. This took ingenuity, courage, and luck, and so far they had remained undetected. Under an innocent and misleading name, Nugent's organization carried out all kinds of missions, dangerous, complicated, tedious, and sometimes downright illegal. But it had never before had to deal with keeping a six-month-old baby out of the hands of those who wanted to kill her.

On Saturday, Malcolm was free, once he'd done his morning tasks at the Trout, to cross the bridge and call at the priory.

He knocked on the kitchen door and went in to find Sister Fenella scraping some potatoes. There was a neater way to deal with potatoes, as he knew from his mother's example, and given a sharp knife, Malcolm could have shown the good nun, but he held his peace.

"Have you come to help me, Malcolm?" she said.

"If you like. But I was really going to tell you something."

"You could prepare those Brussels sprouts."

"All right," said Malcolm, finding the sharpest knife in the drawer and pulling several sprout stalks across the table in the pale February sunlight.

"Don't forget the cross in the base," said Sister Fenella.

She had told him once that this put the mark of the Savior on each sprout and made sure the Devil couldn't get in. Malcolm was impressed by that at the time, but he knew now that it was to help them cook all the way through. His mother had explained that, and said, "But don't you go and contradict Sister Fenella. She's a sweet-hearted old lady, and if she wants to think that, don't upset her."

Malcolm would have put up with a good deal rather than upset Sister Fenella, whom he loved with a deep and uncomplicated devotion.

"Now, what were you going to tell me?" she said as Malcolm settled on the old stool beside her.

"You know who we had in the Trout the other night? There was three gentlemen taking their dinner, and one of them was Lord Nugent, the lord chancellor of England. Ex–lord chancellor. And that's not all. They were looking across here to the priory and they were ever so curious. They asked all kinds of questions—what sort of nuns you were, whether you had any guests here, what kind of people they were—and finally they asked if you'd ever had a baby staying—"

"An infant," put in Asta.

"Yeah, an infant. Have you ever had an infant staying here?"

Sister Fenella stopped scraping. "The lord chancellor of England?" she said. "Are you sure?"

"Dad was, because he saw his picture in the paper and recognized him. They wanted to eat by theirselves in the Terrace Room."

"The lord chancellor himself?"

"Ex–lord chancellor. Sister Fenella, what does the lord chancellor do?"

"Oh, he's very high up, very important. I wouldn't be surprised if he had something to do with the law. Or the government. Was he very grand and proud?"

"No. He was a gentleman, all right, it was easy to tell that, but he was nice and friendly."

"And he wanted to know . . ."

"If you'd ever had an infant staying at the priory. I 'spect he meant staying here to be looked after."

"And what did you tell him, Malcolm?"

"I said I didn't think so. Have you, ever?"

"Not in my time. Goodness me! I wonder if I ought to tell Sister Benedicta."

"Prob'ly. What I thought was, he might be looking for somewhere to put an important infant, if it was convalescing, maybe. Maybe there's a royal infant that we don't know about because it was ill, right, or maybe got bitten by a snake—"

"Why bitten by a snake?"

"'Cause its nursemaid wasn't paying attention, prob'ly reading a magazine or talking to someone, and this snake comes along and there's a sudden scream and she turns round and there's the baby with a snake hanging off it. She'd be in awful trouble, the nursemaid—she might even go to prison. And when the baby was cured of the snakebite, it'd still need convalescing. So the king and the prime minister and the lord chancellor would all be looking for somewhere to convalesce it. And naturally they wouldn't want a place that had no experience of babies."

"Yes, I see," said Sister Fenella. "That all makes sense. I think I really ought to tell Sister Benedicta, at least. She'll know what to do."

"I should think that if they were serious, they'd come and ask here. I mean, we see a lot in the Trout, but the real people to ask would be here, wouldn't they?"

"Unless they didn't want us to know," said Sister Fenella.

"But they asked if I ever spoke to you, and I said I did, quite a lot, being as how I work for you. So they'd expect me to say something, and they didn't ask me not to."

"That's a good point," said Sister Fenella, and she dropped the last scraped potato into the big saucepan. "It does sound curious, though. Perhaps they'll write to the Lady Prioress rather than call in person. I wonder if it's really sanctuary they're asking about."

"Sanctuary?" Malcolm liked the sound of the word, and he could see how to spell it already, in his imagination. "What's that?"

"Well, if somebody broke the law and was being hunted by the authorities, they could go into an oratory and claim sanctuary. That means that they'd be safe from arrest as long as they stayed there."

"But that baby couldn't have broken the law. Not yet anyway."

"No. But it was for refugees too. People who were in danger through no fault of their own. No one could arrest them if they

17

were in sanctuary. Some of the colleges used to be able to give sanctuary to scholars. I don't know if they still do."

"It wouldn't be a scholar either—the baby, I mean. D'you want me to do all these sprouts?"

"All but two stalks. We'll keep them for tomorrow."

Sister Fenella gathered up the discarded sprout leaves and cut the stalks in half a dozen pieces and put them in a bin for stock.

"What are you going to do today, Malcolm?" she said.

"I'm going to take my canoe out. The river's a bit high, so I'll prob'ly have to be careful, but I want to clean it out and make it shipshape."

"Are you planning any long voyages?"

"Well, I'd like to. But I can't leave Mum and Dad, because they need my help."

"They'd be anxious about you too."

"I'd send letters."

"Where would you go?"

"Down the river all the way to London. Maybe as far as the sea. I don't suppose my boat'd be very good at a sea voyage, though. She might overturn in a big wave. I might have to tie her up and go on in a different boat. I will one day."

"Will you send us a postcard?"

"Course I will. Or you could come with me."

"Who'd cook for the sisters, then?"

"They could have picnics. Or eat at the Trout."

She laughed and clapped her hands. In the weak light that came through the dusty windows, Malcolm saw how chapped and cracked the skin of her fingers was, how red and raw. Every time she puts them in hot water it must hurt, he thought, but he had never heard her complaining.

* * *

That afternoon, Malcolm went to the lean-to beside the house and hauled the tarpaulin off his canoe. He inspected it from stem to stern, scraping off the green slime that had accumulated during the winter, examining every inch. Norman the peacock came along to see if there was anything to eat, and shook his feathers with a rattle of displeasure when he found there wasn't.

All the timbers of *La Belle Sauvage* were sound, though the paint was beginning to peel, and Malcolm thought he might scrape off the old name and go over it again, better. It was in green, but red would stand out more clearly. Maybe he could do a few odd jobs for the boatyard at Medley in exchange for a small tin of red paint. He pulled the canoe down the sloping lawn to the river's edge and half thought of going down the river right then and bargaining, but put that aside for another day and instead paddled upstream a little way before turning right into Duke's Cut, one of the streams that connected the river and the Oxford Canal.

He was in luck: there was a narrowboat about to enter the lock, so he slipped in beside it. Sometimes he'd had to wait for an hour, trying to persuade Mr. Parsons to operate the lock just for him, but the lockkeeper was a stickler for the regulations, as well as for not doing more work than was necessary. He didn't mind Malcolm having a ride up or down if there was another boat going through, though.

"Where you off to, Malcolm?" he called down as the water gushed out at the far end and the level sank.

"Going fishing," Malcolm called back.

It was what he usually said, and sometimes it was true. Today, though, he couldn't get that tin of red paint out of his mind, and he thought he'd paddle along to the chandlery in Jericho, just to get an idea of the price. Of course, they might not have any, but he liked the chandlery anyway.

Once on the canal, he paddled steadily down past garden allotments and school playing fields until he came to the northern edge of Jericho: small terraces of brick houses where the workers from the Fell Press or the Eagle Ironworks lived with their families. The area was half-gentrified now, but it still held old corners and dark alleys, an abandoned burial ground and a church with an Italianate campanile standing guard over the boatyard and the chandlery.

There was a towpath on the western side of the water—Malcolm's right—but it needed clearing. Water plants grew thickly at the edge, and as Malcolm slowed down, his eye was caught by a movement among the reeds. He let the canoe drift to a halt and then silently slipped in among the stiff stems and watched as a great crested grebe scrambled up onto the towpath, waddled ungracefully across, and then dropped into the little backwater on the other side. Keeping as quiet as he could and moving very slowly, Malcolm wedged the canoe even deeper into the reeds and watched the bird shake its head and paddle across the water to join its mate.

Malcolm had heard that there were great crested grebes here, but he'd only half believed it. Now he had proof. He'd definitely come back a little later in the year and see if they were breeding.

The reeds were taller than he was as he sat in the canoe, and if he kept very still, he thought he probably couldn't be seen. He heard voices behind him, a man's and a woman's, and sat like a statue as they walked past, absorbed in each other. He'd passed them further back: two lovers strolling hand in hand, their dæmons, two small birds, flying ahead a little way, pausing to whisper together, and flying on again.

Malcolm's dæmon, Asta, was a kingfisher just then, perching on the gunwale of the canoe. When the lovers had passed, she flew up to his shoulder and whispered, "The man just along there—watch. . . ."

Malcolm hadn't seen him. A few yards ahead on the towpath,

just visible through the reed stems, a man in a gray raincoat and trilby hat was standing under an oak tree. He looked as if he was sheltering from the rain, except that it wasn't raining. His coat and hat were almost exactly the color of the late afternoon: he was almost as hard to see as the grebes—harder, in fact, thought Malcolm, because he didn't have a crest of feathers.

"What's he doing?" whispered Malcolm.

Asta became a fly and flew as far as she could from Malcolm, stopping when it began to hurt, and settled at the very top of a bulrush so she could watch the man clearly. He was trying to remain inconspicuous, but being so awkward and unhappy about it that he might as well have been waving a flag.

Asta saw his dæmon—a cat—moving among the lowest branches of the oak tree while he stood below and looked up and down the towpath. Then the cat made a quiet noise, the man looked up, and she jumped down to his shoulder—but in doing so, she dropped something out of her mouth.

The man uttered a little grunt of dismay, and his dæmon scrambled to the ground. They began to cast around, looking under the tree, at the edge of the water, among the scrubby grass.

"What did she drop?" Malcolm whispered.

"Like a nut. About the size of a nut."

"Did you see where it went?"

"I think so. I think it bounced off the bottom of the tree and went under the bush there. Look, they're pretending not to look for it. . . ."

They were too. Someone else was coming along the path, a man and his dog dæmon, and while the man in the raincoat waited for them to pass, he pretended to be looking at his watch, shaking his wrist, listening to it, shaking his wrist again, taking the watch off, winding it. . . . As soon as the other man had gone past, the raincoat man fastened the watch on his wrist again and went back to looking for the object his dæmon had dropped. He was anxious—it was easy to see that—and his dæmon had apology in every line of her body. Between the two of them, they looked the picture of distress.

"We could go and help," said Asta.

Malcolm was torn. He could still see the grebes, and he very much wanted to watch them, but the man seemed as if he needed help, and Malcolm was sure Asta's eyes would find the thing, whatever it was. It would only take a minute or so.

But before he had the chance to do anything, the man bent and scooped up his cat dæmon and made off quite quickly down the towpath, as if he'd decided to go and get help. At once Malcolm backed the canoe out of the reeds and sped towards the spot under the oak tree where the man had been standing. A moment later he'd jumped out, holding the painter, and Asta in the shape of a mouse shot across the path and under the bush. A rustling of leaves, a silence, more rustling, more silence while Malcolm watched the man reach the little iron footbridge to the piazza and climb the steps. Then a squeak of excitement told Malcolm that Asta had found it, and squirrel-formed, she came racing back, up his arm and onto his shoulder, and dropped something into his hand.

"It must be this," she said. "It *must* be."

At first sight it was an acorn, but it was oddly heavy, and when he looked more closely, he saw that it was carved out of a piece of tight-grained wood. Two pieces, in fact: one for the cup, whose surface was carved into an exact replica of the rough overlapping scales of a real one and stained very lightly with green, and one for the nut, which was polished and waxed a perfect glossy light brown. It was beautiful, and she was right: it had to be the thing the man had lost.

"Let's catch him before he gets across the bridge," he said, and put his foot down into the canoe, but Asta said, "Wait. Look."

She'd become an owl, which she always did when she wanted to see something clearly. Her flat face was looking down the canal, and as Malcolm followed her gaze, he saw the man reach the middle of the footbridge and hesitate, because another man had stepped up from the other side, a stocky man dressed in black with a light-stepping vixen dæmon, and Malcolm and Asta could see that the second man was going to stop the raincoat man, and the raincoat man was afraid.

They saw him turn and take a hasty step or two and then stop again, because a third man had appeared on the bridge behind him. He was thinner than the other man, and he too was dressed in black. His dæmon was a large bird of some kind on his shoulder. Both of the men looked full of confidence, as if they had plenty of time to do whatever they wanted. They said something to the raincoat man, and each took one of his arms. He struggled for a futile moment or two, and then seemed to sag downwards, but they held him up and walked him across the bridge, into the little piazza below the church tower, and away out of sight. His cat dæmon hurried after them, abject and desperate.

"Put it in your insidest pocket," Asta whispered.

Malcolm put the acorn into the inside breast pocket of his jacket and then sat down very carefully. He was trembling.

"They were arresting him," he whispered.

"They weren't police."

"No. But they weren't robbers. They were sort of calm about it, as if they were allowed to do anything they wanted."

"Just go home," said Asta. "In case they saw us."

"They weren't even bothering to look," said Malcolm, but he agreed with her: they should go home.

They spoke quietly together while he paddled quickly back towards Duke's Cut.

"I bet he's a spy," she said.

"Could be. And those men—"

"CCD."

"Shh!"

The CCD was the Consistorial Court of Discipline, an agency of the Church concerned with heresy and unbelief. Malcolm didn't know much about it, but he knew the sense of sickening terror the CCD could produce, through hearing some customers once discuss what might have happened to a man they knew, a journalist; he had asked too many questions about the CCD in a series of articles and had suddenly vanished. The editor of his paper had been arrested and jailed for sedition, but the journalist himself had never been seen again.

"We mustn't say anything about this to the sisters," said Asta.

"Specially not to them," Malcolm agreed.

It was hard to understand, but the Consistorial Court of Discipline was on the same side as the gentle sisters of Godstow Priory, sort of. They were both parts of the Church. The only time Malcolm had seen Sister Benedicta distressed was when he'd asked her about it one day.

"These are mysteries we mustn't inquire into, Malcolm," she'd said. "They're too deep for us. But the Holy Church knows the will of God and what must be done. We must continue to love one another and not ask too many questions."

The first part was easy enough for Malcolm, who was fond of most things he knew, but the second part was harder. However, he didn't ask any more about the CCD.

It was nearly dark when they reached home. Malcolm dragged *La Belle Sauvage* out of the water and under the lean-to at the side of the inn and hurried inside, his arms aching, and raced up to his bedroom.

Dropping his coat on the floor and kicking his shoes under the bed, he switched on the bedside light while Asta struggled to pull the acorn out of the insidest pocket. When Malcolm had it in his hand, he turned it over and over, examining it closely.

"Look at the way this is carved!" he said, marveling.

"Try opening it."

He was doing that as she spoke, gently twisting the acorn in its cup without any success. It didn't unscrew, so he tried harder, and then tried to pull it, but that didn't work either.

"Try twisting the other way," said Asta.

"That would just do it up tighter," he said, but he tried, and it worked. The thread was the opposite way.

"I never seen that before," said Malcolm. "Strange."

So neatly and finely made were the threads that he had to turn it a dozen times before the two parts fell open. There was a piece of paper inside, folded up as small as it could go: that very thin kind of paper that Bibles were printed on.

Malcolm and Asta looked at each other. "This is someone else's secret," he said. "We ought not to read it."

He opened it all the same, very carefully so as not to tear the delicate paper, but it wasn't delicate at all: it was tough.

"Anyone might have found it," said Asta. "He's lucky it was us."

"Luckyish," said Malcolm.

"Anyway, he's lucky he hadn't got it on him when he was arrested."

Written on the paper in black ink with a very fine pen were the words:

> We would like you to turn your attention next to another
> matter. You will be aware that the existence of a Rusakov
> field implies the existence of a related particle, but so far such
> a particle has eluded us. When we try measuring one way,

*our substance evades it and seems to prefer another, but
when we try a different way, we have no more success. A
suggestion from Tokojima, although rejected out of hand by
most official bodies, seems to us to hold some promise, and
we would like you to inquire through the alethiometer about
any connection you can discover between the Rusakov field
and the phenomenon unofficially called Dust. We do not
have to remind you of the danger should this research attract
the attention of the other side, but please be aware that they
are themselves beginning a major program of inquiry into this
subject. Tread carefully.*

"What does it mean?" said Asta.

"Something to do with a field. Like a magnetic field, I s'pose. They sound like experimental theologians."

"What d'you think they mean by 'the other side'?"

"The CCD. Bound to be, since it was them chasing the man."

"And what's an aleth—an althe—"

"Malcolm!" came his mother's voice from downstairs.

"Coming," he called, and folded the paper back along the same creases before putting it carefully back in the acorn and screwing it shut. He put it inside one of the clean socks in his chest of drawers and ran down to start the evening's work.

Saturday evening was always busy, of course, but today conversation was subdued: there was a mood of nervous caution in the place, and people were quieter than usual as they stood at the bar or sat at their tables playing dominoes or shove-ha'penny. In a moment of pause, he asked his father why.

"Shh," said his father, leaning over the bar. "Those two men by the fire. CCD. Don't look now. Mind what you say near them."

26

Malcolm felt a shiver of fear that was almost audible, like the tip of a drumstick drawn across a cymbal.

"How d'you know that's what they are?"

"The colors of his tie. Anyway, you can just tell. Watch other people around them— Yes, Bob, what can I get you?"

While his father pulled a couple of pints for a customer, Malcolm gathered empty glasses in a suitably inconspicuous manner, and he was glad to see that his hands remained steady. Then he felt a little jolt of Asta's fear. She was a mouse on his shoulder, and she had looked directly at the men by the fire and seen that they were looking at her, and they *were* the men from the bridge.

And then one of them beckoned with a crooked finger.

"Young man," he said. He was addressing Malcolm.

Malcolm turned his head and looked at them properly for the first time. The speaker was a stoutish man with deep brown eyes: the first man from the bridge.

"Yes, sir?"

"Come here a minute."

"Can I get you anything, sir?"

"Maybe, maybe not. I'm going to ask a question now, and you're going to tell me the truth, aren't you?"

"I always do, sir."

"No, you don't. No boy always tells the truth. Come here— come a bit closer."

He wasn't speaking loudly, but Malcolm knew that everyone nearby—and his father, especially—would be listening intently. He went where the man beckoned and stood near his chair, noticing the scent of cologne that emanated from him. The man was wearing a dark suit and a white shirt, with a navy-blue-and-ocher-striped tie. His vixen dæmon lay at his feet, her eyes wide open and watching.

"Yes, sir?"

"I reckon you notice most people who come in here, don't you?"

"I reckon so, sir."

"You know the regulars?"

"Yes, sir."

"You'd know a stranger?"

"Probably I would, sir."

"Now, then, a few days ago, I wonder if you saw this man come into the Trout."

He held up a photogram. Malcolm recognized the face at once. It was one of the men who'd come with the lord chancellor: the dark-eyed man with the black mustache.

So perhaps this wasn't going to be about the man on the towpath and the acorn. He kept his expression stolid and bland.

"Yes, I saw him, sir," said Malcolm.

"Who was he with?"

"Two other men, sir. One oldish, and one tall and sort of scholarly."

"Did you recognize either of them? Seen them in the paper, anything like that?"

"No, I didn't, sir," said Malcolm, slowly shaking his head. "I didn't recognize any of them."

"What did they talk about?"

"Well, I don't like to listen to customers' conversations, sir. My dad told me it's rude, so—"

"You can't help overhearing things, though, can you?"

"No, that's true."

"So what did you overhear them say?"

The speaker's tone had become quieter and quieter, drawing Malcolm closer. Conversation at the nearby table had nearly ceased, and he knew that everything he said would be audible as far as the bar.

"They talked about the claret, sir. They said how good it was. They ordered a second bottle with their dinner."

"Where were they sitting?"

"In the Terrace Room, sir."

"And where's that?"

"Down that corridor. It's a bit cold in there, so I said they might like to come in here by the fire, but they didn't want to."

"And did you think that a bit odd?"

"Customers do all kinds of things, sir. I don't think about it much."

"So they wanted a bit of privacy?"

"It might have been that, sir."

"Have you seen any of the men since?"

"No, sir."

The man tapped his fingers on the table.

"And what's your name?" he said after a pause.

"Malcolm, sir. Malcolm Polstead."

"All right, Malcolm. Off you go."

"Thank you, sir," said Malcolm, trying to keep his voice steady.

Then the man raised his voice a little and looked around. As soon as he spoke, everyone else fell silent in a moment, as if they'd been waiting for it to happen.

"You've heard what I've been asking young Malcolm here. There's a man we're eager to trace. I'm going to pin his picture up on the wall beside the bar in a minute, so you can all have a look at it. If any of you know anything about this man, get in touch with me. My name and address are on the paper too. Mind what I say. This is an important matter. You understand that. Anybody wants to talk to me about this man, they can come and do so once they've looked at the picture. I'll be sitting here."

The other man took the piece of paper and pinned it on the corkboard, where the notices of dances, auction sales, whist drives, and so on were displayed. To make room, he tugged down a couple of other notices without looking at what they were.

"Hey," said a man standing nearby, whose big dog dæmon was bristling. "You put them notices back up, what you just pulled down."

The CCD man turned to look at him. His crow dæmon opened her wings and uttered a soft "Kaark."

"What did you say?" said the first CCD man, the one who'd stayed by the fire.

"I said to your mate, Put them notices back, what you just pulled down. This is our notice board in here, not yours."

Malcolm drew back towards the wall. The customer who'd spoken was called George Boatwright, a high-colored and truculent boatman whom Mr. Polstead had had to throw out of the Trout half a dozen times; but he was a fair man, and he'd never spoken roughly to Malcolm. The silence in the bar now was profound, and even customers in other parts of the inn had become aware that something was happening, and had come to the doorway to watch.

"Steady, George," murmured Mr. Polstead.

The first CCD man took a sip of his brantwijn. Then he looked at Malcolm and said, "Malcolm, what's that man's name?"

But before Malcolm could even think what to say, Boatwright himself answered in a loud, hard voice: "George Boatwright is my name. Don't try and put the boy on the spot. That's the way of a coward."

"George—" said Mr. Polstead.

"No, Reg, I'll speak for meself," said Boatwright. "And I'll do this too," he added, "since your sour-faced friend don't seem to have heard me."

He reached up to the wall, tore down the paper, and crumpled it up before throwing it into the fire. Then he stood, swaying slightly, in the middle of the room and glared at the chief CCD man. Malcolm admired him greatly at that moment.

Then the CCD man's vixen dæmon stood up. She trotted elegantly out from under the table and stood with her brush sticking straight out behind her and her head perfectly still, looking Boatwright's dæmon in the eye.

Boatwright's dæmon, Sadie, was much bigger. She was a tough-looking mongrel, part Staffordshire terrier, part German shepherd—part wolf, for all Malcolm knew—and now, by the look of things, spoiling for a fight. She stood close by Boatwright's legs with all her fur bristling, her lips drawn back, her tail slowly swinging, a deep growl like distant thunder coming from her throat.

Asta crept inside Malcolm's collar. Fights between grown-up dæmons were not unknown, but Mr. Polstead never allowed anything to get that far inside the inn.

"George, you better leave now," he said. "Go on, hop it. Come back when you're sober."

Boatwright turned his head blurrily, and Malcolm saw to his dismay that the man was indeed a little drunk, because he was slightly off balance and had to take a step to right himself—but then everyone saw the same thing: it wasn't the drink in Boatwright, it was the fear in his dæmon.

Something had terrified her. That brutal bitch whose teeth had met in the pelts of several other dæmons was cowering, quivering, whimpering, as the vixen slowly advanced. Boatwright's dæmon fell to the floor and rolled over, and Boatwright was cringing back, trying to hold his dæmon, trying to avoid the deadly white teeth of the vixen.

The CCD man murmured a name. The vixen stood still, and then backed away a step. Boatwright's dæmon lay curled up on the floor, trembling, and Boatwright's expression was piteous. In fact, after one glance Malcolm preferred not to look, so as not to see Boatwright's shame.

The trim little vixen trotted neatly back to the table and lay down.

"George Boatwright, go and wait outside," said the CCD man, and such was the dominance he had now that no one thought for a moment that Boatwright would disobey and take off. Stroking and half lifting his dæmon, who snapped at him and drew blood from his trembling hand, Boatwright made his miserable way to the door and through to the dark outside.

The second CCD man produced another notice from his brief-case and pinned it up like the first one. Then the two of them finished their drinks, taking their time, and gathered their coats before going out to deal with their abject prisoner. No one said a word.

THREE

LYRA

It turned out that instead of waiting obediently for the CCD men to come out and take him away, George Boatwright had vanished. Good for him, thought Malcolm, but no one talked about it or wondered aloud what had happened to him. That was the way of things with the CCD: it was better not to ask, better not to think about it.

The atmosphere in the Trout was subdued for some days afterwards. Malcolm went to school, did his homework, fetched and carried at the inn, and read over and over again the secret message in the acorn. It wasn't an easy time; everything seemed hung about with an unhappy air of suspicion and fear, quite unlike the normal world, as Malcolm thought of it, the place he was used to living in, where everything was interesting and happy.

Besides, the CCD man had been asking about the lord chancellor's companion, and *his* interest had been in the matter of whether the priory had ever looked after an infant; and Malcolm thought that the care of infants was probably not the sort of thing the CCD usually bothered with. Acorns containing secret messages, perhaps, but they hadn't mentioned anything like that. It was all very puzzling.

In the hope of seeing someone else either leaving or collecting a message from the oak tree, Malcolm went there several times over the next few days, covering up his interest in that little stretch of the canal by watching the great crested grebes. The other thing he did was to hang about in the chandlery. It was a good place to watch the piazza; people were always going back and forth or stopping to drink coffee in the café opposite. They sold all kinds of boat-related stuff in the chandlery, including red paint, of which he bought a small tin and a fine brush to go with it. The woman behind the counter soon realized that his interest didn't stop at red paint.

"What else you looking for, Malcolm?" she said. Her name was Mrs. Carpenter, and she'd known him ever since he was allowed to go out in the canoe on his own.

"Some cotton cord," he said.

"I showed you what we've got yesterday."

"Yes, but maybe there's another reel somewhere . . ."

"I don't understand what's wrong with the one I showed you."

"It's too thin. I want to make a lanyard, and it's got to be a bit heavier than that."

"You could always double it. Use two strands instead of one."

"Oh, yeah. I suppose I could."

"How much d'you want, then?"

"About four fathoms."

"Doubled, or single?"

"Well, eight fathoms. That should be enough if I double it."

"I should think it would be," she said, and measured the cord and cut it.

It was a good thing Malcolm had plenty of money in his tin walrus. Once he'd got the cord stowed away tidily in a big paper bag, he peered out the window, looking left and right, as he'd been doing for the previous quarter of an hour.

"Don't mind me asking," said Mrs. Carpenter, and her drake dæmon murmured in agreement, "but what are you looking for? You been staring out there for ever such a long time. You meeting someone? They not turned up?"

"No! No. Actually . . ." If he couldn't trust Mrs. Carpenter, he thought, he couldn't trust anyone. "Actually, I'm looking for someone. A man in a gray coat and hat. I saw him the other day and he dropped something and we found it, and I want to give it back to him, but I haven't seen him since."

"That's all you can tell me about him? A gray coat and hat? How old was he?"

"I didn't see him clearly. I suppose he was about the same age as my dad. He was kind of thin."

"Where did he drop this thing you've got? Along the canal?"

"Yes. Under a tree back down the towpath . . . It's not important."

"It's not this chap, is it?"

Mrs. Carpenter brought the latest *Oxford Times* out from under the counter and folded it back to an inside page before holding it out for Malcolm to see.

"Yes, I think that's him. . . . What's happened? What's . . . He's been *drowned?*"

"They found him in the canal. Looked as if he'd just slipped in, apparently. You know how rainy it's been, and they don't look after the towpath as they ought to—he's not the first to lose his footing and fall in. Whatever he lost, it's too late to give it back now."

Malcolm was reading the story with wide eyes, gulping the words down. The man's name was Robert Luckhurst, and he'd been a scholar of Magdalen College, an historian. He was unmarried, and was survived by his widowed mother and a brother. There would be an inquest in due course, but there were no signs that his death was anything other than an accident.

"What was it he dropped?" said Mrs. Carpenter.

"Just a little ornament kind of thing," said Malcolm in a steady voice, though his heart was thumping. "He was throwing it up and catching it as he went along, and then he dropped it. He looked for it a bit, and then it started raining and he left."

"What were you doing?"

"I was watching the great crested grebes. I don't suppose he saw me. But when he left, I went to see if I could find it and I did, so I've been looking for him ever since to give it back. But I can't now."

"What day was it you saw him?"

"I think . . ." Malcolm had to think quite hard. He looked at the paper again to see if it said when the man's body had been discovered. The *Oxford Times* was a weekly, so it could have been any day in the past five or six. With a jolt, he realized that Luckhurst's body had been found the day after he had seen him being arrested by the CCD men.

They couldn't have killed him, could they?

"No, it was a few days before this," he lied with great assurance. "I don't suppose it was connected at all. There's lots of people who walk along the towpath. He might have done it every day, like for exercise. He wasn't very bothered about losing it, because he left as soon as it started raining."

"Oh, well," said Mrs. Carpenter. "Poor man. Perhaps they'll take a bit more care of the towpath now it's too late."

A customer came in, and Mrs. Carpenter turned to deal with him. Malcolm wished he hadn't told her about the man and the thing he'd dropped; if he'd had his wits about him, he could have pretended that he'd been looking for a friend. But then she'd never have told him about the story in the paper. This was all very difficult.

"Bye, Mrs. Carpenter," he said as he left, and she waved vaguely as she listened to the other customer.

"I wish we could ask her not to say anything," Malcolm said as they turned the canoe round.

"Then she'd think it was even more worth noticing, and remember it specially," said Asta. "That was a good lie you told."

"I didn't know I could do that. Best to do it as little as possible."

"And remember exactly what we've said each time."

"It's raining again. . . ."

He paddled steadily up the canal, with Asta perching close to his ear so they could whisper together.

"Did they kill him?" she said.

"Unless he killed himself . . ."

"It *might* have been an accident."

"It's not likely, though. Not after the way they got hold of him."

"And what they did to Mr. Boatwright . . . They'd do *anything*. Torture, anything, I bet."

"So what could the message mean?"

They came back to that again and again. Malcolm had copied it so that he didn't have to keep unfolding the paper in the acorn, but even writing the words out himself didn't help make much sense of them. Someone was asking someone else to ask a question, and it was about measuring something, but more than that was hard to work out. And then there was the word *Dust*, with a capital *D*, as if it wasn't ordinary dust but something special.

"D'you think if we went to Magdalen College and asked the other scholars . . ."

"Asked them what?"

"Well, sort of detective questions. Work out what he did—"

"He was a historian. That's what it said."

"*An* historian. We could work out what else he did. What friends he had. Maybe talk to his students, or some of them, if we could find them. Whether he came back to college that evening after we saw them grab hold of him, or whether that was the last anyone saw of him. That sort of thing."

"They wouldn't tell us even if they knew. We don't look like detectives. We look like a schoolkid. And then there's the danger."

"The CCD . . ."

"Of course. If they hear we've been asking about him, wouldn't they get suspicious? Then they'd come and search the Trout and find the acorn, and then we'd be in real trouble."

"Some of the students who come in the Trout wear college scarves. If we knew what the Magdalen one was like . . ."

"That's a good idea! Then if we ask anything, it could seem like just being nosy. Or gossip."

It was raining even harder now, and Malcolm found it difficult to see ahead. Asta became an owl and perched on the prow, her feathers shedding the water in a way she'd discovered when she was trying to become an animal that didn't yet exist. The best she could do so far was to take one animal and add an aspect of another, so now she was an owl with duck's feathers; but she only did it when no one but Malcolm was looking. Guided by her big eyes, he paddled as fast as he could, stopping to bail out the canoe when the rain had filled it to his ankles. When they got home, he was soaked, but all she had to do was shake herself and she was dry again.

"Where've you been?" said his mother, but not crossly.

"Watching an owl. What's for supper?"

"Steak and kidney pie. Wash your hands. Look at you! You're soaking wet! You make sure you change into something dry after you've eaten. And don't leave your wet things on the bedroom floor."

Malcolm rinsed his hands under the kitchen tap and wiped them perfunctorily on a tea towel.

"Have they found Mr. Boatwright yet?" he said.

"No. Why?"

"They were all talking about something exciting in the bar. I could tell something was up, but I couldn't hear any details."

"There was a famous man in earlier. You could have waited on him if you weren't watching your blooming owls."

"Who was it?" said Malcolm, helping himself to mashed potato.

"Lord Asriel, the explorer."

"Oh," said Malcolm, who hadn't heard of him. "Where's he explored?"

"The Arctic mostly, so they say. But you remember what the lord chancellor was asking about?"

"Oh, the infant? If the sisters had ever had an infant to look after?"

"That's right. It turns out it's Lord Asriel's child. His love child. A little baby girl."

"Did he tell people that?"

"Course not! He never said a word about that. Well, he wouldn't go blabbing about that in a public bar, would he?"

"I dunno. Prob'ly not. So how d'you know—"

"Oh, you just put two and two together! The story about how Lord Asriel killed Mr. Coulter, the politician—that was in the papers a month back."

"If he killed someone, why en't he—"

"Eat your pie. He en't in prison because it was a matter of honor. Mr. Coulter's wife had the baby, Lord Asriel's baby, and then Mr. Coulter came charging down to Lord Asriel's estate and burst in, threatening to kill him, and they fought and Lord Asriel won and it turned out there's a law allowing a man to defend himself and his kin—that'd be the child, the baby—so he wasn't put in gaol nor hanged, but they fined him all his fortune, near enough. Eat your pie—come on, for goodness' sake!"

Malcolm was enthralled by this tale, and plied his knife and fork with only half his attention.

"But how d'you know he's come here to put his infant with the sisters?"

"Well, I don't, but it must be that. You can ask Sister Fenella next time you see her. And stop calling it an infant. No one talks like that. She's a baby still. Must be—oh, six months old, I suppose. Maybe a bit more."

"Why isn't her mother looking after her?"

"Lord, I don't know. Some say she never wanted anything more to do with the child, but maybe that's just gossip."

"The nuns won't know how to look after her, if they've never done it before."

"Well, they won't be short of advice. Give me your plate. There's rhubarb and custard on the side there."

As soon as possible, which was three days later, Malcolm hurried to the priory to learn more about the child of the famous explorer. Sister Fenella was his first port of call, and as the rain flung itself against the window, they sat at the kitchen table and kneaded some dough for the priory's bread. After Malcolm had washed his hands three times, making little change to their appearance, Sister Fenella gave up telling him.

"What *is* that in your fingernails?" she said.

"Tar. I was repairing my canoe."

"Well, if it's only tar . . . They say it's healthy," she said doubtfully.

"There's coal-tar soap," Malcolm pointed out.

"True enough. But I don't think it's that color. Never mind, the rest is clean enough. Knead away."

As he pulled and pushed at the dough, Malcolm pressed the nun with questions. Was it true, about Lord Asriel's baby?

"Well, and what have you heard about a baby?"

"That you're looking after it because he killed a man and the court took all his money away. And that was why the lord chancellor was asking about it in the Trout the other day. So is it true?"

"Yes, it is. A little baby girl."

"What's her name?"

"Lyra. I don't know why they didn't give her a good saint's name."

"Will she be here till she's grown up?"

"Oh, I don't know, Malcolm. . . . Harder with that now. Teach it who's boss."

"Did you see Lord Asriel?"

"No. I tried to peep along the corridor, but Sister Benedicta had the door firmly closed."

"Is she the person who's in charge of her?"

"Well, she was the sister who spoke to Lord Asriel."

"So who looks after the baby and feeds her and all that?"

"We all do."

"How do you know how to do all those things? I wondered because . . ."

"Because we're all maiden ladies?"

"Well, it's not the usual thing you get nuns doing."

"You'd be surprised at what we know," she said, and her elderly squirrel dæmon laughed, and so did Asta, so Malcolm did too. "But, you know, Malcolm, you mustn't say anything about the baby. It's a great secret that she's here. You mustn't breathe a word about it."

"Lots of people know already. My mum and dad know, and customers . . . They've all been talking about it."

"Oh, dear. Well, perhaps it doesn't matter, then. But you'd better not say any more. Perhaps that would be all right."

"Sister Fenella, did any men from the CCD come the other night? You know, the Consist—"

"The Consistorial Court of Discipline? Lord preserve us. What have we done to deserve that?"

"I don't know. Nothing. There were some men, two of them, in the Trout the other night, and everyone was afraid of them. They were asking about one of the men who came with the lord chancellor. And Mr. Boatwright stood up to them and they were going to arrest him, but he disappeared. Probably ran away. He might be living in the woods."

"Goodness me! George Boatwright the poacher?"

"You know him, then?"

"Oh, yes. And now he's in trouble with the . . . Oh, dear. Oh, dear."

"Sister, what does the CCD *do*?"

"I expect they do God's work," she said. "It's too hard for us to understand."

"Did they come here?"

"I wouldn't know, Malcolm. Sister Benedicta would have seen them, not me. And she would have kept it to herself, like the brave lady she is, and not troubled anyone else."

"I just wondered if they had anything to do with the baby."

"Well, I wouldn't know, and I wouldn't ask. Come on, that's enough with that dough."

She took it from him and slapped it hard on the stone working surface. Malcolm could see she was troubled, and he wished he hadn't asked about the CCD.

Before he left, Sister Fenella took him along to see Lyra. The baby was asleep in the nuns' parlor, the room where they received visitors, but Sister Fenella said it would be all right if he was very quiet.

He tiptoed after her into the room, which was cold and smelled of furniture polish, and miserably gray in the light from the rain-washed window. In the middle of the floor stood a crib of heavy-looking oak, and inside it there lay a baby, asleep.

Malcolm had never seen a baby at close quarters, and he was struck at once by how real she seemed. He knew that would be a silly thing to say, so he held his tongue, but that was his impression all the same: it was unexpected that something so small should be so perfectly formed. She was as perfectly made as the wooden acorn. Her dæmon, the chick of a small bird like a swallow, was asleep with her, but as soon as Asta flew down, swallow-shaped too, and perched on the edge of the crib, the chick woke up and opened his yellow beak wide for food. Malcolm laughed, and that woke the baby, and seeing his laughing face, she began to laugh too. Asta pretended to snap at a tiny insect and thrust it down the baby dæmon's gaping mouth, which satisfied him, making Malcolm laugh harder, and then the baby laughed so hard she got hiccups, and every time she hicked, the dæmon jumped.

"There, there," said Sister Fenella, and bent to pick her up; but as she lifted the baby, Lyra's little face crumpled into an expression of grief and terror, and she reached round for her dæmon, nearly twisting herself out of the nun's arms. Asta was ahead of her: she took the little chick in her mouth and flew up to place him on the baby's chest, at which point he turned into a miniature tiger cub and hissed and bared his teeth at everyone. All the baby's dismay vanished at once, and she lay in Sister Fenella's arms, looking around with a lordly complacency.

Malcolm was enchanted. Everything about her was perfect and delighted him.

"Better put you down again, sweetheart," said Sister Fenella. "Shouldn't have woken you, should we, darling?"

She laid the baby in the crib, tucking her up and taking the greatest care not to brush a hand against her dæmon. Malcolm supposed the prohibition against touching another person's dæmon was true for babies as well; in any case, he would never have dreamed, after those few minutes, of doing anything to upset that little child. He was her servant for life.

FOUR

UPPSALA

In a comfortable study at the University of Uppsala, in Sweden, three men sat talking as the wild rain lashed the windows and the wind sent occasional puffs of smoke back down the chimney to disturb the fire in the iron stove.

The host was called Gunnar Hallgrimsson. He was a bachelor, a man of sixty or so, plump and sharp-witted. He was a professor of metaphysical philosophy at the university. His dæmon, a robin, stayed on his shoulder and said little.

One of his guests was a university colleague, Axel Löfgren, professor of experimental theology. He was thin, taciturn but amiable, and his dæmon was a ferret. He and Hallgrimsson were old friends, and their habit of teasing each other was usually in full flow after a good dinner, but it was moderated this evening by the presence of the third man, a stranger to them both.

The visitor was about the same age as Hallgrimsson, but he looked older; certainly his face bore the marks of more experience and trial than did the professor's smooth cheeks and unlined brow. He was a gyptian of the people of Eastern Anglia, a man called

Coram van Texel, who had traveled much in the far north. He was lean and of middle height, and his movements were careful, as if he thought he might break something inadvertently, as if he was unused to delicate glasses and fine tableware. His dæmon, a large cat with fur of a thousand beautiful autumnal colors, stalked the corners of the study before leaping gracefully to Coram's lap. Ten years after this evening, and again ten years after that, Lyra would marvel at the coloring of that dæmon's fur.

They had just dined. Coram had arrived that day from the north, with a letter of introduction from an acquaintance of Professor Hallgrimsson's, the consul of the witches at the town of Trollesund.

"You'll take some Tokay?" said Hallgrimsson, sitting down after looking through the window along the rain-swept street, and then pulling the curtains across against the draft.

"That would be a rare pleasure," said Coram.

The professor turned to a small table no more than an arm's length from his comfortable chair and poured some golden wine into three glasses.

"And how is my friend Martin Lanselius?" the professor continued, handing a glass to Coram. "I must say, I never thought he would end up in the diplomatic service of the witches."

"He's thriving," said Coram. "In fine fettle. He's making a study of their religion."

"I've often thought the belief systems of the witch clans would reward investigation," said Hallgrimsson, "but my own studies led me elsewhere."

"Even further into the void," said the professor of experimental theology, taking a glass from his host.

"You must excuse my friend's absurdities. Your good health, Mr. Van Texel," said Hallgrimsson, taking a sip.

"And yours, sir. By God, this is fine."

"I'm glad you think so. There is a wine merchant in Buda-Pesth who sends me a case of it every year."

"We don't taste it very often," said Löfgren. "Every time I see a bottle, there's less in it than there was before."

"Oh, nonsense. Now, what can we do for you here in Uppsala, Mr. Van Texel?"

"Dr. Lanselius told me about the instrument you have, the truth measurer," said the gyptian. "I was hoping to consult it."

"Ah. Tell me about the nature of your inquiry."

"My people," said Coram, "the gyptian people, are under threat from various political factions in Brytain. They want to restrict our ancient freedoms and limit the activities we can take part in—buying and selling, for instance. I want to know which of these threats can be dealt with by opposition, which by negotiation, and which can't be dealt with at all. Is that the sort of question your instrument could answer?"

"In the right hands, yes. Given enough time, I could even make a rough attempt at interpreting it myself."

"You mean you're not an expert reader?"

"By no means expert."

"Then—"

"Let me show you the instrument, and perhaps you will understand the problem."

The professor opened a drawer in the little table and brought out a leather box, circular in shape and about the size of the palm of a man's hand, and three fingers deep. Löfgren pulled out a tapestry-covered stool, and Hallgrimsson placed the box on it and lifted the lid.

Coram leaned forward. In the soft naphtha light, something gleamed richly. The professor adjusted the lampshade so that the light fell full on the stool, and took the instrument out of its box.

His short stubby fingers were touching the instrument with what looked to Coram like the tenderness of a lover, as if he thought it was alive.

It was a clock-shaped device of bright gold, with a crystal face uppermost. At first, Coram could see little but a beautiful complexity, until the professor began to point things out.

"Around the edge of the dial—you see?—we have thirty-six pictures, each painted on ivory with a single hair. And around the outside we have three little wheels a hundred and twenty degrees apart, like the knobs you use to wind a watch. This is what happens when I turn one."

Coram leaned closer, and his dæmon stepped off his lap and stood on the arm of the chair so that she could see too. As the professor turned the wheel, they saw a slender black hand, like a minute hand, detach itself from the complicated background and move around the dial with a series of clicks. The professor stopped when it was pointing at a tiny picture of the sun.

"We have three hands," the professor said, "and we point each at a different symbol. If I were framing your question, I would probably include the sun in the three symbols I chose, because it stands, among other things, for kingship and authority, and by association, for the law. The other two"—he turned the other wheels, and the hands moved obediently round the dial—"would depend on which aspect of your question we wanted to deal with first. You mentioned buying and selling. Somewhere in the griffin range of meanings, those actions occur. Why? Because griffins are associated with treasure. I would also guess that the third hand should point to the dolphin, whose primary meaning is water, because your people are water dwellers, no?"

"That's true. I begin to see."

"Let's try, then."

The professor moved the second hand to the griffin and the third to the dolphin.

"And then this happens," he said.

A needle so slender that Coram hadn't seen it at all, and of a mid-gray color, began to move, apparently of its own accord, slowly, hesitating, and then swung round very quickly, stopping here and there before moving on again.

"What's that doing?" said Coram.

"Giving us the answer."

"You got to be quick, en't you?"

"Your mental faculties have to be calm, but alert. I have heard it compared to the way in which a hunter will lie in wait, ready to pull the trigger at any moment, but without any nervous excitement."

"I understand," said Coram. "I've seen archers in Nippon do something similar."

"Really? I would like to hear about that. But the mental attitude is only one aspect of the difficulty. Another is this: that each symbol has a very deep range of meanings, and they are only made clear in the books of readings."

"How many meanings?"

"Nobody knows. Some have been explored to the depth of a hundred or more, but they show no sign of coming to an end. Perhaps they go on forever."

"And how were these meanings discovered?" put in Löfgren.

Coram looked at the professor; he'd thought Löfgren was familiar with the alethiometer, as Hallgrimsson was, and believed in its powers, but there was a tone of skepticism in his question.

"By contemplation, by meditation, by experiment," said Hallgrimsson.

"Oh. Well, I believe in experiment," said Löfgren.

"I'm glad to hear you believe in something," said his friend.

"These meanings—the relation between them—if they work by kinds of similarity," said Coram, "they could go on a lot past a hundred. There's no end to finding similarities, once you start looking for 'em."

"But what matters is not the similarities your imagination finds, but the similarities that are implicit in the image, and they are not necessarily the same. I have noticed that the more imaginative readers are often the less successful. Their minds leap to what they think is there rather than waiting with patience. And what matters most of all is where the chosen meaning comes in the hierarchy of meanings, you see, and for that there is no alternative to the books. That is why the only alethiometers we know about are kept in or by great libraries."

"How many are there, then?"

"We think there were six made. We know where five of them are: there is this one in Uppsala, there is one in Bologna, one in Paris, the Magisterium has one in Geneva, and there is one in Oxford."

"Oxford, eh?"

"In the Bodleian Library. It is a remarkable story. When the Consistorial Court of Discipline was gathering its power in the last century, the prefect of the court heard of the existence of the Bodleian alethiometer and demanded its surrender. The librarian refused. The convocation of the university, the governing body, ordered him to comply. Instead, what he did was to conceal the instrument in the hollowed-out pages of a work of experimental theology, of which they already had several identical copies, and place it on the open shelves in plain view—but, of course, impossible to find among the million or more volumes in the library. That time the Consistorial Court gave up. Then they came a second time. The prefect sent a body of armed men to the library and threatened the librarian with death if it was not given up. Again the librarian refused, saying that he had not taken up his office in order to give away the contents of the library, and that he had a sacred duty to conserve and protect them for scholarship. The officer in charge ordered his men to arrest the librarian and bring him out into the quadrangle to be shot. The librarian took his place in front of the firing squad and faced the officer for the first time—they had negotiated only by messenger previously, you see—and they recognized each other as old college friends. The officer was abashed, the story says, and would not give the order, and instead stood his men down and went to drink brantwijn with the librarian. The outcome was that the alethiometer remained in the Bodleian Library, where it is still, the librarian retained his position, and the officer was ordered back to Geneva, where shortly afterwards he died, apparently by poison."

The gyptian gave a long, low whistle.

"And who reads the Oxford one now?" he said.

"There is a small body of scholars who have made it their object of study. I have heard there is a woman of great gifts who has made considerable progress in the principles. . . . Ralph? Relph? Something like that."

"I see," said Coram, sipping his wine and looking closely at the alethiometer. "You said there were six of these, Professor, and then you told me the whereabouts of five of 'em. Where is the sixth?"

"Well might you ask. No one knows. Well, I daresay *somebody* knows, but I don't think any scholar knows. Now, if we could come back to your question, Mr. Van Texel: it's a complicated one, but that's not the main problem. The problem is that our leading scholar is not here. He is in Paris, spending a sabbatical term in the Bibliothèque Nationale. I am too slow and clumsy to find my way from one level to another, and to see the connections and estimate where I should look next in the books. I would read it for you if I could, of course."

"Despite the danger?" said Coram.

The professor said nothing for a few moments. Then he said, "The danger of . . ."

"Of summary execution," said Coram, though he was smiling.

"Oh, yes. Aha. Well, I think those days are behind us, fortunately."

"Let's hope so," said Löfgren.

Coram took another sip of the golden wine and sat back in the chair as if he was contented and comfortable. The fact was that the alethiometer, pretty though it was, had little interest for him, and the question he had posed to Professor Hallgrimsson was a blind: the gyptians were perfectly capable of working out the answer for themselves, and indeed they already had. Coram was up to something else altogether, and now he had to maneuver the conversation towards a different matter.

"I daresay you have a lot of visitors," he said.

"Well, I don't know," said the professor. "No more than most universities, I suppose. Of course, we do specialize in one or two areas, and that brings interested scholars from quite some distance. Not only scholars either."

"Explorers, I expect."

"Among others, yes. On their way to the Arctic."

"I wonder if you've met a man called Lord Asriel. He's a friend of my people, a notable explorer in that part of the world."

"He has been here, but not recently. I did hear . . ." The professor looked awkward for a second, and then his eagerness overcame his reluctance. "I don't listen to gossip, you understand."

"Oh, neither do I," said Coram. "Sometimes I overhear it, though."

"Overhear!" said Löfgren. "That is very good."

"Yes, I *overheard* a remarkable story about Lord Asriel not long ago," Hallgrimsson said. "If you have just come from the north, perhaps it won't have reached you yet. . . . It seems that Lord Asriel has been involved in a murder case."

"Murder?"

"He had a child with a woman who was married to someone else, and then he killed the woman's husband."

"Good God!" said Coram, who knew the story well already. "How did that come about?"

He listened to the professor's version of the tale, which differed only slightly from the one he knew, waiting for the opportunity to steer the conversation the way of his question.

"And what happened to the child?" he said. "With its mother, I expect?"

"No. I think the court has custody. For the moment, at any rate. The mother is a remarkably beautiful woman, but not one in whom, shall we say, the flame of motherhood burns very brightly."

"You speak as if you've met her."

"Indeed we have," said Hallgrimsson, and if Coram had had to describe his expression, he would have said that the scholar was preening himself just a little. "We have dined with her. She visited us just a month ago."

"Did she really? And was she off exploring too?"

"No, she came to consult Axel here. She is a remarkable scholar herself, you know."

This was the moment.

"She came to consult you, sir?" said Coram to the experimental theologian.

Löfgren smiled. Coram noticed that his bony face was actually showing a faint blush.

"I used to think my old friend here was immune to the charms of the fair sex," said Hallgrimsson. "In years gone by, Mr. Van Texel, he would hardly have noticed that she was a woman. But this time I think the dart of Cupid might actually have penetrated his carapace."

"I don't blame you, sir," said Coram to Löfgren. "Speaking for myself, I've always found great intelligence in a woman a highly attractive feature. What did she want to consult you about, if I may ask?"

"Oh, you won't get anything out of him," said Hallgrimsson. "I've tried. Anyone would think he had signed an oath of secrecy."

"Because you would make a joke of it, you old buffoon," said Löfgren. "She came to ask me about the Rusakov field. Do you know what that is?"

"No, sir. What is it?"

"You know what a field is, in natural philosophy?"

"I've got a vague idea. It's a region where some force applies. Is that it?"

"That will do. But this field is like no other we know of. Its discoverer, a Muscovite called Rusakov, was investigating the mystery of consciousness—human consciousness—that is, of why something entirely material, such as a human body—including the brain, of course—should be able to generate this impalpable, invisible thing, *awareness*. Is it material, this consciousness we have? We can't weigh it or measure it. Is it something *spiritual*, then? Once we use the word *spiritual*, we don't have to explain anymore, because it belongs to the Church then, and no one can question it. Well, that's no good to a real investigator of nature. I won't go into all the steps Rusakov took, but he finally arrived at the extraordinary idea that consciousness is a perfectly normal property of matter, like mass or anbaric charge; that there is a field of consciousness that pervades the entire universe, and that makes itself apparent most fully—we believe—in human beings. Precisely *how* is a question that is now being investigated with urgent excitement by scientists in every part of the world."

"Every part of the world, that is, where they are allowed to," said Hallgrimsson. "So you see, Mr. Van Texel, how easily this must attract the attention of the Consistorial Court."

"I do, sir. It must have shaken the Church to its foundations. And this was what the lady came here to ask about?"

"It was," said Löfgren. "Mrs. Coulter's interest was unusual in someone who was not a professional scholar. She asked several very perceptive questions about the Rusakov field and human consciousness. I showed her my results, she absorbed everything I could tell her with instant understanding, and then she seemed to lose interest in me, to my sorrow, and started to flatter my colleague here."

"Had she heard about this wine, then, sir?" said Coram.

"Ho ho! No, it wasn't the wine, and it wasn't my many personal attractions. She wanted to consult the alethiometer about her daughter, Mr. Van Texel."

"Her daughter?" said Coram. "You mean the child she had by—"

"By Lord Asriel," said Hallgrimsson. "Indeed. The very same. She wanted me to use the alethiometer to find out where the child was."

"She doesn't know?"

"Oh, no. It—I suppose I mean *she*—is under the supervision of the courts of law, but of course she could be anywhere. Apparently, it's a matter of some secrecy. And now—remember you are just *overhearing* this, Mr. Van Texel—the mother has discovered that the child is the subject of a prophecy by the witches. She did not tell us that. We—ahem—*overheard* it from one of her servants. Mrs. Coulter is very eager to discover more about this, and especially to find out where the child is, so as to take her back into her . . .

I was going to say into her *care*, but I think it would be more like *custody*."

"I see," said Coram. "And what did this prophecy say? Did you happen to overhear that?"

"No, alas. I believe it was simply that the child was of supreme importance in some way. That is all we heard. And her mother does not know what the prophecy foretells. Yes, a very remarkable woman. But should we now be expecting a call from the agents of the Consistorial Court, Mr. Van Texel?"

"I hope not. But these are trying times, Professor."

Coram had asked enough; he had learned what he wanted to. After a few more minutes of conversation, he stood up.

"Well, gentlemen," he said, "I'm greatly obliged to you. A splendid dinner, some of the finest wine I've ever tasted in my life, and a look at that remarkable instrument."

"I'm very sorry I could do no more for you than roughly sketch how it works," said Professor Hallgrimsson, getting to his feet with a little effort. "But at least you have seen the difficulties."

"Indeed, sir. Has it stopped raining yet, I wonder?"

Coram went to the window and looked out at the street: empty to left and right, and very dark between the streetlamps, the roadway glistening wet.

"Can I lend you an umbrella?" said the professor.

"No need for that, thank you. It's dry enough now. Good night, gentlemen, good night to you, and thank you again."

And now came the second problem Coram had to deal with.

The rain had stopped, but the air was heavy with moisture and bitterly cold. A nimbus of mist surrounded every streetlight so that they looked like golden dandelion seed heads, and the drip of water from the eaves was unceasing as Coram and Sophonax walked slowly along the riverfront.

"Want to come up, Sophie?" said Coram, because dæmon or not, Sophonax was a cat, and the pavements were drenched; but she said, "Better not."

"He still there?" Coram murmured.

"He's keeping out of sight, but he's there."

Since they had left Novgorod the previous week, Coram had known they were being followed. It was time to put a stop to it.

"Same one, eh?"

"That dæmon can't hide," said Sophonax.

Coram was moving in a roundabout way towards the narrow little boardinghouse near the river where he'd rented a room, and now he slowed down by the water's edge, where half a dozen barges were tied up at a stone embankment. It was half past midnight.

He paused there, hands on the wet iron railing, looking out across the black water while his dæmon wound herself round his legs, pretending to pester for attention but really watching every movement behind them.

To get to the boardinghouse, they'd have to cross a little iron footbridge that spanned the river, but Coram didn't go that way. Instead, when Sophonax said, "Now," he turned away from the river and walked swiftly across the road and into an alley between two stone-fronted buildings that might have been banks or government offices. He had noticed this alley before, when coming along the river towards the university—a quick glance, an almost automatic registering of possibility—and he'd seen that it was open at the other end. He wouldn't get trapped here, but he might ambush whoever was following him. As soon as he was in the shadows, he ran on soft feet for the large rubbish bins halfway down, almost invisible in the darkness on the right-hand side.

There he crouched and reached inside the sleeve of his coat for the short, heavy stick of lignum vitae he carried along his left forearm. He knew how to use it in at least five lethal ways.

Sophonax waited till he had the stick ready before leaping up to his shoulder, and then, after delicately testing the top of the nearest dustbin in case it was loose, she climbed up there and lay flat, staring at the entrance to the alley with her cat eyes wide. Coram watched the other end, which opened into a narrow street of office buildings.

What happened next would depend on how skillfully the other man's dæmon could fight. They had once overpowered a Tartar and his wolf dæmon when they were younger, and Sophonax was afraid of nothing, and swift and very strong; in a fight to the death, the great taboo against touching another person's dæmon didn't count for much. In fighting for their life, Sophonax had more than once had to scratch and bite with fury at the hideous touch of a stranger's hand and then afterwards wash herself in a near frenzy to get rid of the taint.

But this dæmon . . .

Sophie whispered, "There."

Coram turned, careful and slow, and saw in silhouette against the lighted embankment the small head and hulking shoulders of a hyena. She was looking directly at them. She was a brute such as Coram had never seen: malice in every line of her, jaws that could crack bones as if they were made of pastry. She and her man were clearly trained at the business of following, because Coram was trained at the business of spotting it, and admired their skill; but as Sophie remarked, it wasn't easy for such a dæmon to remain inconspicuous. As for what they wanted, Coram had no idea; if they wanted a fight, they'd get one.

He tightened his grip on the fighting stick; Sophie readied herself to spring. The hyena dæmon came forward a little, emerging into a full silhouette, and the man stepped silently forward after her. Coram and Sophie both spotted the pistol in his hand the moment before he flattened himself against the wall of the alley and disappeared into shadow.

Silence, apart from the eternal drip of water from the roofs.

Coram wished that Sophie had hidden behind the bin with him rather than crouching on the lid. She was too exposed—

A sound like a man spitting a pip—it was a gas pistol—followed at once by a great clatter as the bullet hit the dustbin and sent it tumbling over Coram and rolling across the alley. In the same instant, Sophie leapt away and landed by Coram's side. A gas pistol wasn't accurate over a distance but was deadly enough at close range: they'd have to neutralize it. They kept perfectly still. Slow footsteps came towards them, and they could hear the snuffling, grunting sounds of that creature and the clicking of her claws on the pavement, and then Coram thought, *Now!* and Sophie sprang directly at where the hyena's head would be, claws out, and the man fired the gas pistol again twice, and one bullet scorched its way across Coram's scalp. But it gave him a fix on where the man was, and he lunged forward and slashed with his stick at the darkness, connecting with something—arm? hand? shoulder?—and knocking the gun away.

Sophie's claws, all of them, were firmly fixed in the hyena's scalp and throat. The dæmon was shaking her head wildly, trying to dislodge her, and smashing her against the wall and the ground again and again. Coram saw the man's shadow reach down as if to pick up the gun, and he sprang forward to lash down with the stick but missed and slipped on the wet ground and fell at the man's feet, rolling away at once and kicking out hard towards where the gun had fallen.

His foot connected with something that skittered away over the cobbles, and the man kicked him in the ribs, horribly hard, and then grappled closely with him, trying for a choke hold, and he was wiry and tough, but Coram still had the stick in his hand and stabbed up with it as hard as he could into the man's midriff. A gasping cough and the grip weakened, and then Coram felt a shock as the hyena finally managed to slam Sophie loose, tearing out a corner of her fur between those brutal teeth, and immediately fastened her massive jaws around Sophie's head.

Instantly Coram twisted upright. The man fell away, and Coram swung his arm with every gram of strength he had towards the hyena. He had no idea where he hit her and was only concerned that he didn't fatally damage Sophie, but the blow that landed was a cruel one: he heard bones snapping and saw in the dimness Sophie trying to tear herself away from the hideous jaws. Merciless now, Coram balanced and took aim, and lashed again and again at the hyena's now-broken leg. He didn't let up because the hyena had only to crush her mouth shut and he and Sophie would die in a moment.

So as the hyena opened her great jaws to scream, Sophie twisted away and scratched at the man's hand, tearing his skin and drawing blood, even at the cost of her own disgust; and the man, crying out as the dæmon's pain made his own nerves throb with agony, pulled away and dragged the hyena with him. The dæmon snarled and snapped her jaws in a frenzy of pain and misery, and Coram would have followed them and attacked the man himself, now that they were wounded, except when he tried to stand up, he fainted and fell down again.

He came to only a few moments later, in a sudden silence. Apart from himself and Sophie, the alley was empty. His head was spinning. He tried to sit up, but Sophie said, "Lie down. Let the blood back in your brain."

"Have they gone?"

"They ran away. Well, he did. I don't think she'll ever run again. He was carrying her, and she was mad with pain."

"Why . . ." He couldn't finish, but she understood.

"You've lost a lot of blood," she said.

He hadn't felt much pain till she said that, but then he felt the line the bullet had made through his scalp suddenly reminding him of itself, and the warm wetness on his neck and shoulders beginning to turn cold as the fighting passion subsided, and he lay back to gather his strength. Then he sat up carefully.

"You hurt bad?" he said.

"I would have been. If those jaws had closed, I don't think they'd ever have opened again."

"We should have finished him. Damn, they were good, though. Think he was a Muscovite?"

"No. Don't ask me why. Maybe . . . French?"

Coram stood up, holding on to the wall. He looked out towards both ends of the alley and said, "Come on, then. Back to bed. I don't think we did very well there, Sophie."

His ribs hurt furiously; he thought one of them might be broken. His scalp was bleeding thickly and felt as if a red-hot iron had been pressed against it. He scooped up his dæmon and she attended to the scalp wound, licking and cleaning him tenderly as they walked back to their boardinghouse.

After a wash in the only water available, which was icy cold, he put on a clean shirt and sat down at the little table. By the light of a candle, he composed a letter, saying everything as briefly as possible.

> *To Lord Nugent:*
>   *The lady came to Uppsala to consult the professor of experimental theology, Axel Löfgren. She asked him "several very perceptive questions" about the Rusakov field and its relation to human consciousness. He suspects she was acting on behalf of the CCD. Furthermore, she*

wanted a Professor Hallgrimsson to use his alethiometer
to tell her where her child was. He either could not or
would not, but in any case he did not. Apparently, the
lady had heard that the child was the subject of a witches'
prophecy, but she did not know what it foretold. You
will remember our good friend Bud Schlesinger. I spoke
with him at the house of Martin Lanselius in Trollesund.
He has gone further north to ask about this among
some witches he knows and will contact you as soon as
he returns. One further matter: I was followed from
Novgorod by a man whose dæmon was a hyena. I did
not recognize him, but he bore himself like a thoroughly
trained agent. We fought and he got away, though the
dæmon is wounded. I am curious about him.

CvT

Then he set about the laborious task of transcribing it into code and addressed it in an ordinary envelope to an insignificant part of central London. He carefully burned the original, and then he went to bed.

FIVE

THE SCHOLAR

Dr. Hannah Relf sat up and pressed her hands into the small of her back, stretching painfully. She had been sitting for too long; she wanted to walk briskly for half an hour, but time with the Bodleian alethiometer was limited: there were half a dozen other scholars using it, and she couldn't afford to waste some of her precious allocation in exercising. She could take a walk later.

She bent from side to side, loosening her spine, stretched her arms above her head and rotated her shoulders, and eventually felt a little less stiff. She was sitting in Duke Humfrey, the oldest part of the Bodleian Library in Oxford, and the alethiometer lay on the desk in front of her among a scatter of papers and a heap of books.

The work she was doing was threefold. There was the part she was supposed to be doing, the part that justified her time with the instrument, which was an investigation into the hourglass range of meanings. Already she had added two more floors, as she thought of them, to the levels of significance reaching down into the invisible depths, and she was on the track of a third.

But second, there was the secret work she was doing on behalf of an organization known to her as Oakley Street; she supposed from its address, though there wasn't an Oakley Street in Oxford, so it was possibly in London. She'd been recruited for this two years before by a professor of Byzantine history named George Papadimitriou, who had assured her (and she believed him) that the work was both important and on the side of liberalism and freedom. She realized that Oakley Street was a branch of some sort of secret service, but since all she did was interpret the alethiometer on their behalf, she knew very little more. However, she read the papers, and it wasn't hard for an intelligent person to see what was going on in the politics of her country. The questions Oakley Street asked her were varied, but a lot of them had recently trod closely towards subjects that were forbidden by the religious authorities; she knew quite well that if the CCD, or anyone like it, were to find out what she was doing, she would be in serious trouble.

And third, and most urgent, there was a question she had been asking for a week: *Where was the acorn?* She had no idea how the message in its little carrier had always arrived so dependably behind the stone in the University Parks, or wherever she was to collect it, but it should have appeared some time ago. And now she was becoming anxious.

Hence the question she was asking. It hadn't been easy to frame, and the answer wasn't easy to interpret, but then they never were, though she was becoming more sure-footed among the levels of meaning than she used to be.

But this afternoon, as the gray light faded outside the six-hundred-year-old windows of Duke Humfrey and the little anbaric lamp above the desk glowed more warmly, she thought she had the final part of an answer. After a week's labor, she had the three stark images: boy—inn—fish. If she was a really practiced reader, she thought, each of those ideas would be surrounded by a phalanx of qualifying detail, but there it was: that was all she had to go on.

She pulled a clean piece of paper towards herself and drew lines downwards to divide it into three columns. The first one, *Boy*, she left blank. She knew no boys, except her sister's four-year-old son, and it wasn't going to be him. She left the *Inn* column empty too. How many inns did she know? Not many, actually. She liked to sit in a beer garden with a companion and a glass of wine, but only in good weather. *Fish:* that was probably the easiest to start with. She wrote down as many names of fish as she could think of: herring, cod, sting-ray, salmon, mackerel, haddock, shark, trout, perch, pike . . . What else was there? Sunfish—flying fish—stickleback—barracuda . . .

"Chub," said her dæmon, who was a marmoset.

Down it went, though it didn't help. Her dæmon knew no more than she did, of course, though each sometimes remembered things the other had forgotten.

"Tench," he said.

As far as her official work went—the extension of the hourglass range—she could discuss it with five or six other scholars, but her secret work was secret, and not a word about it passed her lips, except to her dæmon. This question was a part of that, so silence had to reign here too.

She yawned, stretched again, stood up, and walked slowly down the length of the library and back again, thinking as strongly as she could of absolutely nothing. That didn't work either, but when she sat down again, there came into her mind the image of a peacock on a river terrace, and herself among a group of friends, and the peacock's effrontery in snatching a sausage roll out of the very fingers of her neighbor and then trying to run away with it, encumbered by his ridiculous tail. That had happened years ago, when she was an undergraduate. Where had that happened? What was the name of the inn? Was it an inn, or a restaurant, or what?

She looked up at the staff desk. The assistant was checking some request slips, and there was no one else around.

Hannah got up and walked along to her without hesitation, because if she'd hesitated, she wouldn't have done it.

"Anne," she said, "I think I'm going gaga. What's the name of that pub with the river terrace and the peacocks? Where is it?"

"The Trout?" said the assistant. "It's at Godstow."

"Of course! Thanks. Stupid of me."

Hannah tapped her forehead and went back to her desk. She carefully folded up the paper she'd begun to make the list on and put it in an inside pocket. She'd destroy it later. Her trainers had been very severe about not leaving behind any written clues to what you were doing, but she had to have paper to think with, and so far she'd been meticulous about burning it.

She worked for another half an hour and then returned her books and the alethiometer to the desk. Anne put the books on the reserved shelf and pressed a buzzer, which would sound in the senior assistant's office. The alethiometer was kept in a safe in there, and the senior assistant had to put it away himself, which he did with an air of solemnity that Hannah enjoyed very much.

But she didn't stay to watch this time. She gathered her papers together, put them in her bag, and left the library.

The Trout, she thought. *Tomorrow*.

The next day was a Saturday, and a rare dry day with occasional bursts of sunlight. Towards midday, Hannah found her bicycle, and having pumped up the tires, she rode up the Woodstock Road and turned left at the top for Wolvercote and Godstow. She rode briskly, her dæmon sitting in the basket on the handlebars, and arrived at the Trout feeling a little out of breath and warm enough to take her coat off at once.

She ordered a cheese sandwich and a glass of pale ale and sat outside on the terrace, which wasn't crowded by any means but wasn't deserted either. Most people had probably decided to play it safe with the weather and stay indoors.

Hannah ate her sandwich slowly, ignoring the attentions of Norman (or Barry) and reading a book. It was nothing to do with work: it was a thriller, of the sort she liked, with a mysterious death, skin-of-the-teeth escapes, and a haughty and beautiful heroine whose function was to fall in love with the saturnine but witty hero.

She had finished her sandwich, to Norman's disgust, and was just draining the last of her beer when, as she'd hoped, a boy appeared.

"Can I bring you any more to eat or drink, miss?" he said.

His tone was polite and interested, slightly to her surprise, as if he really wanted to help. He was about eleven, she guessed, a stocky, strong-looking boy, ginger-haired. A nice boy, friendly, intelligent.

"No, thanks. But . . ." How should she say it? She'd rehearsed it often enough, but now her voice sounded thin and nervous. Quiet, she thought, quiet.

"Yes, miss?"

"Do you know anything about an acorn?"

It had an extraordinary effect. The color drained out of his face, and his eyes seemed to flash with understanding, and then fear, and then determination. He nodded.

"Don't say anything now," Hannah said quietly. "In a minute I'm going to leave, but I'll forget this book and leave it on my chair. You'll find it and look for me, but I'll be gone. My address is inside the cover. Tomorrow, if you can, bring it to my house in Jericho. And . . . and the acorn. Can you do that? We can talk there."

He nodded again.

"Tomorrow afternoon," he said. "I can do it then."

He had recovered his color: ruddy, or even lionlike, she thought.

She smiled and went back to reading as he gathered up her plate and glass, and then she went through a pantomime of putting on her coat, looking for her purse, leaving a tip, gathering her bag, and going out, leaving her book on the chair pushed under the table.

The next day, she could hardly settle to anything. In the morning she fussed with her little garden, pruning this, repotting that, but her mind wasn't on it. Then it started to rain, so she went inside and made some coffee and did what she had never done in her life: tried the newspaper crossword.

"What a stupid exercise," said her dæmon after five minutes. "Words belong in contexts, not pegged out like biological specimens."

She threw the paper aside and lit a fire in the little hearth, and then found that she'd forgotten her coffee.

"Why didn't you remind me?" she asked her dæmon.

"Because I'd forgotten it too, of course," he said. "Settle down, for goodness' sake."

"I'm trying," she said. "I seem to have forgotten how."

"It's stopped raining. Go and finish pruning the clematis."

"Everything will be drenched."

"Do the ironing."

"There's only one blouse to do."

"Write some letters."

"Don't want to."

"Bake a cake to give that boy a slice of."

"He might come while I'm still making it, and then we'd have to make conversation for an hour and a half till it was ready. Anyway, we've got some biscuits."

"Well, I give up," he said.

At midday, she toasted a cheese sandwich in her mother's blackened old device that hung by the fire. Then she made some more coffee and drank it this time, and then she felt a little more on top of things and managed to read for an hour or so. The rain had started up again.

"He might not come at all if it's pouring like this," she said.

"Yes, he will. He'll be too curious not to."

"You think so?"

"His dæmon changed four times while we were speaking to him."

"Hmm," she said, but there was something in what Jesper had observed. Frequent changes of shape in a child's dæmon, and a wide variety of forms to assume, were a good indicator of intelligence and curiosity. "And you think . . ."

"He'll want to know what it means."

"He was frightened. He went pale."

"Only for a moment. Then his color came back, didn't you see? Sort of ruddy."

"Well, we'll know in a few minutes," she said, seeing him at the gate. "Here he comes now."

She stood up even before the door knocker rapped, and put her book down on the little side table before smoothing her skirt and touching her hair. For heaven's sake, what was there to be nervous about? Well, quite a lot, actually. She opened the door.

"You must be soaking wet," she said.

"Well, I am a bit," said the boy, shaking his waterproof coat outside before letting her take it. He looked at the neat carpet, the polished floorboards, and took his shoes off too.

"Come in and get warm," she said. "How did you get here? You didn't walk?"

"In my boat," he said.

"Your boat? Where is it?"

"She's tied up at the boatyard. They let me leave her there. I thought I better bring her up on the bank and turn her upside down, because if she gets full of water, it takes ages to bail her out. She's called *La Belle Sauvage*."

"Why?"

"That was the name of my uncle's pub. My dad's brother was an innkeeper too, and he had a pub at Richmond and I liked the name."

"Was there a nice sign?"

"Yes, it was a beautiful lady, and she'd done something brave, only I don't know what that was. Oh—here's your book. Sorry it's a bit wet."

They were sitting on either side of the fire, and he was steaming prodigiously.

"Thank you. Perhaps you'd better put it on the hearth."

"It was a good idea to leave it like that so I knew where to come."

"Tradecraft," she said.

"Tradecraft? What's that?"

"A way of . . . oh, passing messages, that kind of thing. By the way, what's your name?"

"Malcolm Polstead."

"And . . . the acorn?"

"How did you know to ask me?" he said, not moving.

"There's a way of . . . There's an instrument. . . . Well, I found out by myself. No one else knows. What can you tell me about the acorn?"

He reached into an inside pocket. Then he held out his hand, and the acorn was resting in his palm.

She took it tentatively, thinking he might snatch it back, but he didn't move. What he did was watch closely as she unscrewed it. Then he nodded.

"I was watching," he said, "to see if you knew which way it un-screwed. It fooled me at first because I never came across anything that unscrewed clockwise. But you knew straightaway, so I reckon this must be for you."

And he brought out the tightly folded sheet of India paper just as the two halves of the acorn fell apart in her hands, showing it to be empty.

"If I'd tried to unscrew it the wrong way . . . ," she said.

"Then I wouldn't have given you the paper."

He handed it to her, and she unfolded it, scanned it quickly, and tucked it in the pocket of her cardigan. Somehow the boy seemed to be in charge, which hadn't been her intention. Now she had to decide what to do about it.

"How did you come across this?" she said.

He told her the whole story, from the moment Asta had spot-ted the man under the oak tree to the story Mrs. Carpenter in the chandlery had shown him in the *Oxford Times*.

"My God," she said. She had gone pale. "Robert Luckhurst?"

"Yes, from Magdalen. Did you know him?"

"Slightly. I had no idea he was the one who . . . We're not sup-posed to know each other, and I'm certainly not supposed to tell you this. What happened usually was that he'd put the acorn in a dead-letter drop and I'd collect it from there, and then put it back in another place when I'd written a reply. I never knew who put it there or collected it."

"That's a good system," he said.

She wondered if she'd already said more than she should. She hadn't expected to tell him anything, but then she hadn't expected him to know so much.

"Have you told anyone else about this?" she said.

"No. I don't think it's safe."

"Well, you're right." She hesitated. She could thank him and send him away now, or . . . "Would you like something hot to drink? Some chocolatl?"

"Oh, yes, please," he said.

In the little kitchen she put some milk on to boil and then looked at the message again. Was there anything compromising in it? It was quite clear that the alethiometer was involved, and the identities of the alethiometer specialists in Oxford were no secret. As for Dust, it meant big trouble.

She mixed the cocoa powder with a little sugar and poured in the hot milk, making some for herself as well. The boy knew so much already that she had to trust him. There was little choice.

"You got a lot of books," he said as she came back. "Are you a scholar?"

"Yes, I am. At St. Sophia's."

"Are you an historian?"

"Sort of. A historian of ideas, I suppose. An historian." She switched on the standard lamp beside the fire, and instantly the room became warmer, the weather outside darker and colder. "Malcolm, this message . . ."

"Yeah? Yes?"

"Have you made a copy of it?"

He blushed. "Yes. But I've hidden it," he said, "under a floorboard in my bedroom. No one knows that space is there."

"Will you do something? Will you burn your copy?"

"Yes. I promise."

His dæmon and hers had established a friendship already, it seemed: Jesper was sitting on top of a glass case of ornaments and curiosities, and Asta, in the form of a goldfinch, was perching there too as he quietly explained about the Babylonian seal, the Roman coin, the harlequin.

"Is there anything you want to ask me?" she said.

"Yes. Lots. Who made the acorn?"

"Well, that I don't know. I think they're sort of standard issue."

"What's the instrument? When I asked how you knew it was me that had the acorn, you said there was an instrument. Is that the althee—almeth—"

"The alethiometer . . . yes."

She explained what it was and how it worked, and he followed closely.

"A-lee-thee-ometer . . . Is that the only one there is?"

"No. There were six originally. The others are all in other universities. Except one, anyway, which is lost."

"Why don't they make another one? Or lots of them?"

"They don't know how to anymore."

"They could take it apart and look. If they didn't know how to make a clock, and they had one that worked, they could take it apart very carefully and make a drawing of every separate part and how they joined up, and then make more parts like that and make another clock. It'd be complicated, but it wouldn't be hard."

This was all safe. If she could keep him on this subject, she'd have nothing to worry about.

"I think there's more to it than that," she said. "I think parts of it are made of an alloy that can't be made anymore. Perhaps the metal's very rare—I don't know. Anyway, nobody has."

"Oh. That's interesting. I'd like to have a look at it someday. How things fit together—I love looking at that."

"Where do you go to school, Malcolm?"

"Ulvercote Elementary. That's the old name for Wolvercote."

"Where will you go when you leave that school?"

"What school, you mean? I dunno if I will. Prob'ly if I get an apprenticeship . . . Maybe my dad would like me just to work at the Trout."

"What about going to a senior school?"

"I don't think they've thought of that."

"Would you like to? Do you like school?"

"Yes, I prob'ly would. Yes, I would. But it's not very likely."

His dæmon was listening closely. She flew to his shoulder and whispered something, and he very slightly shook his head. Hannah pretended not to see and bent to put a log on the fire.

"What did the message mean by the 'Rusakov field'?" said Malcolm.

"Ah. Well, I don't really know. It's not necessary for me to know everything when I consult the alethiometer. It seems to know what it needs to."

"'Cause the message said, 'When we try measuring one way, our substance evades it and seems to prefer another, but when we try a different way, we have no more success.'"

"Have you memorized the whole message?"

"I didn't set out to. I've just read it so much, it memorized itself. Anyway, what I was going to say was, that sounds a bit like the uncertainty principle."

She felt as if she was walking downstairs in the dark and had just missed a step.

"How do you know about that?"

"Well, there's lots of scholars come to the Trout, and they tell me things. Like the uncertainty principle, where you can know some things about a particle, but you can't know everything. If you know *this* thing, you can't know *that* thing, so you're always going to be uncertain. It sounds like that. And the other thing it says, about Dust. What's Dust?"

Hannah hastily tried to recall what was public knowledge and what was Oakley Street knowledge, and said, "It's a kind of elementary particle that we don't know much about. It's not easy to examine, not just because of what it says in this message, but because the Magisterium . . . D'you know what I mean by the Magisterium?"

"The sort of chief authority of the Church."

"That's right. Well, they strongly disapprove of any investigations into Dust. They think it's sinful. I don't know why. That's one of the mysteries that we're trying to solve."

"How can knowing something be sinful?"

"A very good question. Do you talk to anyone at school about this sort of thing?"

"Only my friend Robbie. He doesn't say very much, but I know he's interested."

"Not to the teachers?"

"I don't think they'd understand. It's just that being at the Trout, I can talk to all kinds of people."

"Very useful too," Hannah said. An idea was beginning to form in her mind, but she tried to push it away.

"So you think when he mentions Dust, he's talking about elementary particles?" said Malcolm.

"I expect so. But it's not my area, and I don't know for sure."

He stared into the fire for a while. Then he said, "If Mr. Luckhurst was the person who passed the acorn back and forth from you, then . . ."

"I know. How am I going to contact the—the other people? There's another way. I'll have to use that."

"Who are the other people?"

"I can't tell you because I don't know."

"How was it all set up in the first place?"

"Someone asked me to help."

He sipped his chocolatl and seemed to be considering things deeply.

"And the enemy," he said carefully, "that's the Consistorial Court, isn't it?"

"Well, you've seen enough to realize that, and you've seen how dangerous they are. Promise me you won't do anything else to link you with me or the tree by the canal. Anything dangerous at all."

"I can promise to *try*," he said, "but if it's secret, I won't know if I'm doing anything dangerous or not."

"Fair enough. And you won't tell anyone what you know already?"

"Yes, I can promise that."

"Well, that's a relief to me."

But all the time the *idea* kept nagging at her.

"Malcolm," she said, "when those two CCD men came to the Trout and arrested Mr. . . ."

"Mr. Boatwright. But he got away."

"Yes, him. They weren't asking about this sort of thing, were they?"

"No. They asked about a man who came to the Trout a few nights before. With the ex–lord chancellor. A man with a black mustache."

"Yes, I remember you mentioned him. You do mean the ex–lord chancellor of England? Lord Nugent? Not just someone who was nicknamed the lord chancellor, as a joke?"

"Yes, it was Lord Nugent, all right. Dad showed me his picture in the paper later."

"D'you know why the CCD men were asking about him? Was it about a baby?"

Malcolm was taken aback. He'd been on his guard not to say anything about Lyra, as Sister Fenella had advised him; but then the old lady had realized that lots of people knew already, and she'd said that perhaps it didn't matter.

"Er . . . how d'you know about the baby?" he said.

"Is it something secret? To tell the truth, I heard someone talking about it when I was in the Trout yesterday. Somebody was saying that the nuns . . . I can't remember exactly, but a baby came into it somehow."

"Well," he said, "seeing as how you've heard of it already . . ." He told her how it had begun, from the three guests peering through the window of the Terrace Room to his glimpse of the little baby Lyra and her fierce dæmon.

"Well, that *is* interesting," she said.

"You know the law of sanctuary?" he said. "'Cause Sister Fenella told me about sanctuary, and I wondered if they were going to put the baby there because of that. And she said there were some colleges that could do sanctuary as well."

"I think they all could in the Middle Ages. There's only one that still maintains the right to do that."

"Which one is that?"

"Jordan. And they've used it too, quite recently. Mainly for political reasons these days. Scholars who've upset their governments can claim scholastic sanctuary, like seeking asylum. There's a sort of formula: they have to claim the right to sanctuary in a Latin sentence, which they speak to the Master."

"Which one's Jordan?"

"The one in Turl Street with the very tall spire."

"Oh, I know. . . . D'you think those men could have been asking for sanctuary—for the baby, I mean?"

"I don't know. I really don't know. But it's given me an idea. And I'm going to contradict what I said just now, because I'd like to keep in touch with you, Malcolm, after all. You like reading, don't you?"

"Yeah!" he said.

"Well, let's pretend this: I left my book behind and you brought it back to me—that's perfectly true. You saw all my books, we got talking about books and reading and so on, and I offered to lend you some. To be a sort of library. You could borrow a book or two and bring them back when you've finished and choose some more. That would be a good reason for coming here. Shall we pretend that?"

"Yes," he said at once. His dæmon, a squirrel now, sat on his shoulder and clapped her paws together. "And anything I see or hear—"

"That's right. Don't go looking—don't put yourself in any danger at all. But if you do overhear something interesting, you can tell me about it. And when you come here, we'll talk about books anyway. How's that?"

"That's great! It's a brilliant idea."

"Good. Good! Well, we might as well start now. Look, here are my murder mysteries—d'you like that sort of thing?"

"I like all kinds."

"And here are my history books. Some of them might be a bit dull—I don't know. Anyway, the rest are a mixture of all sorts. Take your pick. Why not find one novel and one something else?"

He got up eagerly and scanned the shelves. She watched, sitting back, not wanting to force anything on him. When she was a young girl, an elderly lady in the village where she grew up had done the same for her, and she remembered the delight of choosing for herself, of being allowed to range anywhere on the shelves. There were two or three commercial subscription libraries in Oxford, but no free public library, and Malcolm wouldn't be the only young person whose hunger for books had to go unsatisfied.

So she felt good at seeing him so keen and happy as he moved along, picking out books and looking at them and reading the first page and putting them back before trying another. She saw herself in this curious boy.

At the same time, she felt horribly guilty. She was exploiting him; she was putting him in danger. She was making a spy out of him. That he was brave and intelligent made it no better; he was still so young that he was unconscious of the chocolatl remaining on his top lip. It wasn't something he could volunteer for, though she guessed he would have done so eagerly; she had pressured him, or tempted him. She had more power, and she had done that.

He chose his books and tucked them away tightly in his knapsack to keep them dry, they agreed when he should come again, and he went out into the damp, dark evening.

She drew the curtains and sat down. She put her head in her hands.

"No point in hiding," said Jesper. "I can see you."

"Was I wrong?"

"Yes, of course. But you had no choice."

"I must have."

"No, you had to do it. If you hadn't done it, you'd have felt feeble."

"It shouldn't be about how we feel—guilty, feeble—"

"No, and it isn't. It's about wrong and less wrong. Bad and less bad. This is about as good a cover as anyone could find. Leave it at that."

"I know," she said. "All the same . . ."

"Tough," he said.

SIX

GLAZING SPRIGS

Malcolm decided to tell his parents about the scholar whose book he'd returned, and about her offer to lend him others, so that he wouldn't be hiding anything except the most important thing of all. He showed his mother the first two books as she dished up the lamb stew that was his supper.

"*The Body in the Library*," she read, "and *A Brief History of Time*. Don't bring 'em in the kitchen, though. They'll get all spotted with grease and gravy. If someone lends you something, you have to look after it."

"I'll keep 'em in my bedroom," said Malcolm, tucking them back in the knapsack.

"Good. Now hurry up—it's busy tonight."

Malcolm sat down to his supper.

"Mum," he said, "when I leave Ulvercote Elementary, am I going to senior school?"

"Depends what your dad says."

"What d'you think he'd say?"

"I think he'd say eat your supper."

"I can eat and listen at the same time."

"Pity I can't talk and cook, then."

The next day, the nuns were busy and Mr. Taphouse was at home, so Malcolm had no excuse to go to the priory. Instead, he lay in his bedroom reading the books one after the other, and then when it stopped raining, he went out to see if it was dry enough to paint the boat's name in his new red paint, but it wasn't. So he went moodily back to his bedroom and set about making a lanyard with his cotton cord.

During lunchtime he carried drinks and food to customers in the bar as usual, and when he was attending to the fire, he happened to see something that surprised him. Alice, the washer-up, came into the bar with two handfuls of clean tankards and was leaning forward to put them on the bar when one of the men sitting nearby reached out and pinched her bottom.

Malcolm held his breath. Alice didn't show the slightest reaction at first, but made sure the glasses were safely on the bar before she turned round.

"Who done that?" she said calmly, but Malcolm could see that her nostrils were flared and her eyes narrowed.

None of the men moved or spoke. The man who had pinched her was a plump middle-aged farmer called Arnold Hemsley, whose dæmon was a ferret. Alice's dæmon, Ben, had become a bulldog, and Malcolm could hear his quiet growl, and saw the ferret trying to hide in the man's sleeve.

"Next time that happens," Alice said, "I won't even try and find out who done it; I'll just glass the nearest one of yer." And she took a tankard by the handle and smashed it on the bar, leaving a jagged edge of handle in her bony fist. The shards of glass fell on the stone floor in the silence.

"What happened here?" said Malcolm's father, arriving from the kitchen.

"Someone made a mistake," said Alice, and she tossed the broken handle into Hemsley's lap. He pulled away in alarm, tried to catch it, and cut himself. Alice walked away indifferently.

Malcolm, crouching in the fireplace with the poker in his hand, heard Hemsley and his friends muttering together. "She's too young, you bloody fool— She wants to watch herself— It was a stupid thing to do; she en't old enough— Deliberately provoking me— She wasn't, en't you got no sense?— Leave her alone, she's old Tony Parslow's girl. . . ."

But his father told him to sweep up the broken glass before he could hear any more, and the men soon stopped talking about it anyway, because all anyone really wanted to talk about was the rain and what it had been doing to the water levels. The reservoirs were full, and the River Board had had to release a lot of water into the river and keep the sluice gates open. Several meadows were flooded around Oxford and Abingdon, but that was nothing unusual; the trouble was that the water wasn't draining away, and further down the river a number of villages were under threat.

Malcolm wondered whether to make notes of all this in case it was important, but decided not to. There'd be conversations like this in every pub on every river in the kingdom. It was strange, though.

"Mr. Anscombe?" he said to one of the watermen.

"What's that, Malcolm?"

"Has it ever been as wet as this before?"

"Oh, yeah. You look at the lockkeeper's house at Duke's Cut. On the wall there they've got a board showing how high the water came in the floods of— When was it, Dougie?"

"It was 1883," said his companion.

"No, more recent than that."

"Then '52, was it? Or '53?"

"Summin' like that. Every forty, fifty years or so there's a monstrous flood. They oughter get it sorted out by now."

"What could they do, though?" said Malcolm.

"Dig more reservoirs," said Dougie. "There's always a demand for water."

"No, no," said Mr. Anscombe, "the problem is the river. They oughter dredge it proper. You seen them dredgers at work down by Wallingford—little flimsy things. They en't man enough for the job. They'd be swep' away theirselves if a really big flood come along. The problem is when you get a big mass of water coming down off the hills, it's held up by the riverbed not being deep enough, and it spreads out instead."

"If they en't taking precautions past Abingdon already," said Dougie, "they bloody oughter be. All them villages down there— they're all vulnerable. See, if they'd dug two or three big reservoirs higher up, the water wouldn't be wasted either. It's a precious resource, water."

"Yeah, it would be in the Sahara Desert," said Mr. Anscombe, "but what're you going to do? Send it there by post? There's no shortage of water in England. It's the river depth that's the problem. Dredge it all out proper, and it'll flow down to the sea good as gold."

"The land's too level this side the Chilterns," said someone else, and began to explain more, but Malcolm was called away to take some beer to the Conservatory Room.

The first thing Malcolm heard that was worth reporting came not from the Trout but from Ulvercote Elementary School. Long periods of rain were the teachers' despair, as the children couldn't go out and the teachers had to supervise indoor play, and everybody became frustrated and fretful.

In the crowded, noisy, stuffy playtime classroom, Malcolm and three friends had turned two desks around back to back and were playing a form of table football, but Eric's dæmon had some exciting and mysterious news that Eric wasn't trying very hard to suppress.

"What? What? What?" said Robbie.

"I'm not supposed to say," said Eric virtuously.

"Well, just say it quietly," said Tom.

"It's not *legal* to say it. It's against the law."

"Who told you, then?"

"My dad. But he told me not to repeat it."

Eric's father was the clerk of the county court and often passed on news of particularly juicy trials to Eric, whose popularity increased in proportion.

"Your dad's always saying that," Malcolm pointed out, "but you always tell us anyway."

"No, this is different. This is *really* secret."

"He shouldn't have told you, then," said Tom.

"He knows he can trust me," said Eric, to a chorus of jeers.

"You know you *are* going to tell us," said Malcolm, "so you might as well do it before the bell goes."

Eric made a great performance of looking around and leaning in close. They all leaned in too.

"You know there was that man who fell in the canal and drowned?" he said.

Robbie had heard about it, Tom hadn't, and Malcolm just nodded.

"Well, there was his inquest on Friday," Eric went on. "And everyone thought he'd drowned, but it turned out he was strangled before his body entered the water. So he never fell in. He was murdered first, and then the murderer chucked him in the canal."

"Wow," said Robbie.

"How'd they know that?" said Tom.

"There was no water in his lungs. And there was marks on his neck where the rope had been."

"So what's going to happen next?" said Malcolm.

"Well, it's a police case now," said Eric. "I don't suppose we'll hear any more till they catch the murderer and he goes on trial."

At that point, the bell went, and they had to put their game away and turn the desks around and settle down, sighing heavily, to French.

Malcolm made straight for the newspaper when he got home, but there was no mention of the body in the canal. *The Body in the Library*, however, was gripping, and he finished it after he was supposed to put his light out. It was a good deal less horrible, somehow, despite the violence done to the victim in the book, than the thought of that poor man who'd lost the acorn: unhappy, frightened, and, finally, strangled to death.

Once that thought had got hold of Malcolm, he found it hard to struggle loose. If only he and Asta had offered to help at once! They would have found the acorn, the man would have got away quickly, the CCD men wouldn't have arrested him, he'd still be alive. . . .

On the other hand, the CCD men might have been watching all the time. They might have been going to arrest him whatever happened. It was the *loneliness* of his death that upset Malcolm most.

After school the next day, Malcolm went to the priory to see how the baby was. The answer was that she was fine, and currently asleep, and no, he couldn't see her.

85

"But I've got a present for her," said Malcolm to Sister Benedicta, who was working in the office. Sister Fenella was busy elsewhere, apparently, and couldn't see him.

"Well, that's very kind of you, Malcolm," said the nun, "and if you give it to me, I'll make sure she gets it."

"Thank you," said Malcolm. "But maybe I'll leave it till I can give it to her myself."

"As you please."

"Is there anything I can do while I'm here?"

"No, not today, thank you, Malcolm. Everything's fine."

"Sister Benedicta," he persisted, "when they were deciding whether to put the baby here, was it the ex–lord chancellor who decided? Lord Nugent?"

"He had a part in the decision, yes," she said. "Now, if—"

"What's the lord chancellor's job?"

"He's one of the chief law officers of the Crown. He's the Speaker of the House of Lords."

"Why was it his job to decide about this baby, then? There must be loads of babies. If he had to decide where each of them should go, he wouldn't have time to do anything else."

"I'm sure you're right," she said, "but that's the way it was. Her parents are important people, mind you. That had something to do with it. And I hope you haven't been talking about it. It's supposed to be confidential. It's certainly private. Now, Malcolm, I really must get these accounts in order before Vespers. Off you go. We'll talk another day."

She'd said "Everything's fine," but it wasn't. Sister Fenella should have been cooking by now, and there were sisters he didn't know very well hurrying along the corridors, looking anxious. He'd have worried about the baby, but Sister Benedicta always told the truth; all the same, it was troubling.

Malcolm went outside into the drizzle of the dark evening and saw a warm light glowing in the workshop. Mr. Taphouse, the carpenter, must still be there. He knocked on the door and went in.

"What're you making, Mr. Taphouse?" he said.

"What's it look like?"

"Looks like windows. That one looks like the kitchen window. Except . . . No, they're going to be shutters. Is that right?"

"That's it. Feel the weight of that, Malcolm."

The old man stood the kitchen-window-shaped frame upright in the middle of the floor, and Malcolm tried to lift it.

"Blimey! That's heavy!"

"Two-inch oak all round. Add the weight of the shutter itself, and what'll you have to be sure of?"

Malcolm thought. "The fixing in the wall. It'll have to be really strong. Is it going inside or out?"

"Outside."

"There's nothing but stone to fix it to there. How are you going to do that?"

Mr. Taphouse winked and opened a cupboard. Inside, Malcolm saw a new piece of large machinery, surrounded by coils of heavy wire flex.

"Anbaric drill," said the carpenter. "You want to give me a hand? Sweep up for me."

He closed the cupboard and handed Malcolm a broom. The floor was thick with shavings and sawdust.

"Why . . . ," Malcolm began, but Mr. Taphouse was too quick for him.

"You may well ask," he said. "Every window shuttered to that quality, and no one tells me why. I don't ask. I never ask. Just do what I'm told. Doesn't mean I don't wonder."

The old man lifted the frame and stood it against the wall with several others.

"The stained-glass windows too?" asked Malcolm.

"Not them yet. I think the sisters believe they're too precious. They reckon no one'd try and damage them."

"So these are for protection?" Malcolm sounded incredulous, and he felt it too: Who on earth would want to hurt the nuns, or break their windows?

"That's my best guess," said Mr. Taphouse, putting a chisel back into its rack on the wall.

"But . . ." Malcolm couldn't think how to finish.

"But who'd threaten the sisters? I know. That's the question. I can't answer it. There's something up, though. They're afraid of something."

"I thought it felt a bit funny in there just now," said Malcolm.

"Well, that's it."

"Is it anything to do with the baby?"

"Who knows? Her father's made hisself a nuisance to the Church in his time."

"Lord Asriel?"

"Thassit. But you want to keep your nose out of that sort of thing. There's some things it's dangerous to talk about."

"Why? I mean, in what way?"

"That's enough. When I say that's enough, that's enough. Don't be cheeky."

Mr. Taphouse's dæmon, a ragged-looking woodpecker, clacked her beak crossly. Malcolm said no more, but swept up the shavings and the sawdust and tipped them into the bin next to the offcuts, from which Mr. Taphouse would feed the old iron stove the next day.

"Good night, Mr. Taphouse," said Malcolm as he left.

The old man grunted and said nothing.

Having finished *The Body in the Library*, Malcolm returned to *A Brief History of Time*. It was harder going, but he expected it to be, and the subject was exciting even if he didn't understand everything the author said about it. He wanted to finish it before Saturday, and just about managed it.

Dr. Relf was replacing a broken pane of glass in her back door when he arrived. Malcolm was interested at once.

"How did that happen?" he said.

"Someone broke it. I bolt the door top and bottom, so they wouldn't have been able to get in anyway, but I think they were hoping the key was in the lock."

"Have you got some putty? And some glazing sprigs?"

"What are they?"

"Little nails without heads that hold the glass in place."

"I thought the putty did that."

"Not by itself. I can go and get some for you."

There was an ironmonger's in Walton Street, about five minutes' walk away, which was one of Malcolm's favorite places after the chandlery. He'd cast a quick glance at Dr. Relf's tools, and she had everything else necessary, so it wasn't long before he returned with a little bag of glazing sprigs.

"I seen—I saw—Mr. Taphouse doing this once at the priory. He's the carpenter," he explained. "What he did was— Look, I'll show you." To avoid bashing the glass with the hammer as he tapped the glazing sprig into the frame, he put the sprig along the glass with its point in the wood, then held the side of a chisel against the other end of it so he could tap the hammer against that to drive it home.

"Oh, that's clever," said Dr. Relf. "Let me have a go."

When he was sure she wouldn't break the glass, Malcolm let her finish while he softened and warmed the putty.

"Should I have a putty knife?" she said.

"No. An ordinary eating knife'll do. One with a round end's best."

He'd never actually done it himself, but he remembered what Mr. Taphouse had done, and the result was perfectly neat.

"Wonderful," she said.

"You have to let it dry and get a bit of a skin before you can paint it," he said. "Then it'll be all weatherproof and everything."

"Well, I think we deserve a cup of chocolatl now," she said. "Thank you very much, Malcolm."

"I'll tidy up," he said. That was what Mr. Taphouse would have expected. Malcolm imagined him watching, and giving a stern nod when everything was put away and swept up.

"I've got two things to tell you," he said when they were sitting down by the fire in the little sitting room.

"Good!"

"It might not be good. You know the priory, where they're looking after the infant, the baby? Well, Mr. Taphouse's making some heavy shutters to go over all their windows. He doesn't know why—he doesn't ask why anything—but they're so heavy and strong. When I was there the other day, the sisters were kind of anxious, and then I found him making the shutters. You could do with some here. Mr. Taphouse said the nuns were probably afraid of something, but he couldn't guess what it was. I don't know if I asked him the right questions. . . . Maybe I should've asked if one of the windows had been broken, but I didn't think of that."

"Never mind. That is interesting. Do you think they were protecting the baby?"

"Bound to be, partly. But they got all sorts of things to protect there, like crucifixes and statues and silver and stuff. If it was just burglars they were worried about, though, I dunno if they'd bother with the sort of shutters that Mr. Taphouse was making. So maybe they're worried about the baby mostly."

"I'm sure they would be."

"Sister Benedicta told me that it *was* Lord Nugent, the ex–lord chancellor of England, who decided to put the baby there. She didn't say why, and sometimes she gets cross if I keep on asking. And she said the baby was confidential as well. But so many people know about her already I thought it wouldn't matter much."

"I expect you're right. What was the other thing?"

"Oh, yes . . ."

Malcolm told her what Eric's father, the clerk of the court, had passed on about the man in the canal. Her face grew pale.

"Good God. That's appalling," she said.

"D'you think it might be true?"

"Oh. Well—don't you?"

"The thing is, Eric does exaggerate a bit."

"Oh?"

"He likes to show off about what he knows, what his dad's heard in court."

"I wonder if his dad *would* have told him that sort of thing."

"Yes, I think he would. I've heard him talk like that about things that have happened, trials and that. I think he'd be telling the truth to Eric. But maybe Eric . . . I dunno, though. I just think that poor man—he looked so unhappy. . . ."

To Malcolm's intense embarrassment, his voice shook, his throat tightened, and he found tears flowing from his eyes. When he'd been moved to tears at home, when he was much younger, his mother had known what to do: she gathered him into her arms and rocked him gently till the crying faded away. Malcolm realized that he'd wanted to cry about the dead man since the moment he'd heard about him, but of course he couldn't possibly tell his mother about any of this.

"Sorry," he said.

"Malcolm! Don't say sorry. *I'm* sorry that you're mixed up in this. And actually, now I think we'd better stop. I've got no business asking you to—"

"I don't want to stop! I want to *find out*!"

"It's too dangerous. If anyone thinks you know anything about this, then you're in real—"

"I know. But I am anyway. I can't help it. It certainly en't your fault. I'd have seen all those things even if it weren't for you. And at least I can talk to you. I couldn't talk to anyone else, not even Sister Fenella. She wouldn't understand at all."

He was still embarrassed, and he could tell that Dr. Relf was embarrassed too, because she hadn't known what to do. He wouldn't have wanted her to embrace him, so he was glad she hadn't tried to do that, at least, but it was still an awkward little moment.

"Well, promise me you won't *ask* anything," she said.

"Yeah, all right, I can promise that," he said, meaning it. "I won't start any asking. But if someone else says something . . ."

"Well, use your judgment. Try not to seem interested. And we'd better get on and do what our cover story says we're doing, and talk about books. What did you think of these two?"

Malcolm had never had a conversation like the one that followed. At school, in a class of forty, there was no time for such a thing, even if the curriculum allowed it, even if the teachers had been interested; at home it wouldn't have happened, because neither his father nor his mother was a reader; in the bar he was a listener rather than a participant; and the only two friends with whom he might have spoken seriously about such things, Robbie and Tom, had none of the breadth of learning and the depth of understanding that he found when Dr. Relf spoke.

At first, Asta sat close on his shoulder, where she'd gone as a little ferret when he had found himself crying; but little by little she felt easier, and before long she was sitting beside Jesper, the kind-faced marmoset, having their own quiet exchange while *The Body in the Library* was discussed and *A Brief History of Time* touched on with wary respect.

"You said last time that you were a historian of ideas," said Malcolm. "An historian. What sort of ideas did you mean? Like the ones in this book?"

"Yes, largely," she said. "Ideas about big things, such as the universe, and good and evil, and why things exist in the first place."

"I never thought about why they did," said Malcolm, wondering. "I never thought you could think things like that. I thought things just were. So people thought different things about 'em in the past?"

"Oh, yes. And there were times when it was very dangerous to think the wrong things, or at least to talk about them."

"It is now, sort of."

"Yes. I'm afraid you're right. But as long as we keep to what's been published, I don't think you and I will get into much trouble."

Malcolm wanted to ask about the secret things she was involved with, and whether they were part of the history of ideas, but he felt that it was better to stick to books for now. So he asked if she had any more books about experimental theology, and she found him one called *The Strange Story of the Quantum*, and then she let him scan the shelves of murder stories, and he picked out another by the author of *The Body in the Library*.

"You got lots of hers," he said.

"Not as many as she wrote."

"How many books have you read?"

"Thousands. I couldn't possibly guess."

"Do you remember them all?"

"No. I remember the very good ones. Most of my murders and thrillers aren't very good in that way, so if I let a little time go by, I find I've forgotten them and I can read them again."

"That's a good idea," he said. "I prob'ly better go now. If I hear anything else, I'll save it up and tell you. And if you get another broken window—well, you can prob'ly mend it yourself, now I showed you about glazing sprigs."

"Thank you, Malcolm," she said. "And please—once more—be careful."

That evening, Hannah didn't go into her college for dinner as usual. Instead, she took a note to the porter's lodge at Jordan College and went home to make herself some scrambled eggs. Then she drank a glass of wine and waited.

At twenty past nine, there was a knock at the door, and she opened it at once and let in the man who was waiting outside in the rain.

"I'm sorry to bring you out on a night like this," she said.

"Sorry to be brought," he said. "Never mind. What's this about?"

His name was George Papadimitriou, and he was the professor of Byzantine history who had first recruited her for Oakley Street two years before. He was also the tall scholarly-looking man who had had dinner with Lord Nugent at the Trout.

She took his coat and shook off the worst of the rain before hanging it on the radiator.

"I've done something stupid," she said.

"That's not like you. I'll have a glass of whatever that is. Go on, then, tell me."

His greenfinch dæmon touched noses courteously with Jesper and then perched on the back of his chair as he sat down by the fire with his wine. Hannah filled her own glass again and sat down in the other chair.

She took a deep breath and told him about Malcolm: the acorn, her asking the alethiometer, the Trout, the books. She edited it very carefully, but she told him everything he needed to know.

He listened in silence. His long, dark, heavy-eyed face was serious and still.

"I read about the man in the canal," he said. "Naturally, I didn't know he was your insulator. I hadn't heard about the strangling either. Any chance that this is just a child's fantasy?"

"It could be, of course, but not Malcolm's. I believe him. If it's a fantasy, it's his friend's."

"It won't be reported in the press, of course."

"Unless it's *not* the CCD behind it. Then they won't be afraid and it won't be censored."

He nodded. He hadn't wasted time agreeing with her that she'd been stupid and chastising her for it and threatening reprisals; all his intellect was focused now on dealing with the situation, with this curious boy and the position she'd put him in.

"Well, he could be useful, you know," he said.

"I know he could be *useful*. I saw that from the start. I'm just angry with myself for putting him at risk."

"As long as you cover it all, there won't be much risk to him."

"Well . . . it's affecting him. When he was telling me about the strangling, he found himself crying."

"Natural in a young child."

"He's a sensitive boy. . . . There's something else. He's very close to the nuns at Godstow Priory, just across the river from the Trout. And it seems that they're looking after the child who was the subject of that court case, the daughter of Lord Asriel."

Papadimitriou nodded.

"You knew about it?" she went on.

"Yes. In fact, I was discussing the matter with two colleagues in a room at the Trout. And it was your Malcolm who was serving us. That'll teach me a lesson."

"So it was you—and the lord chancellor? Was he right about that?"

"What did he tell you?"

She went over it briefly.

"What an observant boy," he said.

"He's an only child, and I think he was fascinated by the baby. She's—I don't know—six months old or thereabouts."

"Who else knows she's there?"

"The boy's parents, I suppose. Presumably some of the customers of the pub, the villagers, servants . . . It didn't seem to be a secret."

"Normally a child would be in the care of its mother, but in this case the woman didn't want it and said so. Custody would then fall to the father, but the court forbade it, on the grounds that he was not a fit person. No, it's not a secret, but it might become important."

"One more thing," said Hannah. She told him about the CCD men who tried to arrest George Boatwright, and their interest in the men who had been in the Trout. "That must have been you and Lord Nugent," she said. "But they were asking about another man."

"There were three of us," said Papadimitriou. He finished the wine.

"Another glass?" she said.

"No, thank you. Don't call me again like this. The porter at Jordan is a gossip. If you want to contact me, put a card on the notice board outside the History Faculty Library, saying simply 'Candle.' That will be a signal to go to the next Evensong at Wykeham. I shall be sitting alone. You will sit next to me and we can talk quietly under the music."

"Candle. I understand. And if you want to contact me?"

"If I do, you will know about it. I think you did well to recruit this boy. Look after him."

SEVEN

TOO SOON

The headquarters of the secret service that employed Hannah Relf was known to its agents as Oakley Street for the simple reason that that respectable Chelsea thoroughfare was nowhere near it and had nothing to do with it at all.

That was not known to Hannah, though. She had never been to the headquarters of the service, and as far as she was aware, the words Oakley Street, wherever that was, meant no more than a straightforward address. Apart from Professor Papadimitriou, almost her only contact with the service was the acorn. She gathered it with its query, and left it with her reply, in one of a number of different hiding places that Oakley Street called left-luggage boxes. The person who left it for her and took it away again, the late Mr. Luckhurst, was known as an insulator: neither of them knew the other, which meant that they wouldn't be able to reveal anything if questioned.

The one other way of talking to Oakley Street was through a cataloger at the Bodleian Library. What she had to do was submit a query about the catalog number of a particular book, which would tell him that she wanted to pass a message to the service. The book didn't matter, but the author's name did: the first letter of the surname was a code that indicated the matter she wanted to talk about.

Accordingly, she submitted her query on the official form, and the following day she received a note inviting her to meet the cataloger, Harry Dibdin, in his office at eleven a.m.

Dibdin was a thin, sandy-colored man, whose dæmon was a bird of some tropical kind she didn't know. He shut the door and lifted a pile of books off the visitor's chair before offering her a cup of coffee.

"Cataloging queries can take time," he said. "And we always pay scrupulous attention to the views of distinguished scholars."

"In that case, I'd like some coffee, thank you," she said.

He plugged in an anbaric kettle and fussed with some cups.

"You can talk in here with perfect confidence," he said. "No one can hear us at all. You wanted to contact Oakley Street. What's it about?"

"My insulator has been murdered. I'm pretty sure of that. By the CCD. For the time being, I've got no way of contacting my clients."

She meant the four or five Oakley Street officers who sent her questions in the acorn.

"Murdered?" said Dibdin. "How do you know?"

She told him the story. By the time she finished, he had poured the coffee and handed her a cup.

"If you'd like milk, I'll have to go and hunt for some. I've got sugar, though."

"Black is fine. Thank you."

"Are your clients in a hurry?" he said, sitting down. His dæmon fluttered an exotic tail and settled on his shoulder.

"If they were in a hurry, they wouldn't be consulting the alethiometer," she said. "But it's not something I want to postpone if I can help it."

"Quite. Are you sure that Oakley Street doesn't know about your insulator?"

"No. I'm not sure of anything. But when a system that's worked for eighteen months suddenly goes wrong—"

"You're worried about what he might have given away before they killed him?"

"Of course. He didn't know me, but he knew where all the left-luggage boxes were, and they could watch them."

"How many did you use?"

"Nine."

"In strict rotation?"

"No. There was a code, which—"

"Don't tell me what it was. But it meant you could pick up or drop a message and go straight to the right box? And he'd do the same?"

"Yes."

"Well, nine . . . They won't have enough agents to watch nine boxes twenty-four hours a day. Wouldn't do any harm to find some new ones, though. Let Oakley Street know through me where they are. And if the insulator didn't know you, you're in no danger."

"So for the moment . . ."

"Do nothing more than look for the new boxes. When Oakley Street's put a new insulator in place, I'll let you know."

"Thanks," she said. "Actually, there was something else I was wondering about."

"Go on."

"Is the lord chancellor, Lord Nugent—ex–lord chancellor—an Oakley Street man?"

Dibdin blinked, and his dæmon shifted her feet.

99

"I don't know," he said.

"Yes, you do. And by the way you reacted, I can tell that he is."

"I didn't say that."

"Not in so many words. Here's another question: What's the significance of the child of a man called Lord Asriel and a woman called Mrs. Coulter?"

He said nothing for several seconds. Then he rubbed his jaw, and his dæmon chirruped something quietly in his ear.

"What do you know about a child?" he asked.

"That child is in the care of some nuns at Godstow. She's a baby—six months old or so. Why is Lord Nugent interested in her?"

"I can't imagine. How do you know he is?"

"I think he was responsible for getting her placed there."

"Perhaps he's a friend of the parents. Not everything's connected to Oakley Street, you know."

"No. You're probably right. Thanks for the coffee."

"A pleasure," he said, opening the door for her. "Anytime."

As she made her way back to Duke Humfrey, she resolved never to mention Oakley Street to Malcolm. He didn't need to know anything about that. And she would have to subdue the guilt she felt about asking him to spy; there was nothing about this business that was comfortable, nothing at all.

Malcolm spent some time helping Mr. Taphouse with the shutters. He liked the new anbaric drill very much, and when Mr. Taphouse, after much pestering, let him try it, he liked it even more. They put up all the shutters that Mr. Taphouse had made, and then went back to the workshop and made some more.

"Had to pay a fortune for this oak," the old man grumbled. "Sister Benedicta don't like paying so much, but I says to her deal's deal and oak's oak, and she saw the sense in the end."

"It's only as strong as the fixing anyway," said Malcolm, who'd heard Mr. Taphouse say those words many times.

"Yeah, but big wood like this'll hold a big fixing. It'd take a long time with a screwdriver to get them screws out the wall."

"I was thinking," said Malcolm, "about these screws, right. You know when the slot gets worn away, it's much harder to undo, because the screwdriver can't bite?"

"What about it?"

"Well, s'pose we filed the head of the screw so you could do it up but not undo it?"

"How d'you mean?"

Malcolm put a screw in the vise and filed away part of the head to show Mr. Taphouse what he meant.

"See, you can turn it to screw it in, but there's nothing to turn against if you want to unscrew it."

"Oh, yeah. That's a good idea, Malcolm. A very good idea. But suppose Sister Benedicta changes her mind next year and tells me to take 'em all down again?"

"Oh. I hadn't thought of that."

"Well, let me know when you have," said the old man.

His dæmon cackled. Malcolm wasn't put out; he liked his idea and thought he could work on it to improve it. He put the screw in his top pocket and helped Mr. Taphouse with the next shutter.

"You going to varnish 'em, Mr. Taphouse?" he said.

"No. Danish oil, boy. Best thing there is. You know what you got to watch out for with Danish oil?"

"No. What?"

"Spontaneous combustion," the old man said roundly. "You put it on with a rag, see, and if you don't soak the rag in water after you've finished and dry it flat, it'll catch fire all by itself."

"What did you call it? Spon—"

"Spontaneous combustion."

Malcolm said it again for the pleasure of it.

After the carpenter had gone home, Malcolm went to the priory kitchen to talk to Sister Fenella. The old nun was cutting up a cabbage, and Malcolm took a knife and helped her.

"What have you been up to, Malcolm?" she said.

"Helping Mr. Taphouse," he said. "You know those shutters he's making, Sister Fenella? Why are you having shutters put up?"

"It was some advice we had from the police," she said. "They came and saw Sister Benedicta and told her there'd been a lot of burglaries in Oxford recently. And they thought of all the silver and plate and the precious vestments and so on, and advised us to put up some extra protection."

"Not for the baby, then?"

"Well, it'll protect her as well, of course."

"How is she?"

"Oh, she's very lively."

"Can I see her again?"

"If there's time."

"I made her a present."

"Oh, Malcolm, that's kind. . . ."

"I've got it here. I always carry it, just in case I can see her."

"Well, that's very good of you."

"So can I see her?"

"Well, all right. Have you done that cabbage?"

"Yes, look."

"Come along, then."

She put her knife down and wiped her hands, and led him down the corridor to the room where they'd been before. The crib stood in the middle of the floor, and one gloomy lamp was all the illumination in the room, so the baby was in semi-darkness. She was making all kinds of baby noises to her dæmon, who stood on his hind legs as a rat and stared at Sister Fenella and Malcolm before fleeing to the pillow and making chirruping noises into Lyra's ear.

"She's teaching him to talk!" Malcolm said.

With the greatest of care Sister Fenella lifted her up, and Lyra's rat dæmon leapt onto her tiny shoulder and became a shrew.

Malcolm took out his present. It was the lanyard he'd made, tied to a little ball of beechwood that he'd rounded and sanded carefully. He'd consulted his mother, who'd said, "As long as it's too big to swallow, it's probably safe."

"I was going to paint it," he told Sister Fenella, "but I know babies chew things and there's all kinds of stuff in paint that might not be good for her. So I sanded it as smooth as I could. She won't get splinters or anything. And if she swallows the lanyard, you can use the ball to pull it out again. It's really safe."

"Oh, it's lovely, Malcolm. Look, Lyra! It's a— It's a block of— What is it?"

"Beech. See, you can tell by the grain. It's really smooth. And the way it's tied, it'll never come off."

Lyra seized the lanyard at once and put it in her mouth.

"She likes it!" said Malcolm.

"She might—I don't know—if she tries to swallow the string, she might choke. . . ."

"I suppose that's a possibility," Malcolm granted reluctantly. "Maybe she ought to wait and have it later. Or else you could bring her crib in the kitchen, and if she started to make choking noises, you could save her right away. I bet her dæmon'd make a racket if she started to choke. What's his name?"

"Pantalaimon."

"He could probably pull it out."

"It's not safe," said Asta firmly. "Give it to her when she's older."

103

"Oh, well," said Malcolm, and he tried to take the lanyard away gently. Lyra didn't care for that and started to object, but then Malcolm pretended to get hiccups and she laughed so much she forgot the lanyard and let go.

"Can I hold her?" he said.

"Better sit down first," said Sister Fenella.

He sat on an upright chair and held out his arms, and Sister Fenella put Lyra very carefully on his lap. Her little dæmon scampered up and down to avoid touching Malcolm, but Lyra herself was intrigued by this change of perspective and gazed calmly around, and then focused her eyes on Malcolm himself.

"That's Malcolm," said Sister Fenella in a soft bright voice. "You like Malcolm, don't you?"

Malcolm felt that, nice as the old nun was, she didn't know the best way of speaking to a baby. He looked down at the little face and said, "Now, see, Lyra, I made you that lanyard and the beechwood ball, but you're not old enough for it yet. That was my fault. I didn't think you'd probably choke on the lanyard. Well, you might not, but it's too dangerous at the moment. So I'll keep it till you're old enough to play with it without stuffing it in your mouth all the time. When you're old enough, I'll show you how to make one. It's quite easy when you know how. I made it with cotton cord, but you could use anything—twine, marline. . . . I'll take you for a ride in *La Belle Sauvage* when you're a bit older, how's that? That's my boat. I s'pose you better learn to swim first. We'll do that in the summer, all right?"

"I think she'll still be a little young . . . ," said Sister Fenella, and then she stopped because they heard voices in the corridor. "Quick!" she whispered, and took the baby from Malcolm's arms just as the door opened.

"Oh! What is this boy doing here?"

The speaker was a woman with tightly rolled gray hair and a hard face. She was not a nun, but the dark blue suit she wore looked like a uniform of some kind, and in the lapel was a small enamel badge showing a gold lamp with a little red flame coming out of it.

"Sister Fenella?" said Sister Benedicta, entering behind her.

"Oh! Well—Malcolm— This is Malcolm—"

"I know who Malcolm is. What are you doing?"

"I made a present for the baby," Malcolm said, "and I asked Sister Fenella if I could give it to her."

"Let me see," said the stranger.

She examined the wooden ball and the soggy string with some distaste.

"Not at all suitable. Take it away. And you, young man, go home. This is none of your business."

When Lyra heard the woman's harsh tone, her face crumpled, her dæmon burrowed his face into her neck, and she began to cry quietly.

"Bye, Lyra," Malcolm said, and squeezed her little hand. "Bye, Sister Fenella."

"Thank you, Malcolm," the old nun managed to say, and Malcolm noticed how frightened she was.

Sister Benedicta took Lyra away from Sister Fenella, and the last thing Malcolm heard as he left the priory was the baby wailing properly.

That was something else to tell Dr. Relf, he thought.

EIGHT

THE LEAGUE OF ST. ALEXANDER

At lunchtime on Monday, Malcolm was squatting in a corner of the playground, one of his non-unscrewable screws in one hand and his Swiss Army knife in the other, trying to work out a way of undoing them. Around him the shouts and screams of children playing and running about echoed from the school's brick walls, and a cold wind carried the noise away over Port Meadow.

Out of the corner of his eye, he saw someone sidling up to him, and he knew who it was without looking. It was Eric, whose father was the clerk of the court.

"I'm busy," Malcolm said, knowing too that Eric would take no notice.

"Hey, you know that man who was murdered? The one who was strangled and thrown in the canal?"

"You're not supposed to talk about him."

"Yeah, but you know what my dad heard?"

"What?"

"He was a spy."

"How do they know?"

"My dad couldn't tell me that, 'cause of the Official Secrets Act."

"Then how could he tell you the man was a spy in the first place? En't that an official secret?"

"No, 'cause if it was, he wouldn't be able to tell me, would he?"

Malcolm thought Eric's father would find a way to tell him anything if he wanted to.

"Who was he a spy for, then?" he said.

"I dunno. Dad couldn't tell me that either."

"Well, who d'you reckon?"

"The Muscovites. They're the enemy, en't they?"

"He might have been a spy for us, and it was the Muscovites who killed him," Malcolm pointed out.

"Well, what was he spying *on*, then?"

"I dunno. He was on holiday, prob'ly. Spies have got to have holidays, same as everyone. Who else you told?"

"No one yet."

"Well, you better be careful. I hope your dad's right about the Official Secrets Act. You know what the penalty for breaking it is?"

"I'll ask him."

"That's a good idea. But in the meantime, it'd be safer if you didn't tell anyone. There's spies everywhere."

"Not in school!" Eric scoffed.

"Teachers might be spies. What about Miss Davis?"

Miss Davis was the music teacher, the shortest-tempered person Malcolm had ever known.

Eric thought about it. "Maybe," he said. "But she stands out too much. A real spy'd be less conspicious. Blend in more."

"That might be a clever disguise, though. You'd expect a spy to be all quiet and sort of camouflaged, so if you saw Miss Davis screaming and banging the piano lid, you'd think she couldn't possibly be a spy, only she was all the time."

"Well, what would she spy on?"

"She'd do it in her spare time. She could go anywhere and spy on anything. *Anyone* could be a spy—that's the point."

"Well," said Eric, "maybe. But the man in the canal was *definitely* a spy."

In the form of a mouse, Eric's dæmon climbed up to his shoulder and said, just loud enough for Malcolm to hear, "Dad never said exactly that the man was a spy. Not exactly."

"Near enough," said Eric.

"Yeah, but you exaggerate."

"What did he say, then?" said Malcolm.

"What he said was: I wouldn't be surprised if he was a spy. Same thing."

"Not quite."

"The point is, why did he say that?" said Asta, who'd been following all this closely as a robin, her head turning sharply from one to the other.

"Exactly. Thank you," said Eric ponderously. "He knew something that made him think it was likely. So it prob'ly is."

"Can you find out?" said Malcolm.

"Dunno. I could ask him. But I got to be suitable about it. Can't just come out with a question."

"What d'you mean, 'suitable'?"

"*You* know. Not obvious."

"Oh, right," said Malcolm. *Subtle* was the word Eric wanted, probably. And he'd probably meant *conspicuous* earlier.

The bell rang at that point, and they had to line up in their classes and go in for the long, dreary afternoon. The usual way this happened was that the teacher on playground duty inspected the lines, told off anyone who was talking or fooling around, and dismissed the classes one at a time. Today, however, something different happened.

The teacher waited till everyone was still and quiet, and then stood still himself and looked past them at the school building. That made several heads turn, Malcolm's among them, and they saw the headmaster coming out, his gown flapping in the wind. And there was someone with him.

"This way," snapped the duty teacher, and they looked forward again before Malcolm could make out who the extra person was.

A moment later she was walking out in front of the class lines with the headmaster, and he recognized her at once as the woman who'd come to the priory, and who'd frightened Lyra with her harsh voice. She wore the same dark blue suit, had the same tightly rolled hairstyle.

"Listen carefully," said the headmaster. "When you go in, in a few moments, you will not go to your classes. You will go into the hall, just as you do for morning assembly. Go in as usual, sit down quietly, and wait. Anyone making a noise will find themselves in trouble. Class Five, lead off."

Malcolm could hear whispers around him: "Who's she? What's going to happen? Who's in trouble?"

He watched the woman closely without seeming to. She was scanning all the classes in front of her, her cold eyes raking through them as they stood and moved off in their lines. When her head turned his way, he made sure he was standing behind Eric, who was a little taller.

The hall was where the lunch ladies set out the tables for school lunch, and the aroma hung around all afternoon. That day, boiled cabbage had featured prominently on the menu, and not even the jam roll that had come after it did anything to dispel the heavy atmosphere. The hall was also where they had gym classes, and underneath the food smell there was an aromatic reminder of several generations of sweaty children.

As his class entered the hall, Malcolm looked at the line of teachers sitting along the back. Their faces were expressionless for the most part, as if this wasn't unusual at all but some quite normal part of a normal day, except that Mr. Savery, the math teacher, was scowling, with a look of deep disgust. And then in the instant before he sat, Malcolm saw the face of Miss Davis, the music teacher, because it caught the light, and it did that because her cheeks were wet with tears.

Malcolm noted all these things and imagined himself writing them down, as he would later, to tell Dr. Relf.

When all the children were sitting and still and silent, all the more quiet because of their sense that something unusual was happening, the headmaster came in and everyone stood up. The woman was with him.

"All right, sit down," he said.

When everything was quiet again, he said, "This lady is Miss Carmichael. I'll let her explain what she's doing."

Then he sat, gathering his gown around him, his crow dæmon in her usual position on his left shoulder. And Malcolm had something else to write later, because his face was as thunderous as Mr. Savery's. The woman couldn't see that, or else she ignored it; she waited for absolute silence, and then she began.

"You know, children, how our Holy Church has many different parts within it. Together they make up what we call the Magisterium, and they all work together for the good of the Church, which is the same as the good of every one of us.

"The part I represent is called the League of St. Alexander. I expect some of you have heard of St. Alexander, but perhaps your lessons haven't got that far yet, so I'll tell you his story.

"He lived in North Africa with his family a long time ago. It was a time when the Holy Church was still struggling against the pagans, those who worshipped evil gods, or those who believed in no god at all. And the little boy Alexander's family was one of those who worshipped an evil god. They didn't believe in Jesus Christ, they had an altar in the cellar under their house where they made sacrifices to the evil god they worshipped, and they mocked those who were like us, who worship the true God.

"Well, one day Alexander heard a man talking in the marketplace. He was a missionary. He had braved all the dangers of land and sea to take the story of Jesus Christ and the message of the true religion to the lands around the Mediterranean Sea, the lands where Alexander and his family lived.

"And Alexander was so interested in what the man said that he stayed and listened. He heard the story of Jesus's life and death, and how he rose from the dead, and how those who believe in him will have eternal life, and he went up to the preacher and said, 'I would like to be a Christian.'

"He wasn't the only one. A lot of people were baptized that day, including the governor of the province, who was a wise man called Regulus. Regulus ordered that all his officials should become Christians, and they all did.

"But there were a lot of people who didn't. A lot of people liked the religion they knew and didn't want to change. Even when Regulus made laws forbidding the pagan religion and compelling people to be Christian for their own good, they kept to the old wicked ways.

"And Alexander saw that he could do something to serve God and the Church. He knew some people who pretended to be Christian but really still worshipped the old gods, the evil gods. His own family, for instance. They had given shelter to a number of pagan people down in their cellar, people who were wanted by the authorities, people who had wickedly refused to hear the holy word of the Scriptures, the sacred word of God.

"So Alexander knew what he must do. Very bravely he went to the authorities and told them about his family and the pagans they were sheltering, and the soldiers went to the family's house in the middle of the night. They knew which house it was because Alexander took a lamp up onto the flat roof and signaled to them. The family was arrested, the pagans in the cellar were taken captive, and the next day they were all put to death in the marketplace. Alexander was given a reward, and he went on to become a great hunter of atheists and pagans. And after his death many years later, he was made a saint.

"The League of St. Alexander was set up in memory of that brave little boy, and its emblem is a picture of the lamp he carried up onto the roof to signal where to come.

"Now, you might think that those days are long ago. We don't have pagan altars in our cellars anymore. We all believe in the true God. We all cherish and love the Church. This is a Christian country in a Christian civilization.

"But there are still enemies of the Church, new ones as well as old ones. There are people who say openly that there is no God. They become famous, some of them; they make speeches and write books, or even teach. But they don't matter very much. We know who they are. More important are the people we *don't* know about. Your neighbors, your friends' parents, your own parents, the grown-ups you see every day. Have any of them ever denied the truth about God? Have you heard anyone mocking the Church or criticizing it? Have you heard anyone telling lies about it?

"The spirit of little St. Alexander lives on today in every boy or girl who is brave enough to do what he did and tell the Church authorities about anyone who is working against the true faith. It's vital work. It's the most important thing you could ever do. And it's something that every child ought to think about.

"You can join the League of St. Alexander today. You'll get a badge, like the one I'm wearing, to wear yourself and show what you think is important. It doesn't cost anything. You can be the eyes and the ears of the Holy Church in the corrupt world we live in. Who would like to join?"

Hands went up, many hands, and Malcolm could see the excitement on the faces all around him; but the teachers, apart from one or two, looked down at the floor or gazed expressionlessly out the windows.

Eric's hand went up at once, and so did Robbie's, but they both looked at Malcolm to see what he was going to do. The fact was that Malcolm would have liked one of those badges very much. They looked very handsome, but all the same, he'd rather not join this league. So he kept his hand down, and seeing that, the other two dithered. Eric's hand came down and then went up again less certainly. Robbie's came down and stayed down.

"I'm so pleased," said Miss Carmichael, looking around the hall. "God will be very happy to know that so many boys and girls are eager to do the right thing. To be the eyes and ears of the Authority! In the streets and the fields, in the houses and the playgrounds and the classrooms of the world, a league of little Alexanders watching and listening for a holy purpose."

She stopped there, turned to the table next to her, and picked up a badge and a sheet of paper.

"When you go back to your classes in a minute, your teachers will have these forms. They will tell you how to fill them in. When you've done that, they'll give you a badge. And you'll be a member of the League of St. Alexander! Oh, and there's one other thing you'll be given. This little booklet"—she held one up—"is very important. It tells the story of St. Alexander, has a list of the rules of the league, and has an address to write to if you see anything wrong, anything sinful, anything suspicious, anything you think the Holy Church would like to know.

"Now put your hands together and close your eyes. . . . Dear Lord, let the spirit of your blessed St. Alexander enter our hearts, that we may have the clear sight to perceive wickedness, the courage to denounce it, and the strength to bear witness, even when it seems most painful and difficult. In the name of the Lord Jesus Christ, amen."

A murmur of "amen" followed from most of the children. Malcolm lifted his head and looked at the woman, who seemed to be looking straight back at him, so he felt horribly uneasy for a moment; but then she turned to the headmaster.

"Thank you, Headmaster," she said. "I leave it in your hands."

She walked out. The headmaster stood up, stiffly and wearily.

"Lead off, Class Five" was all he said.

NINE

COUNTERCLOCKWISE

On Saturday, Malcolm had a lot to tell Hannah. He told her about Eric's father and his guess that the murdered man had been a spy; he told her about the woman in the priory, and about everything she'd said on that strange afternoon in the school hall, and about how many of his classmates had signed up for the League of St. Alexander.

"And the next day, when they all came to school with their badges on, the headmaster talked about them in assembly. He said they had never allowed badge wearing in the school, and he wasn't going to start now. Everyone wearing a badge had to take it off. What they did at home was their own business, but no one was allowed to wear one at school. And he said the form they'd signed had no legal something—no legal force or something—and it meant nothing. Some people tried to argue with him, but he punished them and took their badges away.

"And then some of the kids who had joined the league said they were going to report him, and they must have done, because on Thursday the head wasn't at school, nor yesterday. Mr. Hawkins—

he's the deputy, and he was in favor of the league—he took the assembly yesterday, and he said that Mr. Willis had made a mistake, and that people could wear the badges if they wanted to. He found the box of badges in the headmaster's study and gave them all out again."

"What do the other teachers think of this league?"

"Some like it and some don't. Mr. Savery, the math teacher, hates it. Someone asked him during a lesson what he thought about it, and they must have guessed he was against it because he said he thought the whole thing was disgusting, it was a celebration of a nasty rotten little sneak who got his parents killed. I think one or two people saw it differently after that and they took their badges off when no one was looking and pretended they'd lost 'em. No one actually said they agreed with Mr. Savery 'cause then they'd get reported themselves."

"But you haven't joined?"

"No. I suppose about half the kids have and the other half haven't. I didn't like *her*—that was one reason. Another was I didn't . . . Well, if I thought my parents were doing something wrong, I still wouldn't want to tell on 'em. And . . . I suppose I reckon this league has got something to do with the CCD."

It had occurred to Malcolm already, and it came back to him now, that what he was doing in talking to Dr. Relf was very like what St. Alexander was celebrated for. What was the difference? Only that he liked and trusted Dr. Relf. But he was no less a spy for that.

He felt uncomfortable, and she noticed.

"Are you thinking—"

"I'm thinking that I'm sneaking to you, really."

"Well, it's true in a way, but I wouldn't call it sneaking. I have to report the things I find out, so I'm doing the same sort of thing. The

116

difference is that I think the people I work for are good. I believe in what they do. I think they're on the right side."

"Against the CCD?"

"Of course. Against people who kill and leave bodies in the canal."

"Against the League of St. Alexander?"

"One hundred percent against it. I think it's a loathsome idea. But what about those forms you said people had to sign? Didn't they have to take them home for their parents to look at?"

"No, because she said that this was a matter just for children, and if St. Alexander had had to ask his parents, they'd have said no. Some of the teachers didn't like it, but they had to go along with it."

"I must try and find out about this league. It doesn't sound good to me at all."

"I don't know why she came to the priory to see Lyra. She's too young to join anything."

"It's interesting, though," said Dr. Relf, getting up to make some chocolatl. "But we'll talk about books now. How are you getting along with the quantum one?"

Hannah had been busy in the past few days seeking out a number of new left-luggage boxes. Once she'd found half a dozen, she went to Harry Dibdin at the Bodleian Library with another cataloging query.

"Glad you came," he said. "They've found you another insulator."

"That was quick."

"Well, things are hotting up. You must have noticed."

"Actually, I had. Anyway, if there's an insulator in place, I can use these new boxes straightaway. Harry . . . you've got children at school, haven't you?"

"Two of them. Why?"

"Have they heard of the League of St. Alexander?"

"Yes, now that you mention it. I said no."

"They came home and asked?"

"They were full of it. I told them it was a horrible idea."

"D'you know where it started? Who's behind it?"

"I imagine the usual sources. Why?"

"It's something new. I'm just curious. You said things were hotting up—this is part of it. In your children's school, was there a woman called Carmichael involved?"

"I don't know. They just said it had been announced. I don't get told details."

She told him what had happened at Ulvercote Elementary School.

"And this is your young agent reporting?" he said.

"He's very good. But he's worried now that he's doing that very thing—spying on people and telling me."

"Well, he is."

"He's very young, Harry. He's got a conscience."

"You have to look after him."

"I know," she said. "No one can advise me, but I have to advise him. No, don't get up. Here's the list of my new drops. Bye, Harry."

The report she wrote took up four sheets of the special India paper she used, even cramming her writing as tightly as she could and using a super-sharp hard pencil. It wasn't easy to fold it small enough to fit inside the acorn, but she got it in eventually, and then went for a walk in the Botanic Garden, where a space under a particular thick root inside one of the hothouses was the first left-luggage box.

Then she went back to the work she should have been doing with the alethiometer. She had fallen behind; it was beginning to look as if she'd hit an obstacle, or had fallen out of sympathy with the instrument. She would have to be careful. There was a monthly meeting of the alethiometer research group coming up, when they compared results and discussed lines of approach, and if she had nothing to say, her privileges might be withdrawn.

Malcolm's headmaster, Mr. Willis, was still away on Monday, and on Tuesday Mr. Hawkins, the deputy head, announced that Mr. Willis wouldn't be coming back, and that he would be in charge himself from then on. There was an intake of breath from the pupils. They all knew the reason: Mr. Willis had defied the League of St. Alexander, and now he was being punished. It gave the badge wearers a giddy sense of power. By themselves they had unseated the authority of a headmaster. No teacher was safe now. Malcolm watched the faces of the staff members as Mr. Hawkins made the announcement: Mr. Savery put his head in his hands, Miss Davis bit her lip, Mr. Croker, the woodwork teacher, looked angry. Some of the others gave little triumphant smiles; most were expressionless.

And there was a sort of swagger among the badge wearers. It was rumored that in one of the older classes, the Scripture teacher had been telling them about the miracles in the Bible and explaining how some of them could be interpreted realistically, such as Moses's parting of the Red Sea. He told them that it might just have been a shallow part of the sea and that a high wind would sometimes blow the water away, so it was possible to walk across. One of the boys had challenged him and warned him to be careful and held up his badge, and the teacher had backed down and said that he was only telling them that as an example of a wicked lie, and the Bible was right: the whole deep sea had been held apart for the Israelites to cross.

Other teachers fell into line as well. They taught less vigorously and told fewer stories, lessons became duller and more careful, and yet this seemed to be what the badge wearers wanted. The effect was as if each teacher was being examined by a fierce inspector, and each lesson became an ordeal in which not the pupils but the teachers were being tested.

The badge wearers began to put pressure on the other children too.

"Why aren't you wearing a badge?"

"Why haven't you joined?"

"Are you an atheist?"

When Malcolm was challenged, he just shrugged and said, "Dunno. I'll think about it." Some children said that their parents hadn't let them join, but when the badge wearers smiled with triumph and wrote down their names and addresses, they became frightened and took a badge when they were told to.

A few teachers held out. Malcolm stayed behind after a woodwork class one day; he wanted to ask Mr. Croker about his one-way screw idea. Mr. Croker listened patiently, then looked around and, seeing the woodwork room empty except for the two of them, said, "I see you're not wearing a badge, Malcolm."

"No, sir."

"Any reason?"

"I don't like 'em, sir. I didn't like *her*—that Miss Carmichael. And I did like Mr. Willis. What's happened to him, sir?"

"We haven't been told."

"Is he going to come back?"

"I hope so."

Mr. Croker's dæmon, a green woodpecker, drilled vigorously into a waste piece of pine with a sound like a machine gun. Malcolm wanted to talk more about the badge business, but he didn't want to get Mr. Croker into trouble.

"These screws, sir—"

"Oh, yes. You invented that idea yourself, did you?"

"Yes, sir. But I can't think of how to undo 'em."

"Well, someone beat you to it, Malcolm. Look . . ."

Mr. Croker opened a drawer and found a little cardboard box of screws with ready-filed one-way heads, just like the one Malcolm had made in Mr. Taphouse's workshop, but much neater.

"Blimey," said Malcolm. "And I thought I was the first person to think of 'em. But how d'you undo them?"

"Well, you need a special tool. Hang on. . . ."

Mr. Croker fumbled through the drawer and brought out a tin box with half a dozen short steel rods in it. Each rod had a threaded end that narrowed to a point, and the other end was shaped to fit into a carpenter's brace. They varied in thickness as much as the most common sizes of screws.

Malcolm picked out the largest, and then saw something about the screw thread.

"Oh! It goes backwards!"

"That's it. You drill a hole down the middle of the screw you want to get out, not very far, and then you screw one of these into it the same way as if you're unscrewing, and once it bites, it'll bring the original one out with it."

Malcolm was overcome with admiration. "That's brilliant! That's genius, that is!"

He was so impressed that he very nearly told Mr. Croker about the wooden acorn that unscrewed the wrong way too. He stopped himself just in time.

"Well, Malcolm," said Mr. Croker, "I'm never going to use these. You're a good craftsman—you take them, and the screws as well. Go on, they're yours."

"Oh, thank you, sir," said Malcolm. "That's really kind. Thank you."

"That's all right. Dunno how long I'll last here. Just like to think these tools are in the hands of someone who appreciates 'em. Go on, bugger off now."

By the end of the week, Mr. Croker had vanished too. So had Miss Davis. The school was placed in some difficulty, what with the need to replace them at such short notice, and Mr. Hawkins, the new head, spoke about it during assembly, choosing his words with care.

"You will have noticed, boys and girls, that some of our teachers are no longer with us. Of course, it's right and proper that the staff of a school should change from time to time, have a natural turnover, but it does create temporary difficulties. Perhaps it would be a good idea if this turnover came to a halt now, for a while, so we can settle down into our normal pattern of work again."

Everyone knew that this was a plea to the badge wearers, but of course he couldn't beg them directly. Malcolm wondered whether it would work. As the week went past, he listened and watched, and soon he saw different factions emerging. One group was all for pushing on zealously, and talked openly about reporting Mr. Hawkins himself for speaking like that. Another group said that they should hold their hand and build on their first great success by reminding the teachers who was really in charge, and operating a series of public warnings to keep them in line.

Eventually the second group seemed to prevail. No more teachers were denounced directly, but two or three were made to stand up in assembly and apologize for this or that misdeed.

"I'm truly sorry that I forgot to start that lesson with a prayer."

"Let me apologize to the whole school for expressing doubt about the story of St. Alexander."

"I acknowledge that I was wrong to tell off three members of the league for what I thought was bad behavior during a lesson. I realize it wasn't bad behavior at all, but a perfectly justified discussion about important matters. Please forgive me."

Malcolm told his parents about these extraordinary events, and they were angry, but not angry enough—or perhaps too busy—to do as some parents had done and go to the school and complain. One evening that week, some people were talking about it in the bar, and Malcolm's father called him to come and tell them what he'd seen in Ulvercote Elementary, because it seemed that similar things were happening at other schools in the city.

"Who's behind it—that's what I'd like to know," said a man whose children went to West Oxford Elementary.

"Have you heard who's behind it, Malcolm?" asked Mr. Partridge, the butcher.

"No," said Malcolm. "The badge people just report who they want to, and things happen to them. There's some parents been taken, as well as teachers."

"But who do they report to?"

"I've asked, but they won't tell me till I wear a badge."

The fact was that he'd more than once thought of joining the League of St. Alexander so that he'd know more about it, and have more to tell Dr. Relf. The thing that stopped him was that the badge wearers seemed to have to give up a lot of spare time to go to Church meetings, which again were secret and not to be spoken about, and Malcolm didn't want to do that.

There was one way he could find out, though. Eric, having dithered about joining, had finally committed himself, and now wore a badge proudly. He hadn't changed much, of course, and Malcolm found that if he asked the right questions, Eric would tell him things that were supposed to be secret, because the pleasure of knowing secrets was doubled by telling them to people. Malcolm began by saying that he was interested in joining the league, but that he wasn't sure about it. Soon Eric had told him most of what there was to know.

"If you were going to denounce Mr. Johnson, like," Malcolm said, naming a teacher whose pious fervor made him the least likely candidate, "who would you tell?"

"Ah, well. There's a proper procedure. You can't just go and tell on someone you don't like. That would be wrong. If you have sound reasons and clear knowledge of incorrect or wrongful behavior"—the way he said it made it sound like a formula he'd memorized—"you write their name on a piece of paper and send it to the Bishop."

"What bishop? The bishop of Oxford?"

"No. The Bishop, he's called. I think he's the bishop of London, maybe. Or maybe somewhere else. You just write their name and send it to him."

"But anyone could do that. I could do that to Mrs. Blanchard for giving me detention."

"No, 'cause that's not wrongful behavior. Not sinful, like. If she was to teach you atheism, though, that would be wrongful. You could name her then, all right."

Malcolm didn't press any more on that occasion. It was like fishing; you had to be *suitable*, as Eric would have said.

"You know Miss Carmichael, right," Malcolm said the next day. "I think I seen her before she came to the school. I think she was at the priory talking to the nuns."

"Maybe she wants to get them to take in some teachers and people who need reeducating," said Eric.

"What's reeducating?"

"Oh, being taught what's right."

"Oh. Is she the boss of the whole league?"

"No. She's a deacon. She can be a deacon but not a priest, because she's a woman. I 'spect her boss is the Bishop."

"Is the Bishop the boss of the league?"

"Well, I'm not s'posed to tell you that," said Eric, which only meant that he didn't know. "Actually, I'm not s'posed to talk to you at all unless I'm persuading you to join the league."

"Well, you are," said Malcolm. "Everything you say is persuading me."

"You going to wear a badge, then?"

"Not quite yet. Maybe soon."

Malcolm wasn't going to find out what the woman had been doing at the priory until he spoke to the nuns, so on Thursday evening he ran there through the rain and knocked on the kitchen door. As soon as he got inside, he noticed a strong smell of paint.

"Oh! Malcolm! You gave me a start," said Sister Fenella.

Malcolm had been careful about startling Sister Fenella ever since she'd told him she had a weak heart. When he was younger, he'd thought her heart was weak because she'd had it broken a long time ago, when she was a girl, and that's why she'd become a nun. A young man had broken it, she'd told him. Malcolm saw now that she didn't mean it literally, but the poor old lady was easily startled, and now she sat down and breathed quickly, her face pale.

"Sorry," he said. "I really didn't think that would startle you. I'm sorry."

"There, there, dear, it's all right. No harm done. You come to help me with these potatoes?"

"Yes, I'll do them," he said, taking up the knife she'd dropped. "How's Lyra?"

"Oh, babbling away. She jabbers all the time to that dæmon, and he jabbers back—like a pair of swallows. I don't know what they can be saying to each other, and I don't suppose they do either, but it's very pretty to hear."

"They're making up a private language."

"Well, if it doesn't turn into proper English soon, they might get stuck."

"Will they?"

"No, dear, I don't expect so, not really. All babies do that sort of thing. It's part of how they learn."

"Oh . . ."

The potatoes were old and full of black patches. Sister Fenella had just ignored that and dropped them in the pot as they were, but Malcolm cut around the worst bits. Sister Fenella began to grate some cheese.

"Sister Fenella, who was that lady who was here the other day?"

"Well, I'm not sure, Malcolm. She came to see Sister Benedicta, and they didn't tell me why. I expect she had something to do with Child Services."

"What are they?"

"They're the people who make sure that children are being looked after properly, I think. I expect she came to check on us, to make sure we were doing it right."

"She came to our school," said Malcolm, and he told Sister Fenella all about it. The old lady listened so intently that she stopped grating the cheese. "Have you ever heard of St. Alexander?" Malcolm said to end with.

"Well, there are so many saints, it's hard to remember them all. All doing God's work in different ways."

"But he told on his parents, and they were executed."

"Oh, that doesn't happen anymore. And it's hard to understand some things, dear. Even if it doesn't sound right, it doesn't mean that good won't come of it. These things are too deep for us to understand."

"I've done all these potatoes. Shall I do some more?"

"No, that's enough, dear. If you'd like to polish the silver . . ."

But the kitchen door opened then, and Sister Benedicta came in.

"I thought I heard you, Malcolm," she said. "May I borrow him for a moment, Sister Fenella?"

"Oh, of course, Sister, yes, do. Thank you, Malcolm."

"Evening, Sister Benedicta," Malcolm said as he followed the nun down the corridor to her little parlor. He listened for Lyra's babbling but heard nothing.

"Sit down, Malcolm. Don't worry—you're not in trouble. I want you to tell me about that woman who was here the other day. I believe she's been to your school. What did she want?"

For the second time that evening, Malcolm told the story of the League of St. Alexander, and the headmaster, and the other teachers who'd gone missing, and the whole affair.

Sister Benedicta listened without interrupting. Her expression was stern.

"So what was she doing here, Sister Benedicta?" he said when he'd finished. "Was she asking about Lyra? Because she's too young to join anything."

"Quite so. Miss Carmichael's business with us is concluded, I hope. But I'm concerned to hear about these children who are being encouraged to behave badly. Why has nobody told this to a newspaper?"

"I dunno. Maybe—"

"*Don't* know."

"I don't know, Sister. Perhaps the newspapers aren't allowed to print it."

"Yes, possibly so. Well, thank you, Malcolm. You'd better get back to your parents now."

"Can I see Lyra?"

"Not now. She's asleep. But look—come with me."

She led him back down the corridor and stopped at the door of the room Lyra had been in.

"What d'you think of this?" she said.

She opened the door and switched on the light. A miraculous change had taken place: instead of the gloomy paneling, the walls were painted a bright, cheerful cream, and there were some warm rugs on the floor.

"I thought I could smell paint! This is lovely," he said. "Is this her room for good now?"

"It was wrong for a little child as it was. Too dark. This is better, don't you think? What else do you think she might need in here?"

"A little table and chair for when she's older. Some nice pictures. And a bookshelf, 'cause I bet she's going to like looking at books. She can teach her dæmon to read. And a toy box. And a rocking horse. And—"

"Well, can you and Mr. Taphouse get on and make some of those things?"

"Yes! I'll start tonight. He's got some lovely oak."

"He's already gone home. Tomorrow, perhaps."

"Right. We'll do that. I know *exactly* what she needs."

"I'm sure you do."

"Sister Benedicta," he said before she switched the light off, "why is Mr. Taphouse making shutters?"

"Security," she said. "Good night, Malcolm."

He had a lot to tell Dr. Relf on Saturday. For a while he thought he wouldn't be able to get to her, though, because the river was so full and fast-flowing that it was hard to make it to Duke's Cut, and then the canal itself was brimful and disturbed by the burden of water that had flowed into it from the heavy rain of the past weeks.

He found Dr. Relf filling sandbags. Several jute bags lay on a pile of sand in her little front garden, and she was trying unsuccessfully to fill the first one.

"If you hold it," said Malcolm, "I'll put the sand in. It's almost impossible for one person on their own. I suppose if you made a frame to hold it . . ."

"No time for that," said Dr. Relf.

"Has there been a flood warning?"

"A policeman came to the door last night. It seems they expect a flood soon. I just thought it would be sensible, so I got a builder to drop off some sand. But you're right, it's very difficult for one pair of hands."

"Have you been flooded before?"

"No, but I haven't lived here very long. I think the previous owner was."

"The river's very full."

"Are you safe, in that boat of yours?"

"Oh, yeah. Safer'n being on land. If you float on top of the water, it won't harm you."

"I suppose so. But do take care."

"I always do. You ought to sew up the ends of these. You need a sailmaker's needle."

"I'll have to make do with what I've got. There, that's the last one."

It had begun to rain hard, so having stacked the sandbags neatly beside the door, they hurried inside. Over the usual mugs of chocolatl, Malcolm, who was well rehearsed now, told her of the latest developments.

"I did wonder," he said, "whether it might be a good idea to join this league so's I'd have more to tell you about it, but—"

"No, don't," she said at once. "Remember, I just want to know what you find out in the normal course of things. Don't go looking specially for anything. And I think if you got involved with these people, they wouldn't let you leave. Just talk to Eric from time to time. But I've got some information for you, Malcolm. The person behind the League of St. Alexander is Lyra's mother."

"*What?*"

"That's right. The mother who didn't want her. Mrs. Coulter, that's her name."

"Maybe that was why Miss Carmichael was at the priory, to see if they were looking after Lyra properly so she could tell her mother. . . . Blimey."

"I wonder. It doesn't sound as if Mrs. Coulter is very concerned about the child one way or the other. Perhaps Miss Carmichael wanted to get hold of her for some other reason."

"Sister Benedicta got rid of her anyway."

"I'm glad to hear it. Any news of the CCD men? Have you seen them around again?"

"No, I en't, and no one at the Trout has either, not since George Boatwright got away."

"I wonder how he's getting on."

"I 'spect he's wet," said Malcolm. "If he's hiding in the woods, he's probably wet through and freezing cold."

"I expect he is. Now, what about your books, Malcolm?"

TEN

LORD ASRIEL

When Malcolm showed Mr. Taphouse the new tool Mr. Croker had given him, and they'd tried it with the help of the anbaric drill, the old man was impressed enough to let him file down the heads of several screws for use in the shutters he was about to put up.

"They won't get in now, Malcolm," he said, as if he'd thought of the idea himself.

"But who are *they*?" said Malcolm.

"Malefactors."

"What are malefactors?"

"Evildoers. Don't they teach you nothing at that school?"

"Nothing like that. What sort of evildoers?"

"Never you mind. Get on and do us another dozen screws, will you?"

Malcolm counted them out and put the first one in the vise while Mr. Taphouse put a second coat of Danish oil on the finished shutters to keep them safe from the weather.

"Course, there's other sorts of evildoers than human ones," the old man said.

"Is there?"

"Oh, yes. There's *spiritual* evil as well. Take more'n an oak shutter to keep that out."

"What d'you mean by spiritual evil? Ghosts?"

"Ghosts are the least of it, boy. Night-ghasts, specters, apparitions—all they can do is say boo and frighten you."

"You ever seen a ghost, Mr. Taphouse?"

"Yes. Three times. Once in the graveyard over at St. Peter's in Wolvercote. Another in the Old Gaol in town."

"What were you in gaol for?"

"I wasn't in gaol, you half-wit. It was the Old Gaol, after they built the new one. I was working there one winter's day, taking down some of the old doors and that so they could paint it up nice and make it into offices or whatever. There was this one room— big tall place, high ceiling, only one window very high up, and that was all thick with cobwebs, and this dismal gray light coming in. I had to take down this big platform, oak beams, heavy stuff, I didn't know what it was. Had a sort of trapdoor in the middle. Well, I was down on the floor, setting up my sawhorse, and I heard this tremendous bang from behind me, where the platform was. So I jumped and turned round, and damn me if there wasn't a rope hanging through the trapdoor with a dead man on the end of it. That was the execution chamber, see, and the platform was the scaffold."

"What did you do?"

"I fell to me knees and I prayed like fury. When I opened me eyes, it was gone. No rope, no dead man, and the trapdoor was closed."

"Blimey!"

"Give me a proper turn, it did."

"You never knelt down and prayed—you fainted clean away," said the old man's woodpecker dæmon from the workbench.

"Well, you may be right," he said.

"I remember, because I fell off the sawhorse," she said.

"Cor," said Malcolm, deeply impressed. And then, ever practical, he said, "What did you do with the wood?"

"I burned it all. Couldn't use it. Soaked in misery, it was."

"Yeah, I bet. . . . And where was the third ghost you saw?"

"Right in here. In fact, now I think of it, it was right where you're standing. It was the most horrible thing I ever saw. It was indescribable. How old d'you think I am, eh?"

"Seventy?" said Malcolm, who knew well that Mr. Taphouse had had his seventy-fifth birthday the previous autumn.

"See, that's what terror does to you. I'm thirty-nine, boy. I was a young man till I saw that apparition right there, exactly where you're standing. Turned me hair white overnight."

"I don't believe you," said Malcolm, half sure.

"Suit yourself. I shan't tell you any more. How you doing with them screws?"

"I think you're just making it up. I've done four."

"Well, get on with—"

But before he could finish, there came a furious knocking at the door, and a desperate fumbling with the handle. Malcolm was already primed for fear and felt his skin prickle all over and a lurch in his stomach. He and the old man looked at each other, but before either could say a word, Sister Fenella called, "Mr. Taphouse! Come quickly! Please come and help!"

Without hurrying, Mr. Taphouse picked up a stout hammer and opened the door. Sister Fenella stumbled into the workshop and seized him by the arm.

"Come quickly!" she said, her voice high and quavering, every limb trembling, her face white.

She didn't see Malcolm standing behind him, file in hand. He followed the two of them out quietly.

"What's the trouble?" said the old man as she hurried him along the path to the priory kitchen.

Malcolm's first thought was that a pipe had burst, but that wouldn't account for the old nun's terror. Then he thought there must be a fire, but there was no smell of smoke, no glare of flame. She was gabbling something to Mr. Taphouse, but he couldn't make it out either, because he said, "Slow down, Sister. Slow down. Take a breath and speak slowly."

"Some men—wearing uniforms—they came in and they want to take Lyra away—"

Malcolm could hardly stifle a cry. They probably wouldn't have heard him anyway, over the sound of their feet on the gravel path, and Sister Fenella's panic, and Mr. Taphouse's hearing wasn't all that good in the first place; but nothing was going to prevent Malcolm from following. He wished he'd picked up a hammer like the old man.

"They say who they were?" said Mr. Taphouse.

"No—or at least I didn't understand—like soldiers, or police, or something—oh, dear—"

They were entering the kitchen as she said that. She clutched one hand to her heart and felt around with the other, and Malcolm darted to bring her a chair. She sank onto it, her breathing fast and shallow. Malcolm thought she might die, and he wanted to do something immediately to save her life, but he didn't know what he could do; and in any case there was Lyra. . . .

Sister Fenella gestured shakily towards the corridor. She couldn't say anything.

Mr. Taphouse set off, slow and steady, and he didn't seem to mind Malcolm coming too. In the corridor outside the room that was now Lyra's, there was a group of nuns, all of whom Malcolm knew well, and they were crowding nervously around the door, which was closed.

"What's going on, Sister Clara?" said Mr. Taphouse.

Sister Clara was plump and red-faced and sensible. She jumped slightly and turned round to whisper, "Three men in uniform—they say they've come to take the baby away. Sister Benedicta is talking to them. . . ."

A man's voice was rumbling behind the door. Mr. Taphouse moved towards it, and the nuns all shuffled out of his way. Malcolm went with him.

The old carpenter knocked firmly three times, and then opened the door. Malcolm heard a man's voice saying, "But we have all the authority we need—"

Mr. Taphouse said, "Sister Benedicta, do you need my help?"

"Who is—" the man began, but Sister Benedicta spoke over him.

"Thank you, Mr. Taphouse. Please stay outside, if you'd be good enough. But leave the door open, because these gentlemen are about to go."

"I don't think you quite understand the situation," said another man's voice, educated and pleasant.

"I understand it perfectly," she said. "You are going to go away, and I don't expect you to come back."

Malcolm marveled at the clarity and calm in her voice.

"Let me explain again," said the second man. "We have a warrant from the Office of Child Protection—"

"Oh, yes, the warrant," said Sister Benedicta. "Let me see it."

"I have shown it to you already."

"I want to see it again. You didn't give me a chance to read it properly."

There was the sound of a piece of paper being unfolded, and then a few seconds' silence.

"What is this office, of which I have never heard?" she said.

"It's under the jurisdiction of the Consistorial Court of Discipline, of which I expect you *have* heard."

And then Malcolm, peering around the edge of the door, saw Sister Benedicta tear the sheet of paper into several pieces and throw them into the fire. One or two of the nuns gasped. The men watched, narrow-eyed. Their uniforms were black, and two of them hadn't taken their caps off, which Malcolm knew was bad manners, apart from anything else.

Then Sister Benedicta picked up Lyra with the utmost care and held her tight.

"Did you seriously think for one moment," she said, sounding fierce now, "that I would let this little baby, who has been given into our care, be taken away by three strangers on the strength of a single piece of paper? Three men who practically forced their way into this holy building without any invitation? Who frightened the oldest and the least well of us with threats and weapons—yes, weapons—waving your guns in her face? Who do you think you are? What do you think this place is? The sisters have been giving care and hospitality here for eight hundred years. Think what that means. Am I going to abandon all our holy obligations because three bullies in uniform come shouldering their way in and try to frighten us? And for a helpless baby not six months old? Now go. Get out and don't come back."

"You haven't heard—"

"Oh, now, go on—tell me I haven't heard the last of it. Get out, you bully. Take your two thugs and go home. And you might think of praying to the good Lord and asking for forgiveness."

All this time Malcolm had heard Lyra and her little dæmon chattering away in their pidgin English. Now, for some reason, they stopped, and a thin, uncertain sobbing began to come from her instead. Holding her tight, Sister Benedicta stood firm and faced the men, who had no choice; they turned sullenly and came towards the door. Mr. Taphouse stepped back to make room for them, and so did Malcolm and the nuns, so that there was almost a guard of dishonor for the men to walk through.

Once they'd gone, all the nuns flooded into the baby's room and surrounded Sister Benedicta, uttering little words of sympathy and admiration, stroking Lyra's head. Her crying stopped, and Malcolm saw her smile and laugh and preen herself, as if she had done something splendid.

Mr. Taphouse took him by the shoulder and pulled him gently away. As the two of them made their way back to the workshop, Malcolm asked, "Were *they* malefactors?"

"Yes, they were," the old man replied. "Time to clear up now. Leave them screws till next time."

He wouldn't say any more, so Malcolm helped sweep up and tidy, and fetched a bucket of water for the rags Mr. Taphouse had been wiping the Danish oil on with, to stop them spontaneously combusting. Then he went home.

"Mum, what's the Office of Child Protection?"

"Never heard of it. Eat your supper."

In between mouthfuls of sausage and mash, Malcolm told his mother what had happened. She had seen Lyra herself now—had even held her—and so she realized what it would have meant for the nuns to be deprived of her.

"Wicked," she said. "What happened to Sister Fenella?"

"She wasn't in the kitchen when we went back through. She probably went to bed. She was well scared."

"Poor old lady. I'll take her round some cordial tomorrow."

"Sister Benedicta didn't budge an inch. You should have seen the malefactors when she tore their warrant up."

"What d'you call 'em?"

"Malefactors. Mr. Taphouse told me that word."

"Hmm" was all she said to that.

While Malcolm and his mother talked, Alice had been washing the dishes in her silent, sullen way, and she and Malcolm had been pointedly ignoring each other, as usual. But just then Mrs. Polstead left the kitchen to fetch something from the cellar, and to Malcolm's great surprise, Alice's dæmon growled.

Malcolm looked up, astonished. The dæmon was in the form of a big rough-coated mongrel, sitting behind Alice's legs. The hair on his neck was bristling, and he was looking up at Alice, who wiped a wet and soapy hand on her dress before stroking his head with it.

Alice said, "I know what the Office of Child Protection is."

Malcolm had a mouthful of food, but he managed to say, "What is it?"

Her dæmon said, "Bastards," and growled again.

He didn't know how to reply, and the dæmon said no more. Then Malcolm's mother came back, the dæmon lay down, and Malcolm and Alice resumed their mutual silence.

There weren't many customers in that evening, so there was little for Malcolm to do. He went to his room and wrote a list of the principal rivers of England for geography homework before drawing them on a map. There were more of them than he'd thought. He supposed that they must all be full, like the Thames, if it had been raining everywhere as it had been here in the south. And if they were, then the sea itself would get fuller. He wondered how *La Belle Sauvage* would float at sea. Could he paddle across to France? He opened his atlas to the page showing the English Channel and tried to measure it with his dividers and the miniature scale at the foot of the page, but it was all too small to read properly.

But no, it wasn't too small. There was something in the way. Something was flickering and swimming exactly on the spot he was looking at, so that he couldn't see it clearly, though everything around it seemed clear, at least until he moved his gaze to look at something else and the flickery thing moved too. It was always in the way, and he could see nothing behind it.

He brushed the page, but there was nothing there. He rubbed his eyes, but it still didn't go away. In fact, it was even more curious because he could still see it when his eyes were closed.

And it was very slowly getting bigger. It wasn't a spot anymore. It was a line: a curved line, like a loosely scribbled letter C, and it was sparkling and flickering in a zigzag pattern of blacks and whites and silvers.

Asta said, "What is it?"

"Can you see it?"

"I can feel something. What can you see?"

He described it as well as he could. "And what can you feel?" he added.

"Something strange, like a sort of far-off feeling . . . as if we're a long way apart and I can see for miles and everything's very clear and calm. . . . I'm not afraid of anything, just calm. . . . What's it doing now?"

"Just getting bigger. I can see past it now. It's getting closer, and I can see the words on the page and everything through the middle of it. It's making me feel dizzy, a bit. If I try and look at it directly, it slides away. It's about this big now."

He held out his left hand with the thumb and forefinger curved round, indicating the gap between them to be about as long as the thumb itself.

"Are we going blind?" said Asta.

"I don't think so, 'cause I can see perfectly well through it. It's just getting closer and bigger, but sort of sliding out of the way too, out towards the edge . . . as if it's just going to float past and behind my head."

They sat in the quiet little room, in the warm lamplight, and waited until the sparkling line had drifted closer and closer to the edge of his vision, and eventually just beyond it, and then was gone. Altogether, from beginning to end, the experience lasted about twenty minutes.

"That was very strange," he said. "Like spangled. Like that hymn—you remember: *And the Hornèd moon at night, 'Mid her spangled sisters bright.* It was spangled."

"Was it real?"

"Of course it was real. I saw it."

"But *I* couldn't see it. It wasn't outside. It was in you."

"Yeah . . . but it *was* real. And you were feeling something. That was real too. So it must be part of it."

"Yeah . . . I wonder what it means."

"Maybe . . . I don't know. Maybe nothing."

"No, it must be something," she said firmly.

But if it did mean something, they couldn't imagine what. And before they could think about it anymore, there was a knock on his door, and the handle turned.

It was his father.

"Malcolm, you en't in bed yet—good. Come downstairs for a minute. There's a gentleman wants a word with you."

"Is it the lord chancellor?" said Malcolm eagerly, jumping up and following his father out.

"Keep your voice down. It en't the lord chancellor, no. He'll tell you who he is if he wants to."

"Where is he?"

"In the Terrace Room. Take him a glass of Tokay."

"What's that?"

"Hungarian wine. Come on, hurry up."

"Has it suddenly got busy or something?"

"No. Gentleman wants to see you, that's all. Mind your manners and tell the truth."

"I always do," said Malcolm automatically.

"News to me," said his father. But he ruffled Malcolm's hair before they entered the bar.

The Tokay was a rich gold color and smelled sweet and complicated. Malcolm was seldom tempted by the drinks they sold in the Trout: beer was bitter, and wine was usually sour, and whisky was abominable. But if he could find the bottle later, he'd take a sip of this, all right, once his father's back was turned.

Malcolm had to stand in the corridor outside the Terrace Room for a moment to regain his sense of reality. His mind was still absorbed by the spangled ring. He took a deep breath and went in.

The gentleman waiting gave him a start, though all he was doing was sitting by the cold fireplace. Perhaps it was his dæmon, a beautiful silvery spotted leopard, or perhaps it was his dark, saturnine expression; in any event, Malcolm felt daunted, and very young and small. Asta became a moth.

"Good evening, sir," he said. "Your Tokay what you ordered. Would you like me to make up the fire? It's ever so cold in here."

"Is your name Malcolm?" The man's voice was harsh and deep.

"Yes, sir. Malcolm Polstead."

"I'm a friend of Dr. Relf," said the man. "My name is Asriel."

"Oh. Er—she hasn't told me about you," Malcolm said.

"Why did you say that?"

"Because if she had, I'd know it was true."

The leopard growled, and Malcolm took a step backwards. But then he remembered how Sister Benedicta had faced down the men and stepped forward again.

Asriel gave a short laugh.

"I understand," he said. "You want another reference? I'm the father of that baby in the priory."

"Oh! You're *Lord* Asriel!"

"That's right. But how are you going to test the truth of *that* claim?"

"What's the baby's name?"

"Lyra."

"And what's her dæmon called?"

"Pantalaimon."

"All right," said Malcolm.

"All right now? You sure?"

"No, I en't *sure*. But I'm more sure than I was."

"Good. Can you tell me what happened earlier this evening?"

Malcolm went through it as fully as he could remember.

"The Office of Child Protection?"

"That's what they called themselves, sir."

"What did they look like?"

Malcolm described their uniforms. "The one who took his cap off, he seemed like he was in charge. He was more polite than the others, more sort of smooth and smiling. But it was a real smile, not a fake one. I think I'd even've liked him if he'd come in here as a customer—that sort of thing. The other two were just dull and threatening. Most people would've been dead scared, but Sister Benedicta wasn't. She faced 'em off all by herself."

The man sipped his Tokay. His dæmon lay with her head up and her front paws stretched out ahead of her, like the picture of the Sphinx in Malcolm's encyclopedia. The black-and-silver patterns on her back seemed to flicker and shimmer for a moment, and Malcolm felt as if the spangled ring had changed its form and become a dæmon, but then Lord Asriel spoke suddenly.

"Do you know why I haven't been to see my daughter?"

"I thought you were busy. You probably had important things to do."

"I haven't been to see her because if I do, she'll be taken away from there and put in a much less congenial place. There'll be no Sister Benedicta to stand up for her there. But now they're trying to take her anyway. . . . And what was that other thing I've heard about? The League of St. Alexander?"

Malcolm told him about that.

"Disgusting," said Asriel.

"There's plenty of kids at my school joined. They like being able to wear a badge and tell the teachers what to do. Excuse me, sir, but I told Dr. Relf about all this. Didn't she tell you?"

"Still not quite sure about me?"

"Well . . . no," said Malcolm.

"Don't blame you. You going to go on visiting Dr. Relf?"

"Yes. Because she lends me books as well as listening to what's happened."

"Does she? Good for her. But tell me, the baby—is she being well looked after?"

"Oh, yes. Sister Fenella, she loves her like—" He was going to say *like I do*, but thought better of it. "She loves her a lot. They all do. She's very happy—Lyra, I mean. She talks to her dæmon all the time, just jabber jabber jabber, and he jabbers back. Sister Fenella says they're teaching each other to talk."

"Does she eat properly? Does she laugh? Is she active and curious?"

"Oh, yeah. The nuns are really good to her."

"But now they're being threatened. . . ."

Asriel got up and went to the window to look at the few lights from the priory across the river.

"Seems like it, sir. I mean, Your Lordship."

"*Sir* will do. D'you think they'd let me see her?"

"The nuns? Not if the lord chancellor had told them not to."

"And he has, eh?"

"I couldn't say, sir. What I think is they'd do anything to protect her. Specially Sister Benedicta. If they thought anyone or anything was a danger to her, they'd . . . I suppose they'd do anything, like I said."

"So you know them well, these nuns."

"I've known 'em all my life, sir."

"And they'd listen to you?"

"I suppose they would, yes."

"Could you tell them I'm here and I'd like to see my daughter?"

"When?"

"Right now. I'm being pursued. The High Court has ordered me not to go within fifty miles of her, and if I'm found here, they'll take her away and put her somewhere else where they aren't so careful."

Malcolm was torn between saying, "Well, you ought not to risk it, then" and simple admiration and understanding: of course the man would want to see his daughter, and it was wicked to try to prevent him.

"Well . . ." Malcolm thought, then said, "I don't think you could see her right now, sir. They go to bed ever so early. I wouldn't be surprised if they were all fast asleep. In the morning they get up ever so early too. Maybe—"

"I haven't got that long. Which room have they made into a nursery?"

"Round the other side, sir, facing the orchard."

"Which floor?"

"All their bedrooms are on the ground floor, and hers is too."

"And you know which one?"

"Yes, I do, but—"

"You could show me, then. Come on."

There was no refusing this man. Malcolm led him out of the Terrace Room and along the corridor and out onto the terrace before his father could see them. He closed the door very carefully behind them and found the garden brilliantly lit by the clearest full moon there'd been for months. It felt as if they were being lit by a floodlight.

"Did you say there was someone pursuing you?" said Malcolm quietly.

"Yes. There's someone watching the bridge. Is there any other way across the river?"

"There's my canoe. It's down this way, sir. Let's get off the terrace before anyone sees us."

Lord Asriel went beside him across the grass and into the lean-to where the canoe was kept.

"Ah, it's a proper canoe," said Lord Asriel, as if he'd been expecting a toy. Malcolm felt a little affronted on behalf of *La Belle Sauvage* and said nothing as he turned her over and let her slip silently down the grass and onto the water.

"First thing," he said, "is we'll go downstream a short way, so's no one can see us from the bridge. There's a way into the priory garden on that side. You get in first, sir."

Asriel did so, much more capably than Malcolm had anticipated, and his leopard dæmon followed, with no more weight than a shadow. The canoe hardly moved at all, and Asriel sat down lightly and kept still as Malcolm got in after him.

"You been in a canoe before," Malcolm whispered.

"Yes. This is a good one."

"Quiet now . . ."

Malcolm pushed off and began to paddle, staying close to the bank under the trees and making no noise whatsoever. If there was one thing he was good at, this was it. Once they were out of sight of the bridge, he turned the boat to starboard and made for the other shore.

"I'm going to come up alongside a willow stump," he said very quietly. "The grass is thick there. We'll tie her up and go across the field, behind the hedge."

Lord Asriel was just as good at getting out as he'd been at getting in. Malcolm couldn't imagine a better passenger. He tied the boat to a stout willow branch growing from the stump, and a few seconds later they were moving along the edge of the meadow, under the shade of the hedge.

Malcolm found the gap he knew about and forced his way through the brambles. It must have been harder for the man, being bigger, but he didn't say a word. They were in the priory orchard; the lines of plum trees and apple trees, of pear trees and damson trees, stood bare and neat and fast asleep under the moon.

Malcolm led the way around the back of the priory and came to the side where the window of Lyra's nursery would be, if it hadn't been hidden by the new shutters. They did look remarkably solid.

He counted once more to make sure it was the right one, and then tapped quietly on the shutter with a stone.

Lord Asriel was standing close by. The moon was shining full on this side of the building, so they would both be clearly visible from some way off.

Malcolm whispered, "I don't want to wake any of the other nuns, and I don't want to startle Sister Fenella because of her heart. We got to be careful."

"I'm in your hands," said Lord Asriel.

Malcolm tapped again a little harder.

"Sister Fenella," he said quietly.

No response. He tapped a third time.

"Sister Fenella, it's me, Malcolm!"

What he was really worried about was Sister Benedicta, of course. He dreaded to think what would happen if he woke her, so he kept as quiet as he could while still trying to wake Sister Fenella, which was not easy.

Asriel stood still, watching and saying nothing.

Finally Malcolm heard a stirring inside the room. Lyra gave a little mew, and then it sounded as if Sister Fenella moved a chair or a small table. Her soft old voice murmured something, like a word or two of comfort to the baby.

He tried again, just a little louder. "Sister Fenella . . ."

A little exclamation of shock.

"It's me, Malcolm," he repeated.

A soft noise, like the movement of bare feet on the floor, and then the click of the window catch.

"Sister Fenella—"

"Malcolm? What are you *doing?*"

Like him, she was whispering. Her voice was frightened and thick with sleep. She hadn't opened the shutter.

"Sister, I'm sorry, I really am," he said quickly. "But Lyra's father's here, and he's being pursued by—by his enemies, and he really needs to see Lyra before—before he goes on somewhere else. To—to say good-bye," he added.

"Oh, that's nonsense, Malcolm! You know we can't let him—"

"Sister, please! He's really in earnest," Malcolm said, finding that phrase from somewhere.

"It's impossible. You must go away now, Malcolm. This is a bad thing to ask. Go away before she wakes up. I daren't think what Sister Benedicta—"

Malcolm didn't dare think it either. But then he felt Lord Asriel's hand on his shoulder, and the man said, "Let me speak to Sister Fenella. You go and keep watch, Malcolm."

Malcolm moved away to the corner of the building. From there he could see the bridge and most of the garden, and he watched as

Lord Asriel leaned towards the shutter and spoke quietly. It was a whisper; Malcolm could hear nothing at all. How long Asriel and Sister Fenella spoke he couldn't have guessed, but it was a long time, and he was shivering hard when he saw, to his amazement, the heavy shutter move slowly. Lord Asriel stood back to let it open, and then stepped in again, showing his open, weaponless hands, turning his head a little to let the moonlight fall clearly on his face.

He whispered again. Then there was a minute—two minutes, perhaps—in which nothing happened; and then Sister Fenella's thin arms held out the little bundle, and Asriel took it with infinite delicacy. His leopard dæmon stood up to put her forepaws on his waist, and Asriel held the baby down so she could whisper to Lyra's dæmon.

How had he persuaded Sister Fenella? Malcolm could only wonder. He watched the man lift the baby again and walk along the grass between one bare flower bed and the next, holding the bundle high so he could whisper to her, rocking her gently, strolling along slowly in the brilliant moonlight. At one point he seemed to be showing the moon to Lyra, pointing up at it and holding her so she could see, or perhaps he was showing Lyra to the moon; at any rate he looked like a lord in his own domain, with nothing to fear and all the silvery night to enjoy.

Up and down he strolled with his child. Malcolm thought of Sister Fenella waiting in fear—in case Lord Asriel didn't bring her back, in case his enemies attacked, in case Sister Benedicta suspected something was up. But there was no sound from the priory, no sound from the road, no sound from the man and his baby daughter in the moonlight.

At one point the leopard dæmon seemed to hear something. Her tail lashed once, her ears pricked, her head turned to face the bridge. Malcolm and Asta turned immediately, ears and eyes tightly focused on the bridge, every separate stone of which was clearly outlined in black and silver; but nothing moved, and there was no sound but the call of a hunting owl half a mile away.

Presently the leopard dæmon's statuelike stillness melted, and she moved away once more, lithe and silent. Malcolm realized that that was true of the man as well—during their journey over the river and through the meadow, into the orchard and up to the priory wall, he had not heard the slightest sound of footsteps. Asriel might as well have been a ghost, for all the sound he made.

He was turning now at the end of the walk and making for Sister Fenella's window again. Malcolm watched the bridge, the garden, what he could see of the road, and saw nothing wrong; and when he turned, Asriel was handing the little bundle up through the window, whispering a word or two, and silently swinging the shutter closed.

Then he beckoned, and Malcolm joined him. It was very difficult to make no noise at all, even on grass, and Malcolm watched to see how the man set his feet down: there was something leopard-like about it—something to practice himself anyway.

Back through the orchard, to the hedge, through the brambles, into the meadow, across to the willow stump—

Then a stronger, yellower light than the moon stabbed the sky. Someone on the bridge had a searchlight, and Malcolm heard the sound of a gas engine.

"There they are," said Asriel quietly. "Leave me here, Malcolm."

"No! I got a better idea. Take my canoe and go down the river. Just get me back across to the other side first."

The idea occurred to Malcolm in the same moment he said it. "You sure?"

"You can go downstream a long way. They'll never think of that. Come on!"

He stepped in and untied the painter, holding the boat tight to the bank while Asriel got in too; then Malcolm paddled swiftly and as silently as he could across to the inn garden, though the current wanted to whirl him out into the open water, where they'd be visible from the bridge.

Asriel caught hold of the fixed line on the little jetty as Malcolm got out; and then Malcolm held the boat while the man sat in the stern, took the paddle, and held out his hand to shake.

"I'll get her back to you," he said, and then he was gone, speeding with long, powerful strokes down the river on the swollen current, the leopard dæmon like a great figurehead at the prow. *La Belle Sauvage* had never gone so fast, Malcolm thought.

ELEVEN

THREE LEGS

In the days that followed, Malcolm thought a lot about the strange half hour or so with Lord Asriel in the moonlit priory garden. He and Asta discussed it endlessly. It wasn't something he could talk about to anyone but his dæmon; he certainly couldn't mention it to his father and mother. They were always too busy with the inn to notice much about him, except whether he needed a wash or wasn't doing his homework; he knew they wouldn't realize that his canoe was gone, for example. He told no one about it except Dr. Relf. Getting to her house in Jericho would be a land-based business until Lord Asriel managed to send *La Belle Sauvage* back to him, and when he knocked at the familiar door on Saturday, he was later than he usually was.

"You lent him your boat? That was generous," she said when she'd heard the story.

"Well, I trusted him. 'Cause he was good with Lyra. He showed her the moon and kept her warm and didn't make her cry, and obviously Sister Fenella must have trusted him to let him hold her. I couldn't believe it at first."

"He's hard to say no to. I'm sure you did the right thing."

"He knows how to paddle a canoe, all right."

"D'you think these enemies of his were the same people who tried to take Lyra away from the priory? The Court of Protection, or whatever it was?"

"The Office of Child Protection. I don't think so. I thought he was going to take Lyra away himself to keep her safe from them, but he must have thought she was safer where she was than with him. So he must be in a lot of danger. I hope *La Belle Sauvage* doesn't get bullet holes in her."

"I'm sure he'll look after her. Now, what about some new books?"

Malcolm went home with a book about symbolic pictures, because what Dr. Relf had told him about the alethiometer had intrigued him greatly, and a book called *The Silk Road*. For some reason he thought it was going to be a murder story, but it turned out to be a true description, by a modern traveler, of the trade routes across Central Asia from Tartary to the Levant. He had to look those places up in his atlas when he got home, and soon realized that he needed a better atlas.

"Mum, for my birthday, can I have a big atlas?"

"What d'you want that for?"

She was frying some potatoes, and he was eating rice pudding. It was a busy night, and he'd be needed in the bar before long.

"Well, to look things up," he said.

"I expect so," she said. "I'll talk to Dad about it. Come on, get that finished."

The steamy, noisy kitchen was the safest place in the world, it seemed to him. Safety had never been anything to think about before; it was something you took for granted, like his mother's endless, effortless, generous food, and the fact that there would always be hot plates ready to serve it on.

So he knew that *he* was safe, and that Lyra was safe in the priory, and that Lord Asriel was safe because he'd escaped his pursuers; but there was danger all around, just the same.

The next day was Sunday, and the rain was coming down harder than ever. Hannah Relf made an inspection of the sandbags protecting her front door and went along to the end of the street to see how much the level of the canal had risen. She was alarmed to see, beyond the canal, the entire stretch of land called Port Meadow, acres of open ground, invisible under a gray and rain-swept wilderness of water. The wind gave it the appearance of flowing, although she knew it couldn't be: a great mass of water flowing inexorably towards the houses and businesses of Jericho behind her.

It was too bleak and depressing to stand and look at for long, and besides, the rain was coming down harder than ever, so she turned back, intending to shut her door and put another log on the fire and sit with her studies and a cup of coffee.

But there was a van outside her house, an unmarked vehicle that nevertheless said "official" in every line of the gray unwindowed metal of the bodywork.

"Cross over," said her dæmon. "Just walk naturally and go on past."

"What are they doing?" she whispered.

"Knocking. Don't look."

She tried to keep a steady pace. She had nothing to fear from the police, or from any other agency, except that like every other citizen she had everything to fear. They could lock her up with no warrant and keep her there with no charge; the old act of habeas corpus had been set aside, with little protest from those in Parliament who were supposed to look after English liberty, and now one heard tales of secret arrests and imprisonment without trial, and there was no way of finding out whether the rumors were true. Her association with Oakley Street would be no help; in fact, if anyone found out about it, it might even make things worse. These agencies and half-hidden powers were fiercely rivalrous.

But she couldn't walk in the rain all afternoon. It was absurd. Besides, she had friends. She was a highly respectable member of a great Oxford college. She would be missed; questions would be asked; she knew lawyers who could get her out of any cell in a matter of hours.

She turned back and made straight for her house. Splashing through the water that already lay an inch or two deep on the pavement, she called out when she was close enough: "Can I help? What do you want?"

The man knocking turned and looked. She stood at the gate, trying to seem as if she wasn't afraid.

"This your house, ma'am?"

"Yes. What is it you want?"

"We're from Environmental Protection, ma'am. Just calling on all the houses in this street and the others to see if you're all right in case we get any flooding."

The speaker was a man in his forties, whose dæmon was a bedraggled-looking robin. The other man was younger. His dæmon was an otter, and she had been standing on the sandbags outside Hannah's door. When Hannah spoke, the dæmon flowed over to the young man, who picked her up.

"I—" Hannah began.

"These sandbags are leaking, ma'am," the young man said. "They'll let water in down in that corner."

"Oh. Well, thank you for letting me know."

"All right round the back?" the other man said.

"Yes, that's sandbagged as well."

"Mind if we have a look?"

"No, I suppose not. . . . Round this way."

She led them along the narrow space between her house and next door's fence, and stood back while they looked at the sandbags at the foot of the back door. While the younger man examined the gap between the door and the frame, the older man said, pointing next door: "Any idea who lives there, miss?"

Miss, now, she thought.

"It's a man called Mr. Hopkins," she said. "He's rather old. I think he's gone to stay with his daughter."

He peered over the fence. The house was dark and quiet.

"No sandbags there," he said. "Charlie, we better put a few bags here, front and back."

"Righto," said Charlie.

"Is it going to flood, then?" Hannah asked.

"No way of telling, really. The weather forecast . . ." He shrugged. "Best to be ready, I always think."

"Quite true," she said. "Thank you for checking."

"'S all right, miss. Ta-ta."

They splashed away to their van. Hannah pulled and pushed and kicked at the corner they'd said was leaking, to redistribute the sand, and then went inside and locked the door.

Malcolm was keen to speak to Sister Fenella and ask her what Lord Asriel had said to her in the night, but she simply refused to talk about it.

"If you want to help, peel those apples" was all she said.

He had never known her to be so stubborn. She didn't even acknowledge his questions. Finally he felt he was being rude, and also felt that he should have realized that from the first, so he kept quiet and peeled and cored the Bramley apples, all misshapen and full of brown spots. The nuns sold their best specimens and kept the less perfect ones to eat themselves, though Malcolm thought Sister Fenella's pies tasted pretty good, whatever the apples looked like. She generally kept back a small slice for him.

When enough minutes had gone by, he said, "I wonder what Mr. Boatwright's doing."

"If they haven't caught him, I expect he's still hiding in the woods," said Sister Fenella.

"He might be in disguise."

"What d'you think he'd disguise himself as?"

"As a . . . I don't know. His dæmon would have to be disguised as well."

"Much easier for children," said her squirrel dæmon.

"When you were little, what sort of games did you play?" said Malcolm.

"Our favorite game was King Arthur," said the old lady, putting down her rolling pin.

"How did you play that?"

"Pulling the sword out of the stone. You remember, no one else could pull it out, and he didn't know it was impossible and he just put his hand on the hilt, and out it came. . . ."

She took a clean knife from the drawer and thrust it into the big lump of pastry she hadn't yet rolled.

"There, now you pretend you can't pull it out," she said, and Malcolm went into a pantomime of vast effort, straining and grunting and gritting his teeth and hauling at the knife without moving it at all. Asta joined in, heaving at his wrist as a monkey.

"And then the boy Arthur goes to fetch his brother's sword—" said Sister Fenella's dæmon.

"—and he sees the sword stuck in the stone and thinks, Oh, I'll

156

take that one," said Sister Fenella, and her dæmon finished, "And he set his hand on the hilt, and it came out—just like that!"

Sister Fenella pulled out the knife and waved it in the air.

"And so Arthur became the king," she said.

Malcolm laughed. She was contracting her features in what she thought was a majestic frown, and the squirrel dæmon ran up her arm and stood on her shoulder in triumph.

"Were you always King Arthur?" said Malcolm.

"No. I always wanted to be. Usually I was a squire or someone lowly."

"We played on our own, though, too," said her dæmon. "You were always King Arthur then."

"Yes, always," she said, and wiped the knife clean and put it back in the drawer. "What games do you play, Malcolm?"

"Oh, I suppose exploring games. Discovering lost civilizations and stuff like that."

"Going up the Amazon in your canoe?"

"Er—yeah. That sort of thing."

"How is your boat these days? Is she surviving the winter?"

"Well . . . I lent her to Lord Asriel. When he came and saw Lyra."

She said nothing and went back to rolling the pastry. Then she said, "I'm sure he was very grateful."

But her tone was as close as she ever got to being severe.

After they left the kitchen, Asta said, "She was embarrassed. She was ashamed because she knew she'd done something wrong."

"I wonder if Sister Benedicta found out."

"She might stop Sister Fenella from looking after Lyra altogether."

"Maybe. But maybe she hasn't found out."

"Sister Fenella would confess."

"Yes," Malcolm agreed. "She probably would."

They didn't look in on Mr. Taphouse because there was no light in his workshop. He'd probably gone home early.

"No—wait," said Asta suddenly. "There's someone there."

It was dusk already; the gray rain-sodden sky was ushering darkness in the better part of an hour before it was really due. Malcolm stopped on the path to the bridge and peered back towards the dark workshop.

"Where?" he whispered.

"Round the back. I saw a shadow. . . ."

"It's all shadows."

"No, like a man—"

They were about a hundred yards from the workshop. The gravel path lay open and clear in the gray twilight and the little glow of yellow from the priory windows. Nothing moved. And then from behind the workshop came, in a sort of lurching limp, a shape the size of a large dog, but hunched and heavy in the shoulders, which stood and stared at them directly.

"It's a dæmon," Asta breathed.

"A dog? And what's—"

"Not a dog. That's a hyena."

"And it's got . . . It's only got three legs."

The hyena didn't move, but behind it the shape of a man detached itself from the darkness of the building. He looked directly at Malcolm, though Malcolm couldn't see his face at all, and then merged back into the shadow.

But his dæmon stayed where she was, and then spread her two back legs and pissed right in the middle of the path. Her heavy-jawed face never moved as she glared at Malcolm; all he could see of it were two glints where her eyes caught the light. She took a lurching step forward, propping her weight on her one front leg, and looked at Malcolm for a moment more before turning and loping clumsily back into the shadow.

The little episode shook Malcolm considerably. He'd never seen a maimed dæmon before, or a hyena, or felt such a wave of malevolence. Nevertheless . . .

"We've got to," said Asta.

"I know. Be an owl."

She changed at once, and sat on his shoulder, staring intently at the dark shape of the workshop.

"Can't see them," she whispered.

"Don't take your eyes off that shadow. . . ."

He moved back along the path, or rather along the grass beside the gravel, and came to the kitchen door again, fumbling at the handle and almost falling inside.

"Malcolm," said Sister Fenella. "Have you forgotten something?"

"Just something I need to tell Sister Benedicta. Is she in her office?"

"I expect so, dear. Is everything all right?"

"Yes, yes," said Malcolm, hurrying to the corridor. The smell of paint was still faintly apparent near Lyra's nursery. He knocked on Sister Benedicta's door.

"Come in," she said, and blinked in surprise when she saw him. "What is it, Malcolm?"

"I saw— I just— We were going home past Mr. Taphouse's workshop and we saw a man—and his dæmon was a hyena with three legs—and they—"

"Slow down," she said. "Did you see them clearly?"

"Only the dæmon. She—she had three legs, and she . . . I didn't think they ought to be there, so— I mean, I thought you ought to know, so you could make extra sure the shutters were locked."

He couldn't tell her what the hyena had done. Even if he'd found the right words, he wouldn't have been able to express the contempt and hatred in the action. He felt soiled and belittled by it.

She must have seen something of that in his face because she put down her pen and stood up to put a hand on his shoulder. He couldn't remember her ever touching him before.

"And yet you came back to warn us. Well, Malcolm, that was a good deed. Now let's go and make sure you get home safely."

"You're not going to come with me!"

"You wouldn't like me to do that? Very well, I'll watch you from the door. How would that be?"

"Be careful, Sister! He— I don't know how to say it— Have you ever heard of a man with a dæmon like that?"

"One hears all sorts of things. The question is whether they matter. Come along."

"I didn't want to frighten Sister Fenella."

"That was good of you."

"Is Lyra—"

"She's asleep. You can see her tomorrow. And she's perfectly safe behind Mr. Taphouse's shutters."

They went through the kitchen, where Sister Fenella watched them, puzzled, and Sister Benedicta stood at the door.

"Would you like a lantern, Malcolm?"

"Oh, no, thanks, really. There's enough light . . . and Asta can be an owl."

"I'll wait till you're on the bridge."

"Thank you, Sister. Good night. You better lock all the doors."

"I will. Good night, Malcolm."

What she could actually do, if the man leapt out and attacked him, Malcolm didn't know, but he felt protected by the nun's attention, and he knew she wouldn't take her eyes off him till he was on the bridge.

When he was, he turned and waved. Sister Benedicta waved back and went inside and closed the door.

Malcolm ran home, with Asta flying ahead of him. They tumbled into the kitchen together.

"About time," said his mother.

"Where's Dad?"

"On the roof, signaling to Mars. Where d'you think?"

Malcolm ran into the bar and then stopped dead. Sitting on a stool, with his elbow on the counter, was a man Malcolm had never seen before, and at his feet lay a hyena dæmon with one foreleg.

The man had been talking to Malcolm's father. There were half a dozen other drinkers there, but none of them were close by; in fact, a couple of men who were always found standing by the bar were sitting at a table in the far corner, and the rest were near them, almost as if they wanted to be as far away from the stranger as they could get.

Malcolm took this in at once, and then saw the expression on his father's face. The stranger was looking at Malcolm, and behind him his father was looking down with weary, helpless loathing. When the stranger turned back, Mr. Polstead lifted his head and forced a bright smile.

"Where you been, Malcolm?" he said.

"Usual place," Malcolm muttered, and turned away. The hyena dæmon clacked her teeth—big sharp yellow teeth in a small head. She was astonishingly ugly. Whatever had robbed her of her right foreleg would have suffered for it, if those teeth had met in its flesh.

Malcolm went to the tables across the room.

"Anything I can get you, gentlemen?" he said, conscious that his voice was shaking a little as it fell into the silent room.

He took orders for two more pints, but before he could leave, one of the drinkers surreptitiously took hold of his sleeve.

"Just mind *him*," came a whisper from the table. "Watch your step with that man."

Then the man let go and Malcolm took the glasses down to the other end of the bar. Asta, of course, had been looking at nothing else, and since she was a ladybug, the direction of her gaze wasn't obvious.

"I'll go and look in the Terrace Room," said Malcolm to his father, who nodded briefly.

There was no one in the Terrace Room, but there were two empty glasses on the table. He picked them up and whispered to Asta, "What does he look like?"

"Actually, he's sort of friendly and interested, as if he's listening while you're telling him something he wants to know about. There's nothing really wrong about *him*. It's her. . . ."

"They're one person, en't they? *We* are!"

"Yeah, course, but . . ."

There were a few empty glasses in other places around the pub, and Malcolm took his time collecting them.

"There's hardly anyone here," he said to Asta.

"We won't have to stay in the bar, then. Go upstairs and write it down. Something to tell Dr. Relf."

He took the glasses into the kitchen and began to wash them.

"Mum," he said, "there's a man in the bar. . . ." He told her what had happened as he left the priory, again leaving out what the dæmon had done on the path. "And now he's here! And Dad looks ever so fed up. And no one else wants to go near him."

"You went and told Sister Benedicta? She'll make sure they're all shut up safe."

"But who is he? What's he do?"

"Goodness knows. If you don't like the look of him, stay away from him."

That was the trouble with his mother: she thought an instruction was an explanation. Well, he'd ask his father later.

"There's hardly anyone in tonight," he said. "Not even Alice."

"I said she needn't bother to stay on, since it was so quiet. If that man makes a habit of coming here, it'll be like this every night. Dad'll have to tell him to stay away."

"But why—"

"Never mind why. Got any homework?"

"Some geometry."

"Well, you might as well eat your supper now and get it over with."

Supper was cauliflower with cheese sauce. Asta perched on the table as a squirrel and toyed with a nut. Malcolm hurried through the meal and burned his mouth, but soothed it with a piece of cold plum pie and cream.

The glasses he'd washed had drained dry, so before going upstairs, he took them back to the bar. There were a few more people in, but the man with the hyena dæmon was still sitting on his stool at the counter, and the new arrivals were at the other end, ignoring him.

"Everyone seems to know about him," Asta grumbled. "Except us."

The hyena dæmon hadn't moved. She lay there gnawing and licking at the stump of her missing leg, and the man sat still, one elbow on the bar, looking all around with an air of mild and knowing interest.

Then something surprising happened. Malcolm was sure no one else could see: his father was chatting with the newcomers at the other end of the bar, and the men at the tables were playing dominoes. Afire with curiosity, Malcolm couldn't help staring at the man. He was about forty, Malcolm thought, with black hair and bright brown eyes, and all his features were clear and easy to see, as if he was a very well-lit photogram. He was wearing the sort of clothes a traveler might wear, and he might have been handsome, except that there was a kind of vigor and rough mischief about him that that word didn't do justice to. Malcolm couldn't help liking him.

And the man saw him looking, and smiled, and winked.

It was a smile of warmth and complicity. It seemed to say, We know a thing or two, the pair of us . . . , meaning him and Malcolm. There was knowledge in his expression, and enjoyment. It invited Malcolm into a little conspiracy of acquaintance against the rest of the world, and Malcolm found himself smiling back. Under normal circumstances, Asta would have flown down at once to talk to the dæmon, from politeness, even though she was frightening and ugly, but these circumstances weren't normal. So it was just the curious boy and the man with the complicated, attractive face, and Malcolm had to smile in return.

Then it was over. Malcolm left the clean glasses on the bar and turned to go upstairs.

"I can't even remember what he's wearing," he said once the bedroom door was shut.

"Something dark," said Asta.

"D'you think he's a criminal?"

"Bound to be. But she . . ."

"She's horrible. I've never seen a dæmon so different from their person before."

"I wonder if Dr. Relf will know who he is."

"I shouldn't think so. She knows professors and scholars and people like that. He's different."

"And spies. She knows spies."

"I don't s'pose he's a spy. He's too obvious. Anyone would notice a dæmon like that."

Malcolm turned to his homework, constructing figures with his ruler and compasses, a task he normally enjoyed, but he couldn't focus on it at all. That smile was still dazzling him.

Dr. Relf had never heard of anyone with a dæmon that was maimed in that way.

"It must happen, though, occasionally," she said.

Then Malcolm told her what the dæmon had done on the path, and that puzzled her even more. Dæmons were as keen on privacy as people were, being people themselves, of course.

"Well, it's a puzzle," she said.

"What d'you think it means?"

"Quite right, Malcolm. Treat it like a question for the alethiometer. See if we can work out what it all signifies. What she did on the path was an expression of contempt, wasn't it?"

"Yeah, I thought so."

"For you, who were watching, and for the place where she was— for the priory. Perhaps for the nuns and all the things they represent. Then . . . a hyena is a scavenger. It feeds on carrion and dead bodies left by other animals, as well as killing prey itself."

"So it's disgusting, but useful too," said Malcolm.

"So it is. I hadn't thought of that. And it laughs."

"Does it?"

"The 'laughing hyena.' Not really a laugh, but a cry that sounds like it."

"Like the crocodile crying tears when it doesn't mean it."

"Hypocritical, you mean?"

"Hypocritical," said Malcolm, relishing the word.

"And the man kept out of sight, you said."

"In the shadow, anyway."

"Tell me about the smile."

"Oh, yes, it was the strangest thing he did. He smiled and winked. No one else saw it. It was as if he was letting me know that he knew something I knew and no one else did. It was a secret between us. But not . . . You know how that sort of thing could make you feel creepy or dirty or guilty. . . ."

"But it wasn't like that?"

"It was happy, sort of. Really friendly and nice. And I can't hardly believe it now, but I couldn't help sort of liking him."

"But his dæmon kept gnawing at her leg," said Asta. "I was watching. It was still raw—the stump, I mean. Sort of bloody."

"What could that mean?" said Malcolm.

"She—he—they're vulnerable, perhaps?" said Dr. Relf. "If she lost another leg, she wouldn't be able to walk at all. What an awful situation."

"He didn't look worried, though. He didn't look as if anything would worry him or frighten him ever."

"Did you feel sorry for his dæmon?"

"No," said Malcolm decisively. "I felt glad. She'd be much more dangerous if she wasn't hurt like that."

"So you're in two minds about this man."

"Exactly."

"But your parents . . ."

"Mum just said keep away, and didn't say why. Dad obviously hated him being in the bar, but he had no reason to ask him to leave, and the other customers hated him being there too. I asked Dad later, and all he said was that he was a bad man and he wasn't going to let him in the pub again. But he didn't tell me what he'd done, or why he was bad, or anything. I think it was just something he felt."

"Have you seen him since?"

"It was only the day before yesterday. But no."

"Let me see what I can find out," said Dr. Relf. "Now, what about your books this week?"

"The symbolic pictures one was difficult," said Malcolm. "I didn't understand most of it."

"What *did* you understand?"

"That . . . things can stand for other things."

"That's the main point. Good. The rest is a matter of detail. No one can remember all the meanings of the alethiometer pictures, so we need the books to be able to read it."

"It's like a secret language."

"Yes, it is."

"Did someone make it up? Or . . ."

"Or did they discover it? Was that what you were going to say?"

"Yes, it was," he said, a little surprised. "So which is it?"

"That's not so easy. Let's think of another example—something else. You know the theorem of Pythagoras?"

"The square of the hypotenuse is equal to the sum of the squares of the other two sides."

"That's exactly it. And is that true for every example you've tried?"

"Yes."

"And was it true before Pythagoras realized it?"

Malcolm thought. "Yes," he said. "It must have been."

"So he didn't *invent* it. He discovered it."

"Yes."

"Good. Now let's take one of the alethiometer symbols. The hive, for example, surrounded by bees. One of its meanings is sweetness, and another is light. Can you see why?"

"Honey for the sweetness. And . . ."

"What are candles made of?"

"Wax! Beeswax!"

"That's right. We don't know who first realized that those meanings were there, but did the similarity, the association, exist before they realized it, or not until then? Did they invent it or discover it?"

Malcolm thought hard.

"That's not quite the same," he said slowly. "Because you can *prove* Pythagoras's theorem. So you *know* it must be true. But there's nothing to prove with the beehive. You can see the connection, but you can't *prove* . . ."

"All right, put it like this. Suppose the person who made the alethiometer was looking for a symbol to express the ideas of sweetness and light. Could they have chosen just anything? Could they have chosen a sword, for example, or a dolphin?"

Malcolm tried to work it out. "Not really," he said. "You could twist it a lot and *make* them similar, but . . ."

"That's right. There's a natural sort of connection with the beehive, but not with the other two."

"Yeah. Yes."

"So was it invented or discovered?"

Malcolm thought hard again, and then smiled.

"Discovered," he said.

"All right. Next let's try this. Can you imagine another world?"

"I think so."

"A world where Pythagoras never existed?"

"Yes."

"Would his theorem be true there as well?"

"Yes. It would be true everywhere."

"Now imagine that world has people like us in it, but no bees. They'd have the experience of sweetness and of light, but how would they symbolize them?"

"Well, they . . . they'd find some other things. Maybe sugar for the sweetness and something else, maybe the sun, for light."

"Yes, those would work. Let's imagine another world, a different one again, where there are bees but no people. Would there still be a connection between a beehive and sweetness and light?"

"Well, the connection would be . . . here, in our minds. But not there. If we can think about that other world, *we* could see a connection, even if there was no one *there* to see it."

"That's good. Now, we still can't say whether that language you spoke about, the language of symbols, was definitely invented or definitely discovered, but it looks more as if—"

"As if it was discovered," said Malcolm. "But it's still not like Pythagoras's theorem. You can't *prove* it. It depends on . . . on . . ."

"Yes?"

"It depends on people being there to see it. The theorem doesn't."

"That's right!"

"But it's a bit invented as well. Without people to see it, it would just be . . . it might as well not be there at all."

He sat back, feeling slightly dizzy. Her familiar room was warm, the chair was comfortable, the plate of biscuits was to hand. He felt as if this was the place where he was truly at home, more so than his mother's kitchen or his own bedroom, and he knew he would never say that to anyone but Asta.

"I'll have to go soon," he said.

"You've worked hard."

"Was that work?"

"Yes, I think so. Don't you?"

"I suppose so. Can I see the alethiometer?"

"I'm afraid it has to stay in the library. We've only got the one instrument. But here's a picture you can have."

She took a folded sheet of paper from a drawer in the cabinet and gave it to him. Unfolding it, he found the plan of a large circle with thirty-six divisions around the rim. In each of the little spaces was a picture: an ant, a tree, an anchor, an hourglass. . . .

"There's the beehive," he said.

"Keep it," she told him. "I used it when I was learning them, but I know them now."

"Thank you! I'll learn them too."

"There's a memory trick I'll tell you about another time. Rather than memorize them all for now, you could choose one of them and just think about it. What ideas does it suggest? What could it symbolize?"

"Right, I will. There's—" He stopped. The circle in the diagram, divided into its little sections, reminded him of something.

"There's what?"

"It's sort of like something I saw. . . ."

He described the spangled ring that he'd seen on the night Lord Asriel had come to the Trout. She was interested at once.

"That sounds like a migraine aura," she said. "Do you have bad headaches?"

"No, never."

"Just the aura, then. You'll probably see it again sometime. Did you like the other book? The one about the Silk Road?"

"It's the place I want to go to most in the world."

"One day, perhaps, you will."

That evening, someone brought *La Belle Sauvage* back.

TWELVE

ALICE TALKS

Just as Malcolm finished his supper and took his pudding bowl to the sink, there was a knock on the kitchen door—the door to the garden. No one came to that door as a rule. Malcolm looked at his mother, but she was busy at the stove and he was close to the door, so he opened it a little way.

There stood a man he didn't know, wearing a leather jacket and a wide-brimmed hat, with a blue-and-white-spotted handkerchief around his neck. Something about his clothes, or the way he stood, made Malcolm think: gyptian.

"Are you Malcolm?" the man asked.

"Yes," said Malcolm, and at the same moment his mother said, "Who is it?"

The man stepped forward into the light and took off his hat. He was in late middle age, lean and brown-skinned. His expression was calm and courteous, and his dæmon was a very large and beautiful cat.

"Coram van Texel, ma'am," he said. "I've got something for Malcolm, if you'll just excuse him for a few minutes."

"Got something? Got what? Come inside and give it to him here," she said.

"It's a bit big for that," said the gyptian. "It won't take more'n a short while. I need to explain a couple of things."

His mother's badger dæmon had left his corner and come to the door, and he and the cat dæmon touched noses and exchanged a whisper. Then Mrs. Polstead nodded.

"Go on, then," she said.

Malcolm finished drying his hands and went outside with the stranger. It had stopped raining, but the air was saturated with moisture, and the lights through the windows shone on the terrace and the grass with a misty radiance that made everything look as if it was underwater.

The stranger stepped off the terrace and headed towards the river. Malcolm could see the line of the footprints in the wet grass he'd just made coming up.

"You remember Lord Asriel," the stranger said.

"Yes. Is it—"

"He charged me with bringing back your boat, and he said to give you great thanks, and he hopes you'll be pleased with her condition."

As they went beyond the reach of the lights from the windows, the man struck a match and lit a lantern. He adjusted the wick and closed the lens, and a clear beam fell out on the grass ahead and all the way to the little jetty, where *La Belle Sauvage* was tied up.

Malcolm ran to look. The river was full, holding his beloved canoe higher than usual, and he could see at once that she had been worked on.

"The name—oh, thanks!" he said.

Her name had been painted with great skill in red paint and outlined with a fine line of cream in a way that he would never have managed. It stood out proudly against the green of the boat, which itself . . . Ignoring the wet grass, he knelt to look closely. Something was different.

"She's been through the hands of the finest boatbuilder on English waters," said Coram van Texel. "Every inch of her has been looked at and strengthened, and that paint on her now is a special anti-fouling paint that has another virtue too. She'll be the slippiest vessel on the Thames, apart from real gyptian boats. She'll go through the water like a hot knife through butter."

Malcolm touched the canoe in wonderment.

"Now let me show you something else," said the visitor. "See those brackets set along the gunwales?"

"What are they for?"

The man reached down into the canoe and pulled up a handful of long, slender hazel sticks. He took one and handed the rest to Malcolm, then he leaned out and slipped one end into a bracket on the far side of the canoe, bent it towards himself, and put the other end in a bracket on the near side. The result was a neat hoop across the canoe.

"You try another," he said, and shone the lantern on the next bracket. After a few tries Malcolm slipped it in. He found that the stick bent with great ease, but that once both ends were fixed, the stick was completely firm and unmoving.

"What are they for?" he said.

"I won't show you now, but under the thwart amidships you'll find a tarpaulin. A special kind made of coal silk. You put all the rods in place and pull the tarpaulin over and you'll be snug and dry, no matter how much rain comes down. There's fixings along the edge, but you can work out how to do them."

"Thank you!" said Malcolm. "That's—oh, that's wonderful!"

"It's Lord Asriel you must thank. But this is his thanks to you, so you're all square. Now, Malcolm, I need to ask you a question or two. I know you're visiting a lady called Dr. Relf, and I know why. You can tell her about this, and you can tell her about me, and if she needs to know any more, you can just say the words *Oakley Street*."

"Oakley Street."

"Thassit. That'll reassure her. Don't say those words to anyone else, mind. Now, everything you tell her comes back to me in due course, but time's pressing, and I need to know this urgently. I daresay you see most people who come to the Trout?"

"Yes, I do."

"You know a lot of 'em by name?"

"Well, some."

"You ever know of a man by the name of Gerard Bonneville?"

Before Malcolm could answer, he heard the kitchen door open behind him, and his mother's voice calling, "Malcolm! Malcolm! Where are you?"

"I'm here!" he shouted. "I won't be a minute."

"Well, don't, then," she called, and went back inside.

Malcolm waited till she shut the door, and then said, "Mr. Van Texel, what's all this about?"

"I got two warnings for you, and I'll be off."

For the first time Malcolm saw another boat on the water—a long, low-cabined launch with a quiet motor that puttered gently and held it against the stream. It showed no lights, and he could just make out a man's outline at the wheel.

"First," said Van Texel, "the weather's going to improve in the next few days. Sunshine, warm winds. Don't be fooled by it. After that the rain'll come back even harder, and then there'll be the biggest flood anyone's seen for a hundred years, and not a normal flood either. Every river's full to bursting, and a lot of the weirs are about to give way. The River Board en't been doing its job. But more'n that, there's things in the water been disturbed, and things in the sky too, and they're both clear and bright to them as can read the signs. Tell your mother and father. Be ready."

"I will."

"And second, remember that name I said: Gerard Bonneville. You'll know him if you see him because his dæmon's a hyena."

"Oh! Yes! He's been here. A few days ago. His dæmon's only got three legs."

"Has she, now. Did he say anything to you?"

"No. I don't think anyone wanted to speak to him. He was drinking by himself. He looked nice."

"Well, he might try to be nice to you, but don't you go near him. Never let him get you alone. Have nothing to do with him."

"Thank you," said Malcolm. "I won't. Mr. Van Texel, are you a gyptian?"

"Yes, I am."

"Are the gyptians against the CCD, then?"

"We're not all the same, Malcolm. Some are, and some aren't." He turned to the water and gave a low whistle, and instantly the launch turned its head and glided towards the jetty.

Coram van Texel helped Malcolm haul *La Belle Sauvage* up onto the grass and then said, "Remember what I told you about the flood. And about Bonneville."

They shook hands, and the gyptian stepped onto the launch. A moment later the engine sound increased just a little and the boat sped away upstream and was lost in the dark.

"What was that all about?" said his mother two minutes later.

"I lent the canoe to someone, and that man brought it back."

"Oh. Well, get on and take these dinners through. Table by the big fire."

There were four plates of roast pork and vegetables. He could only manage two at a time, as they were hot, but he did that as quickly as he could and then brought the diners three pints of Badger and a bottle of IPA, and the evening was under way, as busy a Saturday as they'd had for weeks. Malcolm looked out for the man with the three-legged hyena dæmon, but there was no sign of him. He worked hard and picked up a lot of tips, which would all go into the walrus.

At one point, he heard some men—familiar customers—talking about the river level, and he stopped to listen in the way he'd always done and that hardly anyone noticed.

"It en't gone up for days," said someone.

"They know how to manage the level now," said another. "Remember when old Barley was in charge of the River Board? He used to panic every time there was a shower."

"It never flooded in his time, mind you," said a third. "This rain what we been having, that's exceptional."

"It's stopped now, though. The Weather Office—"

Jeers from the others.

"The Weather Office! What do they know?"

"They got the latest philosophical instruments. Course they know what's going on in the atmosphere."

"What do they say, then?"

"They say we got fine weather coming."

"Well, they might be right for once. The wind's changed, ennit? This is dry air out the north what's coming along now. You watch—it'll be clear in the morning, and then it won't rain for a month. A whole month of sunshine, boys."

"I en't so sure. My granny says—"

"Your granny? She know more than the Weather Office?"

"If the army and navy listened to my granny instead of the Weather Office, they'd be better off for it. She says—"

"You know why the river en't burst its banks? Scientific management of resources, that's what it is. They know what to do now, better'n in old Barley's time, how to hold it back and when to let it out."

"There's more water up Gloucester way—"

"The water meadows en't taken up a tenth of what they can. I seen 'em far worse—"

"Scientific management of resources—"

"It all depends on the state of the upper atmosphere—"

"It's drying out. You watch—"

"My granny—"

"No, we've had the worst of it now."

"Get us another pint of Badger, would you, Malcolm?"

When Malcolm was going to bed, Asta said, "Mr. Van Texel knows a lot more than they do."

"They wouldn't listen if we warned them, though," he said.

"Don't forget to look up that word. . . ."

"Oh, yeah!"

Malcolm darted into the sitting room and found the family dictionary. He was going to look up the expression Dr. Relf had used when he'd told her about the spangled ring. He knew what *migraine* meant because sometimes his mother had one, only she called it *my-grain* and Dr. Relf had called it *me-grain*. But the other word . . .

"Here it is. I thought so."

Robin Asta peered at the page from his forearm and read, "'Aurora: a luminous celestial phenomenon of anbarical character seen in the polar regions, with a tremulous motion and streamers of light, sometimes known as the northern lights.' . . . You sure that was the word? It sounded more like *Lyra*. Two syllables."

"No, this is it," said Malcolm firmly. "Aurora. It's the northern lights, in my head."

"It doesn't say *spangled*, though."

"Probably it's different each time. It was tremulous and luminous, all right. Whatever causes the northern lights causes the spangled ring, I bet!"

The thought that the inside of his head was in direct contact with the remote skies above the North Pole gave him a feeling of immense privilege and even awe. Asta was still not quite convinced, but he was thrilled.

In the morning he could hardly wait to go out and look at the canoe in daylight, but his father wanted help clearing up in the bar after the busy evening. *La Belle Sauvage* would have to wait.

So he hurried between the tables and the kitchen, jamming his fingers through as many tankard handles as he could or carrying four glasses with one finger in each of three and two in the fourth. When he took them through to Alice in the scullery, where he normally just put them down on the counter and left without saying a word, something made him stop and look at her. She seemed unusually distracted this morning, as if there was something on her mind. She kept looking around, clearing her throat as if to speak, turning back to the sink, glancing at Malcolm. He was tempted to say, "What is it? What's the matter?" but held his tongue.

Then came a moment when his mother was out of the kitchen. Alice looked at Malcolm directly and said under her voice, "Hey, you know the nuns?"

Malcolm was too surprised to answer at first. He had just picked up half a dozen clean glasses that were ready to be taken back to the bar, and he put them down again and said, "In the priory?"

"Course. That's the only ones there are, en't there?"

"No. There's others in other places. What about them?"

"Are they looking after a baby?"

"Yeah."

"You know whose baby it is?"

"Yeah, I do. So what?"

"Well, there's a man who— Tell you later."

Malcolm's mother had come back. Alice tucked her head down and plunged her hands back into the water. Malcolm picked up the glasses again and carried them through, and found his father reading the paper.

"Dad," he said, "d'you reckon there's going to be a flood?"

"Was that what they were on about last night?" said his father, folding back the sports page.

"Yeah. Mr. Addison reckoned there wasn't, 'cause the air from the north was dry and there's going to be a month of sunshine, but Mr. Twigg says his granny—"

"Oh, don't worry about 'em. What's this about your canoe? Your mother tells me some gyptian came to the door last night."

"You remember Lord Asriel? I lent it to him, and that man came to return it."

"I didn't know he was a pal of the gyptians. What'd he want to borrow your canoe for?"

"'Cause he liked canoeing and he wanted to go up the river in the moonlight."

"There's no accounting for some people. You're lucky to get it back. Is it all right?"

"Better than ever. And, Dad, that gyptian man said there was going to be more rain after this bit of sunshine, and then the biggest flood in a hundred years."

"Did he?"

"He said to warn you. 'Cause the gyptians can read the signs in the water and the sky."

"Did you warn those old boys last night?"

"No, 'cause they'd already drunk a bit, and I didn't reckon they'd listen. But he did say to warn you."

"Well, they are water people, gyptians. . . . That's worth knowing, just to think about. But no need to take it seriously."

"He meant it seriously. There'd be no harm in getting ready for it."

Mr. Polstead considered the matter. "True enough," he said. "Like Noah. You reckon me and Mum could fit in the *La Belle Sauvage* along with you?"

"No," said Malcolm firmly. "But you ought to mend the punt. And maybe Mum ought to keep her flour and stuff up here and not in the cellar."

"Good idea," said his father, turning back to the sports page. "You tell her. You cleared the Terrace Room?"

"I'm just going in there."

Seeing his mother come into the bar and start to talk to his father about vegetables, Malcolm took the glasses from the Terrace Room and hurried back to the kitchen.

"What was that about a man?" he said to Alice.

"I dunno if I should say."

"If it's about the baby . . . You said something about the baby, and then a man. What man?"

"Well, I dunno. Maybe I said too much."

"No, you en't said enough. What man?"

She looked around.

"I don't want to get into trouble," she said.

"Well, just tell me. I won't tell on you."

"All right . . . This man, his dæmon's got a leg missing. She's a hyena or something. Horrible ugly. But he's nice, or he seems nice enough."

"Yeah, I've seen him. You met him, then?"

"Sort of," she said, and she was blushing, so she turned away. Her jackdaw dæmon looked down from her shoulder and turned his head away from Malcolm too. Then she went on: "I spoken to him a bit."

"When?"

"Last night. Down Jericho. He was asking about the baby in the priory, the nuns, all that. . . ."

"What d'you mean, 'all that'? What else?"

"Well, he said he was the baby's father."

"He's not! Her father's Lord Asriel. I *know* that."

"He said he was, though, and he wanted to know if they kept her safe in the priory, whether they locked the doors at night—"

"*What?*"

"And how many nuns there were, and that."

"Did he tell you his name?"

"Gerard. Gerard Bonneville."

"Did he say why he wanted to know about the nuns and the baby?"

"No. We didn't only talk about that. But . . . I dunno . . . it gave me a weird feeling. And his dæmon chewing at her bloody leg . . . Except he was nice. He bought me some fish and chips."

"Was he on his own?"

"Well, yeah."

"And you? Did you have any friends with you?"

"What if I did?"

"It might have made a difference in what he said."

"I was on me own."

Malcolm didn't know what else to ask. It was clearly important to find out whatever he could, but his imagination was limited at this point: he couldn't conceive what a grown man would want with a solitary girl at night, or what could pass between them. Nor could he understand why she was blushing.

"Did your dæmon talk to the hyena?" he said after a pause.

"He tried a bit, but she didn't say nothing."

She looked down towards the sink and plunged her hands into the water. Malcolm's mother had come back from the bar. Malcolm carried the clean glasses out, and the moment passed.

But when Alice had finished for the morning and was putting on her coat to leave, Malcolm saw and caught up with her on the porch.

"Alice—wait a minute. . . ."

"What d'you want?"

"That man—with the hyena dæmon—"

"Forget it. I shouldn't have said nothing."

"It's just that someone warned me about him."

"Who?"

"A gyptian man. He said not to go near him."

"Why?"

"I don't know. But he really meant it. Anyway, if you see him again—Bonneville, I mean—can you tell me what he says?"

"It en't your business. I shouldn't have told you."

"I'm worried about the nuns, you see. I know they're worried about safety and that, 'cause they told me. That's why they got the new shutters put up. So if this man Bonneville is trying to find things out about them . . ."

"He was nice. I told you. Maybe he wants to help them."

"Well, the thing is, he came in here the other night and no one would go near him. As if they were frightened. My dad says if he comes again, he en't going to let him in because he keeps other customers away. They know something about him, as if he's been in prison or something. And there's that gyptian man who warned me about him."

"He didn't worry *me*."

"Still, if you see him again, can you tell me?"

"S'pose so."

"And specially if he asks about the baby."

"Why are you so worried about the baby?"

"Because she *is* a baby. There's no one to protect her except the nuns."

"And you think *you* can? Is that it? You're going to save the baby from the big bad man?"

"Just can you tell me?"

"I said I would. Don't go on about it."

She turned away and stamped off quickly in the thin sunshine.

That afternoon, Malcolm went to the lean-to and inspected the improvements to *La Belle Sauvage*. The tarpaulin of coal silk was as light and impermeable (he tried it) as Mr. Van Texel had said, and the clips to attach it to the gunwales were easy to work and firmly fixed. It was water green in color, like the boat herself, and he thought that when it was in place, he and his vessel would be practically invisible.

The current was running very strongly, so he decided not to take her out and try the slippiness of the new paint, but his fingertips told him the difference. What a gift this was!

There were no other surprises in the canoe, so Malcolm pulled the old tarpaulin over it and made sure it was pegged down.

"It might rain again," he said to Asta.

But there was no sign of that. The cold sunshine lasted all day, and the sky was red when the sun went down, meaning more sunshine tomorrow. As the sky was clear, the evening was bitterly cold, and for the first time in weeks, there were only a few customers in the Trout. His mother decided not to roast a joint or make a set of pies because most would remain uneaten. It was going to be ham and eggs that evening, with fried potatoes if you were early and bread and butter if you weren't.

But since so few customers came at all, and since the assistant barman Frank was on duty in case they did, Malcolm and his father and mother sat down together in the kitchen to have supper.

"Might as well finish up these cold potatoes. Can you eat any more, Reg?"

"You bet. Fry 'em up."

"Malcolm?"

"Yes, please."

Into the frying pan they went, sizzling and spitting and making Malcolm's mouth water. He sat there happily with his parents, thinking of nothing, content with the warmth and the smell of frying food.

Then he was aware that his mother had asked him something.

"What?"

"Again, politely," she said.

"Oh. I beg your pardon?"

"That's better."

"The boy's dreaming," said his father.

"I said, what were you and Alice talking about?"

"Was he talking to Alice?" said Mr. Polstead. "I thought there was a noncommunication treaty between those two."

"Nothing in particular," said Malcolm.

"But come to think of it, he spent five minutes yakking to her on the porch when she left," said his father. "Must have been important."

"Not really," Malcolm said, beginning to feel awkward. He didn't want to keep things from his parents, but then they didn't usually have the time to ask anything more than once. A noncommittal answer normally satisfied them. But with nothing else to do this evening, the matter of Malcolm's talking to Alice became of great interest.

"You were talking to her when I came back in the kitchen," his mother said. "I could hardly believe my eyes. Is she getting friendly?"

"No, it's not that," said Malcolm reluctantly. "She was just asking about the man with the three-legged dæmon."

"Why?" said his father. "She wasn't here that night. How'd she know he came in?"

"She didn't till I told her. She told me about him because he'd been asking her about the nuns."

"Was he? When?" said his mother, dishing up the fried potatoes.

"In Jericho the other night. He was talking to her and asking about the nuns and the baby."

"What was he doing talking to her?"

"I dunno."

"Was she on her own?"

Malcolm shrugged. He'd just put a forkful of hot potato in his mouth and couldn't speak. But he did see the glance that passed between his parents: an expression of muted alarm.

When he'd swallowed his mouthful, he said, "What is it about that man? Why did everyone move away from him in the bar? And what if he was talking to Alice? She said he was nice."

"The thing is, Malcolm," said his father, "he's got a reputation for violence. And for . . . for attacking women. People don't like him. You saw the bar the other night. That dæmon—she has a strange effect on people."

"He can't help that," said Malcolm. "You can't help what shape your dæmon settles as, can you?"

"You'd be surprised," came a voice from the floor, gruff and rich and slow. His mother's badger dæmon rarely spoke, but when he did, Malcolm always listened with close attention.

"You mean you can choose?" he said, surprised.

185

"You didn't say you can't choose; you said you can't help. You can help, all right, but you don't know you're doing it."

"But how—what do you—"

"Eat your supper and you'll find out," he said, and trundled back to his bed in the corner.

"Hmm," Malcolm said.

They didn't speak any more about Gerard Bonneville. Malcolm's mother said she was worried about her mother because she hadn't been well, and said she'd go over to her house in Wolvercote the next day and see if she was all right.

"Has she got enough sandbags?" said Malcolm.

"She won't need those anymore," said his mother.

"Well, Mr. Van Texel said people were going to think it had stopped raining, but the rain was going to come back and there was going to be a big flood."

"Is there, indeed?"

"He said to warn you."

"Did you see him, Brenda?" said his father.

"The gyptian? Yes, briefly. Very polite and quiet."

"They do know the rivers."

"So Granny might need more sandbags," said Malcolm. "I'll help her if she does."

"I'll bear it in mind," said his mother. "Have you told the sisters?"

"They'll all have to come over and stay here," said Malcolm. "They'd have to bring Lyra."

"Who's Lyra?" said his father.

"The baby, of course. The one they're looking after for Lord Asriel."

"Oh. Well, there wouldn't be room for 'em all. We're probably not holy enough either."

"Don't be silly," said Mrs. Polstead. "They do the holiness them-selves. They'd just need somewhere dry."

"It probably wouldn't be for long," said Malcolm.

"No, it wouldn't work. But you better tell 'em anyway, like your mum says. What's for pudding?"

"Stewed apple, and lucky to get it," she said.

After he'd dried the dishes, Malcolm said good night and went up-stairs. There was no homework to do, so he took out the diagram Dr. Relf had given him, the one about the symbols on the alethiometer.

"Be systematic about it," said Asta.

He didn't think that deserved an answer, because he was always systematic. They pored over the diagram under the lamplight, and then he wrote down what each of the thirty-six pictures showed, or was intended to show; but they were so small that he couldn't make them all out.

"We'll have to ask her," said Asta.

"Some of 'em are easy, though. Like the skull. And the hour-glass."

But it was laborious work, and once he'd listed all the ones he could recognize and left gaps for the rest, he and Asta both felt they'd spent enough time with it.

They didn't feel like sleep, and they didn't feel like reading, so Malcolm took the lamp and they wandered through the guest bed-rooms in the old building to look across the river. His own bedroom faced the other way, so he couldn't keep a regular eye on the priory, but the guest bedrooms were all on the river side because the view was better; and as there happened to be no one staying, he could go where he liked.

In the highest bedroom, just below the eaves, he turned out the lamp and leaned on the windowsill.

"Be an owl," he whispered.

"I am."

"Well, I can't see you. Look over there."

"I am!"

"Can you see anything?"

There was a pause. Then she said, "One of the shutters is open."

"Which one?"

"Top floor. Second one along."

Malcolm could only just make out the windows because the gate light was on the other side of the building, and the half moon shone on that side too; but finally he made it out.

"We'll have to tell Mr. Taphouse tomorrow," he said.

"The river's noisy."

"Yeah . . . I wonder if they've been flooded before."

"In all the time the priory's been there, they must have been."

"There'd be stories about it. There'd be a picture in a stained-glass window. I'll ask Sister Fenella."

Malcolm wondered what single picture small and clear enough to fit on the dial of the alethiometer could symbolize a flood. Maybe it would be a mixture of two pictures, or maybe it was a lower-down meaning of another one altogether. He'd ask Dr. Relf. And he'd tell her what the gyptian had said about the flood—he must certainly do that. He thought of all those books that would be ruined if her house was flooded. Perhaps he could help take them upstairs.

"What's that?" said Asta.

"What? Where?"

Malcolm's eyes were adjusted to the dark by this time, or as much as they ever would be, but he couldn't see more than the stone building and the lighter shapes of the shuttered windows.

"There! Just at the corner of the wall!"

Malcolm widened his eyes and peered as hard as he could. Was there a movement? He wasn't sure.

But then he did see something at the base of the wall: just a shadow, slightly darker than the building. Something man-sized but not man-shaped—a massive bulk where the shoulders should have been and no head—and it moved with a crabwise shuffle. . . . Malcolm felt a great drench of fear pour over his heart and down into his belly. And then the shadow vanished.

"What was *that?*" he whispered.

"A man?"

"It didn't have a *head*—"

"A man carrying something?"

Malcolm thought. It could have been.

"What was he doing?" he said.

"Going to close the shutter? Mr. Taphouse, maybe?"

"What was he carrying?"

"A bag of tools? I don't know."

"I don't think it was Mr. Taphouse."

"Nor do I, really," said Asta. "It didn't move like him."

"It's the man—"

"Gerard Bonneville."

"Yes. But what's he carrying?"

"Tools?"

"Oh! I know! His dæmon!"

If she lay across his shoulders, she would account for the bulk, and for the fact that they couldn't see his head.

"What's he *doing?*" said Asta.

"Is he going to climb up—"

"Has he got a ladder?"

"Can't see."

They both peered again as fiercely as they could. If it was Bonneville, and he wanted to climb up to the window behind the shutter, he would have to carry his dæmon; he wouldn't be able to leave her on the ground. Every roofer, tiler, and steeplejack had a dæmon who could fly, or one so small she could come up in a pocket.

"We should tell Dad," Malcolm said.

"Only if we're sure."

"We are, though, en't we?"

"Well . . ."

Her reluctance was speaking for his.

"He's after Lyra," he said. "He must be."

"D'you think he's a murderer?"

"Why would he want to kill a baby, though?"

"*I* think he's a murderer," said Asta. "Even Alice was frightened of him."

"I thought she liked him."

"You don't see much, do you? She was scared stiff as well. That's why she asked us about him."

"Maybe he wants to take Lyra because he really is her father."

"Look—"

The shadow appeared around the side of the building again. And then the man staggered, and the burden on his shoulders seemed to squirm away and fall to the ground; and then they heard a hideous high-pitched cry of laughter.

The man and the dæmon seemed to be spinning around in a mad dance. That uncanny laughter tormented Malcolm's ears; it sounded like a high hiccupping yell of agony.

"He's *hitting* her . . . ," whispered Asta, unable to believe it.

When she said that, it became clear to Malcolm too. The man had a stick in his hand, and he had forced the hyena dæmon back against the wall. He was thrashing and thrashing her with fury, and she couldn't escape.

Malcolm and Asta were terrified. She turned into a cat and burrowed into his arms, and he hid his face in her fur. They had never imagined anything so vile.

And the noise had been heard inside the priory. There was a dim light bobbing its way towards the window with the broken shutter, and then it was there, with a pale face beside it, trying to look directly down. Malcolm couldn't tell which of the nuns it was, but then it was joined by another face, and the window swung open, into the dark and the cries of agonized laughter.

Two heads craned out and looked down. Malcolm heard a commanding call and recognized the voice of Sister Benedicta, though he couldn't make out the words. In the dim light from the lantern above, Malcolm saw the man look up, and in that instant the hyena dæmon gave a desperate leap sideways, lurching away from the man, who felt the inevitable heart-deep tug as soon as she reached the limit of the invisible bond that joined every human with their dæmon, and stumbled after her.

She dragged herself away, limping as fast as she could, and the terrible fury of the man came after her, thrashing and beating with his stick, and the frenzied laughter-like agony filled the air again. Malcolm saw the two nuns flinch as they saw what was happening; then they pulled the shutter closed and the light vanished.

Gradually the cries faded. Malcolm and Asta clung together with horror.

"Never . . . ," she whispered.

". . . never thought we'd ever see anything like that," he finished for her.

"What could make him *do* that?"

"And it was hurting him too. He must be insane."

They held each other till the noise of that laughter had entirely gone.

"He must hate her," Malcolm said. "I can't imagine. . . ."

"D'you think the sisters saw him doing it?"

"Yeah, when they first looked. But he stopped for a second when one of them called, and his dæmon got away."

"If it *was* Sister Benedicta, we could ask . . ."

"She wouldn't say. There's things they like to keep away from us."

"If she knew we'd seen it, maybe."

"Maybe. I wouldn't tell Sister Fenella, though."

"No, no."

The man and his tormented dæmon had gone, and there was nothing now but the darkness and the sound of the river; so after another minute Malcolm and Asta crept out of that room in the dark and felt their way to bed.

When they slept, he dreamed of wild dogs, a pack of them, fifty or sixty, all kinds, racing through the streets of a deserted city; and as he watched them, he felt a strange, wild exhilaration that was still there when he woke up in the morning.

THIRTEEN

THE BOLOGNA INSTRUMENT

The philosophical instruments of the Weather Office, so highly regarded by some of the drinkers at the Trout and so disdained by others, did what they always did and told their attendants exactly what they could have seen by looking at the sky. The weather was fair and cold; the sky was clear day and night; there was no prospect of rain. Further out in the Atlantic than they could perceive, there might have been all sorts of bad weather; there might have been the mother of all depressions, and it might have been heading towards Brytain to bring about just the sort of inundation that Coram van Texel had predicted to Malcolm; but there were no instruments that could see it, except perhaps an alethiometer.

So the citizens of Oxford read the weather forecasts in the newspaper, and enjoyed the pale sun on their faces, and began to put their sandbags away. The river was still racing; a dog that fell in the water at Botley was whirled away and drowned before its owner could rescue it. There was little sign of the level going down, but the banks weren't giving way and the roads were dry, so people thought the worst was over.

Hannah Relf sat at home, writing up her latest findings on the depths of the hourglass range of alethiometer meanings. She had plenty to occupy her in the pages of notes she'd been building up.

She worked hard all day, and when there was a knock on the front door in the late afternoon, her thoughts had begun to turn teawards. She pushed her chair back, feeling pleased at the interruption, and went downstairs to open the door.

"Malcolm! What are you— Come in, come in."

"I know it's not the usual day," he said, shivering, "but I thought it was important, so . . ."

"I was just about to make some tea. You've come at the right time."

"I came straight from school."

"Let's go in the sitting room, and I'll light the fire. It's cold."

She'd been working upstairs with a blanket over her knees and a little naphtha stove at her feet, so she hadn't lit the sitting room fire all day and it felt chilly in there. Malcolm stood awkwardly on the hearth rug while she set newspaper and kindling and struck a match.

"I had to come because—"

"Wait, wait. Tea first. Or would you prefer chocolatl?"

"I don't think I ought to stay. I just came to warn you."

"Warn me?"

"There was this man—a gyptian—"

"Come in the kitchen, then. You're not going out without a hot drink—it's too cold. You can warn me while I make it."

She made tea for them both, and Malcolm told her about Mr. Van Texel, and the canoe, and the flood warning.

"I thought the weather was getting better."

"No, he *knows*. The gyptians know all the rivers and the canals, and they know the state of the weirs all the way up to Gloucester. It's coming, all right, and it's going to be the biggest flood for ages. He said there was something in the water and the sky that was disturbed, and no one could tell except the people who could read the signs, and that made me think of you and the alethiometer. . . . So I thought I ought to come and tell you because of that, and because of all these books. I could help you take them upstairs, maybe."

"That's kind of you. But not now. Have you told anyone else about the gyptian's warning?"

"I told my mum and dad. Oh, and he said—the gyptian man—he said he knew about you."

"What was his name?"

"Coram van Texel. He said I was to say *Oakley Street* to you— just that, so's you could believe him."

"Good grief," said Hannah.

"Where is Oakley Street? I don't know a street called that in Oxford."

"No, it's not in Oxford. It just means— Well, it's a sort of password. Did he say anything else? Let's go in and keep the fire going. Bring your tea."

When Malcolm was sitting as close to the fire as he could get, he told her about Gerard Bonneville, and what he'd seen at the priory from the guest room window.

She listened wide-eyed. Then she said, "Gerard Bonneville . . . How odd. I heard that name yesterday. I dined in college and spoke to one of our guests, who's a lawyer. Apparently, Bonneville isn't long out of prison, I think for assault, or grievous bodily harm— something like that—and it was rather a famous case, because the chief prosecution witness was Mrs. Coulter. That's right—Lyra's mother. Bonneville swore in the dock that he'd get revenge."

"Lyra," said Malcolm at once. "He wants to hurt Lyra. Or kidnap her."

"It wouldn't surprise me. He sounds demented."

"He said to Alice that he was Lyra's father."

"Who's Alice? Oh, I remember. Did he really?"

"I'm going to tell the nuns this evening. They need to get that shutter fixed. I'll help Mr. Taphouse."

"Was he going to climb up? Did he have a ladder?"

"We didn't see. But it would make sense."

"They need more than shutters," said Hannah, stirring the fire. "If only one could trust the police!"

"I'll tell the nuns anyway. Sister Benedicta can protect Lyra against anything. Dr. Relf, have you ever heard of anyone hurting their own dæmon before?"

"Not anyone sane."

"It made us think that maybe it was him that cut her leg off."

"Yes, I can see that. How horrible."

They both sat there looking into the fire.

"I'm sure Mr. Van Texel's right about the flood," Malcolm said. "Even though it doesn't look like it now."

"I'll do something about it. I'll start with the books, as you suggest. If necessary, I'll live upstairs till the water goes away. What about the priory?"

"I'll tell them too, but it won't mean much if I say 'Oakley Street' to the nuns."

"No. You'll just have to be persuasive. And you mustn't actually say those words to anyone but me."

"He told me that."

"Then you've heard it from both of us."

"Have you met him? Mr. Van Texel?"

"No, never. Now, Malcolm, if you've finished your tea, I'm going to hurry you away. I've got to go out this evening. Thank you for the warning. I really will take it seriously."

"Thank you for the tea. I'll come on Saturday as usual."

Hannah wondered if Malcolm had told his parents about seeing the man and his dæmon outside the priory. It was the sort of thing that would worry a sensitive child, and she could see that he'd been badly disturbed. She wanted to hear more, especially about this gyptian who knew Oakley Street. Could he be an agent himself? It wasn't inconceivable.

Her engagement this evening was a mysterious one. The problem was that she didn't know where she was going. When she had seen Professor Papadimitriou some days before, he had told her how to contact him. "If I need to contact you," he'd said, "you will know about it."

A card had come that morning. It was a simple white card inside a white envelope, and all it said was "Come to dinner this evening. George Papadimitriou."

Not an invitation, exactly; more of a command. She supposed the dinner would be at his college, where the porter, he'd said, was a gossip, though, of course, there was more than one porter at Jordan; nevertheless, it was puzzling.

But as she was sorting through her not-very-many dresses and deciding that the note to strike should be serious and quiet, her letter box clattered. Her dæmon looked down from the landing.

"Another white envelope," he said.

The card inside said only "28 Staverton Road. 7 p.m."

"Easy enough, Jesper," she said.

At one minute past seven, after a brisk cold walk, she rang the bell of a large, comfortable-looking villa in one of the roads a little way north of Jericho. There was a thickly grown garden heavy with shrubs and trees, hard to see past from the road. She wondered if this was Papadimitriou's own house: it would be interesting to see how this enigmatic figure lived. And who else would be there?

"It's not a *social* invitation," murmured her dæmon. "This is business."

The door was opened by a pleasant-featured woman of forty or so who looked North African.

"Dr. Relf, how nice of you to come! I'm Yasmin Al-Kaisy. Bitterly cold, isn't it? Do put your coat on the chair here. . . . Come through."

There were three other people in the warm drawing room. Professor Papadimitriou was one, and he seemed to be in charge, but then he always did. It was a large, low-ceilinged room, with naphtha lamps on side tables and two or three anbaric standard lamps beside the armchairs. There were numerous pictures—drawings, prints, a watercolor painting or two—all of high quality, as far as Hannah could judge. The furniture was neither antique nor modern, and looked extremely comfortable.

In the warm light, Papadimitriou moved forward to shake Hannah's hand.

"Let me introduce our hosts, first of all: Dr. Adnan Al-Kaisy and Mrs. Yasmin Al-Kaisy," he said. Hannah smiled at the woman who'd opened the door, who was now standing by a table of drinks, and shook the hand of the man: tall, lean, dark, with brilliant eyes and a short black mustache, his dæmon some kind of desert fox.

"This is Lord Nugent," Papadimitriou continued. "And this is our guest, Dr. Hannah Relf."

Hannah had never seen them before, but Malcolm would have recognized the three men as the ones who had come to the Trout and asked about the priory.

"What will you drink, Dr. Relf?" said Al-Kaisy.

"Wine, thank you. White wine."

"We'll eat very soon," said Papadimitriou. "I don't want to waste any time. For our purposes this evening, Hannah, this is Oakley Street. Lord Nugent is the director, and Adnan is his deputy. Everyone here is part of Oakley Street, and knows about you. What we have to do is explain a complicated situation, and then ask you to do something."

"I see," she said. "Well, I shall listen with great interest."

"Shall we sit at the table?" said Al-Kaisy. "Then we can talk without interrupting ourselves to move."

"Very good idea," said Papadimitriou.

"This way," Al-Kaisy said, and led them into a small dining room. The table was set with cold meats and salads so no one would have to fetch and carry food from the kitchen.

"I know it's a cold night," said Yasmin Al-Kaisy, "but this will be quicker, and some of us have to catch a train. Please help yourself."

"As this is Oakley Street," said Papadimitriou, "I suggest that Lord Nugent speaks first. Hannah, you know, of course, that he was the lord chancellor."

"But here I am the director of Oakley Street," said Lord Nugent. He was very tall and thin, and his voice was very deep. His lemur dæmon sprang to an empty chair next to him as he continued. "Dr. Relf, we've been relying on your readings of the alethiometer for a couple of years now. We're grateful for that. You'll have realized that there are other alethiometrists working for us."

"Well, no, I didn't realize that," said Hannah. "I realized very little."

"Readers in Uppsala and in Bologna were also providing their specialized advice. The instrument in Geneva is in the hands of the

Magisterium, and the Paris people are sympathetic to that cause. The Oxford alethiometer is the only other one we know of."

"Since we're now Oakley Street," said Hannah, "may I ask you this: Is there another Oakley Street agent among the Oxford readers?"

"No, there isn't. The other Oxford readers are honest scholars with sound academic reasons for using the instrument."

"Unless one of them is an agent of the Magisterium," said Yasmin Al-Kaisy.

She didn't smile, but Lord Nugent did.

"Unless, of course, that," he said. "So far, things have remained in a sort of balance. But last week the reader in Bologna was murdered, and her alethiometer was stolen. We can only assume it would soon have been on its way to Geneva."

"It *would have been* on its way?"

"A very quick-witted agent of ours was able to deal with the murderer and capture the instrument. It's in that box under the lamp."

Hannah turned to look. On a side table under a naphtha lamp lay a battered wooden box, certainly the right size to contain the instrument she knew. She longed to get up at once and examine this one, and Papadimitriou could tell.

"You can see it after dinner," he said. "As far as we can tell, it hasn't been damaged by its adventures, but you'll be able to tell us for sure."

She felt breathless. Rather than trust her voice, she took a sip of wine and looked back to Lord Nugent.

"What we would like, Dr. Relf," he said, "is your agreement to a proposition. It comes at a cost, so you might need to think about it. And certainly we shall answer any questions you have. Here it is: we would be very glad if you would put your academic work aside and read the alethiometer for us full-time. You would use this instrument. It would be in your care. No one else, of course, would know. You must tell us what problems that would cause you, and of course the decision is entirely yours, but first I'll ask Adnan to say a word about the background and why this matters."

"Before you do, Dr. Al-Kaisy," Hannah said, "I want to ask a question. Perhaps you were going to answer it anyway, but here goes. Lord Nugent just now referred to the Magisterium in a way that made it clear that it was the enemy, and I know that the Consistorial Court of Discipline has been responsible for various . . . um . . . unfriendly things, such as killing the poor man who was my insulator. And there's a revolting organization called the League of St. Alexander now poisoning relations between children and their teachers in various schools. I assume these things are all connected, and I'm glad to fight them. But who are *we*? What is Oakley Street part of? What's the cause that I've been supporting in my work for Oakley Street? It sounds hopelessly naive and stupid when I put it like that, but I've been working . . . well, I've been working blind for the past few years. I've *assumed* that I was on the right side. How could anyone be so ignorant? Well, I could. I find it quite easy. I hope you can make it clear, Dr. Al-Kaisy. But, as I say, perhaps you were going to anyway."

"I hope I was," he said, "but now I shall take extra care." His dæmon, the desert fox, moved to the other side of his chair, from where she could see Hannah, and settled herself neatly. "Oakley Street is a secret agency of government. We were set up with the express purpose of frustrating the work of the agencies you mentioned and several others too. We were created in 1933, just before the Swiss War, when it seemed likely that Brytain would be defeated by the Magisterium's armed forces. As it turned out, we weren't, and some of the credit for our survival belongs to the Office for Special Inquiry, which later became known informally as Oakley Street. Its purpose was to defend democracy in this country, first of all. Then to defend the principles of freedom of thought and expression. We were lucky in our monarchy, I have to say. King Richard was a strong supporter of our activities; the director of Oakley Street is always a Privy Counselor, and the old king had a passionate interest in what we were doing and why. King Michael, perhaps rather less so . . . But the present king seems to share his grandfather's interest and has been very helpful in ways that haven't been made public."

"What does Parliament know about Oakley Street?"

"Very little. Our activities are funded—not very well—out of the general defense fund, through the Cabinet Office. There is a group of MPs, government backbenchers who are passionately pro-Magisterium—I'm sure you would know some of their names—who suspect that something like Oakley Street exists, and would love to expose it and destroy it and put a stop to everything we do. This is a deep and uncomfortable paradox, which will not have escaped you: we can only defend democracy by being undemocratic. Every secret service knows this paradox. Some are more comfortable with it than others."

"Yes," said Hannah. "It is a paradox. And it is uncomfortable. To go back to the instrument from Bologna for a moment: presumably it's really a possession of Bologna University?"

"It was," said Lord Nugent.

"Surely it still is? Legally? Morally?"

"I daresay," said Lord Nugent. "Like Adnan's democratic paradox, this is another ethical problem. The governing body of the university there is now in the hands of a pro-Geneva faction. Our reader was working for us in secret, as you are, and we suspect she was found out and killed on the orders of that very faction. They'd discovered what she was doing, and they killed her for it, and if our agent hadn't managed to step in at once, this instrument would now be in Geneva, helping our enemies."

"Good grief," said Hannah.

She took a sip of her wine and looked clearly at the four others: Nugent, lean and subtle; Yasmin Al-Kaisy, elegant and warmly interested at the same time; Adnan Al-Kaisy, dark-eyed, sympathetic; and Papadimitriou, cool, curious, fierce.

"So, for the moment, the Bologna instrument counts as the spoils of war," Al-Kaisy went on after a pause.

"And this *is* a war? We're fighting a war?" said Hannah. "A secret war?"

"Yes, it is," said Nugent. "And we're asking you to take a more prominent part. We're quite aware of all the implications."

"Implications . . ."

"About your safety, and so on. The last person to do what we'd like you to do was killed, after all. Yes, we see that as clearly as you do. Her position was considerably more exposed than yours will be, mind you. She was in what was effectively an enemy stronghold. We can make sure that you are protected."

"And you'd need me to do this—what, full-time?"

"Remind my colleagues what you do at the moment," said Papadimitriou.

Yasmin Al-Kaisy was putting a glass bowl of some fragrant ice in front of each of them.

"Thank you," said Hannah. "This looks delicious. Well, I do two things. In the small amount of time I have with the Bodleian alethiometer, I'm supposed to be working, like the other members of the group, on one of the symbol ranges of the instrument. My particular symbol is the hourglass. There are twelve of us in the group, and each of us takes one symbol to study, and we meet regularly to compare notes. I have five hours with the instrument each week.

"That's what I do on the surface, so to speak. Officially. But as you know, I also work for Oakley Street. When they—you—send me a specific question to answer, I work on that, taking time out of my five hours. But if I make no progress with my official—my proper—research, I'll be asked to leave the group and let someone else have my alethiometer time. As it is, I'm one of the slowest because of the work I do for you. And that's . . . It's galling."

"It must be," said Al-Kaisy. "But in that case—I mean, if you are known to be slow—it wouldn't be surprising if, say, you voluntarily gave up your five hours with the Bodleian alethiometer. . . ."

"And said that it was too difficult, you mean? And gave up my research?" Hannah dropped the spoon beside her bowl. "Well, no, that would be *possible*. And the humiliation—well, no doubt I could put up with that. But I have a *career*. . . ."

She picked up the spoon again, dropped it once more. She looked at Papadimitriou.

"Professor, *you* can see what this would mean!" she said, and Jesper, expressing her indignation, bristled all over. "You're asking me to do something that led the last person to do it to her death. Simultaneously you'd like me to sabotage my career by seeming to give up a course of research because it was too difficult for me. That's . . . well, both together . . . it's unreasonable, isn't it?"

Papadimitriou pushed his untouched ice aside.

"Yes, it is," he said. "War asks many people to do unreasonable things. And make no mistake, we *are* at war. Hannah, there is no one else who could do this. I know all the Oxford alethiometer group. Frankly—well, covertly—I have been following the group's reports. Your colleagues are diligent and well informed and skillful, but the only one to work with a real degree of insight into the symbols is you. You may be the slowest; you are also, by a long way, the best. Don't worry about your career."

And, of course, Hannah immediately felt ashamed. But there was nothing she thought she could say. She ate a spoonful of ice.

"As for the danger," said Lord Nugent, "I won't deny it. If it becomes known what you're doing—especially that you have the Bologna instrument—you will be at some risk. I shall see to it that someone will be watching. We were watching the Bologna reader, which is how we were able to deal with the matter so quickly once it was . . . once it was too late, of course. But there we were stretched. Here we would not be. You wouldn't be aware of the protection, but it would be there."

"And you would know," said Al-Kaisy, "that you were making a great contribution to the progress of this war, this secret war. You know who the enemy is, so you know what we're fighting. Remember what is at stake. The right we have to speak and think freely, to pursue research into any subject under the sun—all that would be destroyed. That is worth fighting for, don't you agree?"

"Of course I agree," said Hannah fiercely. "You don't have to *persuade* me of something so obvious. What else would I believe? Of *course* I believe that."

She pushed her ice away.

"We realize that very well," said Nugent. "And of course the position we're putting you in is profoundly uncomfortable. Why don't we finish this delicious dessert, and then you can see the instrument from Bologna. I'd be very interested to hear what you make of it."

"How many alethiometers are there?" asked Yasmin Al-Kaisy. "I suppose I should know, but I don't."

Papadimitriou spoke for Hannah, who took back her ice and ate a spoonful. "Five, as far as we know. There are rumors of a sixth, but . . ."

"Why can't we make another?"

"Hannah could tell us more fully, but I think it's to do with the alloy of which the hands or the needles are made. But the instrument itself is only part of the matter. Each one forms a unity with

205

its reader. Neither is complete, when it comes to working, without the other."

"Which is one of the very mysteries we have to solve," said Al-Kaisy.

Lord Nugent got up from the table and brought the little box with the battered corners over to Hannah. It looked like rosewood; a painted design on the top was only just recognizable as a coat of arms.

She lifted the lid and looked at the alethiometer closely before lifting it out of its nest of maroon velvet and setting it on the white tablecloth. It was deeper than the Bodleian instrument, but the golden case was equally worn with handling, and glowed in the lamplight with as much intensity and fire. The thirty-six symbols arranged in their places around the dial were more simply painted, and only in black on white enamel and not in brilliant colors on ivory, as the Bodleian's were; but they looked less like decoration and more like essential qualities. Behind the hands and the needle, an engraving of the sun in splendor occupied the center of the dial.

Hannah felt her hands moving towards it, as if to the face of a lover. The Bodleian alethiometer was beautiful and ornate, and what she felt about it was great respect and even awe. This one was workmanlike, but it suited her in some inexpressible way. It welcomed her hands as if they were the very ones that had worn down the golden case over centuries and smoothed away the knurling of the wheels. As soon as she felt it, she wanted to be alone with it; she wanted to spend hours and days in its company; she wanted it never to be more than an arm's length away.

She let her mind slip into the state of relaxed attention in which she could feel the first ten or twelve layers of meaning below each symbol, and turned one of the hands to the baby, one of whose functions was to stand for the person making the inquiry. The second she turned to the beehive—in this case standing for productive work. The third she set to the apple, locking its meaning in her mind onto the level that stood for a general inquiry of any sort. With the books she could have asked her question more precisely, but this would have to do: Should she accept this challenge or not?

Immediately the needle began to swing round and round, and Hannah counted six revolutions before it settled firmly on the marionette. The sixth level of the marionette range, in a simple reading like this, stood for affirmation: yes, she should.

She looked up, breathed deeply, and blinked as she came out of her slight trance. They were all watching her.

"Yes, I'll do it," she said.

There was no mistaking the relief and pleasure that came into their expressions. Even Papadimitriou smiled like a young boy given a present. What Hannah didn't tell them was that her hands on the instrument felt instantly at home and at work in a way that they never had with the Oxford alethiometer.

And almost in the same moment she saw the problem.

"But . . . ," she said.

"Yes?" said Papadimitriou.

"I can do what I do with the Bodleian alethiometer only because the library has all the books that deal with the deeper layers of the symbol ranges. From memory I can work about a dozen layers deep, but not much more than that. If I'm going to leave the group, I won't be able to use the books without making it obvious that I have access to another alethiometer. And without the books, I won't be any use to you."

The others looked at Papadimitriou. From somewhere the smell of coffee was drifting.

Papadimitriou said, "On the face of it, that does present a problem. But books are easier to duplicate than alethiometers. I shall make it my business to find as many as you need."

"If it becomes known that you're in the market for such books," said Al-Kaisy, "people will put two and two together. A missing alethiometer here, a scholar keenly seeking to acquire certain books there . . ."

"It won't be *this* there," said Papadimitriou. "It'll be several different theres. Don't worry about it."

"We can put out some green paper," said Nugent, accepting a cup of coffee from Yasmin Al-Kaisy.

"Green paper?" said Hannah.

"False rumors. In the early days of Oakley Street, plans for that sort of thing were often sketched out on green paper. We still use the term. We can suggest that we've found the one missing instrument. Or that we've succeeded in making another, or several more. Green paper is sometimes very useful."

"Yes, I see," said Hannah. "Can I be practical again?"

"Please do."

"I shall need an income. If I go back to teaching, which of course I could do, it would give me little time to work for Oakley Street."

"Leave that to me," said Lord Nugent. "An uncle you didn't know very well . . . a legacy—something like that. We haven't got much money, but we can certainly keep you from starvation."

"I hope you can," said Hannah.

She realized that her hands had not left the alethiometer since she'd first touched it. Self-consciously, she took them away and sipped her coffee.

"Practical arrangements," said Yasmin Al-Kaisy. "More practical arrangements. Have you got a safe at your house?"

"No," Hannah said, and couldn't keep a slight laugh from her voice. "I've got nothing valuable."

"You have now. We'll arrange for a new item of domestic apparatus—say, a new central heating boiler, something of that sort—to be delivered and installed in the next two or three days. It won't be a boiler, but it will be a safe. Please keep the alethiometer in that when you're not using it."

"Of course." She thought, It had better be put upstairs, in case of a flood. And that reminded her of Malcolm's warning, and she said, "Lord Nugent, is there an agent of Oakley Street called Coram van Texel?"

"No," he said.

She thought, Interesting. One of them must be lying, and I think it's Nugent. I can ask the alethiometer anyway. She went on: "Or a man called Gerard Bonneville? Has he anything to do with this business?"

"Bonneville the experimental theologian?"

"Was he a scientist? I didn't know. He's got a hyena dæmon with a missing leg."

"He was a leading researcher into the Rusakov business. Dust— that sort of thing. Then he lost his bearings and was jailed for a sex offense, I think. How have you come across him?"

"Apparently, he's in Oxford. He's been to Malcolm's father's pub. Malcolm mentioned him the other day. One more thing: How will we contact one another? In the same way as before?"

"No," said Papadimitriou. "You and I will have to make some arrangement to meet regularly. In your new capacity as an independent scholar, let's say, you've asked my advice about a book you want to write. We meet to talk about your research. Something like that. What are you doing this Friday afternoon?"

"I would normally be working at home."

"Come to Jordan at three o'clock."

"Very well."

"And I wonder if you could make a start on something right away," said Nugent.

"Yes, I suppose I could," she said, "now I've got this."

"It's about the child at the priory. For some reason we don't understand, she's very important to the other side. Can you make general inquiries, or does it have to be a tightly focused question?"

"Both—but the more tightly focused, the longer it takes."

"Make it general, then. We badly need to know why the child is important. If you could frame a question that would get an answer to that, it would be very helpful."

"I'll do my best."

"One more thing," Nugent went on. "Your young friend, the boy from the inn—Matthew, is it?"

"Malcolm Polstead."

"Malcolm. We won't put him in danger, but he could be valuable in a number of ways. Keep in touch with him. Tell him what you think he can keep quiet about. Pick up whatever you can."

Something had happened. The atmosphere in the room had changed quite suddenly. There was an air of— She couldn't understand it. It was as if the others all knew a secret she didn't, and they didn't want to look at her. It couldn't have been Lord Nugent's words, which seemed to be innocuous; or was she missing what they meant?

The moment passed. People got up, good-byes were said, coats found, thanks uttered, and Hannah put the alethiometer in its rosewood box in a cotton shopping bag and set off home.

"Jesper, what happened then?" she said when they'd turned into the Woodstock Road.

"They knew that he meant something underneath what he actually said, and they didn't like it."

"Well, I got that far myself. I wonder what it was."

FOURTEEN

LADY WITH MONKEY

The next day, Malcolm found the nuns busy preparing for the Feast of St. Scholastica. It wasn't actually a *feast*, as Sister Fenella had explained to a disappointed Malcolm on previous occasions; it was a day of celebration. But that meant long services in the oratory rather than well-filled tables in the refectory.

However, Lyra obviously wasn't expected to sing and pray with the sisters, and equally obviously couldn't be left untended while their hymns and psalms and prayers ascended into the infinite, so Sister Fenella was excused the duty of praising the dead saint and detailed to look after the baby while she prepared the evening meal.

Malcolm came into the kitchen just as the old lady was putting a lamb stew to simmer on the range. Pantalaimon, the baby dæmon, set up a brisk chirruping, and Malcolm moved closer so that Asta could perch on the rim of the crib and change into all the birds she knew, one after the other, making Lyra and her dæmon scream with laughter, as if it was the funniest thing in the world.

"We haven't seen you for a day or two, Malcolm," said Sister Fenella. "What have you been up to?"

"Lots of things. Sister Fenella, will Sister Benedicta be able to see me after the service?"

"Not for long, dear. This is a busy day. Can I tell her anything for you?"

"Well . . . I've got to warn her, but I can warn you as well, because it's for all of you."

"Oh, dear. What are you warning us about?"

She settled on her stool and drew the nearest cabbage towards her on the table. Malcolm watched her hands and the old knife unhurriedly shredding it, setting the outside leaves and the heart aside for stock, and reaching for another.

"You know the river's been high?" he said. "Well, everyone thinks that it'll go down, now it's stopped raining, but the rain's going to come back and the river's going to flood more than it's done for years."

"Really?"

"Yes. A gyptian man told me. And they know the river, gyptians. They know all the waters in England. I just wanted to make sure Sister Benedicta knew, so she could make everything safe, specially Lyra. 'Cause you're low-lying here on this bank. I told my dad, and he said you could all come and stay at the Trout, only it probably wouldn't be holy enough."

She laughed and clapped her old red hands.

"I've told other people," Malcolm went on, "but no one believes me, I don't think. I wish you had some boats here. If you could float, you'd be all right in a flood, but . . ."

"We'd all be carried away," said Sister Fenella. "But I shouldn't worry. We had a big flood in . . . oh, fifty years ago—I was a novice—and all the garden was underwater and it came right in and the ground floor was three or four inches deep. I thought it was marvelously exciting, but the older nuns were distressed, so I didn't say anything. Of course, I had nothing to be responsible for in those days. And it soon went down again. So I shouldn't worry too much, Malcolm. Most things have happened before, and we're all still here, by the grace of God."

"There was something else I wanted to tell Sister Benedicta," said Malcolm. "But maybe it'll wait till tomorrow. Is Mr. Taphouse here today?"

"I haven't seen him. I heard he wasn't well."

"Oh . . . I was going to say something to him as well. Maybe I could go and see him, but I don't know where he lives."

"Neither do I."

"I'll have to see Sister Benedicta after all, then. When do they finish worshipping?"

It turned out that the long service finished in twenty minutes' time, which gave the sisters an hour for recreation and exercise, or for getting on with their work in the garden or with the embroidery needle, before sitting down to eat. Malcolm decided to fill the time by teaching Lyra how to talk.

"Now, Lyra, see, I'm Malcolm. That's easy to say. Go on, have a go. Mal-colm."

She stared at him solemnly. Pantalaimon became a mole and buried himself in her blankets, and Asta laughed.

"No, don't laugh," said Malcolm. "Try it, Lyra. Mal-colm."

She frowned and dribbled.

"Well, you'll get the hang of it eventually," he said, patting her cheeks dry with a tea towel. "Try Asta. Go on. As-ta."

She watched him cautiously and said nothing at all.

"Well, she's very advanced for her age, anyway," said Malcolm. "It's really clever for her dæmon to be a mole. How'd they know about moles?"

"That's a mystery," said the old nun. "Only the good Lord knows the answer to that, but that's not surprising, because after all He created everything."

"I remember being a mole," said Geraint, her old dæmon, who normally said very little and just watched everything with his head to one side. "When I was frightened, I used to be a mole."

"But how did you *know* about moles?" said Malcolm.

"You just feel mole-ish," said Asta.

"Hmm," said Malcolm. "Look, he's coming up again."

Pan, no longer a mole but now a rabbit, emerged from the blankets, very close to Lyra, for safety, but very curious.

"Tell you what, Lyra," Malcolm said. "You can teach Pan how to say Malcolm."

The baby and the dæmon gabbled cautiously together. Then Asta became a monkey and stood on her hands, and they both laughed.

"Well, you can laugh, even if you can't talk," said Malcolm. "I 'spect you'll learn soon. What about Sister Fenella? Can you say that? Sis-ter Fen-el-la?"

The little girl turned her head to Sister Fenella and gave a broad happy smile, and her dæmon became a squirrel like Geraint and chattered with glee.

"She's really clever," said Malcolm. He was full of admiration.

At that moment, he heard a stir of talk in the corridor, and the kitchen door opened to let in Sister Benedicta.

"Ah! Malcolm! I wanted to talk to you. Glad you're here. All well, Sister?"

She meant, *All well with Lyra?* but she didn't really listen to the answer. Another nun, Sister Katarina, was coming to keep an eye on the baby while Sister Fenella went to the oratory for a private service of her own, or so Malcolm gathered. Sister Katarina was young and pretty, with large dark eyes, but she was nervous, and she made Lyra nervous too. The baby was really only perfectly happy with Sister Fenella.

"Come along, Malcolm," said Sister Benedicta. "I want a quick word."

It didn't sound as if he was in trouble. It wasn't that kind of summons.

"I wanted to tell you something too, Sister," he said as she closed the office door behind them.

"In a minute. You remember that man you told me about? With the three-legged dæmon?"

"I saw him the other night," said Malcolm. "I was going through the upstairs bedrooms at home looking for something and . . ."

He described what he'd seen. She listened close, frowning.

"A broken shutter? No, it's not broken. Someone forgot to close it. Never mind that. You saw what he was doing to his dæmon—clearly the man is mentally ill, Malcolm. What I wanted to tell you was to keep away from him. If you see him anywhere, just go in the opposite direction. Don't get drawn into conversation. I know how friendly you are with everyone, and that's a virtue, but you have to use judgment as well, which is another virtue. That man is not capable of reason, poor thing, and his obsessions can damage other people, just as they've damaged his dæmon. Now, what did you want to tell me? Was it about him?"

"Partly. But the other part is that there's going to be a flood. A gyptian man told me."

"Oh, nonsense! The weather's changed. It'll be spring before we know it. Thank the good Lord, all that rain's over and done with."

"But he explained—"

"A lot of what the gyptians say is superstition, Malcolm. Listen to it politely, but again—use your judgment. All the forecasts from the Weather Office agree: the heavy rains are over, and there's no danger of flood."

"But the gyptians *know* the rivers and the weather—"

"Thank you for passing on his warning. But I think we're going to be safe. Was there anything else?"

"Is Mr. Taphouse all right?"

"He's a little poorly. Now that all the shutters are up, I've told him to rest for a few days. Off you go, Malcolm. Remember what I told you about the man."

She was very hard to argue with. Not that he wanted to argue; all he was trying to do was warn, as Mr. Van Texel had asked him to do.

That night, he had another dream about wild dogs. Or perhaps it was the same dream: a pack of wild dogs, all kinds of dogs, running with furious speed across a bare plain this time, intent on hunting and killing something he couldn't see. And he was relishing it. It was frightening and exciting at the same time, and he woke sweating and breathing fast, and lay holding tightly to Asta, who, of course, had been dreaming the same dream. He was still thinking about it when they got up much later to go to school.

Having had no success at warning the nuns about the flood, Malcolm tried with his teachers. He had the same response. It was nonsense—it was superstition—the gyptians knew nothing, or they were up to something, or they weren't to be trusted.

"I dunno," said Malcolm to Robbie and Eric and Tom in the playground. "Some people just don't *want* to be warned."

"Well, it doesn't look likely, this flood," said Robbie.

"River's still high," said Tom, who was a faithful follower of whatever Malcolm said. "It wouldn't take much more rain. . . ."

"My dad says you can't believe anything the gyptians say," announced Eric. "There's always a hidden gender with them."

"A what?" said Robbie.

"They got secret plans that no one else knows about."

"Don't talk daft," said Malcolm. "What secret plan could this be?"

"I dunno," said Eric righteously. "That's why it's secret."

"You stopped wearing your league badge," said Robbie. "I bet there's a secret agenda behind that, an' all."

In answer Eric slowly reached up to the lapel of his blazer and turned it back with a finger and thumb. Pinned underneath was the little enamel lamp of the League of St. Alexander.

"Why're you hiding it?" said Malcolm.

"Those of us who have reached the second degree wear it like that," said Eric. "There's a few of us in school, but not many."

"At least if you wear it on the outside, people can see you belong," said Robbie. "But hiding it's sneaky."

"Why?" said Eric, honestly astonished.

"'Cause if you see someone's wearing a badge, you can just not say anything they could report," said Malcolm. "But if they hide it, you could find yourself in trouble without knowing why."

"What is this 'second degree' anyway?" said Robbie.

"I'm not allowed to tell you."

"Bet you will, though," said Malcolm. "Bet you'll tell us before the end of the week."

"I won't," said Eric.

"Yes, you will," said Robbie and Tom together.

Eric stalked away, offended.

The influence of the league had stabilized since its first big successes. Mr. Hawkins, the deputy head who had compromised with it at once, was confirmed as successor to the old headmaster, who had disappeared. Eric said Mr. Willis was at a special training camp, but he was believed as much as he usually was, so no one knew for sure. Some of the teachers who had left in protest or by being required to take leave had come back, sullen or chastened; others had vanished and been replaced. The real authority in the school was held by the never-quite-named, never-quite-described, never-quite-admitted-to group of senior pupils forming the first and most influential members of the league. They met with Mr. Hawkins every day, and their decisions or orders were announced in the next day's assembly. Somehow it was implied that any such proclamation was the direct word of God, so that to disobey or protest was to blaspheme. Many pupils got into trouble before they understood this. Now, though, the understanding had permeated everywhere.

The pupils in this half-secret group were helped and guided by two or three adults, who were rumored to be special governors. They never spoke in assembly, never taught any lessons, hardly ever spoke to a pupil; they patrolled the corridors making notes and were treated with particular obsequiousness by the staff, but no children were told their names or what their functions were. It just became understood.

About half the school had joined the league; of those, a few had fallen away, and of the rest, a few had given in and joined. For the moment nothing more had been seen of the woman who had first come to tell them about it, and absolutely nothing had been said in the newspapers. You could spend quite some time in the school and never hear it mentioned; but all the same, its existence became known to everyone. It was as if it had always been there, as if it would be strange for a school *not* to be pervaded by this half-enthralling, half-frightening miasma. Lessons went on as normal, though each lesson was now preceded by a prayer. The pictures that had hung in the corridors and classrooms—mostly reproductions of famous paintings, or paintings of historical scenes—had been taken down and replaced with posters bearing quotations from the Bible in rather hectoring color. Few pupils were openly naughty anymore—there were fewer fights in the playground, for instance—but everyone seemed guiltier.

On Saturday, Malcolm took *La Belle Sauvage* for her first extended trip since Mr. Van Texel had brought her back. It was just as the gyptian had said: the little craft was stiffer, more responsive, and very much slippier through the water than she'd ever felt before. Malcolm was delighted; he thought he'd be able to paddle for miles without tiring, and camp anywhere, more or less invisibly, and altogether own the water in a quite new way.

"When we need a big boat," he said to the kingfisher-formed Asta as she sat on the gunwale beside him, "we'll go to that gyptian boatbuilder and he can make it for us."

"How will we find him? And what would it cost?"

"Dunno. We could ask Mr. Van Texel."

"How'll we find where he is?"

"Dunno that either. I wonder if he was a spy," Malcolm said after a while. "I mean, Oakley Street . . ."

Asta didn't reply. She was gazing at a small fish. They were on the canal now, which was high itself, but stiller than the river, of course. Malcolm could feel his dæmon's eagerness to plunge into the water and catch the fish, and silently urged her on; but she held back.

They tied up the canoe in their usual place, and the chandler promised to keep an eye on her, and soon they were in Cranham Street.

"What's that?" said Asta as soon as they turned the corner.

A grand gas-powered vehicle was standing right outside Dr. Relf's house. Malcolm stopped to look at it.

"She's got a visitor," said Asta, a jackdaw now.

"Maybe we should wait."

"Don't you want to see who it is?"

"Sort of. I don't want to get in the way, though."

"It's them who's in our way," said Asta. "She's expecting us. We always come at this time."

"No, I got a feeling. . . ."

It was the grandeur of the vehicle that disturbed him. It didn't fit with his knowledge of Dr. Relf. Still, Asta was right: they were expected.

"Well, we'll just have to be polite and keep our eyes open," he said. "Like proper spies."

"We *are* proper spies," said Asta.

There was a chauffeur with a short pipe in his mouth who was lounging outside the car. He gave them an incurious glance as Malcolm rang the bell.

Dr. Relf, looking a little bothered, opened the door.

"We can come back later if—" Malcolm began, but she shook her head firmly.

"No, Malcolm, come in," she said, and Jesper murmured, "But be careful," only just loud enough for them to hear. Then, louder, she said, "My visitor's just going."

Malcolm stepped over the sandbags, and Asta became a robin, and then changed back to a jackdaw. Malcolm was completely at one with her uncertainty, but thought, Stay like that, when she was in her dusty black feathers. And he assumed an expression of dim and mild agreeableness, the next best thing to being invisible.

It was as well he did. In the sitting room Dr. Relf said, "Mrs. Coulter, this is my pupil Malcolm. Malcolm, say hello to Mrs. Coulter."

The woman's name hit Malcolm like a bullet. *This was Lyra's mother.* She was the most beautiful lady he had ever seen: young and golden-haired and sweet-faced, dressed in gray silk, and wearing a scent, just the very faintest hint of a fragrance, that spoke of warmth and sunlight and the south. She smiled at him with such friendliness that he was reminded of that strange moment with Gerard Bonneville. And this was the woman who wanted nothing more to do with her own child! But he wasn't supposed to know that, and nothing would have made him admit that he knew anything about the baby.

"Hello, Malcolm," she said, and held out her hand to shake. "And what's Dr. Relf teaching you?"

"The history of ideas," said Malcolm stolidly.

"You couldn't have a better teacher."

Her dæmon was disconcerting. He was a monkey with long golden fur, and if there was an expression in his black eyes, it was unfathomable. He sat perfectly still on the back of her armchair, and Asta, who out of politeness would normally have flown across to say good day, felt repelled and frightened and stayed on Malcolm's shoulder.

"Are you a scholar too, Mrs. Coulter?" Malcolm said.

"Only an amateur. How did you find a teacher like Dr. Relf?"

"I found a book she'd lost and brought it back. Now I borrow books from her and we talk about them," he said in the sort of polite, neutral tone that he used with customers in the Trout whom he didn't know very well. He was hoping she wouldn't ask where he lived, in case she knew where Lyra was and made the connection; but hadn't they said she had no interest in the child? Perhaps she didn't know and didn't care.

"And where do you live?" she said.

"Down St. Ebbe's," he said, naming a district in the south of the city, and surprising himself by saying it so calmly.

The golden monkey stirred but said nothing.

"And what do you want to do when you grow up?"

Everybody asked that, but somehow he expected something more interesting from her.

"I dunno, really," he said. "Maybe work on the boats or the railway."

"I expect the history of ideas will be very useful, then," she said, smiling sweetly.

That was sarcastic. He didn't like it, so he thought he'd disconcert her.

"Mrs. Coulter," he said, "I met someone the other day who was a friend of yours."

Asta could see Jesper's eyes widen. Mrs. Coulter smiled again, but differently.

"I wonder who that was," she said.

"I don't know his name. He came in our pub. He was talking about you. His dæmon's a hyena with three legs."

That was a horrible shock for her. Malcolm could see it, and Asta could see it, and Dr. Relf and Jesper could see it too—but all that happened was that the golden monkey leaned forward and put both paws on Mrs. Coulter's shoulders, and the faint pink left her cheeks.

"What an extraordinary thing," she said in the calmest tone in the world. "I'm sure I don't know anyone like that. And what pub is this?"

"The Scrivener's Arms," said Malcolm, certain that there was no pub of that name anywhere in the city.

"And what was he saying?"

"Just that he was a friend of yours and he was going to see you soon. I don't think many people believed him, actually, because he hadn't been in before and no one really knew him."

"And do you spend a lot of time chatting in the bar to strangers?"

The color had come back to her cheeks, but where it had been a delicate flush before, it was now a small fierce spot on each cheek-bone.

"No, I just help out in the evenings," Malcolm said in his most equable tone. "I hear lots of people saying all sorts of things. If he comes back, shall I tell him I've seen you and you don't know him?"

"You'd better not say anything. You'd better not listen to non-sense either. I'm sure Dr. Relf would agree."

Malcolm looked at Dr. Relf, who was listening wide-eyed. But she blinked and recovered, and said, "Was there anything else I can help you with, Mrs. Coulter?"

"Not for now," said Mrs. Coulter. The golden monkey had come to sit on her lap and press his face into her hair, as if he was whis-pering. She stroked his fur automatically, and he turned his head to glare at Malcolm with those unfathomable eyes. Malcolm stared back calmly, though he felt anything but calm: if that monkey had a name, it might be Malice, he thought.

Mrs. Coulter gathered the dæmon into her arms and stood up, whispering something to him. Then she held out her hand to Dr. Relf.

"Very kind of you to put up with me calling without any notice," she said, and then turned to Malcolm. "Good-bye, Malcolm" was all she said. She didn't offer to shake his hand.

Dr. Relf showed her to the front door, helped her on with a warm fur coat, and saw her out. Malcolm watched through the window as the chauffeur stood up straight and bustled around be-ing useful.

"Well, what did you say that for?" said Dr. Relf as the great car drew away.

"I didn't want to tell her where I lived."

"But the man with the hyena dæmon! Why on earth—"

"I wanted to see what would happen."

"Malcolm, that was very reckless."

"Yes. But I don't trust her. I wanted to shake her a bit, and I thought that would work."

"It certainly did. But *did* he say anything about her? Did he say he was a friend?"

Malcolm told her what Alice had said about Bonneville. "I just thought," he added, "if she was meaning any harm to Lyra, it might frighten her a bit."

"It frightened *me*," said Dr. Relf. "But tell me again: He said *what*?"

"He said he was Lyra's father."

"Thank goodness you didn't tell her that."

"I wouldn't be that silly," said Malcolm.

"No . . . I need a cup of tea. Let's go in the kitchen."

"What did she come here for?" said Malcolm, sitting on the kitchen stool.

"Well," she said, "to ask about Lyra."

"Really? What did you tell her?"

"It was strange. She seemed to think I had some connection with the child. As I do, I suppose, indirectly, through you. It was . . ." She stopped, holding the kettle in midair, as if struck by a sudden thought. "Yes. It was just as if she'd learned about that from an alethiometer. I wonder! It's exactly the sort of partial knowledge that you get when you're in a hurry, or you're not an expert reader. She was clearly passionately interested in where the child was, and something had told her that I might know."

"But you didn't . . ."

"Of course not. Of course not! She began by asking about the Oxford alethiometer group, about . . . all sorts of things. But politely, as if she wasn't really interested. Then she began to ask about the child who was being held somewhere in Oxford, or near Oxford, as if it was something interesting but not important, except that it clearly was. Jesper was watching her dæmon, who was gripping the back of her chair. . . ."

As she put the kettle on the stove and busied her hands with the tea caddy, she was thinking hard. Malcolm saw, and said nothing.

She didn't speak till they were sitting down beside the fire. Then she took a deep breath.

"Malcolm," she said, "I'm going to take a risk now and tell you some things I shouldn't. You will keep quiet about them? You do understand how important it is?"

"Well, course."

"Yes, of course you do. I just dread putting you in danger, and I don't know whether it's more dangerous for you to know these things or not to."

"Probably more dangerous not to."

"Yes, that's what I think. Well, the fact is, I've left the alethiometer group."

"Why?"

"I was offered a chance to do something else. To work with a different alethiometer, on my own."

"I thought there wasn't many of them."

"This one became free. Unexpectedly."

"That was lucky."

"I don't know. It might be. I think that was one of the things Mrs. Coulter was trying to find out—whether I had it."

"Is she a spy, then?"

"I think so. For the other side."

"Did you hide it from her? I mean, hide that you were doing it?"

"I hope so. That dæmon . . . it's impossible to tell anything from that face."

"He was a bit shocked when I said about Gerard Bonneville."

"Yes, he was. And she was very shocked. I'm still not sure you should have done it."

"We wouldn't have known otherwise."

"Known what?"

"That she knew about him. Oh, you remember I told you about the broken shutter on the priory window, when we saw him hitting his dæmon?"

"Yes."

"Well, it wasn't broken. Sister Benedicta told me someone had forgotten to close it."

"That's interesting. I wonder if someone left it open on purpose."

"That's what we've been thinking," said Malcolm. "But I dunno who would have done that."

Dr. Relf put her teacup down on the hearth.

"Malcolm, you won't tell anyone about the alethiometer business, will you?"

"Absolutely not," he said, surprised she should ask.

"I didn't think you would. But it *is* deadly secret."

"Course I won't," he said.

He ate a biscuit. She went to the window.

"But, Dr. Relf," he said, "can I ask you what you're doing with the new alethiometer? Is it the same as what you did in the group?"

"No, it's not. The people who gave it to me want me to ask about Lyra, among other things."

"What do they want to know about her?"

"She's important in some way they don't understand. And they want me to look into some more questions about Dust."

She had her back to him, and he felt she wasn't happy answering too many questions, but he had to ask one more.

"And is 'they' Oakley Street?"

She turned around. The sky had become dark behind her, and

the only light in the room came from the coal fire in the hearth, so he couldn't see her expression.

"Yes, it is," she said heavily. "But that's not for mentioning, remember."

"No. All right. I won't ask any more questions."

She turned back to the window. "It looks as though your gyptian was right, and it's going to rain again," she said. "Let's finish soon or you'll get soaked. Come and choose a couple of books."

He could tell she was worried, and not wanting to hang around in case he annoyed her, he quickly picked out a murder story and a book about China and said good-bye.

Once the safe had been installed and the break with the alethiometer group was complete, Hannah asked Professor Papadimitriou about that odd moment at the end of the dinner, when no one could look at her, when the atmosphere changed so suddenly.

Papadimitriou explained it. It seemed that sometimes Oakley Street and other secret services had to use blackmail in order to turn an agent on the other side. There was an agent they were targeting at present, for example, who was reputed to have an unhealthy interest in young boys.

As soon as he said that, she saw the trap she'd fallen into, and cried out in dismay, "No! Not Malcolm!"

"Hannah—"

"I won't allow it! You want to offer him up—I don't know—as a *temptation*—and then what? You'll burst into the room and catch the man red-handed? Or worse? You'll have a secret camera installed and take *photograms*? You want to put Malcolm into a situation like that? How despicable. And Nugent said it wouldn't put him in danger—and I *believed* him. God, what a fool!"

"Hannah, he would not be in the slightest danger. It would be so quick, he wouldn't even be aware of what was happening. We'd make sure of that. He's too valuable to risk."

"I won't let it happen. Never. I'd sooner give this alethiometer back and forget I ever had anything to do with—"

"Well, that would be—"

"And you waited till I was *committed* before telling me. Well, now I see what sort of thing I'm committed to."

"Come back when you've calmed down" was all he said.

"I won't calm down. Not about this."

No, of course she'd do anything to keep Malcolm safe from that. And she saw Lord Nugent in a new light too: under that patrician charm and friendliness, he was ruthless. All she could do was ask the alethiometer about it, and make what sense she could out of the swings and pauses of the silvery needle. As ever, the deeper she went, the more questions she saw.

That evening, the rain started in earnest.

FIFTEEN

THE POTTING SHED

When Malcolm went to the priory that afternoon to see if Mr. Tap-house was better, he found the workshop dark and locked up; but in the kitchen he had a surprise, because there was Alice, kneading some dough.

"Oh," he said, because he could think of nothing else.

Alice looked disdainful, as usual, and said nothing.

"Hello, Malcolm," said Sister Fenella. The old lady was sitting by the stove near Lyra's crib, and she didn't look at all well.

"Alice is helping us for a while," the nun went on, her voice light and breathless.

"Oh, right," he said. "How's Lyra?"

"Fast asleep. Come and see."

Lyra's face was pressed into the fur of her kitten dæmon, but not for long, because as soon as Asta flew down to the crib, Panta-laimon woke up and spat fiercely. That woke Lyra, of course, and she started bellowing with all the breath in her little lungs.

"It's all right, Lyra," Malcolm said, "you know who we are. What a racket! I should think they can hear you all the way across the river and into the Trout."

Asta became a young cat and jumped into the crib, taking care to avoid touching Lyra, and picked up Pan the kitten dæmon and gave him a little shake. He was so astonished that Lyra stopped crying at once to see what was happening, and that made Malcolm laugh, and that made Lyra laugh too, her eyes brilliant with tears.

Malcolm was delighted to have this effect. Alice had come over to look.

"Little flirt," said Alice, and went back to her bread.

"Oh, no," said Sister Fenella, "she knows Malcolm, doesn't she, my sweet? We know Malcolm and Asta, don't we?"

"Can I hold her?" said Malcolm.

"It's nearly time for her feed—yes, go on. Can you take her out?"

"Easy," said Malcolm, and while Asta playfully batted the kitten over and over, he reached in and picked the baby up. They were used to it now, and didn't cry with alarm as they'd done at first. Malcolm pulled up a stool with his foot and sat Lyra on his knee next to Sister Fenella. The baby looked around at everything, and then her hand found her mouth and in went a thumb.

"She's so hungry she's eating herself," Malcolm said.

Sister Fenella was stirring a saucepan of milk on the range and testing the heat with her little finger.

"There, that's just right," she said. "Malcolm, dear, can you fill the bottle for me?"

Malcolm passed Lyra to her and poured the milk very carefully into the clean bottle. He wanted to tell Alice what had happened earlier that afternoon with Mrs. Coulter, but not while Sister Fenella was there; and in any case the girl was so haughty and cold he didn't find it easy to say anything to her at all.

When the bottle was ready, Sister Fenella took Lyra in the crook of her arm and settled back to feed her. Malcolm was troubled; the old lady was as sweet and kindly as she always was, but her face was gray and her eyes were red-rimmed and tired.

"I came to see if Mr. Taphouse was better," he said, sitting on the stool again.

"We haven't seen him for a few days. I hope he's all right. I'm sure Mrs. Taphouse would let us know if he was poorly."

"Perhaps he's having a holiday. He got all those shutters done, though, didn't he?"

"Oh, he's a marvelous workman."

"If you need anything else done, I'll do it."

Alice gave a short laugh. Malcolm decided to ignore her.

For a while the only sounds in the kitchen were the rhythmical slapping of Alice's hands on the dough, the subdued crackle of the fire in the range, the contented sucking of Lyra's lips on the rubber teat, and another sound that Malcolm couldn't identify till he realized that it was the faint straining of Sister Fenella's breath. The old lady's eyes were closed, and a little frown of effort drew her brows together.

Then, as Malcolm watched, the bottle slipped out of her hand, very slowly, and the arm holding Lyra fell outward, even more slowly, so he had time to call, "Alice!" and seize the baby before she fell into the hearth.

Lyra howled in protest, but Malcolm had her safe, and caught the bottle too. Alice in a moment caught Sister Fenella by the shoulders and pulled her gently upright, but the old lady was unconscious. Her squirrel dæmon had fainted on her breast.

"What should we—" said Alice.

"You hold her so she doesn't fall, and I'll go and get—"

"Yeah, yeah—go on—"

Malcolm stood up with Lyra. This was interesting enough to

stop the child yelling, but Malcolm clamped the bottle into her mouth anyway, and with Asta, cat-formed, on the floor holding the kitten Pan in her mouth and following closely, he set off down the corridor towards Sister Benedicta's office.

Which was empty, of course. He looked around as if she might be hiding, then shook his head.

"She's not here, Lyra," he said. "Never there when we need her, is she?"

He went out and saw a slender figure further down the corridor.

"Sister Katarina?" he called.

The young nun turned. She seemed more startled than Malcolm expected.

"What? What is it?"

"Sister Fenella's fainted and we need some help—she was feeding Lyra and—"

"Oh! Oh, goodness! What—"

"Call Sister Benedicta, and then come and help in the kitchen."

"Yes! Yes! Of course!"

She turned and hurried away, calling for Sister Benedicta.

"That was Sister Katarina, Lyra," said Malcolm. "She's going to find Sister Benedicta. You just carry on guzzling, girl. Don't you worry about it. We're going back to the kitchen now. Blooming cold out here, en't it?"

Alice had pulled Sister Fenella back into her armchair, but the old nun hadn't woken, and her breathing was loud and difficult.

"Pneumonia," said Alice, still holding her upright. "That's what my gran was like when she got it."

"Did she die?"

"Well, she did in the end, but not of that. Blimey, she needs changing."

She was looking at Lyra, who was determined to drain the bottle.

"Well, I can't do that," said Malcolm.

"Typical."

"Only because I never been shown how."

"'If you need anything else done, I'll do it,'" she mimicked.

"They wouldn't send for a carpenter to do *that*," Malcolm pointed out. "Is there any more milk in the saucepan?"

"Yeah, a bit. Hold her up—here, give her to me—I'll do it. You put the milk in."

"Can you do baby things?"

"I got two little sisters. Course I can."

She did seem to take Lyra in a steady and competent way, and when she patted the child's back, a gigantic burp emerged, which startled her little dæmon into becoming a turkey chick. Malcolm put the saucepan back on the range to heat for a moment.

"Not too hot," said Alice.

"No, no. I saw what she did."

Malcolm's little finger was not very clean, so he sucked it hard first and then held it in the saucepan till the milk was warm enough, and tipped it all into the bottle. Then he hauled Sister Fenella back upright and was putting a cushion behind her head just as Sister Benedicta and Sister Katarina came in.

"See to the baby," Sister Benedicta said, and Sister Katarina tried to take Lyra, but Alice resisted.

"She's settled with me now," she said. "I'll keep her till she's finished."

"Oh—if you're sure—"

Alice looked at her. Malcolm knew that look and was interested to see its effect on someone else. Sister Katarina looked away nervously, and then even pushed the stool a little forward for Alice to sit on. The nun's pug dæmon hid behind her legs.

Sister Benedicta was attending to Sister Fenella. She passed some smelling salts under the old lady's nose, making her flinch and moan, but she didn't wake up.

"Shall I go and get the doctor?" Malcolm said.

"Thank you, Malcolm, but we won't need him tonight," said Sister Benedicta. "Poor Sister Fenella needs rest more than anything else. We'll take her to her bed. Well done, both of you. Alice, give Lyra to Sister Katarina now. You'd better get back to your bread dough. Malcolm, that's all for tonight, thank you. Off you go home."

"If you need anything—"

"Yes, I'll ask you at once. Good night."

She was worried about Sister Fenella, and so was he. But there was no need to worry about Lyra, he thought.

The next day being Sunday, Malcolm had time in the morning to stock the canoe with emergency supplies—just in case, as Asta kept saying. Most important of all was his little toolbox, but he also had an old biscuit tin from the kitchen with other bits and pieces in it. He thought of including some first-aid materials but decided against them on the grounds that he didn't have any, though it would be good to get hold of some one day.

When he'd finished, Alice had arrived for her lunchtime hours in the kitchen. As soon as Malcolm was alone with her, she said, "You seen Sister Fenella this morning?"

"No. But if they needed the doctor, I'd have been sent."

They said nothing while Mrs. Polstead was there, as if they'd agreed to keep a secret, though there was no need to. Malcolm had told his parents what had happened, and they'd been surprised, as Malcolm had been, that Alice was working in the priory kitchen.

"If she can make bread, I might give her some more hours," said his mother.

"She's a dark horse," said his father.

When his mother went out again, Malcolm and Alice both began speaking at once.

"You know what you said about—" said Malcolm, and "That other nun—" said Alice, and then, "All right, you first."

"You know what you said about Gerard Bonneville saying he was Lyra's father?"

"You en't said that to anyone?"

"Just listen," said Malcolm, and he told Alice about his visit to Dr. Relf, and finding Mrs. Coulter there, and what he said to her.

"You didn't say that he said he was—"

"No, course not. Just that he said he knew her. That was enough. She was dead shocked. So I'm sure she knew who he was, all right."

"What was she doing there anyway?"

"She asked Dr. Relf where Lyra was."

"Did she tell her?"

"Dr. Relf? No! She never would." He was going to add, "She's a spy," but held back. He mustn't say anything about that, but it was becoming easier to talk to Alice all the time, so he'd have to be very careful. He went on: "She said she didn't know herself—Dr. Relf, I mean. She was surprised. Mrs. Coulter prob'ly came to see her about the alethiometer."

"What's that?"

He began to explain, and then his mother came back, and it would have looked awkward to stop talking, so he finished his account of the alethiometer and what it did. His mother stopped to listen.

"Is that what you get up to in Jericho?" she said.

"No. It's what she gets up to in the Bodleian Library."

"Stone the crows. Listen, Alice, how would you like some hours in the kitchen here? Not washing up. I mean, preparing food."

"I dunno," said Alice. "Maybe."

"Well, when you've consulted your social diary, let me know."

"I'm working in the priory kitchen now. They might need me more if Sister Fenella's ill."

"See what you can fit in. There's work here, if you'd like it."

"All right," said Alice, not looking anywhere except into the sink, which was full of hot dishwater.

Malcolm's mother blew out her cheeks and rolled her eyes and then went out to the storeroom.

"You said about Sister Katarina," said Malcolm.

"Yeah. She was the one that left that shutter open. She done it for him."

"Really?"

"Yeah, course, really. Don't you believe me?"

"Yeah, I believe you. But how does *she* know him?"

"I'll show you," said Alice, and then said no more.

But before Malcolm left, Alice's dæmon, Ben, spoke to Asta, both being cats at the time. That had never happened before, and Malcolm was amazed, but simply waited till the two dæmons had finished their brief conversation and went out.

"What did he say?" he whispered to Asta as they went through to the bar.

"He said we should go to the priory kitchen about eight o'clock. That's all. He didn't say why."

Eight o'clock was the hour of Compline, as Malcolm knew. All the sisters would be in the oratory for the final service of the day, except for Sister Fenella, he supposed, and Sister Katarina, if she was looking after Lyra.

And the rain had set in with a fury. It fell not in drops but in sheets, and the ground was running with it, so that you couldn't see anything solid: just flowing fields of bitter cold water. With the excuse of homework, Malcolm had gone upstairs by half past seven, and then tiptoed down again, not that anyone would have heard him above the thunderous drumming on the roof and the doors and the windows.

In the storeroom he put on his high boots and his oilskin raincoat and sou'wester, and then he went to the lean-to and put up the coal-silk tarpaulin on *La Belle Sauvage*. Just in case, he thought.

Then, leaning against the wind, with Asta tucked tight into his breast, he fought his way onto the bridge and looked down at the racing water. He remembered what Coram van Texel had said: there were things in the water that had been disturbed, and things in the sky too. . . . He sheltered his eyes with his hand and peered upwards. Almost at once a flash of lightning dazzled him, like an inscription on the heavens of his own private aurora, and such a crash of thunder hammered his ears that he felt dizzy and nearly fell, and he clutched the stone parapet in alarm.

Asta said, "*His chariots of wrath the deep thunderclouds form—*"

Malcolm finished the verse: "*And dark is His path on the wings of the storm.*"

It was so exposed where he stood that he felt genuinely afraid, and he hastened to the other side and into the shelter of the priory walls. The sound of singing came very faintly from the oratory.

He tapped on the kitchen window with a stone to make it easier to hear, and a moment later Alice opened the door and came out. The rain dashed against her and flattened her hair lankly over her cheeks.

"You know the potting sheds?" she said quietly.

"The priory ones?"

"Course, idiot. There's one at the left-hand end. There's a light in it. You can get into the one next door and look through. Go and see."

They had to lean close together to speak, and her breath was warm against his face.

"But what—"

"Just go. I can't stay out here. I'm looking after Lyra."

"But where's Sister Kat—"

She shook her head. Ben and Asta were whispering urgently together. When Alice turned to open the door, Ben leapt into her arms, ferret-formed. Malcolm felt Asta leap up to his shoulder, and then the door was shut again and they were alone.

"What did he say?" he asked for the second time that day.

"He said we've got to be careful and not make a noise. Any noise at all."

Malcolm nodded, and Asta slipped inside his oilskin raincoat and twisted around to look out from under his chin. They set off around the wall of the priory, away from the bridge, towards the garden where Lord Asriel had walked up and down with his daughter in the moonlight. Malcolm had to peer closely at the ground, so thickly was the rain falling, and he felt against his boots a current of water running strongly away from the river. Was it overflowing its banks? He couldn't see, but it must be.

They came to the kitchen garden, and Asta said, "That shed—the last one—there's a light there, like she said."

Sure enough, if he wiped his eyes and sheltered them with his hand for a few seconds, he could make out a dimly flickering light behind the window. It was on the side facing away from the priory.

He knew how the sheds were laid out because he'd helped Sister Martha many times in the garden. The last two were one shed, really, with a thin dividing wall. The doors were each on a simple iron latch. Sister Martha kept them unlocked on purpose: she had no tools worth stealing, she said, and it was too much trouble to fiddle with a key all the time.

Taking the greatest care with the latch, Malcolm opened the door to the shed next to the lighted one. Asta had already become an owl to see better, because Sister Martha used this side to store flowerpots, and if Malcolm knocked a pile of them over, it would make a noise that even the rain wouldn't be able to cover.

He tiptoed through the darkness, which was actually not quite dark: the single layer of planks between this shed and the other had warped in places, letting through the faint yellow glow of a candle that wavered in the strong draft. The thin roof resonated under the rain: it was like being inside a great drum, which might give way any moment under the crazy assault of the drummer.

Malcolm delicately stepped over the flowerpots and put his hands on the planks of the wall. Listening hard, he thought he could hear a voice—two voices—and then, abruptly stifled, that hideous high cackling laugh. Bonneville was there, only feet away. Asta became a moth, and as she settled near another crack in the wall, Malcolm felt a shock as she saw something. He leaned closer and peered through the crack to see Gerard Bonneville and Sister Katarina in a clumsy embrace. She was leaning back against a pile of empty sacks—her bare legs gleamed in the candlelight. The hyena was licking her pug dæmon, who was on his back, squirming with pleasure—

Malcolm carefully took a step back. His mind was calm enough for that, but only just. He moved away from the wall and sat down on an upturned crate at the other end of the shed.

"You saw?" whispered Asta.

"She's supposed to be looking after—"

"That's why he's with her! He wants her to give him Lyra!"

Malcolm felt the inside of his head whirling like leaves in a wind. He couldn't think firmly or clearly about anything.

"What are we going to do?" said Asta.

"If we told Sister Benedicta, she wouldn't believe us. She'd ask Sister Katarina, who'd say it never happened, we were making it up—"

"She knows Sister Katarina left the shutter open."

"And she knows Bonneville's around. But she'd never believe this. And there en't any proof."

"Not yet," said Asta.

"What d'you mean?"

"We know how people make babies, don't we?"

"Oh. Oh! So—"

"So that's what they're doing, and if she gets pregnant, that'd be proof enough, even for Sister Benedicta."

"But not that it was *him*," said Malcolm.

"Well, no."

"And he might have gone by then."

"With Lyra."

"You think *she's* what he wants?"

"Course. Don't you?"

The idea was horrible.

"Yes, I do," Malcolm said. "You're right. He wants Lyra. I just don't understand why."

"Doesn't matter why. Revenge. He might want to kill her, or hold her hostage. To ransom her."

The nun uttered a long, high moan of some emotion Malcolm didn't understand. It sounded through the wall, above the rain, above the wind. He thought of her cry flying through the night sky and making the moon turn her face away, making the owls tremble in their flight.

He discovered that he was clenching his fists.

"Well, we'll have to . . . ," he said.

"Yeah, we'll have to," she said. "Have to something."

"Suppose we do nothing, and he gets hold of Lyra?"

A low rich male laugh came next, not like the hyena's at all, nor like a laugh at something funny either, but like a little gush of satisfaction.

"That's him!" said Asta.

Malcolm said, "If we tell Sister Benedicta, she'll prob'ly think they both done wrong, but she could only punish Sister Katarina. She can't punish him."

"If she believes us. She might not."

"Is this a crime, what they're doing?"

"If she didn't want to, it'd be a crime, I reckon."

"I think she does, though."

"Yeah, so do I. So there's nothing the police could do to him, even if they believed us, even if they could catch him, even if even if."

"But even punishing him's not so important as making sure Lyra's safe. That's the most important thing."

"I suppose so. . . ."

From the direction of the priory building there came a deep rumbling crash—deeper than the thunder, and it lasted longer. It was not like a noise at all to begin with but a movement of the earth, and even the flowerpots clinked and clattered, and some fell over, and still the rumbling went on and the ground went on trembling.

Sister Katarina cried out, "No! No! Let go—please—I must go—"

Bonneville's deep voice murmured something.

"Yes—I promise—but I *must*—"

Suddenly Malcolm leapt up, thinking, *Lyra!*

He shot out the door, crashing it back against the wooden wall, and raced for the priory, ignoring the sheets of water that fell, the water rushing over the path, the man's shout behind, and the crazed "Haaa! Ha! Haaa!" from the hyena dæmon.

Asta raced, greyhound-formed, beside him. As they reached the priory building and rounded the corner, Malcolm realized that the water they were running through was deeper and faster, and that the gatehouse light had gone out—

—because the gatehouse was no longer there. A heap of stones, planks, rubble, boards, and roof tiles lay there instead, illuminated flickeringly from inside the building. As Malcolm stood in shock, a wave broke over the top of the rubble: the river had burst its banks. When the surge reached him, it was as high as his knees and nearly knocked him over.

"Alice!" Malcolm yelled.

From behind him came a wail of terror in the voice of Sister Katarina.

"The kitchen!" cried Asta, and Malcolm struggled to the kitchen door. The water was surging at the foot of it, and when he shoved it open, he found the kitchen already flooded—the fire in the range hissing and steaming, the floor awash.

And there was Lyra's crib actually afloat—actually rocking on the water—and Alice lying dazed across the kitchen table, half under a pile of plaster and beams from the ceiling—

"Alice!" he cried, and she stirred, moaning, but then sat up too quickly and sagged sideways again.

Malcolm snatched Lyra from the crib, Asta darting down to take care of Pan. Malcolm pulled the blankets out after the child and wrapped them around her. All he could see by was the orange glow from the range. Had he got all the blankets? Would she be warm enough?

Alice was groping for the wall and trying to stand up. Suddenly she was hurled aside as the man Bonneville burst in—smashing the door open even against the water at its foot—and, seeing Malcolm, leapt towards him, snarling so vilely that he sounded worse than the dæmon who followed him close—

Malcolm held Lyra tight against his chest—she was crying in fear—

And then Bonneville fell forward with a great splash as Alice smashed his head from behind with a chair. He grabbed at the table but couldn't hold it—all he did was tip it over and fall with a heavy splash beside it. She raised the chair again and brought it down on him again.

"Quick! Quick!" Alice cried, and Malcolm tried to run through the water, but could only manage a horrible slowness as Bonneville's hands and arms and then his blood-streaming head emerged above the table, and then the man slipped and fell back and emerged again, the side of his head a mask of flaring blood.

"Malcolm!" Alice screamed.

He leapt for the door, clasping Lyra tight. The baby was yelling in fury and kicking and waving her little fists.

"Give me that—" the man roared, and then slipped down again, and Malcolm was out the door and running with Alice towards the bridge, but the water slowed them so much it was worse than a bad dream.

No sign of Sister Katarina, no sign of the other nuns—they couldn't all be drowned? Or crushed under fallen timbers? The only other living being was the blood-soaked Bonneville and his limping, lurching dæmon coming out of the kitchen door behind them—

But there was hardly any light to see by, and the air was full of driving, smashing water. By instinct and memory Malcolm stumbled along the path, calling, "Alice! Alice!"

Then he bumped into her and they both nearly fell over.

"Hold on! Don't let go!" he shouted.

Linked by their cold hands, they forced their way through the flood and up onto the bridge. One light from the Trout was still glowing and showed that the parapet and one side of the roadway were gone.

"Careful!" she cried.

"Don't let go!"

They shuffled sideways along the remaining part of the roadway and felt it shake and rumble under their feet. Lyra had stopped crying and found her thumb, and she lay in Malcolm's tight grasp quite happily, interested in everything.

"It's going to go—the bridge!" Alice cried, and then, "He's there! Quick!" as she looked back past Malcolm.

"How could he—"

"Come *on*!"

They stumbled down the steps that led to the terrace of the Trout and found they had to go back—the river was racing over the terrace at the height of a tabletop: it would sweep them off their feet and away in a moment.

"Where? Which way?" shouted Alice.

"Round the other side—maybe the door—"

Malcolm didn't know what he was going to say, because close behind came that terrifying laugh—"Haa! Ha! Haaa!"—and there, full in the gleam of the light hanging over the inn door, was Bonneville's face, astream with water and astream with blood. Alice picked up a loose stone from the parapet, as big as her fist, and hurled it straight at him, and again he fell.

"Quick! Quick!" cried Malcolm, and led them running down the slope towards the other side of the inn, towards the front door, towards safety.

And the door was locked.

Oh, of course, he thought, they think I'm upstairs. . . .

"Mum! Dad!" he yelled, but the wind and the rain and the torrents of the river tore his voice away like a scrap of tissue paper.

Clutching Lyra close with one arm, holding Alice's hand with the other hand, he scrambled along the wall of the pub to the back door. Locked as well.

He shoved Lyra at Alice and picked up a big stone to hammer on the door with. But the roar of the water and the lashing of the trees in the wind were too loud: he could hardly hear the hammering himself. He hit the door time and again, until he couldn't hold the stone anymore. There was no response, and Bonneville was somewhere close, and they couldn't stand and wait for him to find them.

"Come *on*," he said, and Alice followed as he splashed around to the garden, to the storeroom, to the lean-to, where he kept the canoe. In the faint light coming through the rain from the landing window, they saw a peacock drowned and draped over a bush.

In the lean-to, *La Belle Sauvage* sat snugly under her coal-silk canopy.

"Get in. Sit down there and take Lyra. *Don't move*," he said, and pulled back enough of the canopy for Alice to see the bow, and where to step and where to sit. He shoved Lyra at her, and she took her with firm arms, and then he pulled the canopy back over her and got in himself. There was so much water streaming over the grass that he was pretty sure this would work, and indeed *La Belle Sauvage* was straining at her mooring rope already, as if she sensed what Malcolm wanted.

A quick tug—the knot came loose—and Malcolm took the paddle and used it to keep her upright as she began to move, slowly at first and then faster and faster, down the grass slope towards the river.

But the river was coming up to meet them, and suddenly the little boat came free from the grass and surged forward.

They could only go one way. *La Belle Sauvage* sped like a dart over the mad river, down towards Port Meadow, towards the wild waste of water that was sweeping through Oxford, towards whatever lay beyond.

SIXTEEN

THE PHARMACY

Malcolm could see almost nothing. Apart from the profound darkness of the sky and the slashing rain, the canopy obstructed everything ahead. Besides, it caught the wind and made the canoe lurch unpredictably to the left and right, so he would have found it hard to get a visual fix on anything, even if he could see it. For a few minutes he thought he'd made a horrible mistake in embarking in the canoe, and that they'd be drowned for sure; but what else could they have done? Bonneville would have caught them, stolen Lyra, killed her. . . .

He concentrated on keeping the little boat as upright as possible, steering, not paddling. The force of the flood was sweeping them along without any effort from him, but he had no idea where they were or what they might smash into at any moment: a tree, a bridge, a house— He tried to push the thought away.

There was another problem too. Malcolm was sitting at the stern, and in order to keep the paddle in the water, he had to leave his end of the canoe uncovered by the coal-silk tarpaulin, and the unceasing rain was filling the boat so quickly that his feet were already covered.

"As soon as we find something solid, we'll tie up!" he shouted to Alice. "And bail this water out."

"All right" was all she said.

He leaned to the right, trying to see round the canopy, trying to keep the brim of his sou'wester out of his eyes, trying to make out anything in the teeming murk. Something large, tall, dark swept past—a tree? Asta peered ahead, owl-formed, from the rearmost hoop, though the great raindrops slapping at her wide eyes made it almost impossible to see anything.

Then suddenly, "Go left! Go left!" she screeched, and Malcolm dug the paddle into the water and heaved with all his strength as a low-hanging tree slashed its way along the canopy and nearly snatched his sou'wester off his head.

"More trees!" she cried again.

Malcolm dug in the paddle with all his might, shoving desperately against the current, and found the canoe swirling around and bumping and scraping against branches and twigs—and then a thorn-laden branch swept across his face, making him yell, and startling Lyra into loud sobs.

"What is it?" called Alice.

"Nothing. 'S all right, Lyra," he called back, though his eyes were filled with tears of pain and he could hardly think.

But he kept hold of the paddle, and then found a heavy branch nudging at the hoop where Asta was perching, and he seized that and held the canoe still against it.

He dropped the paddle at his feet and groped for the painter with his free hand. He found it, flung it over the branch, and fumbled a bowline with his cold, wet, trembling fingers.

"Under your feet somewhere there's a canvas bucket," he called, and while Alice looked for that, he pulled the canopy back over the last hoop and fixed it around the gunwale, leaving only one fastening open.

"Here y'are," she said, reaching forward. Lyra was still yelling.

He took the bucket and started to bail, tipping the water over the side where the canopy was still undone. It didn't take long. Then he realized his boots were full of water too, so he struggled to pull them off and empty them. He fastened the tarpaulin and leaned back, exhausted, and let Asta explore the scratches on his face with a soft clean puppy tongue. It hurt even more, but he tried not to yelp.

At least with the tarpaulin over the boat, he wasn't out in that brutal rain anymore. It hammered at the coal silk, but not a drop got in.

"Under your seat there's a tin," he said. "I sealed it with tape, so there shouldn't be any water in it. If you pass it here, I'll open it. There's some biscuits in it."

She fumbled around and found the tin. He picked at the tape until he found the end, and opened it. It was perfectly dry. And he'd forgotten: he'd put his Swiss Army knife in there, and a little anbaric torch! He switched it on, dazzled by the brilliance. And it stopped Lyra from crying.

"Give her a biscuit to suck," he said.

Alice took two, one for herself and one for Lyra, who after waving it around doubtfully found her mouth and began to suck with immense pleasure.

Malcolm saw something out of the corner of his eye—or was it in his eye? A little patch of white on the floor of the canoe. And then, without the slightest warning, it became the shimmering, flickering spot of light, floating in the darkness ahead of him. He blinked and shook his head: this wasn't a good time for spangled rings, but it wouldn't go. It floated in midair, scintillating and spinning, flashing and turning.

"What's the matter?" said Alice. She must have felt him shaking his head or sensed that his attention was distracted.

"Something in my eye. I got to keep still."

He sat there in the wet discomfort and tried to feel calm. He did feel something, the kind of thing Asta had described on that evening when it came on them during his geography homework, a sort of peaceful, disembodied floating, in a space that was immense or even infinite in all directions. The spangled ring grew larger, just like before, and as before, he was helpless and paralyzed while it came closer and closer and expanded to fill the entire circumference of his vision, but he was never frightened; it wasn't alarming; in a way it was even comforting, that calm, oceanic drifting. It was his aurora: it was telling him that he was still part of the great order of things, and that that could never change.

He let the phenomenon run its course and came to himself, exhausted, as if the experience had been strenuous and demanding. But the little patch of white was still there on the floor. He felt down and found it: a card of the sort ladies and gentlemen had with their names printed on them. His eyes were still too disturbed to read it, and without a word to Alice he put it in his shirt pocket.

And once all his consciousness was back in the little enclosed space under the canopy, he could easily tell what Alice had made out earlier: Lyra needed changing. Well, there was absolutely nothing they could do about it now.

"What we gonna do?" said Alice.

"Stay awake, that's the first thing. If the water goes down while the canoe's still tied to the branch, we'll get tipped out and left with the canoe halfway up a tree."

"Yeah, that'd be pretty stupid."

Lyra was humming, or saying something to Pantalaimon, or just expressing her pleasure in the soggy biscuit.

"Well, she's easily pleased," said Malcolm.

"We got to change her soon. She'll get sore otherwise."

"That'll have to wait till we can see where we're going. And till we can get some hot water to wash her. As soon as it's morning, we'll see if we can paddle back home."

"He'll still be around," she said.

That was the least of it, Malcolm thought. The force of the flood might prevent them from going back anyway; they might find themselves swept all the way through Oxford and on to . . . where?

"Well, we'll aim for a house or a shop or something where we can get—whatever she needs," he said.

"Yeah," said Alice. "All right."

"There's a blanket down there if you're cold. Wrap it round both of you."

More fumbling, and then she found it.

"It's soaking wet," she said. "You going to stay awake?"

"Yeah. Keep watch. I'll try anyway."

"Well, wake me up when you can't anymore."

He switched the torch off. The canoe certainly wasn't made for sleeping in. Even if he'd wanted to stretch out, there was still an inch or so of freezing water in the bottom that he couldn't get out with the bucket; and even if it had been dry, there was nowhere to rest his head but the wooden seat; and even if even if, as Asta had said earlier.

In fact, there was plenty to complain about. But Alice hadn't complained once. He was impressed, and vowed not to say a word about the pain from the thorn scratches across his face.

He felt her settling down at the other end of the little boat. Lyra had stopped crying, thanks to the biscuit, and was dozing in Alice's arms. Alice had propped herself inside the bow, with her knees up over the front seat, so as to make her body and arms a cradle for Lyra. Her dæmon was squeezed down beside her.

Asta became a ferret and settled around Malcolm's neck.

"Where do you think we are?" she whispered.

"Somewhere down Port Meadow. There's that oratory off to the right with a grove of trees. . . ."

"That's nowhere near the river."

"I don't think there's a river anymore. This is ever so much higher. There's water everywhere."

"Yeah . . . D'you think we'll get swept away?"

"No. We managed to tie up in the dark, didn't we? Once we can see, in the morning, we'll find our way back."

"It's going ever so fast, though."

"Well, we'll stay tied up till it stops, then."

Asta was silent for a few minutes, but he knew she hadn't gone to sleep; he could feel her thinking.

"Suppose it never stops?" she whispered.

"The gyptian man didn't say it'd do that. Just that there was going to be a flood."

"It *feels* as if it's going on forever."

"There isn't enough water in all the world to do that. Eventually it'll stop and the sun'll come out. Every flood stops in the end and goes down."

"This time might be different."

"It won't."

"What's on that card?" she said after a moment. "The one you picked up."

"Oh, yeah . . ."

He fished it out of his pocket, and shading the torch with his hand so it wouldn't wake Alice, he read:

LORD ASRIEL
October House
Chelsea
London

On the back were written the words *With many thanks. If you need my help at any time, be sure to ask. Asriel.*

An idea came to him, glittering, shimmering, spangled with brilliance. Asta knew what it was at once, and whispered, "Don't tell Alice." The idea was to set off over the flood, all the way down the Thames, and find Lord Asriel and take his child to him. It was almost as if that was why Lord Asriel had paid for *La Belle Sauvage* to be improved, as if he knew the flood was coming and had prepared a safe vessel for his daughter, and as if the faithful canoe had given the message to Malcolm. He felt the idea warming him through and through.

And they agreed wordlessly: *Don't tell Alice. Not yet.* He tucked the card back in his pocket and switched off the torch.

The rain was beating on the tarpaulin just as furiously as it had been doing since they started, and if anything, Malcolm thought, feeling cautiously along the painter, the canoe was higher in the tree than it had been when he tied it. Even worse than being tipped out as the water fell would be being dragged below as it rose.

Still, a bowline was a good knot, and he'd be able to undo it in the dark, if he needed to.

"Mind you," he whispered, "a slipped reef knot would be even better. Just one pull . . ."

"Should've practiced," Asta whispered back.

Another few minutes of silence. He felt his head nodding and snapped it upright.

"Don't fall asleep," she urged.

"I'm not sleepy."

"Yes, you are."

Malcolm supposed he replied, but the next thing he knew was when his thorn-slashed face met the gunwale. He'd slipped over little by little till he was almost horizontal.

"Why didn't you wake me?" he whispered to Asta.

"I was asleep too."

He struggled up, blinking and yawning and rubbing his left eye, where the skin wasn't as scratched as the other side was.

"You all right?" came in a quiet voice from Alice.

"Yeah. I just slipped over sideways."

"I thought you was going to stay awake."

"I was awake. I just slipped."

"Yeah."

He settled himself upright again and checked the branch. The boat didn't seem to have gone up or down, but the rain was still hammering on the tarpaulin.

"You cold?" he said.

"Yeah. You?"

"A bit. We need more blankets."

"Dry ones. And cushions or something. It's bloody uncomfortable."

"We'll get 'em in the morning. I'm going to try and paddle back home when I can see where we are," he said. "But we'll get stuff for Lyra first."

They were quiet for a minute. Then she said, "What if we can't get back?"

"We will."

"You hope."

"Well, it's not far. . . ."

"This water's racing along. You can't paddle against that."

"Then we'll hold tight here till it stops."

"But she needs . . ."

"We're not in the middle of nowhere. There's shops and stuff just across Port Meadow. We'll go there as soon as we can see, in the morning."

"Your mum and dad'll worry."

"Nothing we can do about it now. What about yours?"

"Got no dad. Just Mum and my sisters."

"I don't even know where you live."

"Wolvercote. She'll think I've drowned."

"So will the nuns. They'll think Lyra's been carried away. . . ."

"Well, she has been."

"You know what I mean."

"If there's any of 'em survived."

Another minute or two went by. Malcolm heard her dæmon whispering something to her, and heard her whispering back.

Then she said, "Did you go to the potting shed, like I told you?"

Malcolm felt himself blush and was glad of the dark. He said, "Yeah. He was there with Sister Katarina."

"What were they doing?"

"I . . . I couldn't really see."

"I know what they were doing. Bastard. I wanted to kill him, you know, Bonneville, when I hit him."

"Why?"

"'Cause he'd been nice to me. You wouldn't understand."

"No, I don't. But if you did kill him, I wouldn't tell anyone."

"You think he's really after Lyra?"

"Well, *you* told me that."

"D'you think he *could* be Lyra's father?"

"No, I've spoken to Lyra's father. The real one."

"When?"

He told her about the strange nighttime episode in the priory garden, and about lending Lord Asriel the canoe. She didn't scoff in disbelief, as he'd thought she would.

"*What* did he do with her?"

"I told you. He walked up and down, holding her and whispering to her."

They were practically whispering themselves, speaking as quietly as they could under the rain. Alice said nothing for a minute or so.

Then she said, "Did you hear what he was saying?"

"No. I was keeping watch by the priory wall."

"But he looked as if he loved her?"

"Yeah. Certainly."

Another minute went by.

"If we can't get back," she said, "if we just get swept away, right . . ."

"Yeah?"

"What we going to do with her?"

"Prob'ly . . . prob'ly see if we can get to Jordan College."

"Why?"

"Because of scholastic sanctuary."

"What's that?"

He explained as well as he could.

"You reckon they'd take her in? She en't a scholar, or anything like."

"I think if someone asks for sanctuary, they have to take 'em in."

"And how could they look after a baby, anyway? All those colleges are full of old men. They wouldn't know what to do."

"They'd pay someone to do that, prob'ly. They could prob'ly write to Lord Asriel and he'd pay, or else maybe come and get her himself."

"Where is that college, then?" Alice said.

"On Turl Street. Right in the middle of town."

"How'd you know about that sanctuary thing?"

"Dr. Relf told me," he said, and explained how she'd left a book at the Trout with her address in it, and he'd taken it back to her. He said not a word about the acorn or the spying. Talking to Alice was a lot easier in the dark. He spun the story out, even though he'd told it before, thinking it would help to keep her awake, not realizing for a moment that that was her purpose with regard to him.

"Where did you say she lived?"

"In Jericho. Cranham Street. It'll be underwater now—downstairs, anyway. I hope she did what I told her to and moved all her books upstairs."

If in the morning the water on Port Meadow lay calm and still like a great lagoon, and the sun came out and glittered and sparkled on the water, and all the buildings of Oxford shone against the blue sky, as if they'd been freshly painted, it would be easy to get across to the city center and find Jordan College, he thought. And what a delight it would be to paddle towards them, and slip along canal-like streets and tie up by second-floor windows and look at all the odd views and strange reflections. And on the way they'd find somewhere that had the supplies Lyra needed, which would include milk now, because she'd had nothing but a biscuit. And she had to have something clean to drink, because the water they floated on would be full of stirred-up dirt and dead animals. The ghosts of all the animals would be crying under the water. He could hear them now—"Ha! Haa! Haaa!"

Alice was kicking his ankle.

"Malcolm!" she whispered savagely. "Malcolm!"

"Yeah, I'm awake— What's that? Is that him?"

"*Shut up!*"

He strained to hear. That ghastly laugh was unmistakable, but where was it? The rain had not ceased, the wind was still moaning and whistling in the bare boughs all around, but through the chaos of natural sounds Malcolm could make out something different and regular: the splash of oars, the creak of ungreased oarlocks, and that hyena laugh over it all, as if it was mocking Bonneville himself, mocking the flood, mocking Malcolm and his efforts to make the little canoe safe.

Then they heard Bonneville's voice.

"Shut up, you bitch—shut your crazy mouth—filthy noise—bite your other bloody leg off, go on—chew on that—shut up! Stop that goddamn noise!"

It got closer and closer. Malcolm's hand found the Swiss Army knife and opened it silently. He would stab the dæmon first, and then the man. The paddle was at his feet—if he swung it hard, he might knock the dæmon into the water and then the man would be helpless—but he might grab the paddle before Malcolm could do that. . . .

The sounds diminished.

Malcolm heard Alice blow out her breath, as if she'd been holding it in. And Lyra stirred and in her sleep uttered a little whimpering mew, which Alice quickly muffled. Malcolm could see nothing, of course, but it sounded as if Alice had her hand over Lyra's mouth, and then came a sound of contentment from the child. But it was such a quiet sound that only someone actually in the canoe could have heard it, Malcolm thought.

"Has he gone?" Alice whispered.

"I think so," he whispered back.

"Did he have a light?"

"I didn't see one."

"He's just rowing along in the dark?"

"Well, he's mad."

"Didn't see us, though."

"He's not going to leave us alone," said Malcolm after a minute.

"He's not having her either," Alice said at once.

"No."

He listened hard. No oars, no voice, no dæmonic laughter.

Bonneville's boat had been going in the same direction as theirs, which was the same direction as the flood: downriver. But with everything underwater, and all kinds of unpredictable swirls and currents likely to have been born in the darkness, who knew where he might end up? Malcolm longed for the morning with every particle of his body.

"Here," whispered Alice, and he leaned forward to find her hand and took the biscuit she was holding.

He nibbled it slowly, only taking another bite when every crumb of the last one was gone. The sugar slowly worked its way into his system and made him feel a little stronger. There was a whole packet there, enough to last them some time yet.

But his exhaustion was more than a match for the sugar. Little by little his head slipped lower, and Alice said nothing, and Lyra slept on; and soon all three of them were fast asleep.

Malcolm woke when a faint gray light penetrated the tarpaulin. He was bitterly cold, and shivering so hard he was shaking the canoe. At least the drumming of the rain had stopped, and at least the canoe was still lying level on the water.

He carefully unfastened the nearest part of the tarpaulin and lifted it enough to peer out. Through the bare branches he saw a wild waste of gray water, surging from left to right across the wide open space that had been Port Meadow: he could see the city's spires beyond it. Nothing but water: no ground, no riverbank, no bridge. And all speeding with a mighty force, almost silent, certainly irresistible. There was no possibility of paddling against it and making their way back home.

He checked the branch, the knot in the painter, the tree. The canoe was quite handily placed, in fact; luck had been on their side, or a little luck anyway. They were among the crowns of a group of trees surrounding the tower of an old oratory: exactly where he'd thought they were, though it all looked different from high up in a tree. He couldn't remember the name of the place, but it was half-way down Port Meadow towards the south. The main force of the flood was broken up here and baffled by the trees, which was why the canoe hadn't been torn loose and swept away.

They'd have to move soon, though. Malcolm looked at that wild waste, and his heart quailed. His little boat, and all that force of water . . . Calm rivers and still backwaters and shallow canals were one thing. This was another thing entirely.

But it had to be done. By eye he measured the distance between them and the roofs of Oxford, and estimated how far he could steer the canoe across that surging flood. . . . The city was a long way off, with all that water between them.

He pulled himself up, rolled back the tarpaulin, found the paddle. His moving made the boat sway and woke Alice, who was lying with Lyra on her chest. The child was still asleep.

"What you doing?" Alice whispered.

"The sooner we move, the sooner we can sort her out. It's stopped raining, at least."

She lifted the tarpaulin and peered out.

"That's horrible," she said. "You can't paddle across that. Where are we?"

"Sort of near Binsey."

"That's like the bloody German Ocean out there."

"It's not that big. And it'll be a lot easier once we get among the buildings."

"If you say so," she said, closing the tarpaulin again.

"How's Lyra?"

"Soaking wet and stinking."

"Well, we'd better start, then. No point in waiting till the sun comes out."

He reached up to undo the knot. It was closer than it had been when he tied it, so the water was higher.

"What should I do?" said Alice.

"Sit as still as you can. It'll rock a bit, but if you get frightened and panic, it'll be ten times worse. Just sit still."

He could feel the contempt in her eyes, but she said nothing and settled herself more comfortably. The bowline had been pulled tight by the strain on it during the night, but by working it back and forth, Malcolm was able to undo it. That was the thing with a bowline: you could always undo it. Though a slipped reef knot would be quicker, he thought again. Well, next time.

As soon as the painter was free, the canoe began to swing away from the trees. And at once Malcolm began to regret not having rolled back more of the tarpaulin: he could see hardly anything ahead.

"I'm going to undo the tarpaulin," he said. "Not all of it. Just enough so's I can see ahead."

"You should've—"

"I know."

She held her tongue. Malcolm thanked those gyptian craftsmen who'd made the fastenings, because they all came free with great ease. Alice reached up to pull the coal silk back towards herself, and then he could see a lot better.

He took the paddle and tentatively moved the canoe out into the open. Immediately the current seized it and spun it round so the stern was leading, and Malcolm knew his mistake: nothing should be tentative. He dug the paddle in the water till the boat was the proper way round, and to her credit Alice did as he'd told her and said not a word. Then Malcolm tried to strike a course across the open waste of sweeping water and made hardly any progress. He could see the roofs of Jericho, the campanile of St. Barnabas, the great classical building of the Fell Press, the spires and towers of central Oxford itself, but they were far off and unreachable; the flood had its own idea about where the canoe should go.

All right: concentrate on keeping steady, and hope to avoid any underwater snags.

Actually, the thought of striking anything below the surface was so abominable that Malcolm put it out of his head at once. The canoe was whirled forward, with as little purchase on the water as a twig. The flood was carrying them inexorably into the city, but not smoothly or easily, because the buildings broke up the flow and made the water seethe and surge with turbulence. Malcolm couldn't keep the canoe steady: all he could do was stop it from tipping over and hope that they'd find a calmer patch of water near Broad Street and Jordan College. The idea of going all the way to London seemed like a fantasy of the night: Jordan College—sanctuary—safety—that was the priority now.

The great mass of water coming off Port Meadow had forced its way through the grid of narrow streets in Jericho and was racing down the wide boulevard of St. Giles, having been joined by even more powerful streams coming down the Banbury and Woodstock roads. And now Malcolm and Alice could see other people struggling with the flood, some desperately trying to keep their heads above water as they were carried along, some in little boats—punts or dinghies—trying to rescue those in danger of drowning, some clinging to the trees in St. Mary Magdalen's graveyard, some being helped through open windows into Balliol or St. John's colleges. Cries of despair, shouts of encouragement, and the sound of an engine-boat roaring along a side street all mingled with the crash of the water against the ancient stone buildings, and before Malcolm had the canoe ready to turn into Broad Street, *La Belle Sauvage* was nearly capsized by the turbulence.

Alice cried out in alarm. Malcolm dug the paddle into the water with all his strength and kept the little craft upright, but at the cost of missing the turn into Broad Street. Before he could do anything about it, they were already in the Cornmarket.

"Ship Street!" cried hawk Asta, and Malcolm shouted back, "I know—I'm trying—" as he forced the canoe towards the tower of St. Michael Northgate, at the corner of the little street that led directly to Jordan.

But the way was blocked. Part of the tower had fallen, and the flood surged and foamed against the great heap of stones at the entrance to the street. The only way was to go forward again and hope he could turn onto Market Street, but that was foiled too: a large wagon carrying vegetables to the Covered Market had smashed against the shop on the corner. Boxes of cabbages and onions bobbed on the water, and the horse pulling the wagon lay drowned between the shafts. There was no passage through here either.

And the flood bore them on relentlessly, towards the crossroads at Carfax, where again Malcolm tried to force the canoe left and onto the High Street, in the hope of turning onto Turl Street and reaching Jordan that way. But the little vessel had no more headway than a cork. The flood hurled them across the junction and into St. Aldate's, where the downward slope of the street let the water rush on with even greater speed.

"It en't gonna work!" Alice shouted.

Malcolm could hear Lyra crying, not with shrill fear but with a steady note of complaint at the cold and the wet and the incessant lurching of the canoe.

"We'll find somewhere to stop soon, Lyra!" he shouted back.

All around them, buildings lay with smashed windows or fallen walls, and broken doors and uprooted trees raced along on the water. Someone in an engine-boat was trying to maneuver it towards an upstairs window, where a gray-haired woman in a nightdress was calling for help, her terrier dæmon barking madly. Folly Bridge had been swept away altogether, and the Thames was no longer a river but a swollen sea of gray turbulence sweeping from right to left and threatening to overwhelm *La Belle Sauvage* entirely. But Malcolm had time to prepare, and dug the paddle in harder than ever before, and just managed to keep her on a course for the level land further down.

This was a district of suburban streets and small shops, and before long, hawk-eyed Asta, with Ben flying close to her, cried out, "Left! Left!"

There was nothing to impede them this time, and Malcolm brought the canoe into a side street away from the main flood, where it was a little quieter.

"I'm going to bring us in by that green cross!" he shouted. "It's a pharmacy. See if you can grab hold—it's on a bracket—"

Alice sat up, looked around, shifted Lyra to her other side, and reached out to do as he said. They weren't moving very quickly here, and it wasn't hard for her to seize the bracket and hold the boat still against the building. Malcolm leaned out and looked closely down, sideways, down again.

"Does it feel firm?"

"It en't loose, if that's what you mean."

"Right, let go and I'll catch it and tie us up."

She did. The canoe moved along under the green cross, and Malcolm caught hold of the bracket. He tied a bowline again, just in case, because his fingers knew it and he trusted it. They were right next to an upstairs window.

"I'm going to smash the glass," he said. "Cover her face."

He swung the paddle, and the glass fell inward with a crash that might have sounded loud in normal circumstances but that he could hardly hear for the noise of the water. He thought that normally he'd feel guilty about that, but it would be more guilty by far to keep Lyra outside in the cold and the wet.

"I'll go in," he said, but Alice said, "No! Wait."

He looked at her in puzzlement.

"Knock all the glass out first, else you'll get slashed to ribbons," she explained.

He saw the sense of that, and went round the sash frame knocking every shard of glass into the room behind it.

"It's empty," he said. "No furniture or anything."

"I expect they called the movers when they heard the flood was coming," she said.

He was glad she was being sarcastic. It sounded like her again.

When the frame was clear of glass, Malcolm stood up carefully and put both hands on it, then one leg through, and then the other, and then he was in.

"Pass me Lyra," he said.

Alice had to move to the middle of the canoe, which was difficult, and Lyra was squirming and yelling, which didn't help; but after a minute or so of negotiation, while Asta, hawk-formed, carried the protesting swallow-chick Pan, Alice held up the blanket-wrapped child, and Malcolm took her through into the empty room.

"Cor! You smell like a farmyard, Lyra," he said. "That's a champion stink, that is. Well, we'll clean you up soon."

"'We,'" said Alice, now in the room beside him. "I like that *we*. You'll be off tying knots or summink. It'll be me what cleans her up."

"A pharmacy's all right," said Malcolm. "But I wish they sold food. Look, there's a storeroom through there."

It was as good as a treasure-house. In the storeroom was everything needed for baby care, and medicines of all sorts, and even biscuits and various kinds of juice.

"We need hot water," said Alice, unimpressed.

"There might still be some in a tank. I'll go and have a look," said Malcolm, seeing a small bathroom, and becoming suddenly aware that he badly needed to relieve himself. He found that the lavatory flushed, the taps ran, and there was even a trickle of warmish water. He hastened to tell Alice.

"Right," she said. "Now go and find some of them nappies, the ones you throw away. We'll wash her and change her first, and then feed her. If you can find a way of boiling the water, so much the better. And don't drink it."

There were logs and kindling and paper in the fireplace in the empty room, and Malcolm looked for a saucepan or something to boil water in, blessing the farseeing proprietor who had stocked his shop so comprehensively. No doubt there was every kind of domestic utensil downstairs, but as the floodwater had risen to just under the top step of the staircase, there was no way of getting them; and what a stroke of luck that they stored their wares up here rather than in a basement. And there was even a little kitchen, with a gas stove (not working) and a kettle.

He took out his knife and struck the sparker again and again on the rasp, producing a shower of sparks each time, which each time failed to light the paper in the fireplace.

"What you doing?" said Alice, throwing him a box of matches. "Idiot."

He sighed, struck a match, and soon had the fire blazing. He filled the kettle from the cold tap and held it over the flames.

Lyra had been yelling as Alice washed her and put a clean, dry nappy on her, but it was a shout of general anger rather than distress. Her little dæmon, who had been a very disheveled rat, became a miniature bulldog and joined in the row till Alice's greyhound dæmon picked him up and shook him, which startled the child into outraged silence.

"That's better," said Alice. "Now keep quiet. I'll give you a feed in a minute, when that boy's boiled some water."

She took Lyra into the little kitchen and laid her on the draining board while Malcolm nursed the little flames. He had to wrap his hands in the wet blanket to keep them from burning as he held the kettle. There was nowhere to balance it on the fire.

"At least it's drying the blanket," he said to Asta.

"Suppose the shopkeeper comes?" his dæmon said.

"Nobody would expect us not to change and feed a baby. 'Cept maybe Bonneville."

"It *was* him in the night, wasn't it?"

"Yeah. He must be mad. Really mad."

"Are we really going to take her all the way to—"

"Shh."

He looked around, but Alice was in the other room washing Lyra.

"Yes," he whispered. "Got to now."

"Why not tell Alice, then?" she whispered back.

"'Cause she wouldn't want to. She'd stay behind or give us away or something. *And* take Lyra."

The fire was settling into a proper glow, and the heat on his hands and his face made Malcolm all the more aware of how cold and soaking wet the rest of him was. He was shifting uncomfortably when Alice spoke behind him.

"Where's that water?"

"Oh . . . nearly boiling."

"You better boil it for a few minutes. Kill all the germs. Then let it cool. So I reckon it'll be a while yet before I can mix her feed."

"How's she doing?"

"Well, she smells better. But her poor little bum's all sore."

"There must be some cream or something—"

"Yeah, there is. Good thing this is a pharmacy and not a bloody ironmonger's. Don't spill that water."

The water was boiling, and his hand was feeling scorched.

"Can you get me some cold water?" he said. "I need to wet this blanket again. My hand's getting burned."

She went out and came back with a jug. She poured the water carefully over the blanket, and his hand immediately felt worse, more tender altogether. He took the kettle away and looked around.

"What's the matter?"

"I'm going to find something better to hold it with."

He didn't have to look far. In the little pile of logs beside the fire, there was one that, when he propped it against the hearth, was the right height to stand the kettle on, half on and half off the fire.

"If that falls off—"

"I know," he said. "You stay and watch it for a minute."

He stood up and went to look at Lyra, finding her comfortable enough on the floor with a biscuit in her fist. Asta licked the head of the little puppy Pantalaimon, and Lyra responded with a stream of gurgles.

In the storeroom Malcolm found what he was looking for: a pencil. He wrote on the landing wall: "Malcolm Polstead of the Trout Inn at Godstow will pay for any damage and what we have taken."

Then he found a pile of new towels and carried them through to the broken window, where he leaned out and mopped the inside of the canoe.

"Let's try and keep you dry now," he said to her.

The rain had stopped, but the air was saturated, and the wind was whipping spray off the flood. The level had not gone down at all.

"Well, we've only been here half an hour," said Asta.

"I wish we could hide it a bit. If Bonneville goes past the end of the street, he'll see it straightaway."

"But he never saw the canoe in daylight," she pointed out. "It was pitch-dark. We might be in a punt, for all he knows."

"Hmm," said Malcolm, fastening the canopy down all round.

"Here, Malcolm," Alice called. "Come here."

"What?" he said, pulling himself back in through the window.

"Sit on that stool and keep still," she said.

"Why?"

She'd taken the kettle off the fire, so it must have come to a boil. She had a damp cloth in one hand, and with the other she turned his head this way and that, not roughly but firmly, while she dabbed at his face. He realized why as soon as she began.

"Ow!"

"Shut up. You look horrible with all them scratches. Besides, you might get germs in 'em. Keep still!"

He put up with the stinging and held his tongue. When she'd finished cleaning off the dried blood, she dabbed some antiseptic cream on.

"Stop wriggling. It can't hurt that much."

It did, though he would never dream of saying so. He gritted his teeth and put up with it.

"There," she said. "I dunno whether you need a bandage or two—"

"They'll only come off."

"Suit yourself. Now let me have the stool. I got to feed Lyra."

She tested the temperature of the water as Sister Fenella had done, and then sprinkled in some milk powder and stirred it up well.

"Give us that bottle," she said.

Malcolm passed her the bottle and the rubber teat.

"Ought to sterilize everything, really," she said.

He went to pick the child up. Pan was a sparrow chick now, so Asta became a bird too, a greenfinch this time.

"You finished your biscuit?" he said to Lyra. "You won't want any milk, then. I'll have it."

She was full of beans, as his mother would have said. He passed her over to Alice and then went to the window again, because the thought of his mother had brought sudden, helpless tears to his eyes.

"What's the matter?" said Alice suspiciously.

"Stinging."

He leaned out the window, trying to see any sign of movement in the other buildings, but there was none. Windows were curtained or uncurtained, but there were no lights glowing, no sounds apart from the surge and rush of the water.

Then he did see something moving. Asta saw it first and uttered a little gasp and fled to his breast as a kitten, and then he saw it too. It came floating down the street towards them, bumping into the housefronts, dull and soft and half submerged. It was the body of a woman facedown in the water, drowned and dead.

"What should we do?" whispered Asta.

"Nothing we can do."

"I said 'should.' That's different."

"I suppose . . . we *should* pull her out and lay her down. Sort of treat her with respect. I dunno. But if the shopkeeper came back and found a dead woman in his shop . . ."

For a few moments it looked as if the poor dead woman was trying to get lodged between the shopfront and the canoe. Malcolm dreaded having to reach for the paddle and push her away, but in the end the current carried her down the street. Malcolm and Asta stopped looking; it felt disrespectful.

"What happens to dæmons when people die?" Asta whispered.

"I dunno . . . maybe her dæmon was small, like a bird, and he's in her pocket or something. . . ."

"Maybe he got left behind."

But that was too horrible to think about. They looked back once at the dead woman, now some distance away, and tried to think of something else.

"Stores," said Malcolm. "We ought to take as much as we can pack in the boat."

"Why?" demanded Alice. She was standing right behind them, giving Lyra a break. He hadn't known she was there.

"In case we can't get back," said Malcolm calmly. "You saw how strong the flood is. In case we get swept further down where there aren't any shops or houses or anything."

"We could stay here."

"Bonneville's going to find us if we do that."

She thought. "Yeah," she said. "Maybe."

She patted Lyra on the back, and the child burped loudly.

"What's he want her for, anyway?" Alice said.

"He wants to kill her, prob'ly. Vengeance."

"For what?"

"On her parents. I dunno. Anyway . . ."

"Anyway what?"

"That sanctuary thing . . . We prob'ly couldn't have got her into Jordan College, even if we could've reached it, because you have to say something in Latin, and I don't know what it is. So maybe—"

Alice looked at him narrowly. Something had changed.

"What?" he said.

"You never meant to go back, did you?"

"Course I did—"

"No, you didn't. I can read you like a book, you little bastard."

Suddenly she reached forward and snatched the little white card from his shirt pocket. She read both sides, her face pinched with anger, and flung it to the floor.

Then she kicked his leg hard. She couldn't do anything else with the baby in her arms, and now Lyra was picking up her anger and seemed frightened. Malcolm moved out of range.

"You're just imagining—"

"No I en't! You *meant* to, didn't you? Eh? I saw you look at this card in the canoe when you thought I was asleep. And you meant to take me with you to look after the kid."

She kicked him again, and her dæmon growled and tried to seize Asta, who became a bird easily enough and flew up out of reach. Malcolm simply retreated and picked up the stool.

"And what you gonna do with that, eh? Hit me over the head? I'd like to see you try. I'd— Hush, hush, little one. Don't cry now. Alice has just lost her temper with that little piece of sewage over there, but not with you, my lovely. Put that bloody stool down where it was. I haven't finished feeding her. And put another log on the fire."

Malcolm did as she said. When she'd sat down and put the bottle back to Lyra's mouth, he said, "Think what happened last night. We didn't have any choice. We couldn't have done anything different. We had to come to the Trout—there was nowhere else to go, no other way to be safe. There was only the canoe. We had to get in it and—"

"Shut up. Just stop bloody talking. I got to think what to do now."

"We can't stay here. He'll find us."

"Shut up!"

Something was trickling down his forehead into his right eye. It was blood: the scratches had opened up. He mopped it with his handkerchief, which, like everything else, was still damp, and re-treated to the storeroom.

"Well, we knew she had a temper," whispered Asta.

"Hmm."

The fact was, they were both shaken. Alice's fury was harder to face than the dead woman in the water, harder than the thought of Gerard Bonneville.

Malcolm turned to the shelves, but he couldn't see anything. He couldn't think of stocking the canoe or anything else; his mind was swirling like the flood.

"We got to explain," he said quietly to Asta.

"D'you think she'll listen?"

"At least if she's got Lyra on her lap . . ."

He found a bottle of orange juice and twisted the top off.

"What's that for?" snapped Alice when he offered it to her.

"Breakfast."

"Stick it up your arse."

"Just listen. Let me explain."

In return she glared, but said nothing. He went on. "Lyra's in danger wherever she is—wherever in Oxford, anyway. Even if the priory is safe and the nuns are all alive, there's two lots of people, at least, trying to get hold of her. One's Bonneville. I dunno what he's up to, but he wants her, and he's violent and he's mad. He beats his own dæmon. I think it was him that broke her leg so she lost it. We can't let him get hold of Lyra. Then there's the . . ."

"Office of Child Protection," said Asta.

"Office of Child Protection. You heard, when I was telling Mum about them. And your dæmon . . ."

"Oh, yeah," said Alice. "Bastards."

"But there's scholastic sanctuary, right. Like I told you in the night."

"Oh, yeah. *If* it's true. And *if* we could get back to Jordan College, with the flood like this. They'd never let us in anyway. So much for that idea."

"But there's Lord Asriel. Lyra's father. You remember, I told you . . . he's on the other side from the CCD. And he clearly loves her—that's obvious. So I thought we should take her to him because no one else would protect her. The Office of Child Protection people will come back to the priory, and the nuns will be all busy with clearing up and rebuilding and they wouldn't be able to look after her properly, even Sister Benedicta. And then there's Bonneville. He's . . . well, he's wild. He's out of control. He could snatch her anytime. And Sister Katarina, she'd give her away to him. . . ."

Alice considered that, and then said, "What about your mum and dad? Why couldn't they look after her?"

"They got their hands full with the pub. And the CCD could come again. There's no defense against the CCD. If they wanted to search the pub from top to bottom, they could do it, and no one could stop 'em. And then there's the League of St. Alexander. Someone could tell their kid that Lyra was there and the kid might be a member and he'd give her away."

"Hmm," said Alice. She put the bottle down and lifted Lyra up to pat her back. "Well, there's her mother."

"She's on the side of the CCD. She *started* the League of St. Alexander!"

Alice stood and walked up and down slowly. Pantalaimon began a chirruping conversation as a baby swallow, and Lyra joined in, and so did Asta. Alice's dæmon, lying mastiff-shaped on the hearth, opened one eye to look. Malcolm said nothing and kept still. Finally Alice turned and spoke: "How you going to find him, then, this Lord Asriel?"

Malcolm picked up the card. "This is his address," he said.

"That's what made me think of it. Anyway, the gyptians'll know. If we see any gyptians. Besides, he's a famous man. It won't be hard to find him."

Alice snorted. "You're a mooncalf," she said.

"I don't know what one of them is."

"Look in the bloody mirror, then."

He said nothing because it seemed safer. Alice moved to the window and looked out briefly.

"Get me one of them blankets," she said.

He found one, opened it, and put it around her shoulders.

"Why didn't you tell me?" she said.

"'Cause it all happened so quick."

"But you'd been planning it. The stuff you already had in the canoe."

"I wasn't thinking of going away, not yet. I didn't know the flood would come so soon. And if I had, I'd have prob'ly taken Sister Fenella, 'cause I couldn't look after a baby *and* paddle the—"

"*Sister Fenella?* What did I call you? A mooncalf? You're a bloody gormless staring idiot."

"Well, someone—"

"It always had to be me. There en't anyone else."

"Well, why'd you kick me, then?"

"Why didn't you *tell* me? Or *ask* me, better."

"I only just thought of it in the night, when we were tied up to that tree."

She went back to the fire and put the last log on. "So what's the plan, then?" she said.

"Keep going downstream. Keep out of Bonneville's way. Find our way to Lord Asriel."

He had to clean the blood out of his eye again. He wiped his hand on his trousers, which were nearly dry now.

"Sit down and take Lyra," said Alice. "I'm going to put a bandage

275

on there—I don't care what you say. You're going to drive me mad, blinking blood out of your eye all the time."

She did it more gently than before. Then she held out the packet of bandages and the tube of antiseptic cream.

"You can put them in the boat, to start with. And more blankets and some pillows, if they got any. It was bloody freezing last night. And a load of them nappies that you can throw away. And matches. And that saucepan. And all them biscuits . . ."

She went on without a pause, listing so many things that the canoe would have sunk under them all. Malcolm nodded earnestly to everything.

"Well, go on, then," she said.

So he began. He gathered the things in the order he thought them important, so pillows and dry blankets came first, and then nappies and baby milk and other things for Lyra. Alice didn't seem inclined to help, and he dared not ask, so with each armful of cargo he had to lean out the window, pull the canoe close, drop it in, and then climb down and stow it in as shipshape a way as he could. He put a number of blankets in the prow for Alice to sit on, to keep the cold of the water below the hull away from her, and a couple of pillows there for her to lean on.

"She's very strange," Asta whispered when they were outside. "She could have whined and moaned all night, but she said nothing."

"I wish she hadn't kicked me, though."

"But she looked after your scratches. . . ."

"Shh!"

Malcolm had seen a movement at the end of the street, and then it became clearer: a dinghy, with two men in it, neither of them Bonneville. One was rowing, so the other could look forward, and as soon as he saw Malcolm in the canoe, he said something to the rower, who turned to look.

"Hey!" one of them shouted. "What you doing?"

Malcolm didn't answer. Instead, he called in through the window, "Alice, bring Lyra here."

"Why?" she said, but he'd turned away.

The dinghy was much closer: the man was rowing fast. When they were near enough for Malcolm not to have to shout, he said, "We got a baby to look after. We had to go in here because she was freezing."

Alice appeared beside him and saw the men, who were now close enough to reach out and take hold of the canoe.

"What you want?" she said, holding Lyra in her arms; the child was nearly asleep.

"Just making sure everything's all right and no one's doing what they shouldn't," said the man who wasn't rowing.

"You got a baby there?" said the rower.

"It's my sister," said Alice. "Our house was going to fall down when the flood come, so we got away in the boat. But we been out all night and she's ever so cold and we had to stop and find somewhere to feed and change her. If there was someone here, we'd have asked, but the place was empty."

"What you putting in the boat?" the other man asked Malcolm.

"Blankets and pillows. We're going to try and get home because our parents'll be worried. But in case we got to stay in the boat another night—"

"Why don't you just stay here?"

"'Cause of our parents," said Alice. "Didn't you hear? They'll be worried. We got to try and get back soon as we can."

"Where to?"

"You a policeman or something? What's it got to do with you?"

"Sandra, they're just looking after the place," said Malcolm. "We live in Wolvercote. Last night we got swept all down Port

Meadow. We're going to try and get back through the city, but in case we get stuck again . . ."

"What's your name?"

"Richard Parsons. This is my sister Sandra. And the baby's Ellie."

"Where was your mother and father last night?"

"Our grandmother was took ill yesterday. They went to see her, and while they was out, the flood come."

The rower was manipulating his oars to keep the boat still on the water. He said to the other man, "Leave 'em be. They're all right."

"You know it's theft, what you're doing?" the other man said. "Looting?"

"It en't *looting*," said Alice, but Malcolm spoke over her and said, "We're only taking what we need to stay alive and keep the baby fed. And as soon as the flood goes down, my dad'll come down here and pay for what we took."

"If you make your way into town," said the rower, "and find the town hall—you know where that is? St. Aldate's?"

Malcolm nodded.

"There's an emergency station there. It's full of people been flooded out, and plenty of helpers. You'll find everything you need up there."

"Thanks," said Malcolm. "We'll do that. Thank you."

The men nodded and began to row away.

"*Sandra*," said Alice with deep contempt. "Couldn't you think of nothing better than that?"

"No," said Malcolm.

And ten minutes later, they were moving again, Sandra/Alice wrapped up warm in the bow, a clean and dry and fed Lyra/Ellie fast asleep on her chest. *La Belle Sauvage* was lower in the water than she'd been since Malcolm took Sister Benedicta to the parcel depot, but she moved with all her new eagerness and responded to the paddle like a powerful steed to her master's touch on the reins. Well, Malcolm thought, it could all have gone far worse. They were still alive, and they were moving south.

SEVENTEEN

PILGRIMS' TOWER

At about the same time, George Papadimitriou was standing at the window of his rooms at the top of Pilgrims' Tower, the highest set in Jordan College, and looking out at the waste of waters that surrounded the tower and lapped against the windows of the other college buildings. Even in the enclosed quadrangle, the wind was whipping it into spray. The sky was heavy, promising even more rain, and the room was so cold that, in spite of the fire in the hearth, he was wearing his overcoat.

"When should we expect him, do you think?" he said.

"In this flood . . . ," said Lord Nugent, joining him at the window. "Who knows. But he's resourceful."

Nugent had arrived in Oxford the previous evening, an hour or two before the flood struck the city. Oakley Street had heard that Lyra was in danger, and he wanted to make sure of the arrangements for her safety. He would have made his way to the priory already that morning, despite the flood, but for the fact that they were awaiting the arrival of a traveler from the far north, Bud Schlesinger, news of whom had been in Coram van

Texel's coded letter from Uppsala. Schlesinger was a New Dane by birth, and an agent of Oakley Street by training and inclination. He had gone to the north to find out as much as he could about the witches' knowledge of Lyra, because it seemed that the source of much that was said about her came from them. The witches were a great power in those latitudes, and the alliances they made were costly but valuable. Nugent was eager to gain their support, but even more eager to prevent the other side from gaining it.

"I should think every boat that exists will have been requisitioned by the authorities," said Papadimitriou. "They would want to maintain civil order above everything else."

"Oh, he'll get here. Until he does, I'm going to— Wait a minute. Isn't that Hannah Relf down there?"

Papadimitriou peered down at the flooded quadrangle, where a slight figure clothed in oilskins was wading waist-deep towards the tower. She looked up briefly, pushing back her yellow sou'wester, and the two men recognized her at once. Papadimitriou waved, but she didn't see him, and she moved on through the water.

"I'll go down and meet her," Papadimitriou said.

He ran down the steep stairs and found her on the first landing, breathing heavily and unfastening the oilskin coat. Her little dæmon was helping with the buttons.

"Let me give you a hand," he said. "Good Lord, what are you wearing?"

"Salmon-fishing waders," she said. "Never thought I'd need them here."

"Well, this counts as a revelation. I wouldn't have imagined you with a fishing rod in your hands," he said, taking the coat from her. The waders came up to her chest and looked substantial.

"Not mine. They belonged to my brother, who gave up fishing

when he was injured. It's not easy to wear waders with a prosthetic leg. If I sit on the stairs, perhaps you could . . ."

He went down a step or two and tugged hard. She was fully clothed underneath, and must have been extremely uncomfortable.

"Well, good for you," he said.

"Are you very busy? I don't want to interrupt anything, but—"

"You won't. Don't worry."

"I thought I should come and tell you something important."

"Tom Nugent's here. Save your breath to climb the stairs and tell us both when you get there."

Their dæmons climbed ahead of them, talking quietly. Papadimitriou was concerned about Hannah: she was breathing heavily, and her face was flushed.

"You didn't walk all this way?" he said. Then, "Sorry, don't speak. Take it easy. No hurry."

When they reached the top floor, she said, "I begged a lift from a neighbor with an engine-boat. I'm not sure anyone could walk all the way. Have you seen how fast the water's flowing down St. Giles?"

Nugent opened the door, hearing their voices, and said, "Dr. Relf, this is valiant. Come in and sit by the fire and let me give you some of George's brandy."

"Thanks," she said. "I could do with it. I won't stay any longer than I need to."

"You'll stay till you're warm and dry," said Papadimitriou. "It would be good for you to meet Schlesinger, anyway."

She took a glass from Lord Nugent and sipped gratefully. "Who's Schlesinger?"

"An Oakley Street agent with something to tell us, we hope."

"I came because something's happened at the priory," she said. "Late last night. I heard from a neighbor, the man who owns the boat, and he took me up to see what was going on and check whether Malcolm was all right. But it's all such a . . . To start with, the gatehouse and several other parts of the main building have fallen down. So has the bridge across to the inn. Seven of the nuns are dead—drowned—and two others are missing. And the child . . . Well, she's missing too. But here's the point: Malcolm, the boy, you remember, he's disappeared as well. But so has his canoe *and* the girl who was helping out at the priory with the baby. That's the only thing that's giving Malcolm's parents any hope."

"They think he might have . . . what? Rescued the child and floated away?"

"In a word, yes. He was very fond of the baby, very interested in her and everything to do with her. So . . . well, that's what I had to tell you, really."

"Who is this girl?"

"Alice Parslow. Sixteen. She helps out in the inn, and she'd just begun at the priory too. But there's something else that might have a bearing on—"

"Wait a minute. They're *sure* the child is gone? Not buried under the collapsed building?"

"Yes, they're sure, because she was in a wooden crib in the kitchen when the gatehouse fell, in the care of the girl Alice. The crib was still there, but all the blankets had gone. But there's another thing. There was a man who'd shown up at the Trout a few days ago—Malcolm had told me about him for the first time on the day of Dr. Al-Kaisy's dinner. I mentioned him then, but you'd given me so many other things to think about that I didn't ask any further. His name was Gerard Bonneville. He had a hyena dæmon who'd lost a leg, and . . ."

Nugent sat forward.

Papadimitriou said, "How does he fit in? What was he doing?"

"I don't know whether he matters or not," said Hannah, "but Malcolm was afraid of the man because of the way his dæmon behaved. On the day of Dr. Al-Kaisy's dinner, Malcolm told me that he'd seen Bonneville trying to break into the priory the night before. . . . Oh, and the girl Alice had spoken to him, to Bonneville, and she said he'd claimed to be the father of the baby, of Lyra. But do you know anything about him?"

"As a matter of fact, yes," said Nugent. "We've been interested in him for some time. He's a scientist—an authority on elementary particles. Or used to be. He led a group in Paris researching the Rusakov field, that theory about consciousness that has the Magisterium in such a spin. He wrote a paper arguing that there must be a particle associated with the field, and made the extraordinary claim that Dust could be that particle. The gist of it, as far as I can understand it, was that everything is material and that matter itself is conscious. There's no need to bring spirit into the discussion. You can see why the Magisterium is keen to shut him up. He was—well, he is—a brilliant mind. And he's involved with this, with Lyra?"

"But he was in prison," said Papadimitriou. "Wasn't there a court case? Some sexual offense?"

"Yes, that was his downfall. Or part of it. I think Marisa Coulter was involved in some way—perhaps she testified against him— we'll look up the details. And he's claiming to be Lyra's father?"

Hannah said, "So I heard from Malcolm, who heard it from the girl Alice. And Mrs. Coulter does know Bonneville."

"How do you know?"

"She came to my house."

"What? When?" said Nugent.

She told them what had happened on that afternoon, and how Malcolm had spoken to Mrs. Coulter and deflected her questions. "She clearly did know this Bonneville, but she wouldn't admit it.

She wanted to know where the child was. She didn't say it was her own daughter, let alone who the father was. It was a strange conversation altogether. . . . Isn't that someone outside?"

As she said that, there came a knock on the door. Papadimitriou opened it and warmly shook the hand of the man who came in.

"Bud! You made it," he said. "Well done!"

Nugent got up to welcome him. Schlesinger was a man of thirty or so, lean, with fair hair cut very short and a vivid alertness in his expression. His dæmon was a small owl. His cold-weather clothing seemed wet through.

"Hello," he said, seeing Hannah. "Am I interrupting something?"

"No, I think I am," said Hannah. "I'll go now."

"No, Dr. Relf, stay," said Nugent. "This is important. Bud, Hannah is one of us. She knows what this is all about, and she's given us some valuable information. Look, you're soaked. Come near the fire."

Schlesinger shook Hannah's hand and said, "Good to meet you. What are you discussing? Have I missed the best part?"

As Schlesinger took off his outer clothing and sat down next to the fire, Nugent explained the situation, and Hannah listened with professional admiration. An A-plus for that summary, she thought: everything there and in its right relation with everything else, not a redundant word, clarity throughout.

As Lord Nugent spoke, Papadimitriou made a pot of coffee.

"So that's where we are," said Nugent as he finished. "Now, what do you have for us?"

Schlesinger sipped his coffee and said, "Plenty. First, the child. Lyra. There's no doubt she's the daughter of Coulter and Asriel. No one else involved. We'd heard rumors of some prophecy concerning the child, and we knew that the Magisterium was strongly interested in her, so I went north to find out more. The witches of the Enara region had heard voices in the aurora—that's how they put it; I gather it's a metaphor—voices that said that the child was destined to put an end to destiny. That's all. They didn't know what that meant, and I sure as hell don't either. Could be a good thing, could be bad. And the main condition is that she must do this without knowing that she's doing it. Anyway, the Magisterium heard about this prophecy through their own witch contacts, and immediately set about finding the child. That was when we realized that something important was going on, and when you began to look for somewhere to hide her."

"That's right," said Nugent. "Go on."

"Now the second thing: Gerard Bonneville. I knew him a little in Paris, and I heard he'd come to the north, so I asked around quietly among the university people I knew. He'd been in prison for this sexual crime, whatever it was, and he was newly released. He'd been dismissed from his academic post, cut off from access to laboratory facilities and technical help, to libraries, to everything a scientist needs. No one would employ him. He was always a difficult guy to work with—demanding, obsessive, and that dæmon was just so goddamn unpleasant. . . . Three legs, huh? Well, she had a full set of legs when I saw Bonneville last. I think Coram van Texel might know something about that. I saw Coram in Sweden—I guess he told you."

At the mention of Coram van Texel, Hannah glanced at Lord Nugent, who returned her look with bland impassivity.

"But Bonneville saw a way back into favor," Schlesinger went on. "He knew about the witches' prophecy, and he thought if he could get hold of the child, he'd be able to bargain with the Magisterium: give me a laboratory, give me all the help I need, and you can have the child and do what you like with her. So that's what he's after, and why. And do we know where he is now? What's the latest you heard?"

"This is surmise," said Papadimitriou, "but it's likely that he's pursuing the boy and the girl who are looking after Lyra. They have a boat—a canoe, I believe—and Hannah thinks they escaped in that. But, Hannah, where would they go? What would they be looking for?"

"Well," said Hannah, "some time ago now, Malcolm asked me about the idea of sanctuary, because he'd heard about it from one of the nuns, and he asked me if the colleges still offered sanctuary to scholars, and I told him that Jordan used to have some form of it. . . ."

"We still do," said Papadimitriou. "Scholastic sanctuary has to be invoked by asking the Master himself. There's a Latin formula. . . ."

"So I'm sure Malcolm would try to bring her here," Hannah said. "But we've all seen the way the flood is racing through the city. I don't think a canoe could make much headway in this sort of torrent. They'd have to go where the flood took them."

"But a baby is not a scholar," said Papadimitriou. "It wouldn't work."

"If she *were* granted scholastic sanctuary, though, how safe would it make her?"

"Completely. The law has been tested in the courts, and always found to be impregnable. But, as I say—"

"You know," said Schlesinger, sitting forward suddenly, excited, "this makes sense of something else I heard in the north. I was asking about a child—I didn't say girl, on purpose, I said child. Was there a prophecy about a child? And there was one witch—what was she called? Tilda Vasara . . . Queen Tilda Vasara—she told me she'd heard a prophecy about a boy, so I kind of listened politely, but I was really only interested in what they might have to

287

say about a girl. And she said the voices in the aurora had spoken about a boy who had to carry a treasure to a place of safety. Well, I had no interest in a boy, so I clean forgot it till you started talking about a place of safety. Sanctuary. Could this boy of yours be doing that?"

"Yes!" said Hannah. "It's just the sort of way he'd think. He's intensely romantic."

"But in any case, he hasn't brought her here," said Papadimitriou, "so we have to assume that if he was trying to come here, he failed, and they've been carried further downstream. What would his next idea be?"

Hannah found all three men looking at her intently, as if they thought she knew. Well, perhaps she did.

"Lord Asriel," she said. "That night when Lord Asriel came to the priory and saw the baby, and Malcolm lent him his canoe, it made a great impression on him. Malcolm would think that Asriel represented safety for Lyra. I think he'd try and take her to him."

"Would he know where to find him?" said Papadimitriou.

"I don't know. I suppose London . . . but no, I have no idea."

"Anyway," said Schlesinger, "I saw Asriel briefly last night in Chelsea. He's just about to set off for the north again. Even if your Malcolm does get there, Asriel might be gone."

"Unless the flood holds him up," said Nugent, standing. He looked suddenly younger, energized, full of purpose. "Well, everything's clarified. We know what we have to do: we have to set off on the flood and find them before Bonneville does. Bud, how did you travel here?"

"I hired a fast powerboat. I guess the owner's still around; he said he's going to try and pick up some work in Oxford."

"Find him, and set off," said Nugent. "George, you know the gyptians. Use your contacts. Find a couple of boats, for yourself and for me. The Magisterium will be looking for them too. The CCD has a number of riverboats; they'll all be concentrating on this. Hannah, put everything else aside and use the alethiometer to search for them."

"How will I keep in touch with you?" said Hannah.

"You won't," said Lord Nugent. "Whether we're successful or not, you'll be writing the history in due course. Go home, keep dry and safe, and watch the alethiometer. I'll find a way of keeping in contact."

EIGHTEEN

LORD MURDERER

Malcolm had never thought it possible for an entire river, not to say an entire countryside, to disappear under a flood. Where this colossal amount of water had come from was hard to imagine. At one point later in the morning, he put his hand over the side and brought some to his mouth to taste, half expecting to find it salty, as if it was the Bristol Channel pouring its way through to London. But there was no salt; it didn't taste very good, but it wasn't seawater.

"If you was paddling to London," said Alice, "and the river was normal and there wasn't no flood, how long would it take?"

It was the first time she'd spoken since they'd left the pharmacy two hours before.

"Dunno. It's about sixty miles, maybe more, 'cause the river twists and turns. But you'd be going with the current, so . . ."

"Well, how long, then?"

"A few days?"

Alice's expression indicated disgust.

"But this'll be quicker," Malcolm went on, "'cause the current's stronger. Look how fast we're going past those trees."

The summit of a hill stood out above the water, crowned with a clump of trees, mostly oaks, whose bare branches looked mournful against the gray sky. But *La Belle Sauvage* was moving fast; in a minute she had sped past, and the hill was behind them.

"So it shouldn't take that long," he said. "Maybe just a day."

Alice said nothing, but reached down to adjust Lyra's covers. The child was lying between her feet, wrapped up so thickly that all Malcolm could make out was the top of her head and the brilliant butterfly Pantalaimon perching on her hair.

"Is she all right?" he said.

"Seems to be."

Asta was very curious about Pan. She had noticed before that he could change in Lyra's sleep, although he was asleep himself. She had a theory that when he was a butterfly it meant that Lyra was dreaming, but Malcolm was skeptical. Of course, neither of them had the faintest idea what happened when they themselves were asleep; they knew Asta could go to sleep as one creature and wake up as another, but neither of them remembered anything about the change. It was the sort of thing he'd have liked to mention to Alice, but the prospect of her bottomless scorn put him off.

"I bet it *is* a dream," Asta said.

"Who's that?" said Alice sharply.

She was pointing past Malcolm's shoulder, looking some distance back. He turned to look and saw, only just visible through the wet gray air, a man in a dinghy rowing hard towards them.

"Can't see for sure," Malcolm said. "It might be . . ."

"It *is*," she said. "That dæmon's in the front. Go faster."

Malcolm could see that the dinghy was an unhandy vessel, by no means as swift and easy through the water as *La Belle Sauvage*. Still, the man had adult muscles and was plying the oars with determination.

So Malcolm dug the paddle in and urged the canoe forward.

But he couldn't do it for long, because his shoulders and arms, his whole torso and waist, were aching.

"What's he doing? Where is he?" he said.

"He's dropping back. Can't see him—he's behind that hill—keep going!"

"I'm going as fast as I can. But I'll have to stop soon. Besides . . ."

The change in motion had woken Lyra, and she began to cry quietly. They'd have to feed her before long, and that meant tying up the canoe, building a fire, heating the saucepan. And before that, finding somewhere to hide.

Malcolm looked all around while paddling as steadily as he could. They were in a broad valley, probably far above the river-bed, with a wooded slope rising out of the water to the left, and to the right a large house, classical in shape and white in color, on the breast of a green hill on which were more trees. Each side was some way off; it was likely that the man in the dinghy would see them long before they reached a hiding place.

"Make for the house," said Alice.

Malcolm thought that was the better option too, so he paddled the canoe as fast as he could in that direction. As they got closer, he could see a thin column of smoke rising from one of the many chimneys, before being blown away.

"There's people there," he said.

"Good" was all she said.

"If there's people around," said Asta, "he's less likely to . . ."

"Suppose he's already here, and he's one of them?" said Malcolm.

"But that was him back there in the boat," she said. "Wasn't it?"

"Maybe. Too far away to see."

Malcolm was realizing how tired he was. He had no idea how long he'd been paddling, but as he slowed down, nearing the house, he felt more and more hungry and weary and cold. He could barely hold his head up.

Ahead of them a sloping lawn rose directly out of the floodwater and led smoothly up to the white facade of the house, the columns and the pediment. Someone was moving there, behind the columns, but the light was too gloomy to see anything more than the movement. The smoke was rising from a chimney somewhere at the back.

Malcolm brought the canoe to rest against the grass of the lawn.

"Well, what are we s'posed to do now?" said Alice.

The slope was a gentle one, and the edge of the water was some feet further than the canoe could reach.

"Take your shoes and socks off," said Malcolm, hauling off his boots. "We'll pull the canoe up out of the water. It'll slide over the grass easy enough."

There was a shout from the house. A man came out from between the columns and gestured to them to go away. He shouted again, but they couldn't hear what he said.

"You better go up and tell him we got to feed a baby and rest for a while," said Malcolm.

"Why me?"

"'Cause he'll take more notice of you."

They got the canoe out of the water, and then Alice sulkily picked her way up the lawn towards the man, who was shouting again.

Malcolm pulled the canoe away from the water and into ragged shrubbery at the edge of the lawn, and then slumped down beside it. He said to Lyra, "I suppose you're just waking up, are you? It's all right for some. It's a nice life being a baby."

She wasn't happy. Malcolm took her out of the canoe and cuddled her on his lap, ignoring the smell that meant she needed changing, ignoring the heavy gray sky and the cold wind and the distant man in the dinghy, who had come into sight again. He held the little child against his chest and self-consciously kissed her forehead.

"We'll keep you safe," he said. "See, Alice is talking to the man up there. Soon we'll take you there and make a fire and warm some milk. Course, if your mummy was here . . . You never had a mummy, did you? You were just found somewhere. The lord chancellor found you under a bush. And he thought, Blimey, I can't look after a baby, I better take her to the sisters at Godstow. So then it was Sister Fenella who looked after you. I bet you remember her. She's a nice old lady, isn't she? And then the flood came and we had to take you away in *La Belle Sauvage* to keep you safe. I wonder if you'll remember any of this. Prob'ly not. I can't remember anything from when I was a baby. Look, here comes Alice. Let's see what she says."

"He says we can't stay long," she told him. "I says we got to make a fire and feed the baby and we don't want to stay long anyway. I think summing funny's going on. He had a strange look about him."

"Was there anyone else there?" said Malcolm, getting to his feet.

"No. At least I didn't see no one."

"Take Lyra, then, and I'll hide the canoe a bit more," he said, handing over the child. His arms were trembling with fatigue.

Once he had the canoe concealed, he gathered the things they needed for Lyra and made his way up to the house. The great door was open behind the columns, and lingering beside it was the man: a sour-faced individual in rough clothes, whose mastiff dæmon stood close by, watching without moving.

"You en't staying long," the man said.

"Not very long, no," Malcolm agreed. And he recognized something: the man was a little drunk. Malcolm knew how to deal with drunks.

"Lovely house," he said.

"So it may be. It en't yours."

"Is it yours?"

"'Tis now."

"Did you buy it, or did you fight for it?"

"You being cheeky?"

The mastiff dæmon growled.

"No," said Malcolm easily. "It's just with everything changed by the flood, I wouldn't be surprised if you had to fight for it. Everything's different now. And if you fought for it, then it belongs to you, no doubt about it."

He looked down the lawn towards the turbid flood. In the heavy twilight he couldn't see the rowing boat at all.

"It's like a castle," he went on. "You could defend this easy, if you were attacked."

"Who's going to attack it?"

"No one. I'm just saying. You made a good choice."

The man turned and followed his gaze out over the water.

"Has it got a name, this house?" said Malcolm.

"Why?"

"It looks important. It looks like a manor or a palace or something. You could call it after yourself."

The man snorted. It might have been with laughter.

"You could put a notice up at the edge of the water," Malcolm said. "Saying keep out, or trespassers will be prosecuted. You'd have every right to. Like that man over there in the dinghy," he said, because now he could see the boat, still some way off, still moving steadily towards them.

"What's the matter with him?"

"Nothing, till he tries to land and take this house away from you."

"D'you know him?"

"I think I know who he is. And he prob'ly would try and do that."

"I got a shotgun."

"Well, he wouldn't dare land if you threatened him with that."

The man seemed to be thinking about it.

"I got to defend my property," he said.

"Course you have. You got every right to."

"Who is he, anyway?"

"If it's who I think it is, his name's Bonneville. He's not long out of prison."

The mastiff dæmon, following the man's line of sight, growled again.

"Is he after you?"

"Yeah. He's been following us from Oxford."

"What's he want?"

"He wants the baby."

"Is it his kid, then?"

The man's blurred eyes swam towards focus on Malcolm's face.

"No. She's our sister. He just wants her."

"Get away!"

"I'm afraid so," Malcolm said.

"Bastard."

The man in the boat was getting closer, making quite clearly for the lawn, and now Malcolm had no doubt who he was.

"I better get inside, in case he sees me," he said. "We won't make any trouble for you. We'll get away as soon as we can."

"Don't you worry, son," the man said. "What's your name?"

Malcolm had to think.

"Richard," he said. "And my sister's Sandra, and the baby's Ellie."

"Get inside. Keep out the way. Leave him to me."

"Thank you," said Malcolm, and he slipped inside.

The man came inside too, and took a shotgun from a cabinet in a room just off the hall.

"Be careful," said Malcolm. "He might be dangerous."

"*I'm* dangerous."

The man went unsteadily outside. Malcolm looked around quickly. The hall was decorated with ornate plasterwork, cabinets in precious woods and tortoiseshell and gold, statues of marble. The huge chimneypiece was cracked, though, and the hearth was empty. Alice must have found the fire in another room.

Afraid to call out for her, he hurried from room to room, listening hard for the sound of a gunshot; but there was no sound from outside except the wind and the rush of the water.

He found Alice in the kitchen. There was a fire in an iron range, and Lyra sat freshly changed in the center of a large pine table.

"What'd he say?" Alice demanded.

"He said we can stay here and do what we need to. And he's got a shotgun and he's going to defend the house against Bonneville."

"Is he coming? It *was* him in the boat, wannit?"

"Yeah."

The water in the saucepan had been boiling when Malcolm came in. Alice took it off to cool. Malcolm picked up the biscuit that had fallen from Lyra's hand and gave it to her again. She gurgled her appreciation.

"If she drops her biscuit, you ought to tell her where it's gone," he said to Pantalaimon, who instantly became a bush baby and gazed at him with enormous eyes, unmoving and silent.

"Look at Pan," Malcolm said to Alice.

She cast a quick glance, not interested.

"How does he know how to be one of them?" Malcolm went on. "They can't ever have *seen* a whatever-it-is. So how does he know—"

"What we gonna do if Bonneville gets past the man?" said Alice, her voice sharp and high.

"Hide. Then run out and get away."

Her face showed what she thought of that.

"Go and find out what's going on," she told him. "And don't let him see you."

Malcolm went out and tiptoed along the corridor to the main hall. Pressing himself into the shadows beside the door, he listened hard, and hearing nothing, he looked around carefully. The hall was empty. What now?

There was no sound but the wind and the water, no voices, certainly no gunshots. They might be talking at the water's edge, he thought, and keeping to the wall, he moved silently across the marble floor towards the great windows.

But Asta, moth-formed, got there first, and Malcolm felt a horrible shock as she saw something outside and fell off the curtain into his hand.

The man from the house was lying on the grass, with his head and arms in the water beside Bonneville's dinghy, not moving. There was no sign of Bonneville, and no sign of the gun.

In his alarm, Malcolm recklessly went close to the window, peering out to left and right. The only movements were the bobbing of the dinghy, which was tied to a stick Bonneville had driven into the soft lawn, and the swaying this way and that of the top half of the man's body. The light was too gray and dim for him to be sure, but Malcolm thought he could see a current of scarlet trailing away from the man's throat.

He pressed himself against the glass, trying to see where he'd hidden *La Belle Sauvage*. As far as he could tell, the bushes were undisturbed.

Which was the cabinet the man had opened to get the gun? In that room at the other end of the great hall . . .

But Malcolm didn't know how to load and fire one, even if . . .

He ran back to the kitchen. Alice was just pouring the milk into Lyra's bottle.

"What is it?"

"Shh. Bonneville's killed the man and taken his gun, and I can't see him anywhere."

"What gun?" she said, alarmed.

"He had a shotgun. I told you. He was going to defend the place. And now Bonneville's got it and killed him. He's lying in the water. . . ."

Malcolm was looking around, almost panting with fear. He saw an iron ring in a wooden trapdoor, and his panic-strengthened muscles lifted it at once. A flight of steps led down into profound darkness.

"Candles—on the shelf over there," said Alice, scooping up Lyra and the bottle and looking around for anything that would give them away, but there was too much to pick up.

Malcolm ran to the shelf and found a box of matches there as well.

"You go down first. I'll pull the trapdoor after me," he said.

Alice moved cautiously into the dark. Lyra was twisting and struggling, and Pantalaimon was chirruping like a frightened bird. Asta flew to him, perching on Lyra's blanket, and made soft cooing noises.

Malcolm was struggling with the trapdoor. There was a rope handle on the inside, but the hinges were stiff and it was very heavy. Finally he managed to haul it over and let it down as quietly as he could.

The strain of being at a distance from his dæmon was beginning to tell. His hands were trembling and his heart was lurching painfully.

"Don't move any further away," he whispered to Alice.

"Why—"

"Dæmon."

She understood and moved back a step, crowding him slightly as he tried to strike a match. He got a candle lit, and Asta flew back to him, for the little flame itself was enough to distract Lyra. In its light, Alice trod carefully down to the cellar floor.

"All right, Lyra, hush, gal," she whispered, and settled on the cold earth floor with her back against the wall. A noisy sound of sucking came almost at once, and Alice's dæmon settled near the chick-shaped Pan as a crow. The little dæmon's anxious chirruping stopped.

Malcolm sat on the bottom step, looking around. This was a storeroom for vegetables and sacks of rice and other such things: dry enough, but bitterly cold. A low archway led through into a further cellar.

"All he's got to do," said Alice shakily, "is move summing heavy onto the trapdoor and—"

"Don't think about it. There's no point in thinking like that. In a minute I'll go through that archway and see where it leads. There's bound to be another entrance."

"Why?"

"Because a cellar is where they keep wine. And when they send the butler down to fetch up some bottles of claret or whatever, he en't going to struggle with the trapdoor and stumble down the steps, like we did. There'll be a proper staircase somewhere—"

"Shh!"

He sat still, tense and fearful, trying not to let his fear show. Leisurely footsteps moved across the floor above. They stopped at the end of the kitchen and paused, and then crossed the floor again. The steps paused once more, close to the trapdoor.

Nothing happened for a minute. Then there was a sound, as of a wooden chair being pulled out from the table, just that; but they couldn't tell whether Bonneville had put it over the trapdoor, or whether he'd simply moved it and gone out.

Another minute went past, and then another.

With the greatest of care, Malcolm stood up and stepped down to the earth floor. He set the lit candle on the ground near Alice, screwing it into the soil so as to stand securely, and tiptoed under the low archway into the next part of the cellar. Once he was there, he lit another candle. This was a second storeroom, but for unwanted furniture rather than food, so he looked around quickly and moved on through the next archway.

At the other end of this room, there was a heavy wooden door with great iron hinges and a lock as big as a large book. There was no key hanging nearby, and he couldn't tell whether the door was locked, even by looking closely.

And then a quiet voice spoke on the other side. It was Bonneville. Asta, on his shoulder as a lemur, nearly fainted; he caught her and held her close.

"Well, Malcolm," said Bonneville, his voice low and confiding. "Here we are on either side of a locked door, and neither of us has the key. At least I haven't, and I assume you haven't either, because you'd have unlocked it and come through, wouldn't you? That would have been unfortunate for you."

Malcolm had nearly dropped the candle. His heart was beating like the wings of a captured bird, and Asta changed rapidly from lemur to butterfly to crow before becoming a lemur again, crouching on Malcolm's shoulder, her enormous eyes fixed on the lock.

"Don't say a word," she murmured into his ear.

"Oh, I know you're there," said Bonneville. "I can see the light of your candle. I saw you on the terrace talking to our late host—did you know this is an island, by the way? If your canoe should meet with an accident, you'd be marooned. How would you like that?"

Again Malcolm held his tongue.

"I know it's you because it must be you," Bonneville went on. He was speaking confidentially, his voice just loud enough to penetrate the door. "It couldn't be anyone else. That girl is feeding the baby—she wouldn't be prowling around with a candle. And I know you're listening. It won't be long before we're face to face. You won't escape me now. Can you see them, by the way?"

"See who?" Malcolm cursed himself as soon as he spoke. "There's no one here but me," he went on.

"Oh, don't ever think that, Malcolm. You're never alone."

"Well, there's my dæmon—"

"I don't mean her. You and she are the same being, naturally. I mean someone besides you."

"Who d'you mean, then?"

"I hardly know where to start. There are spirits of the air and the earth, to begin with. Once you learn to see them, you'll realize that the world is thronged with them. And then in wicked places like this, there are night-ghasts of many kinds. Do you know what used to go on here, Malcolm?"

"No," said Malcolm, who didn't want to know in the least.

"This is where Lord Murdstone used to bring his victims," said Bonneville. "Have you heard his name? They used to call him Lord Murderer. Not all that long ago either."

Malcolm's heart was beating painfully. "Did he—" He couldn't speak clearly. "Did he own this house?"

"He could do what he liked here," the slow, dark voice went on through the door. "There was no one to stop him. So he used to bring children down here and dismember them."

"Did—what?" Malcolm could only whisper.

"Cut them apart bit by bit while they were still alive. That was his special pleasure. And naturally the horrible agony of those children was too great to disappear forever when they eventually died. It soaked into the stonework. It lingered in the air. There's no clean wind blowing through these cellars, Malcolm. The air you're breathing now was last in the lungs of those tortured children."

"I don't want to hear any more," said Malcolm.

"I don't blame you. I wouldn't want to hear it either. I'd want to stop my ears up and wish it would go away. But there's no escaping it, Malcolm. They're all around you now, the spirits of that agony. They're sensing your fear, and they're flocking towards you to lap it up. Next thing you'll start hearing them—a sort of desperate little whisper—and then you'll begin to see them."

Malcolm was nearly fainting by this time. He believed everything Bonneville was saying; it all sounded so likely that he believed it helplessly and immediately.

Then a little current of air found his candle flame and made it lean sideways for a moment, and he looked at it, and instantly there in his vision was the little floating grain of light and movement, the seed of his aurora. A tiny spring of relief and hope began to flow in his mind.

"You're wrong about the baby," he said, and was surprised to find his voice steady.

"Wrong? In what way?"

"You think she's your child, but she's not."

"Well, you're wrong about her too."

"I en't wrong about that. She's Lord Asriel and Mrs. Coulter's child."

"You're wrong to think I'm interested in her. I might be interested in Alice."

Asta whispered, "Don't let him make us talk about what he wants."

Malcolm nodded. She was right. His heart was pounding.

Then he remembered the message in the wooden acorn and said, "Mr. Bonneville, what's the Rusakov field?"

"What do you know about that?"

"Nothing. That's why I'm asking."

"Why don't you ask Dr. Hannah Relf?"

That was a surprise. He had to answer quickly.

"I have," he said, "but it's not what she knows about. She knows about stuff like the history of ideas."

"Right up her street, I would have thought. Why are you interested in the Rusakov field?"

The spangled ring was growing larger, as it always did. Now it was like a small jeweled serpent twisting and twining for him alone. He went on steadily. "'Cause you know how the gravitational field deals with the force of gravity, right, and the magnetic field deals with that force, so what force is it that the Rusakov field deals with?"

"Nobody knows."

"Is it something to do with the uncertainty principle?"

Bonneville was silent for a few moments. Then he said, "My, my, you are a persistent child. If I were in your position, I'd want to know something quite different."

"Well, I want to know all sorts of things, but in the right order. The Rusakov field is the most important one, 'cause it's connected with Dust. . . ."

Malcolm heard a quiet noise behind him and turned to see Alice coming through the archway, holding the candle. He put his finger to his lips and mouthed in an exaggerated way, "Bonneville," pointing to the door. He gestured: *Go, go!*

Her eyes widened and she stood still.

Malcolm turned back. Bonneville was speaking. He was saying: "Because there are some things you can explain to an elementary school pupil and others that move quickly out of his range. This is one of them. You need at least an undergraduate grasp of experimental theology before the Rusakov field will have the slightest meaning for you. There's no point in even beginning."

Malcolm looked round silently and saw that Alice had gone. "But all the same—" he said, turning back.

"Why were you turning round?"

"I thought I heard something."

"That girl? Alice? Was it her?"

"No, it wasn't. It's just me here."

"I thought we'd disposed of that notion, Malcolm. Those dead children—did I tell you what he did to their dæmons? It was the most ingenious . . ."

Malcolm turned away with the candle held in both hands and went back across the cellar, which, despite his success in distracting the man, and despite his aurora, now glittering at the edge of his vision, was still thronged with almost-visible horrors. He felt forward with his feet, trying to hold his balance and keep the candle alight, and all the time Bonneville's voice spoke on behind the door, and Malcolm mouthed to himself, "Not true! Not true!"

Finally he reached the other room. Alice and Lyra had gone. He almost stumbled up to the flight of steps, held himself steady, and began to climb, silent, careful, slow.

He got to the trapdoor and stopped: Could he hear anything? The urge to fling it open and rush out into the clear air was almost overpowering, but he made himself listen. Nothing. No voice, no footsteps, nothing but the thudding of his own heart.

So he put his back against the trapdoor and pushed up, and up it went, quite smooth and easy, and then a gust of air blew his candle out—but it was all right—there was light coming in through the kitchen window—he could see the table, the walls—and there was the glow of the fire still. He climbed out in a moment, lowered the trapdoor swiftly and silently, and then, before racing to the door and the world outside, stopped.

This was a kitchen, and if the cooks here were anything like his mother or Sister Fenella, there would be a drawer with knives in it. He felt around the table, found a knob, pulled it open, and there they were: an assortment of wooden-handled cooks' knives, all lying ready to hand. He felt through the handles till he came to one that wasn't too long to conceal, whose blade came to a point and not a rounded end.

He put it in his belt behind his back and made for the door and the clear, cold air outside.

In the very last gray of the day, he could see Alice stumbling across the grass in great haste, carrying Lyra. Bonneville's boat was still tied up, but the body of the other man had floated away, and there was no sign of Bonneville himself.

He ran to the dinghy, pulled the stick it was tied to out of the ground, and began to shove the boat out into the current.

But he stopped: there was a rucksack in it, under the thwart. The thought came at once: If we have this, we can bargain with him. So he reached in and swung it up—it was heavy—and out onto the grass, and then pushed the boat away from the land.

He grabbed the rucksack and ran back towards Alice. She had put Lyra down on the grass and was tugging La Belle Sauvage out of the bushes, so Malcolm dropped the rucksack in the canoe and joined her.

But they hadn't moved it a foot before they heard behind them the "Haa! Haa! Haa!" of that abominable dæmon, and turned to see Bonneville sauntering down from the entrance of the house, shotgun under his arm, the dæmon limping and lurching beside him, as if on an invisible leash.

Malcolm let go of the canoe and quickly picked up Lyra, and Alice, turning to see what was happening, said, "Oh, God, no."

There wouldn't be time to get the canoe into the water, and even if they did, the man still had that gun. Although his face was indistinct in the gathering gloom, every line of his body looked as if he knew he'd won.

He stopped a few paces away and moved the gun to his left hand. Was he left-handed? Malcolm couldn't remember, and cursed his carelessness in not noticing.

"Well, you might as well give her to me," Bonneville said. "You've got no hope of getting away now."

"But why d'you want her?" said Malcolm, holding the child even tighter to his chest.

"'Cause he's a bloody pervert," said Alice.

Bonneville laughed gently.

Malcolm's heart was hammering so much it hurt. He felt Alice tense beside him. He was desperate to keep Bonneville looking their way, because the man hadn't yet noticed that his own boat was gone. "What you were saying in there, through the door, it wasn't true," he said.

Malcolm had Lyra in his left arm, tight against his chest. She was quiet; Asta, as a mouse, was whispering to her and Pan. Malcolm felt behind him with his right hand, trying to feel for the knife. But the muscles of his arm were trembling so much that he was afraid he'd drop the knife before he could use it; and did he really intend to stab the man, anyway? He had never deliberately harmed so much as a fly, and the only fights he had had were playground scuffles. Even when he'd knocked the boy into the river for painting an s over the v of SAUVAGE, he'd pulled him out straightaway.

"How would you ever know what the truth was?" said Bonneville.

Malcolm said, "Your voice changes when you say something not true." He was still feeling for the knife, and hoping that Bonneville didn't see him moving.

"Oh, you believe that sort of thing? I suppose you believe that the last thing someone sees is imprinted on their retina?"

Malcolm found the handle of the knife and said, "No, I don't believe that. But why do you want Lyra? What are you going to do with her?"

"She's my daughter. I want to give her a decent education."

"No, she's not. You'll have to give us a better reason than that."

"All right, then. I'm going to roast her and eat her. Have you any idea how delicious—"

Alice spat at him.

"Oh, Alice," he said. "You and I could have been such friends. Perhaps even more than friends. How close we nearly came, you and I! We really shouldn't let such a little thing spoil a beautiful possibility."

Malcolm had got the knife out of his belt. Alice could see what he was doing, dark though it was, and getting darker, and she moved a little closer.

"You still haven't told the truth," said Malcolm, shifting Lyra's weight.

Bonneville stepped nearer. Malcolm held Lyra away from his chest, as if to give her to the man, and Bonneville held out his right arm, as if to take her.

The second he was close enough, Malcolm brought his right hand round and stabbed the knife as hard as he could into Bonneville's thigh. It was the closest part of him. The man roared with pain and staggered sideways, dropping the gun to grab at his leg. His dæmon howled and lurched forward, slipping and falling flat. Malcolm turned around swiftly and put Lyra down—

—and then there was an explosion so loud it knocked him flat.

His head ringing, he pulled himself up to see Alice holding the gun. Bonneville was groaning and rocking back and forth on the grass, clutching his thigh, which was bleeding heavily, but his dæmon lay thrashing, howling, screaming, utterly unable to get up: her one foreleg was smashed beyond repair.

"Take Lyra!" Malcolm shouted to Alice, and scrambled over to seize the painter of the canoe and drag it down over the grass to the water's edge.

Behind him Bonneville was shouting incoherently and trying to haul himself over the ground towards the child. Alice threw the gun into the darkness of the trees and snatched Lyra up. Bonneville tried to grab her as she came near, but she easily evaded him and leapt over the howling dæmon, who twisted and squirmed and fell again, trying to stand up on a leg that was hardly there.

It was horrible to watch: Malcolm had to close his eyes. Then Alice was climbing into the canoe with Lyra secure in her arms, and he pushed off from the grass, and the sweet-natured canoe did his bidding at once and carried them away and onto the breast of the flood.

NINETEEN

THE POACHER

Heavy clouds loomed above, but behind the clouds the moon was nearly full and lent a faint radiance to the whole sky.

Lyra lay awake, happy enough to gurgle with the swaying of the boat. Malcolm's stiff arms and shoulders began to loosen, and the canoe made good speed on the dark water. Alice was looking intently past Malcolm's head towards the house as it vanished behind them. Even in the dimness, Malcolm could see her face, sharp and anxious and angry, and he saw her bend forward to adjust Lyra's blankets and stroke her face.

"D'you wanna biscuit?" she said softly.

He thought she was speaking to Lyra. Then she looked up at him.

"What's the matter? Wake up," she said.

"Oh. Me. Yes, please, I'd like a biscuit. Actually, I'd like a whole plate of steak and kidney pudding. And some lemonade. And—"

"Shut up," she said. "Stupid, talking like that. All we got's biscuits. D'you want one or not?"

"Yes."

She leaned forward and gave him a handful of fig rolls. He ate them in small mouthfuls, taking as long as he could to chew each bite.

"Can you see him?" Malcolm said after five minutes.

"Can't even see the house. I reckon we lost him now."

"But he's mad. Mad people, they don't know when to give up."

"You must be mad, then."

He didn't know what to say to that. He paddled on, though the force of the flood was such that all he had to do was steer and keep the boat's head forward.

"He's prob'ly dead by now," Alice said.

"I was thinking that. He was bleeding a lot."

"I think there's an artery there, in his leg. And that dæmon . . ."

"She can't live, surely. Won't be able to move, neither of 'em."

"We better hope they *are* dead."

The clouds overhead parted from time to time and let the brilliant moonlight through—so bright that Malcolm almost had to shade his eyes. Alice sat up and peered even more fiercely at the water behind them, and Malcolm scanned ahead left and right, looking for somewhere to land and rest; but only isolated clumps of bare trees rose above the racing water. He felt as if he had passed beyond exhaustion into a state of trance, and that minutes went by in which his sleeping body paddled and watched and steered without any influence from his dreaming mind.

The only sound was the wind over the flood, except for a tiny insect buzz that came and went. The floodwater must be breeding pestilence, Malcolm thought. "Better be careful to keep mosquitoes and that away from Lyra," he said.

"What mosquitoes? It's far too cold."

"I can hear one."

"That en't a mosquito," she said, sounding scornful, and she nodded at something behind him.

He turned. The bulky clouds had shouldered one another aside, and the moon shone down over the whole waste of water; and in all that wide emptiness there was only one thing that moved with purpose, and that was an engine-boat a long way behind them. He could only see it because it had a searchlight on the bow, and it was getting very slightly closer every minute.

"Is that him?" Malcolm said.

"Can't be. It's too big. He never had a boat with an engine."

"They haven't seen us yet."

"How d'you know that?"

"'Cause they're moving the searchlight all over the place. And they'd be going a lot faster if they wanted to catch us. We'll have to hide, though, 'cause they'll see us if they get any closer."

He bent his back to paddling harder, even though every bone and muscle in his body ached and he longed to cry with fatigue. He would hate to cry in front of Lyra, because to her he was big and strong, and she would have been frightened to see him frightened, or at least he thought so.

So he gritted his teeth and plunged the paddle into the water with his trembling muscles and tried to ignore the whine of the motor, which was not intermittent anymore, but constant and getting louder.

The flood was taking them into an area of hills and woodlands, hills that crowded closer than before and woodlands that were partly bare and partly evergreen. The clouds drifted over the moon again and darkened everything.

"I can't see 'em," said Alice. "They've gone behind that wood. . . . No, there they are."

"How far back are they, d'you think?"

"They'll catch us in about five minutes."

"I'll pull in, then."

"Why?"

"On the water they could just tip us over. On land we got a chance."

"Chance to *what?*"

"Chance to not die, maybe."

In fact, he was terrified, so much so that he could barely move the canoe forward anymore in case he dropped the paddle. There was a wooded slope to their left—dark trees—and what looked in the gloom like a stone embankment, though it was probably the roof of a big house—anyway, he made for that, and then the moon came out again.

It was no rooftop, simply a flat piece of land in front of the wood. Malcolm drove *La Belle Sauvage* up onto the soft soil, and Alice seized Lyra and stepped out almost in one movement. Malcolm leapt out and turned to look for the launch.

Alice, holding Lyra, had retreated further up the slope, but the open space was not very large: close-branched holm oaks with spiked leaves crowded in on all sides. She clung to the baby and watched fearfully for the launch, moving her weight unconsciously from one foot to the other, shivering, breathing quickly, making a little moaning noise in her throat.

Malcolm had never found it so difficult to move; every muscle quivered. He looked up at the close-leafed trees, dark evergreens that were darker than the sky. The moon shone down with what felt like merciless force, but it was unable to penetrate the canopy of the leaves. He hauled and hauled *La Belle Sauvage* up over the stony ground and into the shadow of the trees just as the search-light appeared from behind a thick wood a couple of hundred yards away and swung towards them.

"Don't move," said Malcolm. "Just keep absolutely still."

"Think I'm stupid?" said Alice, but sotto voce.

Then the light was directly shining at them, dazzling, blinding.

Malcolm shut his eyes and stood like a statue. He could hear Alice whispering, desperate for Lyra to stay quiet. Then the light moved away, and the launch moved past.

When it had gone, the fear Malcolm had been holding down since he stabbed Bonneville came back, and he had to lean forward and be sick.

"Don't worry," said Alice. "You'll feel better in a minute."

"Will I?"

"Yeah. You'll see."

He had never heard that tone in her voice before, or ever expected it. Lyra was grizzling. He wiped his mouth and felt in the canoe for the torch. He switched it on and waved it about to distract Lyra. She stopped crying and held out her hands for it.

"No, you can't have it," he said. "I'm going to find some wood and make a fire. You'll like that. When we're warm, we can . . ."

He didn't know how to finish the sentence. He had never felt so frightened. But why? The danger was gone.

"Alice," he said, "are you scared?"

"Yeah. But not much. If it was just me, I would be. But not so much with us both. . . ."

He set off up the little slope towards the wood. The trees clustered so close and thick that he could hardly force his way between them, and when he did, the leaves scratched his hands and his head; but this was a relief. Any activity was a relief. And there were dry branches enough on the ground, and dry sticks, and soon he'd gathered an armful.

But when he came out of the trees, he found Alice on her feet, desperate.

"What is it?"

"They're coming back—"

She pointed. In the direction they'd come from, there was a light on the water—the searchlight—and although it was still some way off, the boat had the air of something official, the police, the CCD; it was searching for something or someone. It was coming, not fast but inexorably, and it would see them very soon.

And at that there was a rustling among the leaves, and the branches parted, and a man stepped out.

"Malcolm," said the man, "get your boat further in the trees, quick. Bring the baby in here out the way. That's the CCD down there. Come on!"

"Mr. Boatwright?" said Malcolm, utterly astonished.

"Yes, that's me. Now hurry up."

While Alice ran with Lyra up to the shelter of the trees, Malcolm untied *La Belle Sauvage* and, with George Boatwright's help, pulled it up the slope and under the low branches before taking Bonneville's rucksack and turning the canoe upside down in case it rained again.

Meanwhile, the boat with the searchlight was getting closer.

"How d'you know it's the CCD?" he whispered.

"They been patrolling. Don't worry. If we keep still and quiet, they won't stop."

"The baby—"

"Drop o' wine'll keep her quiet," said Boatwright, handing something to Alice.

Malcolm looked around. There was no one to see but Boatwright and a score of shadows, but then the moon went in again and the shadows dissolved in a deeper darkness. The boat with its searchlight moved closer.

"Where's Alice?" Malcolm whispered to Asta.

Almost inaudibly his dæmon murmured, "Further in. Giving Lyra a drink."

The men in the boat had seen something that interested them.

The searchlight was turning towards the shore, and then shining straight up into the trees. Malcolm felt as if every inch of him was visible.

"Keep still and they won't see a thing," muttered George Boatwright from the darkness.

A voice from the boat said, "Is that footprints?"

"Where?" said another.

"On the grass. Down there—look."

The searchlight swung down. The voices spoke again more quietly.

"Will they—" Malcolm began to whisper, but Boatwright's hard smoky-smelling hand shut his mouth.

"Don't bother with it," one of the voices said. "Come on."

Then the light swung away and the engine noise rose, and the boat steadily moved away. A minute later it had vanished on the flood.

Boatwright took his hand away. Malcolm could hardly speak. He was shaking in every limb. He stumbled, and Boatwright caught him.

"When'd you last eat or sleep, eh?" he said.

"Can't remember."

"Well, thassit, then. Come along here and have a bit of stew. Eh, your mum'd be proud of a stew like we got in the cave. Want me to carry that?"

The rucksack was heavy, but Malcolm shook his head, and then said, "No," realizing that subtle gestures were lost in the dark. He struggled to put his arms through the straps, and Boatwright helped him. A few paces further on there was a little clearing, where Alice was sitting on a fallen tree trunk with Lyra, who was fast asleep on her lap. She'd been feeding her with a teaspoon from a bottle of wine.

When Alice saw Malcolm, she got to her feet at once and came to his side, Lyra tight in her arms.

"Here, take Lyra. I got to pee. . . ."

She thrust the child at him and darted into the undergrowth. Trembling or not, Malcolm held on to the child as firmly as he could and listened to her contented breathing. "We ought to've given you wine before," he said to her. "You're sleeping like a baby."

Boatwright said, "Five minutes' walk, lad. You want to bring anything else from the canoe?"

"Will it be safe?"

"It's invisible, son. Can't get safer'n that."

"Good. Well . . . there's things for the baby. Alice knows what they are."

She came back at that moment, brushing her skirt down, and having heard what they said, she gathered an armful of things: a pillow, blankets, the saucepan, a packet of nappies, a box of milk powder. . . . But she was trembling as much as Malcolm.

"Spread that blanket out on the ground," said Boatwright, and when she did, he packed everything in the center, gathered in the four corners, and swung the bundle over his shoulder. "Now follow me."

"You all right carrying her?" Alice whispered.

"For a bit, yeah. She's fast asleep."

"We oughter tried wine before. . . ."

"That's what I thought."

"I dunno what effect it'll have on her insides. Here, let me take her. You got that rucksack. Where'd you get it anyway? Is it his?"

"Yeah," said Malcolm. "From his boat."

He was glad to hand the child over, because the rucksack was heavy. He had no idea why he'd taken it, except as something to bargain with. Perhaps they wouldn't need it now. Maybe Bonne-ville was a spy, in which case Dr. Relf would be interested in it.

But that made his throat catch. Just the thought of those cozy afternoons in that warm house, talking about books, hearing about the history of ideas! And he might have to be a fugitive for the rest of his life, an outlaw, like Mr. Boatwright. It was all very well in the flood, when everything was upside down, but when the water re-treated and normal life emerged . . . Well, actually, nothing would be normal and safe ever again.

After some minutes' walking, they came to a larger clearing in front of a rock that rose sheer from the ground. The moon had come out again, and in its silver light they saw the entrance to a cave half hidden behind the undergrowth. The smoke of a fire was drifting through the air, with various good smells of meat and gravy, and the sound of quiet voices.

Mr. Boatwright lifted a heavy sheet of canvas and held it open for Malcolm and Alice. They went in, and all conversation stopped. In the light of a lantern, they saw half a dozen people, men and women and two children, sitting on the floor or on wooden boxes, eating from tin plates. Beside the fire was a large woman whom Malcolm recognized: Mrs. Boatwright.

She saw Alice first and said, "Alice Parslow? That en't you, is it? I know your mam. And you're Malcolm Polstead from the Trout—well, God bless me. What's going on, George?"

George Boatwright said, "Survivors on the flood, they are."

"You can call me Audrey," said the woman, getting to her feet. "And who's this? He? She?"

"She," said Malcolm. "Lyra."

"Well, she needs a clean nappy. We got warm water over here. You got food for her? It'll have to be milk powder—oh, you got some. That'll do. I'll put a saucepan on to boil while you change her and clean her. Then you can both have a bite to eat yourselves. You floated all the way from Oxford? You must be worn out. Eat, then sleep."

"Where are we?" said Malcolm.

"Somewhere in the Chilterns. That's all I know. Safe for the time being. These other folk, they're all like us, in the same position kind of thing, but you don't inquire too close—it en't polite."

"All right," said Alice.

"Thank you," said Malcolm, and went with Alice to a corner of the cave away from the people who were eating.

Audrey Boatwright brought a lantern and hung it up. In its warm light, Alice set about undoing Lyra's sopping clothes and handing the stinking bundle to Malcolm.

"Her dress and everything's all . . . ," he said.

"I'll wrap her in the blanket for now and dress her properly when it's aired out a bit or washed if we can."

Malcolm took the soggy bundle and carefully separated what was to be thrown away and what was to be washed. He looked around, wondering what they did with rubbish, and found a boy of about his own age looking at him.

"You want to know where to throw it?" the boy said. "Come with me. I'll show you. What's your name?"

"Malcolm. What's yours?"

"Andrew. That your sister?"

"What, Alice? No . . ."

"I mean the baby."

"Oh. We're just looking after her in the flood."

"Where you from?"

"Oxford. You?"

"Wallingford. Look, you can throw that in the pit there."

The boy seemed to want to be helpful, but Malcolm wasn't

inclined to talk. All he wanted to do was sleep. Still, on the principle of not making enemies, he let the boy guide him back to the cave and exchanged a question or two.

"Are you here with your parents?" Malcolm asked.

"No. Just my auntie."

"Did you get flooded out?"

"Yeah. Lots of people in our street got drowned. There's never been such a flood since Noah's time, prob'ly."

"Yeah, I wouldn't be surprised. It won't last long, though, I don't suppose."

"Forty days and forty nights."

"You reckon? Oh—yeah," said Malcolm, remembering his Bible lessons.

"What's the baby's name?"

"Lyra."

"Lyra . . . And who's the big girl? Did you say her name was Alice?"

"She's just a friend. Thanks for showing me the pit. G'night."

"Oh, g'night," said Andrew, sounding a little put out.

Alice was feeding Lyra, sitting under the lantern light, looking exhausted. Audrey Boatwright came over with two tin plates heaped with stew and potatoes, steaming hot.

"Give her to me," she said. "I'll finish her off. You need to eat."

Alice handed the child over without a word, and started to eat, as Malcolm had already done. He had never felt so hungry, never felt his hunger so gratified, not even in his mother's kitchen.

He finished the stew and almost immediately felt his eyes closing. But he managed to force himself awake enough to take Lyra from Audrey, who was patting her back, and carry her to where Alice was already curling up on the floor.

"Here," said Mr. Boatwright, handing him a bundle of blankets and canvas bags roughly filled with hay. With the last of his wake-fulness, Malcolm pushed them into shape and laid them side by side, and then, putting Lyra between them, lay down next to Alice and fell at once into the deepest sleep of his life.

And it was Lyra who woke them when the gray light of a wet dawn crept into the cave. Asta sleepily nipped Malcolm's ear, and he came awake like someone struggling to swim to the surface of a lake of laudanum, where the strongest delights were the deepest and there was nothing above but cold and fear and duty.

Lyra was crying, and Asta was trying to comfort Pan, but the little ferret wouldn't be comforted and burrowed closer around Lyra's neck, only irritating her further. Malcolm, heavy-eyed, forced himself up and rocked the child gently to and fro. That didn't help either, so he picked her up.

"You been productive in the night," he whispered. "I never knew such a fountain of manure. I'll have to see if I can do the changing of the guard myself. Alice is still asleep, see."

She was a little happier in his arms, but not much. She whimpered instead of crying fully, and Pan looked out and let Asta lick his nose.

"What you doing?" mumbled Alice, and instantly her dæmon was awake and growling softly.

"'S all right," said Malcolm. "I'm going to change her, that's all."

"You can't," said Alice, sitting up. "You'll do it all wrong."

"Yeah, I prob'ly would," said Malcolm with some relief.

"What's the time?"

"About dawn."

They spoke in the quietest of whispers; neither wanted to wake the other sleepers. Gathering a blanket around her shoulders, Alice crawled to the fire and put another log on the ashy heap, stirring it until she found a few red embers, and put the saucepan on to heat. There was a cask of fresh water nearby; Audrey had said that anyone who used some had to refill it from the spring outside, so she made sure to do that while waiting for the saucepan to heat up.

Meanwhile, Malcolm walked up and down with Lyra. They went to the mouth of the cave and looked out at the rain, heavy, incessant, falling straight down through the sodden air. They looked back into the cave, where sleepers lay on both sides, some alone, some snuggled up together. There were more of them than he'd been aware of the night before; perhaps they'd already been there, fast asleep, or perhaps they'd come in later on. They might have been poaching. If the flood had forced deer and pheasants as well as people high up above their usual dens and nests, there should be plenty of them around to catch.

He whispered all this to Lyra, rocking her from side to side as he walked about. At one point, Asta whispered, "Look at Pan," and Malcolm noticed that the little dæmon, kitten-shaped, was unwittingly kneading the flesh of Malcolm's hand with his tiny claws. Malcolm felt astonished, shy, privileged. The great taboo against touching another's dæmon was not instinctual but learned, then. He felt a wave of love for the child and her dæmon, but that made no difference to them, because Lyra was still grizzling and Pantalaimon soon let go of Malcolm's hand and became a toad.

And then the fear came back. What they'd done to Bonneville . . . When the CCD men in their boat found the dæmon with the shattered leg and the man with a wound in his thigh, they'd have one more reason to hunt Malcolm and Alice down. Was the knife still in the wound? Was Bonneville actually dead? He couldn't remember. Everything had passed with such nightmarish speed.

"Ready," said Alice very quietly behind him, and he nearly leapt in the air with shock. But she didn't laugh. She seemed to know just what he was thinking, and to be thinking the same herself. The look they exchanged in the mouth of the cave before going back to the fire was something Malcolm never forgot: it was deep and complex and close, and it touched every part of him, body and dæmon and ghost.

He knelt beside her, and he and Asta occupied Lyra's attention while Alice washed and dried her.

"You can see her thinking, even though she hasn't got any words," he said.

"Not this end," said Alice shortly.

One or two sleepers were beginning to stir as the light grew stronger. Malcolm took the bundle to be thrown away and tried to move very quietly as he carried it out to the pit the boy had shown him.

"I didn't see him in the cave," Asta whispered.

"Perhaps he sleeps somewhere else."

They found the rubbish pit and hurried back because the rain was drenching. When they got there, Audrey was holding Lyra, who seemed comfortable enough, even if a little doubtful, while Alice prepared the milk.

"Who's her mother?" Audrey said, settling herself next to the fire.

"We don't know," said Malcolm. "She was being looked after by the nuns at Godstow, so she must be someone important."

"Oh, I know the ones you mean," said Audrey. "Sister Benedicta."

"Yes, she's in charge. But it was Sister Fenella who looked after her mostly."

"What happened?"

"The priory collapsed in the flood. We just got her out in time. Then we got swept away."

"So you don't know who her family is?"

"No," said Malcolm. He was getting better at lying.

Audrey handed the child over to Alice, who had the bottle ready. A little way off, Mr. Boatwright stood up and stretched and went out of the cave, and others were stirring.

"Who is everyone?" said Malcolm. "Is it all your family?"

"There's my son, Simon, and his wife and two little kids. The others are . . . just others."

"There's a boy called Andrew. I spoke to him last night."

"Yes, he's Doris Whicher's nephew. That's Doris over there by the big rock. They come from Wallingford way. My, she's hungry, en't she?" she said admiringly, watching Lyra's lusty guzzling.

Doris Whicher was still asleep. There was no sign of Andrew.

"I don't suppose we'll stay long," said Malcolm. "Just till the rain's stopped."

"You stay as long as you need to. You'll be safe here. No one knows about this place. There's a few of us got reason to be careful who knows where they are, and we en't lost anyone yet."

Mr. Boatwright came out of the rain carrying a dead chicken.

"Know how to pluck a chicken, Malcolm?" he said.

Actually, Malcolm did, because of watching Sister Fenella doing it in the priory kitchen. He'd done it once or twice in his mother's kitchen too. He took the bird, a scrawny item, and set to work while Mr. Boatwright sat down and stirred the fire up before lighting a pipe.

"What'd they say after I vanished, eh?" he said. "Anyone guess where I'd gone?"

"No," said Malcolm. "They all said you were the only person that had ever got away from the CCD. And the officers came back the next day and asked a lot of questions, but no one said anything, except one or two said you had evil dark powers, like making yourself invisible, and the CCD had no hope of finding you, ever."

Mr. Boatwright laughed so much he had to put his pipe down.

"Hear that, Audrey?" he wheezed. "Invisible!"

"I wish you was inaudible sometimes," she said.

"No," he went on, "I been preparing for summat like that. You got to have an escape route, no matter where you are. Always have an escape route. And when the time comes, don't hesitate a single second. Eh, Audrey? We had our escape route and we took it that same night the bastards come to the Trout."

"Did you come straight here?"

"In a manner of speaking. There's hidden pathways and hidden refuges, all across the woods, all across Oxfordshire and Gloucestershire and Berkshire and beyond. You could go from Bristol to London by them hidden pathways and no one'd ever know you were doing it."

"What happened when the flood came?"

"Ah, all we done was go up higher. This spot where we are now is the highest piece of land in Berkshire. We know all the shortcuts and the shallow ways and the deep ways. We can always slip away and they'll never catch us. And the water's on our side, not theirs."

"I don't understand," said Malcolm, turning the chicken over.

"The creatures in the water, Malcolm. I don't mean fish neither, nor water voles; I mean the old gods. Old Father Thames, I seen him a few times, with his crown and his weeds and his trident. He's on our side. The bloody CCD, they won't never win against Old Father Thames. And other beings as well. There was a man with us, he saw a mermaid near Henley. The sea was so full she come right up the river, even that far from the coast, and this chap, he swore to me that if he saw that mermaid again, he'd go off with her. Well, two days later he disappeared, and chances are he did just that. I believe it, anyway."

"If that was Tom Simms," said Audrey, "I'd say he was probably drunk and his mermaid was a porpoise."

"She weren't a porpoise. He spoke to her, didn't he? And she spoke back. She had a voice sweeter than a chime of bells, he said. Ten to one he's living with her now, out in the German Ocean."

"He'll be bloody cold if he is," said Audrey. "Here, give me that chicken. I'll finish it off."

Malcolm had made a reasonable job of it, he thought, but he was glad to let her take over. His hands were numb with cold and he couldn't grip the smaller feathers.

"Get yourself some bread from the bin over there," Audrey told him. "There's cheese in the bin next to it."

The bins were galvanized steel dustbins. In the first one, there were three and a half heavy loaves, hard and stale, and a knife to cut them with. Malcolm cut a thick slice for himself and another for Alice, and carved some cheese to go with them as the woman Doris Whicher woke up nearby and looked around blearily.

"Andrew?" she said. "Where's Andrew?"

"I haven't seen him this morning," Malcolm said.

She rolled over and sat up in a thick smell of alcohol. "Where's he gone?"

"I saw him last night."

"Who are you, then?"

"Malcolm Polstead," he told her. There was no point in giving himself a false name, since Mr. Boatwright knew exactly who he was.

Doris Whicher groaned and lay down again, and Malcolm took the bread and cheese over to Alice. Audrey Boatwright was holding Lyra up and patting her back, and Lyra obliged with a fine expression of wind. Malcolm sat down to gnaw at the bread and cheese and found it hard going, but his stomach was glad of the effort his teeth were making.

And then, once he was able to sit and relax, the realization came back: he had killed Bonneville. He and Alice, they were murderers. The dreadful word was stamped on his mind as if by a printing press on a sheet of paper, and the ink was red. Asta became a moth and flew from his shoulder to Alice's dæmon, and Ben tilted his head as Asta whispered to him. Mrs. Boatwright was walking up and down, showing Lyra to the people who were just waking, and someone else was attending to the chicken, gutting it and jointing it and sprinkling it with flour. If that was going to feed everyone in the cave, Malcolm thought, trying to distract himself, there wouldn't be much on anyone's plate.

But Alice had moved closer, and she was leaning in to whisper something.

"Mr. Boatwright . . . D'you trust him?"

"I . . . think so. Yes."

"'Cause we didn't ought to stay here much longer."

"I think so too. And there's a boy . . ."

He told her about Andrew. She frowned.

"And he en't here now?"

"No. I'm a bit worried."

At that moment, Andrew's aunt stumbled up to the fire and sat down heavily. Alice glared at her. Doris Whicher didn't notice; she was in the throes of a hangover, and the smell of liquor was so strong that Malcolm thought she ought to breathe more carefully near the fire. Her crow dæmon kept falling down and scrabbling up again.

Then she looked at Malcolm and said, "Who was asking me about Andrew? Was it you?"

"Yes. I didn't know where he was."

"Why d'you want to know?"

"'Cause we were talking last night and he said something interesting and I was going to ask him about it."

"Is it that bloody league?"

Every nerve in Malcolm's body sprang awake.

"The League of St. Alexander? Is he a member?"

"Yeah, little bastard. If I says to him once—"

Malcolm got up at once, and Alice, seeing his urgency, followed.

"We got to go," he said. "Right now."

Alice ran to Audrey Boatwright, who was talking to another woman near the cave entrance, jogging Lyra comfortably on her bosom. Malcolm looked around and saw George Boatwright bending some sticks together to make a trap.

"Mr. Boatwright—sorry to disturb you—but we've got to go right away. Can you show us the path down—"

"Don't worry about that CCD boat," said Boatwright confidently. "Chances are, they—"

"No, it's not them. We got to get Lyra away before—"

But there were loud voices behind him. He turned swiftly to see Alice trying to get between Mrs. Boatwright and a man in a dark uniform, and three other men behind him spread out to prevent anyone leaving the cave. And lurking behind them, half ashamed, half proud, was Andrew.

Malcolm ran to help Alice, who was trying to pull Lyra from Audrey Boatwright's arms. But then one of the men grabbed Alice by the neck, and he was shouting, and Malcolm was shouting too, and he didn't know what he was saying. Audrey was trying to shelter Lyra, turning away, trying to move back into the cave, and Mr. Boatwright was trying to help her, and Lyra was screaming in fear. At one moment, Malcolm reached Mrs. Boatwright and had his hands on Lyra and began to lift her away, and the next moment came a shocking blow on his head and he fell sprawling half conscious to the ground; and Alice was biting the arms that held her, and lashing out with both feet, and screaming.

Malcolm dragged himself to his knees, dizzy and weak and almost totally confused. Through the tumult of voices, one voice cried out to him with perfect clarity, that of Lyra, and he called back, "Lyra! Lyra! I'm coming!"

But a heavy weight crashed into him and knocked him flat again. It was Audrey Boatwright, who had lost hold of Lyra and been knocked off her feet by one of the men. Malcolm struggled to get out from under her body, but it was so hard, because she was struggling too, and then he found himself on his knees again, and Alice was lying still on the ground, and so was George Boatwright. Someone was wailing and crying, but it wasn't Lyra; someone else a long way off was shouting, a woman's voice, incoherent with rage and helplessness. Audrey Boatwright began to sob as she found her husband unconscious beside her.

But the dark-uniformed men were gone, and Lyra was gone with them.

TWENTY

THE SISTERS OF HOLY OBEDIENCE

Malcolm tried to step forward, but the cave was revolving in his vision. He missed his footing, found it again, and then fell over completely and nearly vomited. Asta was whispering hoarsely, "It's the blow on the head—you can't stand up yet—lie down and keep still." But he was possessed by a frenzy of fear and rage, and he struggled to get to his feet.

There was Andrew, smiling nervously, but with a righteous smugness in his expression too. He put up his hands in defense. Malcolm knocked them aside and hit him hard in the face, so that he fell over, crying, "Auntie! Auntie!"

"What you done?" said his aunt, but Malcolm didn't know whether she was speaking to him or to Andrew. Perhaps she didn't know either.

Malcolm kicked the boy, and he rolled away, curled up like a wood louse.

"Who were those men?" Malcolm shouted. "Where were they going?"

"None of your— Argh!" cried Andrew as Malcolm kicked him again.

Finally Doris Whicher realized what was happening and hauled Malcolm away.

"Who were they?" Malcolm roared, struggling against the fat arms and the reek of alcohol. "Where are they taking Lyra?"

Andrew had rolled out of reach and tried to stand up, making the most of the blows Malcolm had landed, wincing, limping, touching his face with delicate fingers.

"I think you broke my jaw—"

Malcolm stamped on Doris's foot, and then Alice was there too, slapping and scratching at the boy, then turning to haul at his aunt's shaking arms as they tried to hold on to Malcolm, who tore himself free and rushed to corner Andrew against the rocky wall of the cave. The boy's mouse dæmon was squealing and screaming as she cowered behind his feet.

"No! Don't hit me!"

"Just tell me who they were."

"CCD!"

"Liar. It was the wrong uniform. Who were they?"

"I don't know! I thought they were CCD—"

"Where did you go to find them?"

By this time the other adults had come round to watch and encourage one side or the other. Some of them had not been awake when the men came and needed to have it explained, and George Boatwright was still unconscious, and Audrey was anxiously crying his name as she knelt beside him, so the cave was full of hubbub.

Andrew was sobbing. Malcolm turned away in disgust and sank to his knees, but Asta, cat-shaped, leapt at Andrew's mouse dæmon and bore her to the ground. And there was Ben, hair bristling, growling at the boy with a bulldog ferocity.

But Alice was tugging at Malcolm's arm and making him stand up, so he turned away from the dæmons for a moment.

"Listen," she said, "listen to this man."

The man was small and wiry and dark-haired, and his dæmon was a vixen.

"I seen them uniforms before," he said. "They en't CCD. They're called summing like the Security of the Holy Spirit, summing like that. They guard religious places—seminaries, nunneries, schools, that sort of place. They prob'ly come from Wallingford, from the priory there."

"A priory?" said Malcolm. "With monks or nuns?"

"Nuns," said someone else, a woman whom Malcolm couldn't see. "The Sisters of Holy Obedience."

"How d'you know?" said the man.

"I used to work for 'em," she said, coming out of the shadows and into the gray light near the entrance of the cave. "For the sisters. I used to clean and look after the chickens and the goats."

"Where are they? Where is this place?" said Malcolm.

"Down Wallingford," she said. "You wouldn't miss it. Big white stone buildings."

"And who are these sisters? What do they do?" said Alice, her face pale, her eyes blazing.

"They pray. They teach. They look after kids. I dunno . . . they're fierce."

"Fierce? How?" said Malcolm.

"Stern. Very stern and cruel. I couldn't bear it, so I left," the woman said.

"I seen them guards catching a kid what run away," said the man. "They beat him right there in the street till he fainted. No use trying to interfere—they got all the power they need."

"Is that what you did, then?" said Malcolm, turning to Andrew. "You went and told them about us and the baby?"

Andrew whimpered and wiped his nose on his sleeve.

"Tell 'em, boy," said his aunt. "Stop sniveling."

"I don't want him to hit me again," said Andrew.

"I won't hit you. Just tell us what you did."

"I'm in the league. I had to do what's right."

"Never mind the league. What did you do?"

"I knew you never oughter been looking after a kid that en't yours. You prob'ly stole her or summing. So I told the Office of Child Protection. They came in our school and explained why it was right to tell 'em things like that. I don't know nothing about this Security of the Holy Spirit; I never heard of them. It was the Office of Child Protection."

"Where are they?"

"In the priory."

"Isn't the priory flooded like everywhere else?"

"No, 'cause it's on a hill."

"Who's in charge there?"

"The Mother Superior."

"So you went and told her, did you?"

"The Child Protection people took me to see her. It was the right thing to do," he said quaveringly, beginning to wail.

His aunt hit him, and he choked back his wail with a sniveling cough.

"What did she say, the Mother Superior?" Malcolm demanded.

"She wanted to know who the kid was and where we were and all that. I told her everything I knew. I had to."

"And then what?"

"We said a prayer and then she give me a bed to sleep on for a bit, and then I guided 'em back here."

In the face of the hostility and contempt of almost everyone in the cave, Andrew crumpled and fell to the floor, curled up and sobbing. Almost everyone, because George Boatwright was still unconscious, and Audrey was now increasingly frightened. She knelt beside him, rubbing his hand, stroking his head, calling his name, and looking around to everyone there for help.

Alice saw her and knelt to see if she could do anything, while Malcolm continued to question Andrew.

"Where is this priory? How far away?"

"Dunno . . ."

"Did you walk there and back, or go in a boat?"

"In a boat. Their boat."

"It's not far," said the woman who'd worked there. "It's the highest place. You can't miss it."

"Have they got lots of kids there?" Malcolm asked her.

"Yeah, all ages. From babies right up to sixteen, I suppose."

"What do they do? Teach them, or make them work, or what?"

"Teach 'em, yeah. . . . They prepare them for lives as servants, that kind of thing."

"Boys and girls?"

"Yeah, boys and girls, but after ten years old they keep 'em apart."

"And the babies, do they keep them apart from the rest?"

"There's a nursery just for the young ones, yes."

"How many babies have they got there?"

"Oh, Lord, I don't know. . . . In my time, there was about fifteen or sixteen. . . ."

"Are they all orphans?"

"No. Sometimes if a child is really badly behaved, they take them in. They never get out till they're sixteen. They never see their parents again."

"How many kids altogether, then? Babies and older ones?"

"A hundred, maybe . . ."

"Don't they ever try to escape?"

"They might escape once, but they're always caught, and they never dare to do it again."

"So they're cruel, these nuns?"

"You wouldn't believe how cruel they can be. You wouldn't believe it."

"You—Andrew," said Malcolm. "Have you told on any other kids and got them taken in there?"

"I en't saying," the boy mumbled.

"Tell the truth, you little shit," his aunt said.

"No, I en't, then!"

"Never?" said Malcolm.

"It en't your busi—"

His aunt slapped him. His voice rose in a high wail.

"All right, maybe I have!" he cried.

"Little sneaking shit," she said.

"Who do you speak to when you go to report someone?" said Malcolm, desperately trying to keep his focus. His head was throbbing, and waves of nausea came and went. "Where did you go last night? Who did you speak to?"

"Brother Peter. I en't s'posed to tell you this."

"I don't care what you're s'posed to tell. Who's Brother Peter, and where did you go to find him?"

"He's the director of the Office of Child Protection for Wallingford. They got an office at the priory."

"And he knew you because you'd been to him before?"

At that, Andrew just buried his head in his arms and howled.

There were voices behind Malcolm, excited and relieved, and he turned to see, but felt a bout of pain and nausea in his head as he did, so brutal it was like being hit again. He kept still, knowing that the slightest movement of his head would mean being violently sick.

Alice was beside him, holding his arm.

"Lean on me," she said. "And come over this way."

He did as she told him.

"Lyra," he muttered.

"We know where she is, and she en't going anywhere else. You can't move now, else you'll be sick. Just sit down here."

Her voice was quiet and gentle, and that was so surprising that he let himself be led and tended to.

"Mr. Boatwright's woken up," she said. "He had a crack on the nut, like you did, only worse. Audrey thought he was dead, but he en't. Just keep still now."

"Here," said a woman's voice, and then, "Let him sip this."

"Thank you," said Alice. "Here, Mal, sit up a bit and sip this. But mind, it's hot."

Mal! She had never called him Mal. No one had. He wouldn't let anyone but Alice call him that now. The drink was scalding, and he could only take the smallest sip. It tasted like lemon, the sort of cold remedy his mother sometimes gave him, but there was something else in it.

"I put a bit of ginger with it," the woman said. "Stops you feeling sick. Otherwise, it's a painkiller."

"Thank you," he murmured. He had no idea how he'd had the energy to interrogate Andrew only a minute before.

He sipped a little more of the drink and fell asleep.

It was dark again when he woke up. He was warm, and covered in something heavy with a doggish animal smell. He moved a little, and his head didn't punish him for it, so he moved a little more and sat up.

"Mal," Alice said at once from beside him. "You all right now?"

"Yeah, I think so," he said.

"Stay there. I'll get you some bread and cheese."

She scrambled up, which showed him that she'd been lying beside him. She was more and more surprising. He lay there, slowly waking up, letting the memory of the last day and night slowly wake up too. Then he remembered what had happened to Lyra, and sat up with a convulsive shock. Alice was holding out something for him.

"Here y'are," she said, putting a hunk of bread in his hand. "It's hard, but it en't moldy. D'you want an egg? I can fry you an egg if you like."

"No, thanks. Alice, did we really . . . ," he whispered, unable to say any more.

"Bonneville?" she whispered back. "Yeah, we did. But hush about that. Don't say nothing. It's over."

Malcolm tried to bite a piece off the hunk of bread and found it so hard that it was a serious challenge to his teeth, and thus to the pain in his head. Still, he persevered. Alice appeared again with a mug of something strong and salty.

"What's this?"

"Some sort of stock cube. I dunno. It'll do you good."

"Thank you," he said, and took a sip. "Has it been night for a long time?"

"No. There's people out there poaching or summing. It en't been dark long."

"Where's Andrew?"

"His auntie's guarding him. He won't get out again."

"We got to—" He tried to swallow a lump of bread, and then retrieved it and chewed it a bit more before trying again and continuing hoarsely, "We've got to rescue Lyra."

"Yeah. I been thinking about that."

"First we got to look at the priory."

"And," she said, "we got to know exactly what Andrew told 'em about us."

"D'you think he'd ever tell us the truth?"

"I could get it out of him."

"He's not reliable. He'd say anything to avoid getting hit."

"I'll hit him anyway."

He chewed another mouthful of bread.

"I'd like to ask that lady who worked there," he said. "About where everything is, where the nursery is, how to get there, all that."

"I'll go and get her."

She leapt to her feet and hurried to the fire, where a number of people were sitting and drinking and talking and occasionally stirring a big pot of stew.

Malcolm struggled to sit up a bit higher, and found that although his headache had receded, a number of other aches, all over his body, had come out to claim his attention. He chewed off another piece of cheese and concentrated on that.

Soon Alice came back with the woman who'd spoken up before. Her dæmon was a ferret, who sat nibbling constantly on her shoulder.

"This is Mrs. Simkin," said Alice.

"Hello, Mrs. Simkin," said Malcolm, trying to swallow the cheese, and having to soften it with a sip of the stock-cube drink. "We want to know all about this priory."

"You en't thinking of trying to get in and rescue her?" she said, sitting down nearby. Her hand kept going up to stroke her dæmon, who was very nervous.

"Well, yes," said Malcolm. "We got to. There's no question about it."

"You can't," she said. "It's like a fortress. You'll never get in."

"Well, all right. But what's it like when you *are* in? Where do they keep the kids?"

"There's the nursery—that's where the little ones sleep and get looked after. That's upstairs near where the nuns have their cells."

"*Cells?*" said Alice.

"That's what they call their bedrooms," explained Malcolm. "Can you draw a plan?" he said to the woman.

But she was so doubtful and uneasy that he realized she couldn't read or write, and had no idea of the principles of maps or plans of any sort. He felt embarrassed for asking, and went on quickly: "How many flights of stairs is there?"

"There's one at the front, a big one, and a small one at the back for the cleaners and servants, people like me. And there's another, but I never seen it. Sometimes they have guests—men too—and it wouldn't be right for them to mingle with the nuns, or the servants neither, so they have their own staircase. But that only goes up to the guest rooms, and they're shut off from the rest of the place."

"Right. Now, when you go up the servants' staircase, what do you come to at the top?"

The woman's dæmon whispered to her. She listened and then said, "He's just reminding me. On the first floor there's a small landing and a door that opens on a corridor where the nursery is."

"Anything else in that corridor?"

"There's two cells on the opposite side from the nursery. Whichever nuns are on duty with the little kids, they sleep in there."

"What's the nursery like?"

"It's a big room, with about . . . I dunno, maybe twenty or so beds and cribs."

"Are there that many little kids?"

"Not always. There's usually a bed or two empty, in case any new kids arrive."

"How old are the kids in there?"

"Up to four, I think. Then they're moved to the main block.

The nursery's in the kitchen block, like, right over the kitchen on the ground floor."

"Is there anything else besides the nursery on that corridor?"

"There's two bathrooms on the right, before you get to the nursery. Oh, and an airing cupboard for blankets and that."

"And the cells are on the left?"

"That's right."

"So there's only two nuns looking after the kids?"

"There's another one sleeping in the nursery itself."

The mouse dæmon whispered again.

"Don't forget," the woman said, "they get up ever so early for the services."

"Oh, yeah. I remember. They did that at Godstow."

He thought there wouldn't be much time to find Lyra and get out again, even if he could get in. And all it would take to give them away would be a nervous child crying out at the presence of strangers in the nursery. . . .

He asked the woman about the arrangement of doors and windows in the kitchen, and anything else he could think of. The more he heard, the more difficult it seemed, and the more despondent he became.

"Well, thank you," he said. "That's all very useful."

The woman nodded and went back to the fire.

"What we gonna do?" said Alice quietly.

"Get in and rescue her. But suppose there's twenty kids the same age all lying asleep—how could we tell which was her?"

"Well, *I'd* recognize her. She's unmistakable."

"When she's awake, yeah. Pan would recognize Asta, and Ben too. But if she's asleep . . . We can't wake 'em all up."

"I won't mistake her. Nor will you, actually."

"Let's go now, then."

"You all right to do that?"

"Yes. I'm feeling much better."

In fact, Malcolm was still aching and a little dizzy, but the thought of lounging in the cave while Lyra was captive was too horrible to bear. He stood up slowly and took a step or two towards the entrance, going carefully, making no fuss, saying nothing. Alice was gathering their possessions and wrapping them in the blanket as Boatwright had.

Once they were outside, he said softly to Alice, "Those biscuits she likes—are they still in the canoe?"

"Well, we didn't bring 'em up here. They must be."

"We can give her one of them to keep her quiet."

"Yeah, if . . ."

"Keep a watch out for Andrew."

"Can you remember the way to the canoe?"

"If we keep going down, we'll get there eventually."

That was what he hoped anyway. Even if George Boatwright had fully recovered, which he probably hadn't yet, it wouldn't have been a good idea to ask him to guide them down. He'd have wanted to know where they were going and what they planned to do, and he'd have told them not to.

Malcolm stopped thinking about that. He was discovering a new power in himself: he was able to stop thinking things he didn't want to think. Quite often, he realized as he led the way down the moonlit path, he had pushed aside thoughts of his mother and father and how they must be suffering, wondering where he was, whether he was still alive, how he'd ever find his way back against the flood. He did it again now. It was dark under the holm oaks, so it didn't matter if he made a face of anguish. He could stop that too after a few seconds.

"There's the water," said Alice.

"Let's go carefully. There might be another boat snooping around. . . ."

They stood still just inside the darkness of the trees, watching and listening. The expanse of water was clear ahead of them, and the only sound was its rush against the grass and the bushes.

Malcolm was trying to remember whether they'd left the boat on the left or right of the path.

"D'you remember where . . ."

"There it is now—look," she said.

She was pointing to the left, and as soon as he followed her line of sight, he saw it. The canoe was barely concealed at all, and yet it had been invisible a moment before. The moon was so bright that everything under the trees was caught in a net of confusing shadows.

"You can see better'n I can," he said, and pulled the boat out onto the grass, checking all around and turning her the right way up. He was tender with her, feeling all along her hull, checking that all the hoop brackets were firm, counting the hoops themselves as they lay inside the canoe, making sure the tarpaulin was folded and stowed away neatly. It was all shipshape, and the skin of the hull was undamaged, though the neat gyptian paintwork was a bit scratched.

He pushed her down to the water, and once again he felt as if this inanimate thing was joyously coming alive as she met her own element.

He held the gunwale as Alice got in, and then handed her the rucksack he'd taken from the dead Bonneville.

"Blimey, this is heavy," she said. "What's *in* here?"

"Haven't had time to look. As soon as we've got Lyra and found somewhere safe to stop, we'll open it up and see. Ready?"

"Yeah, go on."

She wrapped a blanket around her thin shoulders and kept watch behind as he began to paddle. The moon was brilliant, the water one sheet of fast-flowing glass. Malcolm felt good to be paddling again, despite his bruises, and he worked their way steadily to the center of the flood. The only sense of speed he had was the cold air against his face and the occasional tremor of the hull as some obstruction far below raised a slight wave in the water.

He had a thousand misgivings. If they were to miss the priory, they would never be able to work their way back against the power of the water. And if they got there and found it guarded? Or impossible to get inside? And suppose . . . And so on. But he thrust all those thoughts aside.

On they sped, and the moon continued to shine. Alice continually scanned the stream behind, on both sides, and as far back as the horizon; but she saw no other boats, no sign of life at all. They said little. Since their fight with Bonneville, something large had changed in the relationship between them, and it wasn't just that she'd started calling him Mal. A wall of hostility had fallen down and vanished. They were friends now. It was easy to sit together.

Something ahead was gleaming, on the horizon, nowhere near yet.

"Is that a light, d'you reckon?" he said, pointing.

She turned and looked.

"Could be. But it looks more like summing's just white, with the moon shining on it."

And there it was again: the spangled ring, his personal aurora. It was so familiar now that he almost welcomed it, in spite of the difficulty it caused in seeing things behind it. And right inside the lovely celestial curve as it grew was the thing Alice mentioned, the great building gleaming white under the moon.

They were going so fast that it soon became clear that she was right: a large building, something like a castle, rising out of the water; but it wasn't a castle because instead of a great keep at the heart of it, there rose the spire of an oratory.

"That's it!" Malcolm said.

"It's bloody immense," she said.

It lay on the left as they floated swiftly towards it. It was built of a light stone that shone almost like snow in the glare of the moon, a vast spreading complex of walls and roofs and buttresses, all surrounding the slender spire. Black windows pierced the flat blank cliffs of white, occasionally flashing a reflection of the moon as the canoe floated by. It was just as bright and just as black as the scintillations on the spangled ring, which was now close enough to be almost out of sight behind him. The building had no windows low enough to climb into, no doors at all, no flights of steps; just immense vertical sheets of white stone, with any break in the smoothness high above anything they could reach from the level of the water. Like a fortress, it seemed designed to repel any attempt to get inside.

Malcolm was holding the canoe back now, trying to resist the power of the flood, and *La Belle Sauvage* responded sweetly. She could almost dance on the water, Malcolm thought, and he stroked the gunwale with love.

"Can you see a way in?" Alice said quietly.

"Not yet. But we won't be going in through the front door anyway."

"S'pose not. . . . It's bloody huge. It goes on and on."

Malcolm was turning the canoe to port to go around and see how far the building extended. As they left the moon behind and passed into the great shadow of the walls, he felt a chill, though he'd been cold enough already, and to be sure, the moon gave no warmth. They were out of the main current here, and he could bring the canoe closer and look up at the towering walls, to see if there was any way in at all, but it seemed to be impossible.

"What's that?" said Alice.

"What?"

"Listen."

He kept still and heard a soft, continual splashing a little way ahead. There was what looked like a broad stone buttress there, running the full height of the wall, and at the top it continued into a stack of chimneys, with the moon shining brightly on them. He thought, They must have a kitchen somewhere, so maybe it's here. . . . And then he saw what was splashing. A square opening near the foot of the wall, in which an iron grating hung loosely, was letting a stream of water spill out and fall in a steady arc.

"Toilets," said Alice.

"No. I don't think so. It's quite clean, look, and it doesn't smell. . . . Must be an overflow or summing."

He paddled on to the next corner, slowly and silently. They were still in the shadow of the moon, but he knew that anything moving attracted the eye, and there were no bushes or reeds to hide among: just the bare water and the bare stone. They would be very easy to see. With infinite caution he edged the canoe past the corner of the great building and looked along what must have been the front.

Alice was gripping the gunwales and peering as hard as she could in the deceptive light. Malcolm turned the boat sideways so that anyone looking from that direction would have had a much smaller silhouette to see. Roughly halfway along the front there was a wide row of steps, surmounted by a portico where classical columns supported a pediment. . . . Was that a figure among the columns?

Alice was twisting right round to look at it. Then she whispered, "There's a man—two men—look, they got a boat. . . ."

There was a powerboat tied up at the base of the steps, and Alice was right: there were two men. As Malcolm looked, they stepped idly out of the line of columns and talked together. They were smoking and had rifles over their shoulders.

With even more care than before, Malcolm maneuvered the canoe around the corner and out of sight.

"What did the man in the cave call them?" he whispered. "The Security of the Holy Spirit—they guard nunneries and monasteries and that. . . . So we can't go in that way."

He looked up at the chimneys again, and an idea came to him.

"If this is the kitchen, right, just inside this wall, 'cause of the chimneys—well, you know in the priory? In Godstow?" He was suddenly excited. "In the old room they called the scullery?"

"I never went in there."

"It's ever so old, and they got this ancient drain—it comes out of a spring, and it runs in a sort of stone channel right across the floor and out the other side, into the river. Sister Fenella sometimes used to throw her washing-up water in it—"

"You think this is summing like that?"

"It could be. This water's clean."

"It's got a bloody great iron grating across it."

"Here, take the paddle and hold the boat up close to it. . . ."

When she had it steady, he stood up and gripped the iron grille, and at once it came loose, in a shower of stone dust and mortar, and fell with a loud splash between the canoe and the wall.

"Blimey!" he said, steadying himself.

"We can't go in there!"

"Why not?"

"Well, for one thing, we wouldn't be able to get out again. There's nothing to tie the boat up to. And s'pose there's another grating at the top, where it comes out the kitchen or the scullery or wherever it is? Anyway, we'd get soaked. It's freezing."

"I'm going to try. You'll have to stay here with the canoe. Just hold it steady and keep warm and wait."

"You can't—" she began, and then bit her lip. "You'll drown, Mal."

"If it gets too difficult, I'll come back and we'll think of something else. Stay close to the wall. Tuck it in close to the chimney stack. I'll be as quick as I can."

He gripped the gunwale of the canoe and thought, Look after her, *Belle Sauvage*.

Then he stood up again and reached up to the opening and took hold of the stone rim. The stream of water wasn't great in volume, but it was cold and it was continuous, and by the time he'd managed to pull himself up, he was soaked to the skin. Asta was already inside the drain as an otter, with her teeth in his sleeve, pulling and pulling, and finally the two of them lay panting on the floor of the drain, trying to keep to one side, out of the flow of water.

"Get up," she said. "You can crawl. It's high enough for that. . . ."

His shins were scraped, his fingernails broken. He knelt gingerly and found, as she said, that there was room to crawl. Asta became some kind of night-dwelling beast and clung to his back, her wide eyes taking in every tiny flicker of light. Before long, though, there was no light left, and they were crawling upwards in total darkness, and Malcolm found himself beginning to get badly frightened. He thought of the great weight of stone above them; he wanted to stand up; he wanted to raise his arms above his head; he wanted much more space than there was. . . .

He was near panic, but Asta whispered, "Not far now— honestly—I can see the light of the kitchen—just a little further—"

"But suppose—"

"Don't suppose anything. Just breathe deeply."

"Can't help shivering—"

"No, but keep going. There's bound to be a range in the kitchen burning all night. Big place like this. You can get warm in a minute.

Just push the thoughts aside, like we learned how to do. Keep going—thassit. . . ."

His hands and legs were numb with cold, but not so numb that he couldn't feel a lot of pain in them under the numbness.

"How are we going to get Lyra down here—"

"We'll find a way. There is a way. We just don't know it yet. Don't stop. . . ."

And after another desperate minute, his eyes began to see what he'd disbelieved that hers could: a glimmer of light on the wet sides of the tunnel.

"There you are," she said.

"Yeah—just hope there isn't—"

A grating at the top like there is at the bottom, he was going to say. But of course there was: if something fell into the drain, the kitchen workers wouldn't want it to disappear. He nearly despaired at that point. Dark bars of iron stood heavy and still between him and the dimly lit scullery beyond. There was no way through. He choked back a sob.

"No, wait," said Asta. She was a rat now, and she scampered up the grating and examined it closely. "They'll need to clean the drain sometimes—they'll need to get brushes and things down here. . . ."

Malcolm pulled himself together. One more sob, of cold as much as of despair, shook his chest, but after that he said, "Yeah, that's right. Maybe . . ."

He gripped the bars, shook them, felt them move. They swung back and forth a tiny way.

"Is there a—at the top—"

"A hinge—yes!"

"So down at the bottom . . ."

Malcolm put his arm through the grating and felt around and, as simply as that, found a heavy iron bolt lying across the bars just above the water, the end deep in a hole in the stone. It was well greased, and it slid out with no effort. The grating swung up towards the kitchen, and Malcolm's numb and trembling hands found a catch above that held it firmly.

A moment later he had scrambled underneath and into the room, which was, as he'd guessed, a scullery, with sinks for washing and racks for drying crockery. After the darkness of the drain, his eyes welcomed the dim light that let him see everything there. The stream ran across the floor, just like the one at Godstow, in a channel lined with bricks. And, mercy of all mercies, there was a range, slumbering but alight, and above it a rack of warming towels, hanging there to dry after having been washed. He tugged off his sweater and his shirt and wrapped a large towel around his shoulders, huddling near the range, rocking back and forth as the cold gradually left his body.

"I'll never be warm again," said Malcolm. "And if I'm shivering like this, I'll never keep quiet in that nursery looking for Lyra. Are you sure we'll recognize her? Babies are all pretty much the same, en't they?"

"I'll recognize Pan, and he'll recognize me."

"If you say so . . . We can't stay here for long."

He was thinking of Alice. It must be nerve-racking for her outside on the water, with nowhere to hide. He dragged his shirt and sweater back on, wet as they were, and shivered again violently.

"Come on, then," said Asta. "Oh, look! That box . . ."

She was a cat now. The box she meant was a wooden thing of the sort that might have contained apples.

"What about . . . Oh, yeah! Right!"

It was big enough for Lyra. If he lined it with towels, she might stay dry as he pulled her down the drain. He dragged some towels off the rack and laid them inside it, ready for her.

"Let's go, then," he said.

He opened the scullery door and listened. Silence. Then, from high above and some way off, a deep bell rang three times. He tiptoed along the stone corridor, making, he hoped, for the back staircase. There were dim anbaric lamps along the wall, which was otherwise bare and whitewashed, with doors to the left and right.

Then the bell rang again, much louder than before, and he heard a choir singing, as if the door to a chapel or an oratory had opened. He looked around—there was nowhere to hide. The singing got louder still, and then to his horror a line of nuns, hands pressed together and eyes lowered, came around a corner and straight towards him. Evidently, like the Godstow nuns, they got up at all times of the night to sing and pray. He was caught. There was nothing he could do but stand and shiver and lower his head.

Someone stopped in front of him. He kept his head low, so all he could see were her sandaled feet and the hem of her habit.

"Who are you, boy? What are you doing?"

"I wet me bed, miss. Sister. Then I got lost."

He tried to sound sorry for himself, and in truth it wasn't hard. He sniffed and wiped his nose on his sleeve, and the next moment there came a resounding slap on the side of his head that sent him staggering to the wall.

"Filthy brat. Go upstairs to the bathroom and wash yourself. Then take an oilcloth and a fresh blanket from the airing cupboard and go back to bed. We'll discuss your punishment in the morning."

"Sorry, Sister . . ."

"Stop whining. Do as I tell you, and don't make a noise."

"I dunno where the bathroom—"

"Of course you do. Up the back stairs and along the corridor. Just keep quiet."

"Yes, Sister."

He dragged his feet in the direction she pointed and tried to look contrite.

"Good! Good!" whispered Asta on his shoulder. She had subdued her natural wish to change into something that could bite and threaten, and remained a robin.

"'S all right for you. It wasn't your head she smacked. The oilcloth'll be useful, though. For the box."

"And the blankets . . ."

He found the staircase easily enough. It was lit, like everything else he'd seen so far, with a dim anbaric bulb, which made him wonder how they still had power.

"Surely in a flood that would be the first thing to go," he said.

"They must have a generator."

They were barely whispering. At the top of the staircase, a drab corridor stretched out ahead, with rough coconut matting on the floor. The light here was even dimmer. Remembering what the woman in the cave had told them, Malcolm counted the doors: the ones on the left were cells for the nuns, and those on the right were first the two bathrooms and then the nursery.

"Where's the airing cupboard?" he whispered.

"There, between the bathrooms."

He opened the little door and was met with a wave of musty heat. Shelves of thin folded blankets rose above a hot-water tank.

"There's the oilcloths," said Asta.

They lay in rolls on the top shelf. Malcolm took one down, together with a couple of blankets.

"Can't carry any more, not with her as well. This'll be hard as it is."

He closed the cupboard silently, and then, with Asta as a mouse, listened as hard as he could outside the nursery. A light snore, which might have been the nun on duty, a little snuffling and whimpering—no more than that.

"No point in waiting," Malcolm whispered.

He turned the handle, trying to do it silently, but the little noise he made sounded to him like a stick banging a bucket. Nothing to be done about it: he slipped inside and shut the door, and then stood absolutely still, assessing the place.

A long room, with a dim anbaric light at each end. A line of cribs along one wall, and small beds along the other, with an adult's bed at the nearer end, where a nun was sleeping and, as he'd heard from outside, gently snoring.

The floor was drab linoleum, and the walls were bare. He thought of the pretty little nursery the nuns had made for Lyra at Godstow and clenched his fists.

"Concentrate," whispered Asta. "She's in one of these cribs."

There were so many things that could go wrong that Malcolm could scarcely manage to push them all aside in his mind. He tip-toed to the first crib and peered in. Asta was a night bird of some kind, perching on the side and looking down. A large heavy child with black hair. No. They shook their heads.

The next: too small.

The next: the head was too round.

The next: too fair.

The next: too big.

The next— The nun in the bed behind them groaned and murmured in her sleep. Malcolm stood stock-still and held his breath. After a moment the woman sighed heavily and fell silent again.

"Come *on*," said Asta.

The next child was the right size and coloring, but she wasn't Lyra. He was surprised: it was easy to tell, after all.

They moved on to the next, and then the door handle turned.

Without thinking, Malcolm darted to the nearest bed against the opposite wall and pulled himself underneath, clutching the blankets and the oilcloth.

Two voices were speaking quietly at the other end of the room, and one was a man's.

Malcolm was already freezing cold, but a shiver took hold of him. Help me stop shivering! he thought desperately, and Asta instantly became a ferret and lay close around his neck.

Footsteps came slowly towards them. The voices continued in a murmur.

"Are you sure about this?" the woman said.

"As sure as I can be. That child is the daughter of Lord Asriel."

"But how did she come to be in a cave in the woods with a lot of poachers and common thieves? It doesn't make sense."

"I don't know how, Sister. We'll never know. By the time we send someone back to interrogate them, they'll have gone. I must say this has been a complete—"

"Keep your voice down, Father."

They both sounded testy.

"Which one is she?" said the priest.

Malcolm lifted his head and watched as the nun led him to the seventh crib from the end.

The priest stood gazing down at the child in the crib. "I'll take her with me in the morning," he said.

"I beg your pardon, Father, but you won't. She is in our care now, and there she will remain. That is the rule of our order."

"My authority outweighs the rule of your order. In any case, I should have thought that the one thing a Sister of Holy Obedience ought to do was obey. I will take this child in the morning, and that is the end of it."

He turned and walked to the end of the room and out the door. One or two of the sleeping children muttered or whimpered in their sleep as he passed, and the nun in the bed at the end gave a soft shuddering snore and turned over.

The nun who had come in remained by the crib for a few moments, and then made her way more slowly to the door. Malcolm could see along the length of the room under the beds, and in the dim light from the corridor he saw her sandaled feet under her long habit as she stopped and turned to look back. She stood there for some time, and he thought, Has she seen me? What's she going to do?

But finally she turned and left and shut the door.

Malcolm thought of Alice, faithfully waiting outside in the cold, cut off from any knowledge of what was happening. How lucky he and Lyra were to have her to rely on! But how long could he stay lying here? Not much longer. He was aching with cold.

Slowly, carefully, he pulled himself out from under the bed. Asta was watching all around, cat-formed, ears pricked. When he stood up, she flew to his shoulder as a wren.

"She's gone down the corridor," she whispered. "Come on!"

Malcolm, shivering hard, tiptoed to the seventh crib. He was about to reach down when Asta said, "Stop—"

He stood back and looked around, but she said, "No—look at her!"

The sleeping child had thick black curls.

"That's not Lyra," he said stupidly. "But she said—"

"Look in the other cribs!"

The next one was empty, but the one after that—

"Is this her?"

He was so bewildered now that he couldn't even guess. It *looked* like Lyra, but the nun had been so sure. . . .

Asta, silent-winged, flew down to the pillow. She bent her head to the little dæmon fast asleep around the child's neck and nudged him gently. The child stirred and sighed.

"*Is* it?" said Malcolm, more urgently.

"Yes. This is Pan. But there's something—I don't know—something not right. . . ."

She lifted the little ferret dæmon's head, and it flopped back as soon as she let go.

"They should have woken," said Malcolm.

"They're drugged. I can smell something sweet on her lips."

That would make it easier, at least, he thought.

"Are you *absolutely* sure it's her?"

"Well, look. Aren't you?"

The light was very dim, but when he peered down close and looked at the child's face, he knew beyond any doubt that this was the Lyra he loved.

"Yes, it's her. Course it is. Well, let's go."

He spread the blankets he was carrying on the floor, and while Asta carefully lifted the sleeping Pan away, he bent and picked up the child, feeling a little surprised at her solidity. She neither stirred nor murmured, but hung in his arms profoundly asleep.

He laid her on the blankets and rolled them around her. Asta, badger-formed now, carried Pan in her mouth, and they made their way silently between the row of cribs and the row of beds, past the sleeping nun at the end of the room, still gently snoring, and opened the door.

Silence. Without waiting a second, Malcolm stepped through and Asta followed, and then they shut the door and tiptoed back towards the stairs.

As they were about to take the first step down, the great bell rang and startled him so, he nearly dropped the clumsy bundle; but it was only telling the time. Nothing happened. They went on down through the kitchen and into the scullery, and found the wooden box where they'd left it.

Malcolm laid Lyra on the table, lined the box with the oilskin, and put the child and blankets inside. Then Asta settled the limp dæmon in his place around Lyra's neck, and Malcolm said, "Ready?"

"I'll go first," said Asta.

Malcolm was shivering so hard he thought he'd never be able to hold the box, but he managed to step into the drain, his back to the way out, and pull the box after him. Once they were under the grating, he reached up and set it free from the catch. He couldn't prevent it from falling with a loud clang and wished he'd left it, but there was nothing to be done.

He clambered backwards down the drain, moaning with cold, bashing his head, scraping his knees, slipping, falling on his face, pushing himself up again, into the darkness, until Asta said, "There it is! We're nearly there!"

He could see a faint light gleaming on the wet walls; he could smell fresh air; he could hear the lapping of water.

"Careful—don't go too fast—"

"Is she there?"

"Course she's there. Alice—Alice—come closer. . . ."

"Took your bloody time, didn't you?" came her voice from below. "Here—gimme your foot—thassit—now the other—"

He felt the rock and swing of the canoe underfoot and let his whole weight down into it. Then he didn't know what to do with the box. He was nearly stupid with exhaustion and fear and cold.

"I got it steady—don't hurry," she said. "Just bring it out slow and careful. No hurry. Got the weight? Take your time. Turn round this way. I got it—I got it—and she slept through all this? Lazy little cow. Come here, sweetheart, come to Alice. Here, Mal, sit down and put them blankets round you. For God's sake, get warm. And eat this—here. I kept it from the cave. If you got summing in your belly, it'll warm you up quicker."

She shoved a lump of bread and a piece of cheese into his hands, and he gobbled down a bit at once.

"Gimme the paddle," he mumbled, and with another bit of bread and cheese in his mouth, the blankets around his shoulders, and the paddle in his hand, he pushed away from the walls of the great white priory and brought the faithful canoe out once more onto the flood.

TWENTY-ONE

THE ENCHANTED ISLAND

Between bites of the bread and cheese and strokes of the paddle, Malcolm told Alice everything that had happened.

"So the priest wanted to take her away," she said, "and the nun showed him the wrong child? D'you think she just didn't know herself which was the right one?"

"No, I think she knew, all right. She was trying to trick him, and it would have worked. Well, it might still work—for a while, anyway. Till he finds out it wasn't Lyra. And the nuns find out that the real Lyra's missing."

"But how could he know it was Lord Asriel's kid who was there in the first place?"

"It must have been Andrew. I had to use our real names 'cause Mr. Boatwright knows who we are, but I should have called Lyra something else. There can't be many Lyras in the world."

"You can't help that. I trusted 'em too. Little toe rag."

"But I can't understand what the nuns were going to do with Lyra if the priest had taken the wrong kid. I mean, they wouldn't have been able to keep her hidden forever. Maybe what she was going to do would have been even worse'n what he was going to do."

"I'd like to see what happens in the morning, though. Pity we can't get 'em all out. Poor little buggers."

He finished the bread and cheese. All he wanted to do was lie down and sleep. He felt on the edge of death with the desire for it, and presently, without his being able to prevent it, his eyes closed.

"Want me to paddle for a bit?" said Alice, waking him up with a start. He nearly dropped the paddle. "You been asleep for a long time."

"No," he said. "I'm all right. But as soon as we find somewhere . . ."

"Yeah. What about that hill over there?"

She pointed, turning around. A wooded hilltop rose out of the water, a little island all on its own, brightly lit by the low-lying moon. The air was warm, and there was a softness about it, almost a fragrance.

Malcolm steered for it, still more than half asleep, and brought *La Belle Sauvage* gently alongside the hill, out of the main current, where little swirls and whirlpools made the canoe dance and lurch and bob, until Alice found a branch to hold on to.

"Just a bit further along—look—there's a sort of little beach," she said, and he pushed the paddle into the water and brought the bow of the canoe firmly up onto a patch of grass. The moon shone directly in at it and helped him see a firm branch to tie the painter to, and then he slumped down in the canoe where he was and closed his eyes and fell asleep.

He must have slept for hours. When he woke up, it felt like a whole season later because he was warm, and the light through the leaves above was bright and sparkling. Leaves! There couldn't be leaves out, not yet! He blinked and rubbed his eyes, but there they were: leaves, and blossoms too. He had to put his hand up against the brilliance. But the brilliance defeated him: there it was inside his eyes, twisting and scintillating like a . . .

It was like an old friend now. Certainly it was a sign of something. He lay stiff and aching where he'd dropped, and slowly let his wits come back to him as the spangled ring expanded and drifted closer and closer, until it vanished past the corner of his eye.

Someone was talking nearby. It was Alice, and a woman was responding. The woman's voice was low and sweet. They were discussing babies. Could he hear Lyra's voice as well, burbling her nonsense? It might have been that, or it might have been the lapping of the water, which sounded like a little stream now, not like a great flood. And birdsong! He could hear a blackbird, and sparrows, and a lark, for all the world as though it was already spring.

There was a warm smell—was that coffee? Or toast? Or both? Either was impossible. Both were inconceivable. But there it was, that fragrance, stronger by the minute.

"I think he's woken up," said the woman's voice.

"Richard?" called Alice quickly.

And he was on his guard at once.

He heard her light footsteps, and then felt her hand on his, and he had to open his eyes properly.

"Richard, come and have some coffee," she said. "Coffee! Think of that!"

"Where are we?" he mumbled.

"I dunno, but this lady, she . . . Come *on*. Wake up!"

He yawned and stretched and made himself sit up.

"How long have I been asleep?"

"Hours and hours."

"And how's—"

"Ellie?" she cut in. "She's fine. Everything's all right."

"And who—" he whispered.

"This lady, it's her place, that's all," she whispered back. "She's really nice. But . . ."

He rubbed his eyes and reluctantly pushed himself up out of the canoe. He'd been so deeply asleep that he could remember no dreams, unless the episode at the white priory had been a dream itself, which seemed not unlikely, now that scraps of it came back to him.

Still heavy and groggy with sleep, he followed Alice (No! What was her name? What was it? Sandra! Sandra!) up the grassy slope to where Lyra/Ellie lay on the grass, with Pan laughing at the flight of a dozen, a score, of large blue butterflies that flickered and fluttered around him. One of them might have been the woman's dæmon.

The woman . . .

She was young, as far as Malcolm could judge, maybe in her twenties, and very pretty, with the sunlight glowing in her golden hair and her light green dress. She was kneeling on the grass in front of Lyra, tickling her, or letting the petals of some sort of blossom fall over her face, or leaning down to let the child play with a long necklace she wore, but Lyra never managed to grasp it. Her hands went right through it, as if it wasn't there.

"Miss," said Alice, "this is Richard."

The woman stood up in one swift, elegant movement.

"Hello, Richard," she said. "Did you sleep well?"

"Very well, thank you, miss. Is it morning or afternoon?"

"Late morning. If Sandra has finished with the cup, you can have some coffee. Would you like some?"

"Yes, please."

Alice filled it for him from a copper pot that hung over a fire that crackled in a ring of stones.

"Thanks. Do you live here?" he said.

"Not all the time. I do when it suits me. Where do you live?"

"In Oxford. Up the river . . ."

She seemed to be listening intently, but not necessarily to his words. Everything about her was pretty and gentle and kind, and yet he felt uneasy.

"And what are you going to do with little Ellie?" she said.

"We're taking her to her father. In London."

"That's a long way," she said, sitting back down and stroking the child's hair. Pan had become a butterfly himself by now and was struggling to fly with the cloud of big blue ones, who fluttered around him, encouraging, helping, lifting, but he couldn't fly very far from Lyra and soon fell back on the grass beside her, as lightly as a leaf. Then he became a mouse and scuttled to her neck.

"Well, yeah, it is," said Malcolm.

"You can rest here as long as you like."

"Thank you. . . ."

Alice was doing something at the fire.

"Here y'are," she said, and held out a plate with a fork and two fried eggs on it.

"Oh, thanks!" he said, and suddenly realized how hungry he was, and ate them up in a moment.

Lyra was laughing. The woman had picked her up and was holding her high and laughing up at her. Pan was a butterfly again, a pure white one, and was dancing in the air with the cloud of blue ones, successfully this time, and Malcolm suddenly thought: Suppose her dæmon is the whole cloud of butterflies, not just one of them?

That made him shiver.

Alice gave him a slice of bread. It was fresh and soft, unlike the brick-hard bread from the cave, and he thought he'd never tasted anything better.

"Miss," he said when he'd finished the bread, "what's your name?"

"Diania," she said.

"Diana?"

"No, Diania."

"Oh. Well, um . . . How far are we from London?"

"Oh, miles and miles."

"Is London closer than Oxford?"

"It depends how you go. By road, yes, it's probably closer. But all the roads in Albion are drowned now. By water, everything is changed. By air, I think we're exactly halfway."

Malcolm looked at Alice. Her expression was neutral.

"By air?" he said to Diania. "You en't got a zeppelin or a gyropter, have you?"

"Zeppelins! Gyropters!" she said, laughing and tossing Lyra up and making her laugh too. "Who needs a zeppelin? Great noisy things."

"But you can't . . . I mean . . ."

"You know, Richard, I've only known you for half an hour, since you woke up, but I can already tell that you're an uncommonly earth-minded boy."

"I don't know what that means."

"Literal-minded. How's that?"

He didn't want to contradict her, because after all she might have been right. He was still a long way from understanding himself, and she was grown up.

"Is that a bad thing to be?" he said cautiously.

"Not for a mechanic, for instance. It would be a good thing, if you were a mechanic."

"Well, I wouldn't mind being a mechanic."

"There you are, then."

Alice was watching this exchange closely. A little frown occupied her forehead, and her eyes were narrowed.

"I'm going to check the canoe," Malcolm said.

La Belle Sauvage was bobbing comfortably on the water, which had lost the racing fury of the past days and was now flowing steadily, faster than the Thames in Port Meadow, but not much. It looked as if it had settled like this forever.

Malcolm checked the canoe over from end to end, taking his time, letting his hands rest on it for longer than he needed to; it calmed his unease. Everything was in order, everything inside was dry and safe, and Bonneville's rucksack was still tucked under the seat.

The rucksack . . .

He lifted it out.

"You going to open it?" said Asta.

"What do you think?"

"I thought it might be like evidence, or something, if they found his body," she said.

"Evidence that we'd . . ."

"Yes. But then I thought we could have picked it up anywhere. Just found it on the bank—summing like that."

"Yeah. It's pretty heavy."

"Might be gold bars in there. Go on."

It was a battered old thing of green canvas, with leather patches on the corners and edges. The buckles were made of tarnished brass. Malcolm unfastened them and pulled back the top. The first thing he found was a sweater of navy-blue wool, which smelled of fuel oil and smokeleaf.

"We could have done with that," he said.

"Well, now we know. . . . Go on."

He laid the sweater on the grass and looked again. There were five folders of faded cardboard, bent or torn at the corners, each one full of paper.

"No wonder it was heavy," he said.

He took out the first folder and opened it. The papers were covered in swift, spidery handwriting, in black ink, which was hard to read; it seemed to be a sort of long argument about mathematics, all in French.

"There's a map," said Asta.

One sheet of paper did have what looked like a plan of a building on it. Rooms, corridors, doorways . . . The explanatory words were in French too, and in different writing. He could understand none of it. There were more plans beside the first one, which looked as if they might be further floors of the same building.

He put them all back and took out the next folder.

"This is in English," he said.

"He *was* English, wasn't he?"

"Bonneville? I suppose he might have been French. Hey, look!"

The first page was typewritten, a title page, and it said: *An Analysis of Some Philosophical Implications of the Rusakov Field, by Gerard Bonneville, Ph.D.*

"The Rusakov field!" said Malcolm. "We were right! He did know about it!"

"And he's got a Ph.D., look. Like Dr. Relf. We ought to take all this to her."

"Yeah," he said. "If we ever . . ."

"What else is in the folder?"

He flipped through it. Densely typed pages, the text broken by equations full of signs he had never seen before; there was no way of understanding it. He looked at the opening paragraph.

Since the discovery of the Rusakov field and the shocking but incontestable revelation that consciousness can no longer be regarded exclusively as a function of the human brain, the search for a particle associated with the field has been energetically pursued by a number of researchers and institutions, without, so far, any indication of success. In this paper I propose a methodology . . .

"Save that for later," Malcolm said. "It'll be interesting, though, I bet."

"What's next?"

The third, fourth, and fifth folders contained only papers that were unreadable. The mixture of letters, numbers, and symbols was like no language Malcolm had ever seen.

"It must be code," he said. "I bet Dr. Relf and Oakley Street could understand it."

There was still something else at the bottom of the rucksack, and it was heavy too. A package wrapped in oilskin, and inside that in thick soft leather, and finally in black velvet, opened up to disclose a square wooden box, as big as the palm of a large man's hand, much decorated with marquetry in exotic patterns.

"Look at that!" Malcolm said, admiring the workmanship. "That must have taken years!"

"How d'you open it?" said Asta, mouse-formed.

He looked all round it and saw no hinges, no clasp, no keyhole, no way in at all.

"Hmm," he said. "Well, if there's no hinges . . ."

"Does the lid just lift off?"

He tried and found it didn't.

"If you were a mechanic—" she said, and got no further before he flicked her off the gunwale. But before she hit the water, she became a butterfly and flew up to perch on his hair.

He turned the box round slowly. He pressed every part of its surface, looking for a secret catch.

"That edge, there," said his dæmon's butterfly voice. "Where it's sort of green."

"What about it?"

"Press it sideways."

He did, quite gently, and then a little more forcefully, and felt something move. A narrow panel that ran the length of the end of the box slid sideways for about the length of his thumbnail.

"Ah," he said. "That's a start."

He pushed it back, and then out again, feeling for some tiny looseness anywhere that might reveal where the next movement came. After a few moments he found it: the opposite side of the box slid downwards for the same distance.

"Getting there," he said.

The first panel slid a little further, and then the other side did the same, and then it happened a third time. But that was all. He could push them in back to the starting point and then out again, but they would only move those three steps, and still the box wasn't open.

He looked all round, felt here and there, and then . . . "Ah," he said, "I got it."

When the side was as far down as it would go, the top could slide out. It was as simple as that.

"Oh!" said Asta. "Is that a . . ."

In a bed of black velvet lay a golden instrument like a large watch or a compass. It was the most beautiful thing Malcolm and his dæmon had ever seen. It was just as Dr. Relf had described it to him, but finer than he could ever have imagined. The thirty-six pictures around the dial were minute and clear, the three hands and the one needle were exquisitely shaped out of some silver-gray metal, and a golden sunburst surrounded the center of the dial.

"That's what it is," he said, and he found he was whispering.

"Hide it. Put it back straightaway," she said. "Look at it later, when we're somewhere else."

"Yeah. Yeah. You're right."

He was bewitched by its beauty, but he did as she said and put it straight back into the box, wrapped it up, and thrust it into the bottom of the rucksack.

"Where can he have got that from?" she whispered.

"Stole it. That's what I reckon."

He fastened the rucksack again and stowed it where it was before, under the thwart.

"Dr. Relf said there was six originally, remember?" he said. "And one was missing, because they knew where five of them were but not the sixth. . . . I bet this is it."

There was silence from further up in the grassy glade where the fire was, and when Malcolm got back there, he saw why: Lyra was asleep on the grass, wrapped in a silken blanket the color of sunshine, and the woman was busy doing something to Alice's hair. Alice was kneeling in front of her, facing away, as the woman bent over her and with deft fingers wove her hair into complex braids, twisting flowers into it as she did. The butterflies were still there. One or two were resting on the sleeping Pan, some on the woman's shoulders and neck, and some tried to settle on Ben, who lay head on paws close to Alice; but whenever they did, he growled very softly and deeply, and they took off again.

Alice's expression was strange. She was embarrassed, but at the same time she was shy and delighted and determined to be as pretty as the woman wanted her to be. The look she gave Malcolm was almost fierce, as if daring him to laugh or roll his eyes, and there was a pleading in it too. Since they had killed Bonneville, they had been close to each other, probably closer than Malcolm had felt to anyone. Now she was being made to look different from the ratty, thin-faced girl with the permanent sneer and the swift frown, his closest friend. Now she was becoming almost pretty. He felt strange about that, and he could tell that she did too.

He looked away.

The woman was murmuring to her, and Malcolm tried not to listen. He moved further away and lay down on the grass. The day was warm, and he was sleepy. He closed his eyes.

Someone was shaking his shoulder. It was Alice.

"Wake up! Mal, we can't stay here. Wake up!"

She was whispering, but he heard every word.

"Why can't we stay here?" he whispered back.

"Come and see what she's doing."

He rolled over and rubbed his eyes. Then he sat up.

"What? Where is she?"

"By the fire. Just come quietly. Don't make a noise."

Malcolm stood up and found himself still dazed with sleep. She caught him before he fell.

"You all right?" she said.

"Just dizzy. What's she doing?"

"I can't . . . But you gotta come and look."

She took his hand as they walked the little way up to the fire. It was late afternoon, nearly evening, and for the first time for months, it seemed to Malcolm, he could see a sunset. The sky was clear in the southwest and the rays of the sun struck through the trees, red, warm, and dazzling. As his senses returned, he looked back at the canoe, and it was still there, and the rucksack was still under the seat. Alice tugged his hand: she didn't want to stop.

The little grassy glade was clearly illuminated, and right in the middle of it sat Diania, bare-shouldered, bare-breasted, with Lyra sucking vigorously at her right nipple. The woman looked up and gave them a smile so strange she might have been inhuman.

"What are you doing?" said Malcolm.

"Why, feeding the child, of course! Giving her good milk. Look at her suck!"

She looked down proudly. The nipple slipped out of Lyra's mouth, and the woman lifted her up to her shoulder and patted her back. Lyra obligingly belched, and the woman promptly brought her down on the other side, and the child's little mouth began to work open and shut even before she found the nipple. Then she closed her eyes and went on sucking vigorously.

Malcolm thought that she never sucked the bottle like that. Asta whispered, "This woman is trying to steal her."

Malcolm tugged at Alice's hand, and together they left the little glade and went back to the canoe.

"She's not good!" said Asta passionately.

"No, she en't," said Alice's dæmon.

"She's not doing her any harm," said Malcolm, but he knew it wasn't true as soon as he said it.

"She's doing that to make her belong to her," said Alice. "She en't normal, Mal. She en't proper human. See them butterflies? Well, which one's her dæmon?"

"I think they all are."

"Well, where were they just now?"

"I . . . They weren't there."

"They were. They were all over Pan. You couldn't hardly see him. She's doing some magic or summing, I swear. You know the fairies, in stories? Well, they take human children."

"But not really," said Malcolm. "Only in stories."

"But story after story, and songs too, they all say that happens. They steal kids and they're never seen again. It's *true*," she said.

"Well, normally . . . ," said Malcolm.

"It's *not* normal!" said Asta. "Nothing's normal. Everything's changed after the flood."

Asta was right—nothing was normal anymore. Malcolm tried to remember the fairy tales he knew. Could you bargain with fairies? Did they keep their promises? There was something about names. . . .

"We've got to get her back," he said.

"Let's just go and ask her," said Alice. "Then we'll know right enough."

"We've got to get ready to go straightaway. If we stay here, she'll just steal Lyra when we're asleep."

"Yeah," said Alice. "But we can't pack all our stuff without her seeing. It's impossible."

"I got an idea," said Malcolm.

Asta flew off his shoulder and began to search for a stone of the right size, while he took the rucksack out of the canoe.

"What you doing?" said Alice. "What's that?"

He opened the box and showed her the alethiometer. Her eyes widened.

"Here's one," said Asta from a little way off, "but I can't . . ."

Alice helped her pull the stone out of the ground and washed it in the water. Meanwhile, Malcolm wrapped the alethiometer in the velvet and the leather and oilskin and stuffed it back into the rucksack. Alice's eyes gleamed with approval as he put the stone in the box and closed it again.

"I'll tell you more later," he said.

Then, alethiometer and box separately in the rucksack over his shoulder, they went back to the glade. The woman was still feeding Lyra, but when they arrived, she took the child away from her breast. Lyra was nearly asleep and utterly replete.

"She won't have had milk like that before," said the woman.

"No, and thank you for feeding her," said Malcolm, "but we're going to go now."

"Won't you stay another night?"

"No. We need to go. It's been kind of you to let us stay here, but it's time we went on."

"Well, if you must, then you must."

"And we'll take Ellie now."

"No, you won't. She's mine."

Malcolm's heart was beating so hard he could hardly stand up. Alice's hand found his.

"We're taking her," she said, "because she's ours. We know what we're doing with her."

"She's mine. She's drunk my milk. Look at how happy she is in my arms! She's going to stay with me."

"Why d'you think you can do this?" said Malcolm.

"Because I want to, and I have the power. If she could speak, she'd say she wanted to stay here too."

"What are you going to do with her?"

"Bring her up to be one of my people, of course."

"But she isn't one of your people."

"She is now she's drunk my milk. You can't alter that."

"Anyway, what people d'you mean?"

"The oldest people there are. The first inhabitants of Albion. She'll be a princess. She'll be one of us."

"Look," said Malcolm, swinging the rucksack down to the ground, "I'll give you a treasure to have instead."

"What sort of treasure?"

"A treasure fit for a queen. You *are* a queen, en't you?"

"Of course."

"Are you a fairy person?"

"Where is this treasure?"

Malcolm brought out the box.

"Let me see," she said.

"Let me hold Ellie, and then you can look properly," said Alice.

But Diania held the child closer and gave Alice a look that frightened her.

"You think I'm stupid? Every trick you can think of, I've seen it and heard it a thousand times before. How would a pair of children like you be in charge of a treasure? It doesn't make sense. No one would give you a treasure to look after."

"Then why are we looking after a baby?" said Alice.

"That's much easier to explain," she said.

And that was the moment Malcolm had been waiting for.

"If you can explain it," he said, "then you can keep her, and the treasure as well."

The woman looked at him and cuddled Lyra closer, rocking her back and forth.

"If I can explain . . ."

"If you can explain how me and Sandra came to be looking after Ellie, then she can stay with you."

The woman was thinking.

"How many chances?" she said. "I want more than one."

"You can have three."

"Three. All right. First: she is your sister, and your parents have died. They left her to you to look after."

"Wrong," said Malcolm. "Two more chances."

"All right . . . Two: you stole her from her crib and you're taking her to London to sell."

"That's wrong too. Only one chance left."

"Only one . . . only one . . . Very well. Let me see. I know! She was in the care of the nuns, and then the flood came, and you and

Sandra took her from her crib and put her in your boat, and you were swept away by the flood and there was a man chasing you, and then you killed him, and then she was taken by the Sisters of Holy Obedience, and you rescued her and brought her here."

"Who did?"

"You did. Richard and Sandra."

"Brought who here?"

"Ellie, of course!"

"Well, you're wrong for the third time," said Malcolm, "because this is Alice, not Sandra, and I'm Malcolm, not Richard, and the baby's not Ellie, she's Lyra. You lost."

And then the woman opened her mouth and uttered a wail so loud and terrible that Malcolm had to cover his ears. She opened her arms, and Lyra fell out and would have hit the ground if Alice hadn't darted in and caught her. The woman put her hands to her head, tears flooded from her eyes, and she flung herself full-length on the grass, weeping with a passion that touched Malcolm's heart with fear.

But he gathered up their blankets and their tin of biscuits and held out the wooden box.

"I promised you a treasure," he said, "and here it is."

The woman was sobbing bitterly; her whole body was heaving with the gulps that racked her.

"Here," he said again, and put it down on the grass.

The woman rolled over onto her back and flung her head from side to side.

"My baby!" she cried. "You're taking my baby away!"

"No, she's not your baby," said Malcolm.

"I waited for a thousand years to hold a baby to my breast! And she's drunk my milk! She's mine!"

"We're going away now. Look, I put the treasure down here."

She sat up, sobbing so much that she could hardly hold her balance. One hand wiped away the tears that flooded her face, and the other felt along the ground till it found the box.

"What is this?"

"I told you. Treasure. We're going now. Thank you for letting us stay for a bit."

The woman got to her knees, and then flung herself at Alice's feet, clinging to her legs. Alice looked alarmed and held Lyra out of her reach.

"*He* doesn't understand—he never would—how could a man understand? But you—"

"No," said Alice.

"Did you look in the glass after I arranged your hair?"

"Yes . . ."

"And did you like it?"

"Yes. But . . ."

"I could make you beautiful. I could make your face so lovely that every man would be your slave. I could do that! I have that power!"

Alice's lips were set tight. Malcolm just looked at her helplessly. Something had told him already that Alice was discontented with her looks. He could read her face now, and he saw a succession of emotions pass over it, some too hard for him to name or to know. Finally it settled into the usual half-sneering contempt.

"You're a liar," she said. "Let go of my legs."

The woman did, sobbing again, but without hope this time. Malcolm felt truly sorry for her. But what could they do?

He quietly walked away. Alice went with him, Lyra silent and asleep in her arms.

He turned around once more and saw the woman sitting up, turning the box over and over in her hands.

"What's she going to do when she opens it?" Alice whispered.

"She never will."

"How d'you know?"

"'Cause she's not a mechanic."

The canoe was safe; he had been anxious about that. He held it steady for Alice, and when she and the child were settled in the prow and the rucksack was stowed under the thwart, he got in himself and took the paddle and propelled *La Belle Sauvage* away from the enchanted island.

TWENTY-TWO

RESIN

In the flood of news that followed the flood of water, news that was full of collapsing buildings, daring rescues, drownings, and disappearances, the information that a religious community near Oxford had been devastated by the deaths of several nuns and the destruction of a medieval gatehouse was a minor item. Many other places and communities had fared even worse. Trying to locate the relevant facts among the immense volume of information was no easy task for the Consistorial Court of Discipline or for Oakley Street; but Oakley Street had a slight advantage, thanks to Hannah Relf, and was able to start searching for a boy and girl in a canoe, with a baby, before the opposition did.

However, the CCD was better resourced. Oakley Street had three vessels—the boat Bud Schlesinger had hired from Tilbury, and two gyptian narrowboats, with Nugent in one and Papadimi-triou in the other—whereas the CCD had seven, including four fast powerboats. On the other hand, in the gyptians the Oakley Street boats had well-informed and greatly experienced guides to all the waterways. The CCD had little to rely on but the fear they caused when they asked questions with their customary force.

So the two sides set out in search of *La Belle Sauvage* and her crew and passengers, the Oakley Street boats from Oxford and the CCD from various points downriver.

But the weather was unhelpful, the flood all-consuming, and the confusion universal. Besides, Lord Nugent soon found himself wondering whether this deluge was altogether natural. It seemed to him and his gyptian companions that the inundation had a stranger source than the weather because it had begun to cause curious illusions and to behave in unexpected ways. At one point, they lost sight of all land altogether and might have been out on the ocean. At another, Nugent was certain that he could see a beast like a crocodile at least as long as the boat shadowing them without ever quite revealing itself; and then one night there were mysterious lights moving below the surface, and the sound of an orchestra playing music such as none of them had heard before.

It wasn't long before Nugent overheard his gyptian companions using a phrase to describe the phenomena, a phrase that was unknown to him. They called the flood and all its effects part of the secret commonwealth. He asked them what that meant, but they would say no more about it.

So they moved on, and still *La Belle Sauvage* evaded them.

The flood was running smoothly, like a great river, such as the Amazon or the Nile, which Malcolm had read about—an unimaginable volume of water carried onwards with no snags, no rocks, no shoals, and no harsh wind or tempest to fling the surface into waves.

The sun went down and gave way to the moon. Malcolm and Alice said nothing, and Lyra slept on. Malcolm thought Alice was asleep too, until some time had gone by.

Then she said, "Are you hungry?"

"No."

"Nor me. I'd've thought we would be, being as we en't eaten anything for hours. . . ."

"Lyra too."

"Fairy milk," she said. "I wonder what it'll do. . . . It'll make her part fairy."

"We ate fairy food too."

"Them eggs. Yeah, I s'pose we did."

They floated on over the moonlight-scintillating water, as if they were sharing the same dream.

"Mal," she said.

"What?"

"How'd you know how to fool her like that? I was thinking it'd never work, but as soon as she realized she'd got the names wrong . . ."

"I remembered Rumpelstiltskin, and I thought names must be important to fairies, so maybe it'd work. But if you hadn't used those fake names in the first place, we wouldn't have been able to try it, even."

They said nothing for another minute, and then Malcolm said, "Alice, are we murderers?"

She thought, and finally said, "He might not be dead. We can't be sure. We didn't want to kill him. That wasn't the plan at all. We were just defending Lyra. En't that right?"

"That's what I try and think. But we're thieves, certainly."

"'Cause of the rucksack? No sense in leaving it there. Someone else would've took it. And if we hadn't had that box . . . Mal, that was brilliant. I couldn't never've thought of that. You saved us then. And getting Lyra out of that big white priory . . ."

"I still feel bad."

"About Bonneville?"

"Yeah."

"I s'pose . . . The only thing to do is—"

"Do you feel bad about him?"

"Yeah. But then I think what he done to Sister Katarina. And . . . I never told you what he said to me, did I?"

"When?"

"That first night I saw him. In Jericho."

"No . . ."

"Nor what he did."

"What did he do?"

"After he bought me fish and chips, he said, 'Let's go for a walk on the meadow.' And I thought, Well, he seems nice. . . ."

"It was nighttime, wasn't it? Why did he want to go for a walk?"

"Well, he—he wanted . . ."

Malcolm suddenly felt foolish. "Oh, right," he said. "I— Sorry. Yeah."

"Don't worry about it. There en't been many boys wanted that with me. Seems I scare 'em off or summing. But he was a proper man, and I couldn't resist. We went down Walton Well Road and over the bridge, and then he kissed me and told me I was beautiful. That's all he did. I felt so many things, I can't tell you, Mal."

Something glittered on her cheek, and he saw to his immense surprise that tears were flowing from her eyes. Her voice was a little unsteady. She went on.

"But I'd always thought that if it ever happened, right, if it ever happened to me, then the other person's dæmon would kind of . . . be nice to my dæmon too. That's what happens in stories. That's what people tell you. But Ben, he . . ."

Her dæmon, greyhound-formed, put his head under her hand. She played with his ears. Malcolm watched and said nothing.

"That bloody hyena," she went on, and she was sobbing now. "That bloody violent . . . It was horrible. . . . It was impossible. She was never going to be nice. *He* was, Bonneville was, he wanted to go on kissing me, but I couldn't, not with *her* growling and biting and . . . and *pissing*. She pissed like it was a weapon. . . ."

"I saw her do that," said Malcolm.

"So I had to say to him, 'No, I can't, no more,' and then he just laughed and pushed me away. And it could have been . . . I thought it was going to be the best thing. . . . And in the end it was just scorn and hate. But I was so torn about it, Mal, 'cause first of all he was so gentle and so sweet to me. . . . He said it twice, that I was beautiful. No one ever said that to me and I thought no one ever would."

She dragged a torn handkerchief from a pocket and mopped her eyes.

"And when that fairy woman done my hair with all them blossoms and that and showed me in the mirror, I thought . . . Well, maybe. I just thought that."

"You *are* pretty," said Malcolm. "Well, I think so."

He tried to sound loyal. He felt loyal. But Alice gave a short, bitter laugh and wiped her eyes again, saying nothing.

"When I first saw him in the priory garden," he said, "I was dead afraid. He just stepped out of the dark and said nothing, and that hyena just stood and pissed on the path. But later that same evening, he came in the Trout and my dad had to serve him. He'd done nothing wrong, Bonneville, nothing that anyone knew about, but the other customers all moved away. They just didn't like him. As if they knew all about him already. But then I came in, and he was so friendly I thought I must be wrong, I'd mistaken what I saw, and he was really nice. And all the time he was after Lyra. . . ."

"Sister Katarina didn't have a chance," said Alice. "She had no hope at all. He could have got anything he wanted."

"He nearly did. If the flood hadn't begun . . ."

"D'you think he really wanted to kill Lyra?" she said.

"It seemed like it. I can't imagine what else he could have wanted. Maybe to kidnap her."

"Maybe . . ."

"We had to defend her."

"Course."

And he knew that they had to—they had no choice. He was perfectly sure about that.

"What was that thing you took out of the box?" Alice asked after a minute or two.

"An alethiometer. I think so, anyway—I never seen one. But there was only six ever made, and they know where five of them are, but one was missing for years. I think maybe this is the missing one."

"What would he have done with it?"

"Maybe he could read it. But you need years of training. . . . He might have tried to sort of use it for bargaining. He was a spy."

"How d'you know?"

"The papers in the rucksack. Loads of 'em are in code. I'll take them to Dr. Relf, if we ever get back. . . ."

"You think we might not?"

"No. I think of course we'll get back. This—what's happening now, on the flood and all—it's a kind of . . . I don't know how to make it clear. It's a kind of between-time. Like a dream or something."

"It's all in our heads? It's not real?"

"No, not that. It's as real as anything could be. But it just seems kind of bigger than I thought. There's more things in it."

He wanted to tell her about the spangled ring, but knew that if he did, the meaning of it would come apart and be lost. That would have to wait till he was more certain of it himself.

"But we're getting closer to London and to Lord Asriel," he said, "and then we'll go back to Oxford 'cause the flood will have gone down by then. And I'll see my . . ."

He was going to say *mum and dad*, but he couldn't say the words, because he found a sob choking his throat, and then another, as the images came pouring into his memory: his mother's kitchen, her calm, sardonic presence, shepherd's pies and apple crumbles and steam and warmth, and his father laughing and telling stories and reading the football results and listening as Malcolm told him about this theory or that discovery and being proud of him; and before he could help it, he was sobbing as if his heart had been broken, and it was his fate to drift forever on a worldwide flood, further and further away from everything that was home, and they would never know where he was.

Only a day or two before, he would rather have had his right arm torn off than cry in front of Alice. This was like being naked in front of her, but strangely it didn't matter, because she was weeping herself. The length of the boat and the sleeping Lyra lay between them, or otherwise, he felt, they would have embraced and wept together.

As it was, they each sobbed for a while, and then quietly, gently, the little storms died down. And still the canoe floated on, and still Lyra slept, and still they felt no hunger.

And still they saw nowhere to land and rest. Malcolm thought the flood must have been at its highest now, because although there were little groups of trees above the water here and there, there was no land to be seen—no islands of the sort they'd rested on before, no hills, no housetops, no rocks. They might have been on the Amazon, which was so wide, Malcolm had read, that from the middle you could see neither of the banks.

For the first time a little question came into Malcolm's mind: Just suppose they did manage to get to London, and that London was still standing after this flood . . . Would it be hard to find Lord Asriel? Malcolm had said glibly to Alice that it would be easy to find him, but would it really?

He dared not close his eyes, tired as he was, for fear of running *La Belle Sauvage* over some dangerous obstacle, and yet he didn't feel inclined to sleep either, because he had passed into a state beyond that, as he was beyond hunger. Maybe sleeping on the fairy's island meant you never needed to sleep again.

And Lyra slept on, calm and silent and still.

When they had been quiet for an hour, Malcolm began to notice a new kind of movement in the water. There was a definite current in the great wide flood, not all of it, but a stream within it moving with what felt like purpose. And they were caught in it.

To begin with, it was very little faster than the vast body of water around them, and it might have been moving like that for some time without their noticing. When Malcolm woke up to it, though, it had already become like a separate river inside the larger one. He wondered whether he should try to paddle out of it and back onto the vast slow mirror of the main flood, but when he tried it, he found *La Belle Sauvage* moved her head almost intentionally to follow the faster stream, and when he'd noticed that, he found that it was too strong for him to paddle against anyway. If they had two paddles, and if Alice was awake— But they didn't. He rested the paddle across his knees and tried to see where they were going.

But Alice was awake.

"What's going on?" she said.

"There's a current in the water. It's all right. It's taking us in the right direction."

She sat up, not quite alarmed but curious.

"You sure?" she said.

"I think so."

The moon had almost set; it was the darkest hour of night. A few stars shone, and their reflections shook and broke up, silver scintillating in the black water. Malcolm looked all around the horizon and saw nothing as clear as an island or a tree or a cliff; but wasn't that something ahead—a thicker blackness at one point?

"What you looking at?" said Alice.

"Dead ahead . . . something . . ."

She turned around, peering back over her shoulder.

"Yeah, there is. Are we going straight for it? Can't you paddle us out of this current?"

"I've tried. It's too strong."

"It's an island."

"Yeah . . . Could be . . . It must be deserted. There's no lights at all."

"We're going to crash into it!"

"The current'll take us round one side or the other," he said, but he was far from certain. It looked exactly as if they were heading directly for the island, and as they got closer, Malcolm could hear something that he didn't like at all. So could Alice.

"That's a waterfall," she said. "Can you hear it?"

"Yeah. We'll have to hang on tight. But it's a fair way off yet. . . ."

And it was, but it was getting closer. He tried again to paddle hard to the right, which his muscles liked better than the left; but as hard as he dug and as fast as he worked, it made no difference at all.

There was another thing about the sound of the waterfall: it seemed to be coming from within the body of the island, deep under the earth. He cursed himself for not noticing the current sooner, and not paddling out while it had still been weak enough to let him.

"Keep your head down!" he shouted, because they were making straight for the dark flank of the island, heavy with vegetation— and the stream was going even faster—

And then there was a crashing and a sweeping of low branches and sharp twigs, and he only just threw his arm up across his face in time, and they were in a tunnel, in the utter dark, and all the clamor of rushing water and booming was resounding from the walls close around their heads.

He nearly shouted, "Hold tight to Lyra!" but he knew he didn't need to tell Alice that. He hooked his left arm through one strap of the rucksack, jammed the paddle tight under his feet, and held on to the gunwales with all his strength—

And the sound of crashing water was almost upon them, and then it was there, and the canoe pitched forward violently and Malcolm was drenched with icy water and shaken hard—Alice cried out in fear—Malcolm yelled, "Hold on! Hold on!"

But then, of all things, came a burst of happy laughter from the child. Lyra was beside herself with glee. Nothing in the world, nothing she had ever seen or heard, had pleased her more than this crazy plunge down a waterfall in the total darkness.

She was in Alice's arms—but was Alice safe?

Malcolm called again, his boy's voice high and frightened over the roar of the water: "Alice—Alice—Alice—"

And then, as suddenly as if a light had been switched on, the canoe shot out of the cavern, out of the cataract, out of the dark, and they were bobbing calmly on a gentle stream flowing between green banks by the light of a thousand glowing lanterns.

"Alice!"

She was lying unconscious with her arms around Lyra. Ben lay beside her, completely still.

Malcolm took up the paddle with shaking hands and moved the

canoe swiftly towards the left-hand bank, where a smooth lawn came down to a little landing. In a moment he'd made the boat fast, Asta had carried Pan up onto the bank, and he had lifted Lyra from Alice's grasp and sat her down on the grass, where she chattered with pleasure.

Then he leaned down into the canoe and moved Alice's head as gently as he could. She had been shaken about so much that her head had crashed into the gunwale, but she was already moving, and there was no blood.

"Oh, Alice! Can you hear me?"

He clumsily embraced her, and then pulled back as she struggled to sit up.

"Where's Lyra?" she said.

"On the grass. She's fine."

"Little bugger. She thought it was fun."

"She still does."

With his help, Alice stumbled out of the canoe and onto the landing, Ben following cautiously. Asta was impatient to go and see to Pan, so they moved up to sit on the grass beside Lyra, exhausted, shaking, and looked around.

They found themselves in a great garden, where paths and beds of flowers were set in immense lawns of soft grass, which glowed a brilliant green in the light of the lanterns. Or were they lanterns? There seemed to be large blossoms on every branch of every tree, glowing with soft, warm light; and there were so many trees that light was everywhere on the ground, though above there was nothing but a velvet black that might have been a million miles away, or no more than six feet.

The lawns sloped up to a terrace that ran along the front of a grand house where every window was brightly lit, and where people (too small to see in detail at that distance) moved about, as if at a ball or a reception for important guests. They danced behind the windows; they stood talking on the terrace; they wandered here and there among the fountains and the flowers in the garden. Scraps of a waltz played by a large orchestra drifted down to the travelers on the grass, and scraps of conversation too, from the people who were walking to and fro.

On the other bank of the little river there was . . . nothing to see at all. A thick fog covered everything beyond the edge of the water. From time to time something would make the fog swirl and seem about to part, but it never did. Whether the opposite bank was like this one—cultivated, beautiful, wealthy—or an empty desert, they couldn't tell.

So Malcolm and Alice sat amazed on the garden side of the river, pointing to this marvel and that: a glowing fountain, a tree laden with golden pears, a school of rainbow-colored fish that sprang up out of the stream, all moving as one, and turned their heads to look at them with their goggle eyes.

Malcolm stood up, feeling stiff and painful, and Alice said, "Where you going?"

"I'm just going to bail the canoe out. Put things out to dry."

The fact was that he was dizzy with all this strangeness, and he hoped that by attending to something dull and workmanlike he'd regain a little balance.

He took out all the wet things, the blankets and pillows and Lyra's sodden clothes, and laid them flat on the planks of the landing. He inspected the tin and found the biscuits shaken to pieces but not damp, and the matches were safe as well. Then he unrolled the coal-silk tarpaulin and laid that out to dry on the grass. The rucksack with its precious cargo, which he'd had over his shoulder, was wet only on the outside; the canvas had been stout enough to protect the folders of paper, and the alethiometer was snug in its oilskin.

He laid everything carefully on the little wooden jetty and made his way back to the others. Alice was playing with Lyra, holding her up so her feet touched the ground, pretending to make her walk. The child was still in high spirits, and blackbird Ben was helping Pantalaimon fly as high as he could, which was not quite high enough to reach the lowest branches of a light-bearing tree.

"What d'you want to do?" said Alice when Malcolm came back.

"Go and see that house. See if anyone there can tell us where Lord Asriel lives. You never know. They all look like lords and ladies."

"Come on, then. You carry her for a bit."

"We might find something to eat too. And somewhere to change her."

Lyra was lighter than the rucksack but awkwarder, because the rucksack's weight was taken on the shoulders, whereas carrying Lyra, Malcolm soon remembered, involved both arms. Nor was she very fragrant. Alice happily took the rucksack, and Malcolm went along beside her, with Lyra squirming and complaining in his arms.

"No, you can't go with Alice all the time," he told her. "You got to put up with me. As soon as we get up to that pretty house on the hill, see, with all those lights, we'll change your nappy and give you a feed. That's all you want. Won't be long now. . . ."

But it was going to take longer than they thought. The path to the palace led through the gardens, among the little trees with lights, past the beds of roses and lilies and other flowers, past a fountain with blue water and then another with water that sparkled and a third that sprayed up not water but something like eau de cologne—and after all that, the travelers seemed not a yard closer to the building on the hill. They could see every window, every column, every one of the steps leading to the great open door and the brightly lit space inside; they could see people moving about behind the tall windows; they could even hear the sound of music, as if a ball was in progress; but they were just as far from the palace as they were when they started.

"This path must be laid out like a sodding maze," said Alice.

"Let's go straight across the grass," said Malcolm. "If we keep it right in front of us, we can't go wrong."

So they tried that. If they came to a path, they crossed it. If they came to a fountain, they went round it and carried straight on. If they came to a flower bed, they went right through it. And still they were no closer.

"Oh, bollocks," said Alice, dropping the rucksack on the grass. "This is driving me mad."

"It's not real," said Malcolm. "Not normal, anyway."

"There's someone coming. Let's ask them."

Wandering towards them was a little group of two men and two women. Malcolm put Lyra down on the grass; she began to wail, so Alice wearily picked her up. Malcolm waited on the path for the people to come closer. They were young and elegant, dressed for a ball, the women in long gowns that left their arms and shoulders bare, the men in black-and-white evening dress, and they each carried a glass. They were laughing and talking in that light, happy way that Malcolm had seen lovers doing, and their bird dæmons fluttered around or settled on their shoulders.

"Excuse me," he said as they approached, "but . . ."

They ignored him and walked closer. Malcolm stepped right in front of them.

"Sorry to bother you, but d'you know how we can—"

They took no notice whatsoever. It was as if he didn't exist, except as an obstacle in the path. Two went on one side of him, laughing and chatting, and two went on the other, hand in hand, murmuring into each other's ears. Asta became a bird and flew up to talk with their dæmons.

"They won't listen! They don't seem as if they can see us at all!" she said.

"Excuse me! Hello!" Malcolm said more loudly, and ran around in front of them again. "We need to know how to get to the house up there, whatever it is. Can you . . ."

And again they walked around him, taking no notice. It was exactly as if he was invisible, inaudible, impalpable. He picked up a little stone from the path and threw it, and it hit one of the men on the back of the head, but it might as well have been a molecule of air, for all the notice he took.

Malcolm looked back at Alice and spread his hands. She was scowling.

"Rude sods," she said.

Lyra was crying properly now. Malcolm said, "I'll light a fire. Then we can warm some water for her, at least."

"Where's the canoe? Can we find our way back to it, or is that going to play tricks with us as well?"

"It's just there—look," he said, pointing back fifty yards or so. "All that walking, and we hardly got anywhere. Maybe it's magic. It doesn't make any bloody sense anyway."

He found that he could return to the canoe in just a few steps. Somehow that wasn't surprising. He gathered everything they needed for the child and made his way back to Alice. He plucked some twigs from the nearest tree and broke off a few short branches, shredding the twigs and placing them as well as he could before striking a match. The fire caught at once. He snapped the branches into shorter pieces, and it was easy, as if they had been designed to break to exactly the right length, and to be dry enough to burn too, just off the tree.

"It doesn't seem to mind us making a fire. It's only going to the house it doesn't want us doing. I'll get some water."

The fountain he walked to was closer than he thought, the water fresh and clean as he filled the saucepan. They'd taken some bottles of water from the pharmacy—it seemed very long ago now—and he refilled those as well.

"Everything's in favor of us, except the house and the people," said Asta.

Several people had walked past the fire, and not one had stopped to ask about it or tell them off. Malcolm had built it on the grass only a few feet from one of the main paths, but, like him, it seemed to be invisible. More young lovers, older men and women too, grave gray-haired statesman-looking figures, grandmotherly women in old-fashioned gowns, middle-aged people full of power and responsibility—all kinds of guests, and not only guests: waiters with trays of fresh glasses of wine or plates of canapés moved here and there among them. Malcolm lifted one of the plates away as the waiter went past and took it to Alice.

"I'm going to change her first," she said, her mouth full of a smoked-salmon sandwich. "She'll be more comfortable then. I'll feed her after."

"D'you need more water? That'll be too hot, what's in the pan now."

But it was exactly right to wash her with. Alice opened Lyra's garments, mopped her clean, dried her easily in the warm air. Then she went to look for somewhere to put the dirty nappy while Malcolm played with the child and fed her bits of smoked salmon. Lyra spat them out, and when Malcolm laughed at her, she frowned and clamped her mouth shut.

When Alice came back, she said, "Have you seen any rubbish bins here?"

"No."

"Nor've I. But when I wanted one, there it was."

It was just one more puzzle. The saucepan had boiled and the water had cooled enough for Lyra's bottle, so Alice filled it and started to feed her. Malcolm wandered about the grass, looking at the little trees with glowing blossoms and listening to the birds that flew and sang in the branches as prettily as nightingales.

Asta flew up to join them, and soon came back.

"Just like you and the people on the path!" she said. "They didn't seem to see me!"

"Were they young birds or grown-up ones?"

"Grown-up ones, I think. Why?"

"Well, everyone we've seen is grown up."

"But it's a sort of grand evening cocktail party kind of thing, or a ball, something like that. There wouldn't be any kids around anyway."

"Still," said Malcolm.

They went back to Alice.

"Here, you do it," she said.

He took Lyra, who had no time to complain before he plugged the bottle in again. Alice stretched out full-length on the grass. Ben and Asta lay down too, both snakes, each one trying to be longer.

"He never used to fool around," said Alice quietly, meaning her dæmon.

"Asta fools around all the time."

"Yeah. I wish . . ." Her voice faltered.

"What?" he said after a few moments.

She looked at Ben and, seeing him fully occupied with Asta, said quietly, "I wish I knew when he'd stop changing and settle."

"What d'you think happens when they stop changing?"

"What d'you mean?"

"I mean, will they stop being able to do it suddenly one day, or will they just do it less and less?"

"Dunno. My mum always said, 'Don't worry about it, it'll just happen.'"

"What would you like him to settle as?"

"Summing poisonous," she said decisively.

He nodded. More people came past, all kinds of people, and among them were faces he thought he remembered, but they might have been customers at the Trout, or people he'd seen in dreams. They might even have been friends from school who'd grown up and were now middle-aged, which would account for the fact that they looked familiar but strange. And there was a young man who looked so much like Mr. Taphouse, only fifty years younger, that Malcolm almost jumped up and greeted him.

Alice was lying on her side watching them all go by.

"Can you see people you know?" he said.

"Yeah. I thought I was asleep."

"Are the young ones older and the old ones younger?"

"Yeah. And some of them are dead."

"Dead?"

"I just seen my gran."

"D'you think *we're* dead?"

Alice was silent for a few moments, and then she said, "I hope not."

"Me too. I wonder what they're all doing here. And who the other people are, the ones we don't know."

"Maybe they're people we will know."

"Or else . . . maybe it's the world where that fairy lady came from. Maybe these people are all like her. It feels a bit like that."

"Yeah," she said. "It does. That's what it is. Except they can't see us, like she could. . . ."

"But we were above the ground then, in *our* world, so we'd've been more solid, like. Down here we're probably invisible to them."

"Yeah. That's probably it. But we better be careful all the same."
She yawned and rolled over onto her back.

Not to be left out, Lyra yawned as well. Pantalaimon tried to be a snake like the other two, but gave up after half a minute and became a mouse instead, and cuddled close against Lyra's neck. She was asleep in a moment, and once Ben had taken his greyhound shape and stretched out against Alice's side, Alice was too.

Without knowing why he was doing it, Malcolm knelt down beside the sleeping Alice and looked at her face. He knew it well, but he'd never looked at her closely before because she would have shoved him away; he felt a little guilty doing it now, while she was unconscious.

But he was so curious. The little frown that lived between her eyebrows had vanished; it was a softer face altogether. Her mouth was relaxed, and her whole expression was complex and subtle. There was a sort of kindness in it, and a sort of lazy enjoyment—those were the words he found to describe it. A hint of a mocking smile lay in the flesh around her eyes. Her lips, narrow and compressed when she was awake, were looser and fuller in sleep, and almost smiling, like her sleeping eyes. Her skin too—or what did ladies call it? her complexion?—was fine and silky, and in her cheeks was a faint flush, as if she was hot, or as if she was blushing at a dream.

It was too close. He felt he was doing wrong. He sat up and looked away. Lyra stirred and murmured, and he stroked her forehead and found it hot, like Alice's face. He wished he could stroke Alice's cheeks, but that image was too troubling altogether. He stood up and walked the little way down to the landing, where *La Belle Sauvage* bobbed gently on the water.

He didn't feel in the least bit sleepy, and his mind was still dwelling helplessly on the thought of Alice's face, and what it might be like to stroke it or kiss it. He pushed that idea aside and tried to think of something else.

So he knelt down to look at the canoe, and there he had a shock because there was an inch of water in the bottom, and he knew he had bailed it out.

He untied the painter and hauled *La Belle Sauvage* up onto the grass and then tipped her over to let the water out. And just as he'd feared, there was a crack in the hull.

"When we came through that cataract," said Asta.

"Must've hit a rock. Bugger."

He knelt on the grass and looked at it closely. One of the cedar planks that formed the skin of the canoe had split, and the paint around it was scraped. The split didn't look very serious, but Malcolm knew that the skin of the canoe flexed a little when it was moving, and no doubt it would go on letting in water till he mended it.

"What do we need?" said Asta, cat-shaped.

"Another plank, best of all. Or some canvas and glue. But we haven't got any of them either."

"The rucksack's made of canvas."

"Yeah. It is. I suppose I could cut a bit off the flap. . . ."

"And look over there," she said.

She was pointing to a great cedar, one of the few coniferous trees among the rest. Partway up the trunk, a branch had broken off, and the wound was leaking golden resin.

"That'll do," he said. "Let's cut a bit of canvas."

The flap of the rucksack was quite long and could easily spare a patch of the right size. Malcolm wondered whether the canvas was really necessary, because the actual waterproofing would be done by the resin, but then he thought of Alice and Lyra as the water slowly came in, and of himself trying more and more desperately to find somewhere to land. . . . He should repair it as well as he could, as well as Mr. Taphouse would. He opened his knife and began to saw at the thick, stiff fabric, cutting out a piece a bit longer than the split in the hull. It was hard work.

"I never thought canvas was so tough," he said. "I should have sharpened the knife."

Asta, now bird-formed, had been sitting on a branch as high as she could get and keeping watch all around. She flew down to his shoulder.

"Let's not be too long," she said quietly.

"Is something wrong?"

"There's something I can't see. Not wrong, exactly, but . . . Just get the resin and we'll go."

Malcolm cut through the last strands of the canvas and set off. Asta darted ahead a little way, becoming a hawk and getting to the tree just before he did. The resin was too high for him to reach without climbing, but he was happy to do that; the massive wide branches, sweeping low over the grass, made it feel totally secure.

He pressed the little piece of canvas into the resin and let it soak up as much as it could. Then he looked out of the tree and across the great lawns and flower beds as far as the terrace and the house beyond it: gracious and comfortable, splendid and generous. He thought that one day he'd come here by right, and be made welcome, and stroll among these gardens with happy companions and feel at ease with life and death.

Then he looked the other way, across the little river. And he was high enough in the tree to see over the top of the fog bank, which only extended upwards for a few feet, as he now discovered; and beyond it he saw a desolation, a wilderness of broken buildings, burned houses, heaps of rubble, crude shanties made of shattered plywood and tar paper, coils of rusty barbed wire, puddles of filthy water whose surfaces gleamed with the toxic shimmer of chemi-cal waste, where children with sores on their arms and legs were throwing stones at a dog tied to a post.

He cried out before he could help it. But so did Asta, and she glided to his shoulder and said, "Bonneville! It's him! On the terrace—"

He turned to look. It was too far to see distinctly, but there was a stir, and people were running towards someone in a chair—a car-riage of some kind—a wheelchair—

"What are they doing?" he said.

He was aware of her attention, of the straightness and speed of it like a lance from her brilliant eyes. He tugged the canvas away from the resin with trembling fingers.

"They're looking this way—they're pointing at where Alice is, at the canoe—they're moving towards the steps—"

Now he could see clearly, and at the center of this activity was Gerard Bonneville. He was directing everyone. They began to carry his wheelchair down the steps of the terrace.

"Take this," Malcolm said, and held out the canvas. It was abominably sticky. Asta pulled it away in her beak and hovered close to the tree as Malcolm clambered down. Once on the ground, he ran to the canoe as fast as he could, and Asta swooped down and laid the resin-soaked canvas where he directed her.

"Will this do by itself?" she said.

"I'll put some tacks in it. It won't be easy—my fingers are too sticky."

Alice had heard them and opened her eyes sleepily.

"What you doing?" she said.

"Mending a hole. Then we got to get away quick. Bonneville's up there by the house. Here, can you open the toolbox for me? And hand me a tack out of the smokeleaf tin in there?"

She scrambled up to do it. He took it stickily and touched the point of the little nail to a corner of the canvas. One tap of the hammer and it stayed in place while he hit it home, and so did the other five he put in.

"Right, let's turn her over," he said, and while he did that, Alice stood on tiptoe to look up at the activity on the terrace, and Malcolm found himself gazing at her slim, tense legs, her slender waist, the slight swell of her hips. He looked away with a silent groan in his chest. What had happened to him? But there was no time to think about that. He tore his mind away and slid the boat down and into the water. Asta was still in her hawk shape, hovering as high above him as she could get and staring fixedly at the terrace.

"What are they doing now?" Malcolm said as Alice threw the blankets into the canoe. Lyra was awake and interested, and Pan was buzzing around her head as a bee.

"They're moving him towards the steps," said Asta in the air above. "I can't see exactly. . . . There's a big crowd around him now, and more people joining them. . . ."

"What we going to do?" said Alice, settling herself into the bow with Lyra on her lap.

"Only thing we can," said Malcolm. "Can't go up a waterfall. Have to see what happens at the other end. . . ."

He pushed away from the landing and watched the resin-mended patch with feverish curiosity.

La Belle Sauvage was moving swiftly over the water, and Malcolm dug the paddle in deep and hard as Asta glided to the gunwale. Alice's Ben was a bird as well, and he too flew down to the safety of her shoulder.

"Shush, honey," Alice said, because Lyra was starting to complain. "Soon be away. Shush now."

They were going past a patch of lawn where there were no trees, and Malcolm felt horribly exposed. There was nothing between them and the house, and as he glanced up, he could see the crowd of people moving towards them, with something in the center of them, a small carriage, and people pointing at them, and a distant laugh: "Haa! Haa! Haaa! Haa-haaa!"

"Oh, God," Alice murmured.

"Nearly there," said Malcolm, because they had come to a group of trees that cut off their view of the house, and the garden was behind them. Vegetation clustered thickly on both banks, and the light that came from the tree lanterns was fading quickly the further away they got, so that almost everything ahead was dark.

Almost everything. But there was enough light still in the air for Malcolm to see ahead of them a great pair of iron-bound doors, heavy with age and draped in moss and weeds, emerging from the stream like the gates of a lock, completely shutting off their escape. There was no way out by water.

TWENTY-THREE

ANCIENTRY

Alice couldn't see why they'd stopped, and twisted round to look.

"Ah," she sighed helplessly.

"Maybe we can open them. There must be a way," said Malcolm, peering as closely as he could to right and left. But there was nothing to be seen but clustering bushes and water weeds and low-hanging boughs of yew. They had left the light from the trees behind, and the darkness here seemed to be not just the absence of light but a positive presence, something exuded from the vegetation and the moisture.

Malcolm listened. The only sounds were those of water dripping, lapping, trickling, and perhaps it was the river making its way through the gaps in the ancient gates, where the wood had rotted away, or perhaps it was the endless drops falling from the leaves all around. There was no sound from behind them.

He brought the canoe tight against the gates and stood carefully to feel how high they were. Too high anyway: he could neither see nor reach any top to them. Nor could he see whether they rolled apart to open, or swung slowly round against the resistance of the water, or even lifted up out of it altogether. But the river was still flowing against them, so it must be going underneath, and if there was any mechanism, it must be controlled from the bank.

Still standing up, with his hands on the cold and slimy wood of the doors, Malcolm looked towards the right-hand bank—

—and had such a shock that he started back, swaying the canoe, almost losing his balance, making Alice cry out in alarm.

"What? What?" she said.

She was clutching Lyra tight, trying to peer through the murk, and Malcolm was shakily sitting down.

"There," he said, and pointed at the thing he'd seen.

Thing? It was the head of a man, but huge, emerging from the water among the reeds. He must have been a giant. His hair was tangled with weeds and seemed to be growing through a rusty crown; his skin was greenish, and his long beard trailed over his throat and down into the water. He was looking at them with mild and peaceful interest. As he stood up higher, they saw that his left hand was clasping the shaft of a— What was it? A spear? No, a trident, as Malcolm saw by looking upwards into the darkness, where three points of reflected light shone dimly.

He looked at the giant's face and thought he could see a glimmer of benevolence there.

"Sir," he said, "we'd like to go through these gates, if you please, because we need to escape from someone who's following us. Can you open them for us?"

"Oh, no, I can't do that," said the giant.

"But they're made to be opened, and we need to go through!"

"Well, I can't do that. Them gates en't bin opened for thousands of years. They're for use only in the case of drought in the daily world."

"But if we could just get through—it would only take a couple of seconds!"

402

"You don't know how deep them gates go, boy. It might be just a couple of seconds to you, but there en't enough numbers to calculate how much water'd get through them in a couple of seconds."

"The flood can't get any worse than it is already. Please, mister—"

"What you got in there? Is that a babby?"

"Yeah, it's the Princess Lyra," said Alice. "We're taking her to her father, the king, and there are enemies after us."

"King of where? What king?"

"King of England."

"England?"

"Albion," said Malcolm desperately, remembering something the fairy woman had said.

"Oh, Albion," said the giant. "Well, why didn't you say?"

"Can you open them, then?"

"No. I got me instructions, and that's that."

"Who gave you those instructions?"

"Old Father Thames hisself."

Malcolm thought he could hear the hyena's laugh, and from the way Alice's eyes opened wide, he knew she could too.

"Anyway," he said, "I shouldn't have asked you, because you probably en't strong enough."

"What d'ye mean by that?" said the giant. "I can open them gates, all right. I done it thousands of times."

"What would make you open them again?"

"Orders, that's what."

"Well, as it happens," said Malcolm, fumbling with trembling hands in the rucksack, "we've got these orders from the king's ambassador in Oxford, kind of a passport, so's we can have safe passage. Look."

He pulled a sheet of paper out of one of the cardboard folders and held it up for the giant to see. It was covered in mathematical formulae. The giant peered down at it.

"Hold it up higher," he said. "And it's the wrong way up. Turn it the other way."

It wasn't, but Malcolm did as he said. He was so close that Malcolm could smell his skin, which was redolent of mud, and fishes, and weeds. The giant peered closer still, mouthing something, as if he was reading it, and then nodded.

"Yes, I see," he said. "That's undeniable. I can't argue with that. Let me see the babby."

Malcolm stuffed the paper back in the rucksack and took Lyra from Alice, holding her high so the giant could see. Lyra looked up at him solemnly.

"Ah," said the giant. "I can see she's a princess, all right, bless her. Can I hold her?"

He held out his great left hand.

"Mal," said Alice quietly, "careful."

But Malcolm trusted him. He laid Lyra on the enormous palm, and she gazed up at the giant with perfect confidence, and Pantalaimon sang like a nightingale.

The giant kissed his right forefinger and touched it to Lyra's head before handing her back, very delicately, to Malcolm.

"Can we go through, then?" said Malcolm, who could hear the hyena again, even closer.

"All right, since you let me hold the princess, I'll open the gates for you."

"And then close them again and not let anyone else through?"

"Unless they got orders like what you have."

"Before you do," said Malcolm, "what is that place back there? That garden?"

"That's the place where people go when they forget. You seen the fog on the other side?"

"Yes. And I saw what was behind it."

"That fog's hiding everything they ought to remember. If it ever cleared away, they'd have to take stock of theirselves, and they wouldn't be able to stay in the garden no more. Back off a bit and give me room."

Malcolm gave Lyra to Alice and backed the canoe a few feet, and the giant stuck his trident in the muddy bank and took a deep breath before sinking under the water. A moment later the gates began to stir, creaking, dripping, and slowly, slowly opening against the current, making the water seethe and churn. As soon as the gap was wide enough, Malcolm drove *La Belle Sauvage* forward and through, and into the darkness beyond. The last thing they heard from the garden under the ground was the hyena's distant laughter dying away as the gates closed behind them.

The tunnel to the outside world took about five minutes to paddle through, but it was pitch-dark, so Malcolm had to go slowly, feeling his way from bump to bump. Finally they came to a mass of hanging vegetation, and the fresh smell of the world outside, and after a brief struggle they were through into the open air of the night.

"I don't get it," said Alice.

"What?"

"We went *down* into that tunnel with the rapids, what led us in there, so we should have had to come *up* to get out of it. But this is the same level."

"Still," said Malcolm. "We're out."

"Yeah. Suppose so. And who was *he*?"

"Dunno. Maybe he's the god of a little tributary, like Old Father Thames is the god of the main river, perhaps. That would make sense. George Boatwright said he'd seen Old Father Thames."

"What was it you said Lyra's father was the king of?"

"Albion. It was something the fairy woman said."

"Good thing you remembered it, then."

He paddled on under the moon. The night was quiet and the flood was as wide as the horizon. Little by little Alice subsided into sleep, and Malcolm wondered about pulling the blanket higher around her shoulders, but it wasn't cold.

After half an hour or so he saw an island ahead, just a low, flat piece of land with no trees or buildings, no cliffs, no bushes—not even any grass, by the look of things. He stopped paddling and let the canoe float gently towards it. Perhaps he could tie up here and lie down and rest, though it did seem horribly exposed. The canopy was ideal for concealing the canoe among vegetation, but against bare rocks it would be visible for miles.

But there was nothing he could do about that. He was aching for sleep. He moved *La Belle Sauvage* towards the shore and found a place where a little beach of bare earth lay between the rocks. He let the bow slide up on the soil, and the canoe came to rest. Alice and Lyra lay fast asleep.

Malcolm laid the paddle down and clambered out stiffly. It was only then that he remembered the hole in the hull, the resin patch, and with a heartbeat of anxiety he bent to look, but it was as dry inside as the rest of the hull. The patch had held.

"It's safe," said a voice from behind him.

He nearly fell over from fear. He spun round at once, ready to fight, and then found Asta, cat-formed, springing into his arms, deadly afraid. Looking at them was the strangest woman they had ever seen. She was about the same age as Lyra's mother, to judge by the look of her in the moonlight, and she wore a little coronet of flowers around her head. Her hair was long and black, and she was dressed in black too, or partially dressed, because she seemed to be wearing clustered ribbons of black silk and very little else. She was looking at him as if she'd expected him, and then he realized that there was something missing: she had no dæmon. On the ground beside her lay a branch of pine. Could her dæmon have that form? He felt a shiver of cold run down his spine.

"Who are you?" he said.

"My name is Tilda Vasara. I am the queen of the witches in the Onega region."

"I don't know where that is."

"It's in the north."

"You weren't here a second ago. Where'd you come from?"

"From the sky."

He caught a slight movement in the corner of his eye and turned to the canoe, where he saw a white bird whispering into the ear of Alice's dæmon, Ben. It was the witch's dæmon, there after all.

"They will sleep for the rest of the night now," said Tilda Vasara. "And the people on that boat will not see you."

She pointed past his shoulder, just as he saw a different light catching her eyes. Malcolm turned to look and saw the searchlight on a boat that was either the same CCD vessel that nearly caught them before or a similar one. It was moving steadily towards the island, and Malcolm had to hold himself still because he longed to fling himself to the ground and hide behind anything: a rock, the canoe, the witch. The boat came nearer, the searchlight sweeping to left and right, almost on course to hit the island, but at the last minute it turned a little to starboard and moved past. In the minute or so when it was coming closer, the light became fiercer and brighter, and he saw the witch's face, quite calm, almost amused, and utterly fearless.

"Why didn't they see us?" he said when it had gone.

"We can make ourselves invisible. Their vision slides over us and over anything nearby. You were quite safe. They can't even see the island."

"You know who they were?"

"No."

"They want to catch that baby and . . . I don't know what. Probably kill her."

She looked down where he was pointing at the sleeping Lyra, the sleeping Alice.

"Is she the baby's mother?"

"No, no," said Malcolm. "Just . . . we're just . . . looking after her. But why did the people in the boat turn away when they got close, if they can't see the island?"

"They don't know why. It doesn't matter. They're gone now. Where are you going?"

"To find the baby's father."

"How will you do that?"

"I know his address, at least. I don't know how we'll find it. But we'll have to."

The white bird flew up to her shoulder. He was of a kind Malcolm didn't know, with a white body and wings and a black head.

"What kind of bird is your dæmon?" Asta asked.

"Arctic tern," she answered. "All our dæmons are birds."

Malcolm said, "Why are you here, so far out of the north?"

"I was looking for something. Now that I've found it, I shall go home."

"Oh. Well, thank you for hiding me."

The moonlight shone full onto her face. He'd thought she was young, or no older than Mrs. Coulter, who he supposed was about thirty; her body was slim and lithe, and there were no lines or wrinkles on her face, and her hair was thick and black, with no gray; but somehow the witch's expression made him think she must be indescribably ancient, perhaps as old as the giant under the water. She looked calm and even friendly, but at the same time she looked merciless. And she was curious about him, as he was about her. For a few moments they looked into each other's eyes with complete frankness.

The witch turned away and bent to pick up the pine branch that lay on the ground beside her. She looked back at him once, and again he had that sense of perfect openness, as if they knew each other very well and there were no secrets between them. Then she sprang into the air, holding the branch in her left hand, as her dæmon skimmed down low over Malcolm and Asta in farewell; and then they were gone. For a long time he looked up as her dark shape grew smaller and smaller against the stars. Then there was nothing to show she had ever been there.

He crouched by the canoe and pulled the blanket higher over Alice's shoulders, tucking it around Lyra's head, making sure she could breathe. Pan was curled up like a dormouse between cat Ben's paws, both fast asleep.

"Are you tired?" he said to Asta.

"Sort of. More than tired. Out the other side of tired."

"Me too."

The island was about the size of two tennis courts side by side, and no part of it rose higher than the height of Malcolm's waist above the flood. It was utterly bare: a platform of tumbled rocks with not a blade of grass to be seen, no tree, no bush, nor any moss or lichen. It might have been a part of the moon. Malcolm and Asta walked all round it in little more than a minute, and that was going slowly.

"I can't see any other land either," he said. "It's like the middle of the sea."

"Except that the water's flowing. This is still the flood."

They sat on a rock and watched it go past, a great black sheet of glass full of stars, with the moon shining both above and below.

"I liked that witch," Malcolm said. "I don't suppose we'll ever see another one. She had a bow and arrows."

"When she said she'd found what she was looking for, d'you reckon that was us?"

"What, she came all this way just to look for us? No. She must've had bigger things than that to do. She was a queen. I wish she'd stopped a little longer. We could've asked her all kinds of things."

They sat for a while, and gradually Malcolm found his eyes closing. The night was quiet and the world was calm, and he realized that whatever he and Asta had said to each other a minute before, he felt more tired than ever before in his life, and what he wanted to do most of all was lose consciousness.

"Better get in the canoe," said Asta.

They settled themselves in the boat, having checked that Alice and Lyra were safe and comfortable, and they fell asleep in a moment.

That night, he dreamed of the wild dogs again, his savage dogs, with bloodstained muzzles and torn ears and broken teeth, with wild eyes and slavering jaws and scarred flanks, howling and barking as they raced around him, surging up to lick his face, thrusting themselves at his hands, rubbing themselves against his legs, a tumult of canine fury, with him at its heart and center, humbling themselves before cat-formed Asta; and as before, he felt no fear, he felt nothing but savage exhilaration and boundless delight.

TWENTY-FOUR

THE MAUSOLEUM

They were tired, they were hungry, they were cold, they were filthy, and they were followed everywhere by a shadow. Heavy clouds filled the sky again. Over the gray waste of water Malcolm paddled all the next day while Lyra cried fretfully and Alice lay indifferently in the bow. Whenever they saw a hilltop or a roof rising above the water, Malcolm stopped, tied up, built a fire, and one or the other of them attended to Lyra. Sometimes Malcolm didn't know whether it was him doing it or it was Alice.

And everywhere they went, something went with them, behind, just beyond the edge of eyesight, something that flickered and vanished and then appeared again when they looked at something else. They both saw it. It was the only thing they talked about, and neither could see it fully.

"If it was night," said Malcolm, "it'd be a night-ghast."

"Well, it en't. Night, I mean."

"I hope it's gone by the time it gets dark."

"Shut up. I didn't want to think about that. Thanks for nothing."

She sounded like the old Alice, the first Alice, scornful and bitter. Malcolm had hoped that that Alice had gone for good, but there she was again, sprawling and scowling and sneering; and he couldn't look at her now anyway without an electric tension in his body that he only part understood, and part delighted in, and part feared. And he couldn't talk to Asta about it because they were all so close together in the canoe; and in any case, he felt that his dæmon was in thrall to it too, whatever it was, this bewitchment.

The landscape was changing as they got further down the great flood towards London. Scenes of devastation began to emerge: the shells of houses, their roofs torn off, furniture and clothing strewn all around or caught in bushes and trees; and the trees themselves, stripped of their branches and sometimes of their bark, standing stark and dead under the gray sky; an oratory, its tower lying full-length on the sodden ground, with enormous bronze bells scattered beside it, their mouths full of mud and leaves.

And all the time, never quite forgotten, never fully seen, the shadow.

Malcolm tried to catch it by turning suddenly to the left or to the right, but all he saw was the swift movement that showed where it had been a moment before. Asta watched behind, but she had just the same experience: whenever she looked, it had just moved away.

"Wouldn't matter if it felt friendly," Malcolm muttered to her.

But it didn't. It felt as if it was hunting them.

Seated as they were, with Alice in the bow looking back over the stern, she was more aware of things behind them than Malcolm was, and two or three times during the day she'd seen something else to worry about.

"Is that them?" she said. "The CCD? Is that their boat?"

Malcolm tried to turn and look, but he was so stiff from paddling that it hurt to twist his body, and besides, the heavy gray of the sky and the dark gray of the wind-whipped water made it hard to see anything. Once he thought he could distinguish the CCD colors of navy blue and ocher, and Asta became a wolf cub and uttered an involuntary little howl, but the boat, if that was what it was, soon faded into the murky haze.

Late in the afternoon the clouds darkened, and they heard a rumble of thunder. It was going to rain.

"We'd better stop next place we see," said Malcolm. "We'll put the tarpaulin up."

"Yeah," said Alice wearily. And then, alarmed: "Look. It's them again."

This time when Malcolm turned round, he saw the beam of a searchlight, brilliant against the gloomy sky, sweeping from left to right.

"They just switched it on," Alice said. "They'll see us any minute now. They're coming fast."

Malcolm dug the paddle into the water with limbs that were trembling with fatigue. There was no point in trying to outpace the CCD boat; they'd have to hide, and the only hiding place in sight was a wooded hill with an overgrown grassy space just above the waterline. Malcolm made for it as quickly as he could. It was getting darker rapidly, and the first big drops of rain splashed onto his head and hands.

"Not here," said Alice. "I hate this place. I dunno what it is, but it's horrible."

"There's nowhere else!"

"No. I know. But it's horrible."

Malcolm brought the canoe up onto the lank and sodden grass under a yew tree, tied the painter urgently to the nearest branch, and hastened to fix the hoops into their brackets. Lyra, feeling raindrops on her face, woke up and protested, but Alice ignored her, pulling the coal silk over the hoops and fastening it as Malcolm instructed her. The sound of the engine grew louder and closer.

They got the canopy fixed and sat still, Alice holding Lyra

tight and whispering to keep her quiet, Malcolm hardly daring to breathe. The searchlight shone through the thin coal silk, illuminating every corner of their little enclosed world, and Malcolm imagined the canoe from the outside, hoping passionately that the regular green shape wouldn't show up in the mass of irregular shadows. Lyra looked around solemnly, and their three dæmons clung together on the thwart. The searchlight shone directly at them for seconds that felt like minutes, but then it swung away and the engine noise changed as the steersman opened the throttle and moved off along the flood. Malcolm could hardly hear it over the rain hammering on the canopy.

Alice opened her eyes and breathed out.

"I wish we'd stopped somewhere else," she said. "You know what this place is?"

"What?"

"It's a graveyard. It's got one of them little houses where they bury people."

"A mausoleum," said Malcolm, who had seen the word but never heard it, and pronounced it to rhyme with *linoleum*.

"Is that what it is? Well, I don't like it."

"Me neither. But there wasn't anywhere else. We'll just have to keep tight in the canoe and go as soon as we can."

"How are we going to feed her, then?" said Alice. "Or wash her? You gonna build a fire in the boat?"

"We'll have to wash her in cold water and—"

"Don't be stupid. We can't do that. She's got to have a hot bottle anyway."

"What's the matter? Why are you angry?"

"Everything. What d'you think?"

He shrugged. There was nothing he could do about everything. He didn't want to argue. He wanted the searchlight to go away and never come back. He wanted to talk about the garden under the ground, and wonder with her what it meant; he wanted to tell her what he'd seen beyond the fog bank. He wanted to tell her about the witch and the wild dogs, and wonder what *they* meant. He wanted to talk about the shadow they felt was following them, and agree that it was nothing and laugh about it. He wanted her to admire him for mending the crack in the hull. He wanted her to call him Mal. He wanted Lyra to feel warm and clean and happy and well fed. But none of that was going to happen.

The rain beat on the coal silk with more force every minute. It was so loud that he didn't even notice Lyra crying until Alice leaned forward and picked her up. Even when she was cross with him, she was always patient with Lyra, he thought.

Maybe there'd be some dry wood under the trees. If he went out now, he could get it inside the boat before it got too wet. Maybe the rain would stop soon.

Presently there came another crack of thunder, but further away, and shortly after that the rain did stop coming down so hard; and then it eased off until the only drops falling on the tarpaulin were what dripped down from the branches above.

Malcolm lifted the edge of the canopy. Everything around was still dripping, and the air was as wet as a sodden sponge, full of the smells of dank vegetation, of rot, of earth crawling with worms. Nothing but earth and water and air, and all he wanted was fire.

"I'm going to look for some wood," he said.

"Don't go too far!" she said, alarmed at once.

"No. But we've got to have some if we want a fire."

"Just don't go out of sight, all right? You got the torch?"

"Yes. The battery's nearly dead, though. I can't keep it on all the time."

The moon was still large and the clouds thin as they raced away after the storm, so there was some light from the sky; but under the yew trees it was horribly dark. Malcolm stumbled more than once on gravestones that had half sunk into the soil or were simply hidden in the long grass, and all the time kept an eye on that little building of stone, where bodies were laid to rot without being buried.

And everything was saturated, whether with rain or dew or the remains of the flood; everything he touched was heavy and soaked and rotten. His heart was just like that. He would never manage to light any of it.

But behind the mausoleum, in the dim light of the torch, he found a stack of old fence posts. They were soaking wet, but when he broke one over his knee—with great effort—he found that, inside, it was dry. He could shave some tinder off it, and there were always Bonneville's notes, five volumes of them.

"Don't think of doing that," whispered Asta. She was a lemur perching on his shoulder, her eyes wide.

"They'd burn well."

But he knew he wouldn't do that, not even if they were desperate.

He gathered up half a dozen of the fence posts and brought them around to the front of the mausoleum, where a thought struck him. He shone the torch at the door; it was closed with a padlock.

"What d'you think?" he whispered to Asta. "Dry wood . . ."

"They can't hurt us if they're dead," she whispered back.

The padlock didn't look very strong, and it was easy to thrust the end of a fence post behind it and pull down hard. The lock snapped and fell away. One push, and the door was open.

Malcolm looked in cautiously. The air smelled of age and dry rot and damp, but of nothing worse than that. In the dimly flickering light, they saw rows of shelves, with coffins neatly placed on them, and the wood of the coffins was perfectly dry, as he found when he touched one.

"I'm sorry," he whispered to the occupant of the first, "but I need your coffin. They'll give you another one, don't worry."

The lid was screwed down, but the screws were brass, so they hadn't rusted tight, and he had his knife with him. Only a few minutes later he had the lid off and split into long pieces. The skeleton inside didn't worry him, he found, partly because he was expecting it, and anyway he'd seen worse than that. It must have been a woman, he thought, because around the neck—or where the flesh of the neck had been long ago—was a golden necklace, and there were gold rings on two of the bony fingers.

Malcolm thought about it, and then lifted them all gently away and tucked them down beneath the frail velvet the skeleton was lying on.

"To keep 'em safe," he whispered. "Sorry about your lid, ma'am, truly sorry, but we need it bad."

He set the pieces of the lid against the stone shelf and splintered them with a series of kicks. The coffin's wood was as dry as its occupant, and perfect for burning.

He closed the mausoleum and hung the broken padlock in place so that it looked, at a quick glance, as if nothing had happened. He turned back towards the canoe, signaling once with the torch to let Alice know he was there, and then he saw the shadow.

It was formed like a man—he only saw it for a second and then it darted away—but he knew it at once: it wasn't a shadow at all. It was Bonneville. It had been crouching beside the boat. There was no one else it could have been. The shock was horrible, and he instantly felt even more vulnerable, not knowing where it had gone.

"Did you see—" he whispered.

"Yes!"

He hurried across the gravestone-strewn grass, falling twice, bashing his knee, with Asta darting beside him as a cat, stopping to help, encouraging, watching all around.

Alice had been singing a nursery rhyme. She heard his panting, stumbling approach and stopped, and called, "Mal?"

"Yeah—it's me—"

He played the feeble torch beam on the canopy and then shone it all around on the dark yews, the dripping branches, the sodden ground.

And of course saw no shadow, no Bonneville.

"Did you find some wood?" said Alice from the canoe.

"Yeah. A bit. Maybe enough."

His voice was shaking, but he could do nothing about it.

"What's the matter?" she said, lifting the canopy. "You see summing?"

She was instantly terrified. She knew quite well what he'd seen, and he knew it.

"No. It was just a mistake," he said.

He looked around again, but it took courage: the shadow—Bonneville—could have been hiding among the darkness under any of the trees, behind any of the four columns at the entrance to the mausoleum, or, in the form of something small, behind any of the gravestones. And where was the hyena dæmon? But no, he must be imagining it. They couldn't just paddle away, because this was the only land they'd seen, and it was dark, and out there on the water was the CCD boat, and Lyra needed food and warmth now. Malcolm breathed deeply and tried to stop himself shaking.

"I'll make a fire here," he said.

With the knife, he split some tinder from one of the splintered planks and set a fire on the grass. His hands were only just strong enough to do the work. But it caught at once, and soon one of their last bottles of water was heating in the little saucepan.

He tried not to look up from the flames. The little flicker of the fire made the surrounding darkness even deeper, and made every shadow move.

Lyra was crying steadily, a quiet lament of unhappiness. When Alice undressed her, she just lay there without even trying to move. Asta and Ben tried to comfort Pantalaimon, but he wriggled free; he wanted to be with the little pale form that could only weep and weep.

The coffin lid burned well, and there was enough of it to warm Lyra's milk, but only just. As soon as Alice had her dressed and feeding, the last of the wood flared up in a single yellow flame and went out, and Malcolm kicked the ashes away and gladly got in the canoe. His arms ached, his back ached, his heart ached; the thought of setting off again over the unforgiving water was horrible, even if there'd been no CCD boat searching for them. Body, mind, and dæmon longed for the oblivion of sleep.

"Is there any of that candle left?" said Alice.

"A bit, I think."

He rummaged among the jumble of stuff they'd taken from the pharmacy so long ago, and found a piece of candle about as long as his thumb. He lit it, let a little molten wax gather around the wick, and tilted it out onto the thwart and set the candle upright in it.

He could still do simple, everyday things, then. He hadn't lost the power to live from second to second and to take pleasure, even, in the warm yellow light that filled the canoe.

Lyra twisted in Alice's arms and looked at the candle. Her thumb found her mouth and she gazed solemnly at the little yellow flame.

"What did you see?" Alice whispered.

"Nothing."

"It was him, wasn't it?"

"It might have . . . No. It just looked like him for a second."

"Then what?"

"Then nothing. It wasn't there. There was nothing there."

"We should've made sure of him. Back there, when he nearly got us. We should've done him in proper."

"When someone dies . . . ," he said.

"What?"

"What happens to their dæmon?"

"They just vanish."

"Don't talk about this!" said Asta, and Alice's terrier dæmon, Ben, said, "Yeah, don't say those things."

"Then when there's a ghost, or a night-ghast," Malcolm said, ignoring them, "is that the dead person's dæmon?"

"I dunno. And could someone's body move around, and do things, if their dæmon was dead?"

"You never get a person without a dæmon. It's impossible because—"

"Shut *up*!" said Ben.

"—because it hurts too much when you try and pull apart."

"But I've heard that in some places there can be people without dæmons. Maybe they're just dead bodies walking around. But maybe—"

"Don't! Stop talking about that!" said Asta, and became a terrier, like Ben, and they growled together. But her voice had been terrified.

Then Lyra complained. Alice turned back to her.

"Listen, darling, your milk's all gone. Special treat now, all right? I got a bag full of canopies."

She reached into the bag and pulled out a bit of toast that had once had a quail's egg on it.

"You eat the toast and I'll find the little egg. Little tiny egg. You'll like that."

Lyra took the toast willingly enough and brought it to her mouth.

"You get them from the garden?" said Malcolm stupidly.

"I nicked a whole lot of stuff from the waiters that went past. They never noticed. There's enough for us an' all. Here y'are."

She leaned forward, holding out something the size of Lyra's palm, brown and squashed. It turned out to be a miniature spicy fish cake.

"I suppose," he said with his mouth full, "if she eats enough toast and stuff, it won't matter so much if we run out of—"

He heard something from outside. But it wasn't "something"; it wasn't just an abstract noise, a sound with no meaning. It was the word *Alice*, and it was spoken softly in the voice of Bonneville.

She froze. He couldn't help looking at her, just as children in a classroom can't help looking at the pupil whose name is spoken by a teacher in the tone that means trouble and punishment. He looked for a reaction, instinctively, and at once regretted it. She was terrified. Her face lost all its color, her eyes widened, she bit her lip. And he had stared at her like the child who was safe. He hated himself.

"You don't have to—" he whispered.

"Shut up! Keep quiet!"

They both listened, sitting like statues, straining to hear. Lyra went on sucking and munching at her toast, unaware of anything wrong.

And there was no voice, just the wind passing through the yew trees, just the occasional lapping of water against the hull.

Something strange was happening to the candle. Its flame was burning, it was giving out light, but it had a shadow. The searchlight was back.

Alice gasped and put her hand over her mouth, then immediately took it away and held it close to Lyra to stifle any cry from her. Malcolm saw it all clearly in the cold glare through the canopy, and he could hear the engine noise too. After a few moments the full beam swung away from them, but there was still light nearby, as if the searchers were looking more slowly along the edge, where the water met the graveyard.

"Here," whispered Alice, "take Lyra, because I'm going to faint."

Very carefully, avoiding the candle, she passed the child to him. Lyra came placidly enough, happy with her toast. Alice was pale, but she didn't look like fainting; he thought if she really felt faint, she wouldn't be able to say so; she'd just sink down into oblivion.

Malcolm watched her closely. It wasn't only the light that had frightened her; there'd been that whisper of her name in Bonneville's voice. She looked at the very edge of terror. She sat back and suddenly turned to her left, the side closer to the bank. She was listening. Malcolm could hear a whisper. Her eyes grew wider, more full of horror, or loathing, and she didn't seem to be aware of him or of Lyra anymore, just of that insistent whisper through the coal silk at her side.

"Alice—" he began again, desperate to help.

"Shut up!"

She put her hands over her ears. Ben, terrier-formed, was standing with his back legs on her lap, his forepaws on the gunwale, intent like her on the whisper, which Malcolm could hear now, though he couldn't distinguish the words.

Expressions flitted over Alice's face like the shadows of swift clouds on an April morning; but these expressions were all fear, or disgust, or horror, and looking at her, Malcolm felt he would never see sunlight on a spring morning again, so deep was the anguish and loathing the girl was feeling.

Then the tarpaulin rippled next to her, and Ben jumped back, and then a slit appeared in the coal-silk canopy as a knifepoint moved down it, and then a man's hand reached through and seized Alice by the throat.

Alice tried to scream, but the grip on her throat choked her voice, and then the hand moved down her front, to her lap, searching for something else, feeling left and right—trying to find Lyra.

Alice was moaning, struggling to get away from the loathsome touch, and Ben, terrier-formed, seized the man's wrist in his teeth, despite the disgust it must have caused him; and then, finding no Lyra, Bonneville's hand grabbed the little dæmon and snatched him out through the slit in the canopy, out into the dark, away from Alice.

"Ben! BEN!" Alice cried, and stumbled up and fell across the thwart and half out of the canoe and then scrambled up and was gone after them. Malcolm reached for her, meaning to hold her back, but she was gone before he could touch her. The hyena dæmon laughed, just a couple of feet from Malcolm's ears, splitting the night with her "Haa! Haaaa! Haaa!" And there was an additional note in the laughter, like a scream of agony.

Lyra, terrified by the sound, began to cry, and Malcolm rocked her closely while he called, "Alice! Alice!"

Asta, cat-formed, put her paws on the gunwale and tried to look out from under the canopy, but Malcolm knew she could see nothing. Pantalaimon was fluttering here and there, a moth, landing on Lyra's hand for a moment and flying away again, blundering close to the candle flame and fleeing in fear, and finally settling on the child's damp hair.

From the direction of the mausoleum there came a high, hopeless cry, not a scream, just a desperate wail of protest. Malcolm's heart clenched.

Then there was just the sound of the baby crying in his arms, and the water lapping, and a soft, keening sob from Asta, a puppy, pressing herself against his side.

I'm not old enough for this! Malcolm thought, almost aloud.

He cuddled the child close and pulled the blanket up around her before setting her down among the cushions. Guilt and rage and fear fought one another in his mind. He thought he'd never been more awake in all his life; he thought he'd never sleep again; he thought this was the worst night he'd ever known.

His head was full of thunder. He thought his skull would crack open.

"Asta—" he gasped. "I've got to go to Alice—but Lyra—can't leave her—"

"Go!" she said. "Yes, go! I'll stay— I won't leave her—"

"It'll hurt so much—"

"But we have to— I'll guard Lyra— I won't move—promise. . . ."

His eyes were streaming with hot tears. He kissed Lyra over and over again, and then held puppy Asta to his heart, to his face, to his lips. He set her down next to the child, and she became a leopard cub, so beautiful he sobbed with love.

And he stood up so carefully, so gently, that the canoe didn't rock or move an inch, and he took the paddle and climbed out.

Immediately the deep pain of separation began, and he heard a stifled moan from the canoe behind him. It was like struggling to climb up a steep slope with his lungs clamoring for air and his heart hammering at his ribs, but it was worse: because inside the pain and coloring it, deepening it, poisoning it, there was the horrible guilt of hurting his dearest Asta so much. She was shaking with love and pain, and she was so brave—her eyes were watching him with such devotion as he slowly, unforgivably wrenched his body away from her, as if he was leaving her behind forever. But he had to. He forced himself through the pain, which he knew was tearing at her leopard form without mercy; he dragged himself away from the little boat and up the slope to the dark mausoleum, because something was doing something to Alice and she was crying in wild protest.

And the hyena dæmon, both her front legs gone, was half standing, half lying on the grass, with Ben, the terrier, in her foul jaws.

Ben writhed and kicked and bit and howled, and the monstrous jaws and teeth of Bonneville's dæmon were closing, slowly, voluptuously, ecstatically, on his little form.

Then the moon came out. There was Bonneville in clear sight, his hands gripping Alice's wrists, holding her down on the steps. The cold light was reflected in the hyena's eyes, and in Bonneville's too, and from the tears on Alice's cheeks. It was the worst thing Malcolm had ever seen, and he tore himself through the pain and lurched and stumbled up the slippery grass and raised the paddle and brought it down on the man's back, but feebly, too feebly.

Bonneville twisted, saw Malcolm, and laughed out loud. Alice cried and tried to force the man away, but he slammed her down hard, and she screamed. Malcolm tried to hit him again. The moon shone brilliantly on the sodden grass, the mossy gravestones, the crumbling mausoleum, the figures in their hideous embrace between the columns.

Malcolm felt something grow inside him that he couldn't argue with or control, and it was like a herd of wild dogs, snarling and howling and snapping, racing towards him with their torn ears and blind eyes and bloodied muzzles.

And then they were all around him and through him and he whirled the paddle again and caught the hyena dæmon on the shoulder.

"Ah," said Bonneville, and fell clumsily.

The hyena growled. Malcolm hit her again, full on the head, and she lurched and slid away, her back legs slipping on the grass, her chest and throat bearing all the weight of her as she crushed little Ben. One more blow from the paddle, and Ben fell out of her jaws and scrambled up towards Alice, but Bonneville saw him and kicked out at him, sending him tumbling away over the grass.

Alice cried out in pain. The dogs howled and snarled, and what happened was that Malcolm whirled the paddle again and caught Bonneville hard on the back of the head.

"Tell me—" Malcolm raged, though he couldn't finish the command, and he tried to hold the dogs back with the paddle, but they surged forward again, and Malcolm struck once more, and the figure fell full-length with a long, expiring moan.

Malcolm turned to the imaginary dogs. He felt his eyes throwing fire. But he also knew in that fraction of a second that without the dogs he would find himself giving way to pity, and only with their help could he punish the figure who had hurt Alice. But if he didn't hold them off, he'd never know what Bonneville could tell him—and yet he didn't know what to ask, and if he held them off for a moment too long, they'd go away and take all that power with them. He thought all that in less than a second.

Malcolm turned back to the dying figure. The dogs howled, and Malcolm whirled the paddle again and struck the arm that came up in defense. He had never hit anything so hard. The figure cried out, "Go on, kill me, you little shit! Peace at last."

The dogs surged again, and the man flinched even before Malcolm had moved. If he hit him again, Malcolm knew, he'd kill him, and all the time the terrible, draining separation pain exhausted him, and the knowledge of his brave abandoned dæmon guarding the little child drenched him with misery.

"What's the Rusakov field?" he managed to say. "Why's it important?"

"Dust . . ." It was the last word Bonneville said, hardly more than a whisper.

The dogs were milling around, leaderless. Malcolm thought of Alice, of the fairy arranging her hair, of her sleep-warmed cheeks, and of how it felt to hold baby Lyra in his arms, and the dogs felt his emotion and turned around and leapt forward once more, through

Malcolm, and he raised the paddle and struck again and again till the Bonneville figure fell still, the groaning stopped, all was silent, the hyena dæmon had vanished, and Malcolm was left standing over the body of the man who had pursued them so madly and for so long.

Malcolm's arms, strengthened by days of paddling, now ached with exhaustion. The weight of the paddle itself was too much for him. He dropped it. The dogs had gone. He sat down suddenly and leaned against one of the columns. Bonneville's body lay half in and half out of the dazzling moonlight. A trickle of blood ran slowly down, joining the rain puddles still lying on the steps.

Alice's eyes were closed. There was blood on her cheek, blood dripping down her leg, blood in her fingernails. She was shaking. She wiped her mouth and lay back on the wet stone, looking like a broken bird. Ben was a mouse, trembling at her neck.

"Alice," he whispered.

"Where's Asta?" she mumbled through bruised lips. "How . . ."

"She's guarding Lyra. We had to sep-separate. . . ."

"Oh, Mal," she said, just that, and he felt that all the pain had been worth it.

He wiped his face.

"We ought to drag him down to the water," he said shakily.

"Yeah. All right. Go slowly. . . ."

Malcolm pulled his painful body upright and bent to grasp the man's feet. He began to pull. Alice forced herself up and helped, hauling at a sleeve. The body was heavy, but it came without resistance, without even snagging on the half-buried gravestones.

They came to the water's edge, where the flood was flowing strongly. The CCD boat and its searchlight had gone. They rolled the dead man clumsily over until the current took him away, and then stood clinging to each other and watching the dark shape, darker on the dark water, drift off with the flood till it had vanished.

The candle was still burning in the canoe. They found Lyra fast asleep and Asta, at the end of her strength, lying beside her. Malcolm lifted up his dæmon and hugged her close, and they both wept.

Alice climbed into the canoe and lay trembling as Ben, terrier-formed, licked and licked at her, cleaning the blood from every part. Then she pulled a blanket over them both and turned away and closed her eyes.

Malcolm picked up the child and lay down with her in his arms and their dæmons between them and the blankets wrapped around them both. The last thing he did was to pinch out the candle.

TWENTY-FIVE

A QUIET RODE

The flood was at its height by this time. All across southern England houses and villages were devastated, large buildings were swept away, farm animals were drowned, and as for people, the number of missing or dead was, for the time being, uncountable. The authorities both local and national had to spend every penny in their treasuries and every second of time in the sole task of dealing with the chaos.

Among all the other activities, desperate and urgent as they all were, the two sides that were searching for Malcolm and Lyra made their way steadily downstream towards the capital city. They followed rumors, of which there were many; they ignored every cry for help from the beleaguered people on all sides; they had eyes and minds only for a boy and a girl in a canoe, with a baby, and for a man with a three-legged hyena dæmon.

Like Lord Nugent, George Papadimitriou had experienced the sense of strangeness and unreality that the flood produced. The gyptian owner of the boat he was traveling on told him that in gyptian lore, extreme weather had its own states of mind, just as calm weather did.

"How can the weather have a state of mind?" said Papadimitriou.

The gyptian said, "You think the weather is only *out there*? It's *in here* too," and tapped his head.

"So do you mean that the weather's state of mind is just *our* state of mind?"

"Nothing is *just* anything," the gyptian replied, and would say no more.

They moved on with the flood, speaking to anyone they could find, asking about the canoe and the boy and the girl. Yes, they'd been seen the day before, but no, it wasn't a canoe, it was a dinghy with an outboard engine. Yes, some people had seen them, but they were dead in their boat, or they were water-ghasts, or they were armed with guns. And over and over again: they were spirits, it was bad luck to talk to them, they came from the fairy world. Papadimitriou accepted all this nonsense with serious attention. The CCD in their search would be hearing the same rumors: the problem was not to judge their truthfulness, but to assess the likely reaction of the other side. Nugent and Schlesinger would be faced with just the same problem.

And every hour they came closer to London.

The morning light, as cold and merciless as it could be, woke Malcolm up far earlier than he liked. Aching in every muscle, and aching in his mind when images of the night came back to him, he struggled to sit up and assemble his senses.

Alice was asleep, and so was the child, still and warm in his arms. He wished he hadn't woken; he knew he'd have to wake them, and he wished he could let them sleep. He looked out from under the canopy. The graveyard looked even worse than it had during the night, when the moonlight had at least given it a silvery coherence. In the cruel light of the morning, it looked squalid, neglected, overgrown, and there was something worse: the steps of the little mausoleum were stained with blood, a great deal of it.

For a moment Malcolm felt sick, and closed his eyes and held himself steady. Then the feeling passed. Moving very slowly so as not to waken Lyra, he laid her down among the blankets and climbed out of the canoe, to stand shivering on the sodden grass, taking Asta in his arms. With her now so close, he felt more shaken, sadder, more guilty, much older. She pressed her cat face into his neck. She had been hurt too when they pulled apart; one day, perhaps, they'd be able to talk about it; but for now he felt full of sorrow and regret that he'd hurt her. If it was like his, the pain she was feeling was so deep that it seemed to inhabit every atom of her.

"We couldn't do anything else," she whispered.

"We had to."

"It's true. We did."

Could he wash the blood away? Would the steps ever be clean again? His body quailed.

"Mal? Where are you?"

Alice's voice was faint. He lifted the canopy and saw her face blurred with sleep and still bloody from the night. He reached into the boat and took one of the crumpled towels and dragged it through the grass to moisten it. She took it silently and dabbed her eyes and cheeks.

Then she climbed out too, very painfully, shivering and teeth chattering, and reached in for Lyra.

The child badly needed a change of nappy. She was drowsy; instead of her usual lively chatter, she grizzled unhappily, and Pantalaimon lay limply as a mouse against her neck.

"Her cheeks are red," Malcolm said.

"Prob'ly caught a cold. And we only got one nappy left. I don't think we can go on much longer."

"Well . . ."

431

"We got to have a fire, Mal. We got to clean her, and we got to feed her."

"I'll get some more wood."

He reached in for the paddle, intending first to wash the blood off it, and found a catastrophe.

"Oh, God!"

"What is it?"

The paddle was broken. What he'd done in the night had snapped the shaft. The blade and the handle still held together, but only just; any strain, the slightest push against the water, would break it off entirely. Malcolm turned it over in his hands, dismayed beyond expression.

"Mal? What's the matter?" and then: "Oh, God, what's happened?"

"The paddle's broken. If I use it, it'll just snap. I wish I . . . I wish I'd . . . If only I'd . . ."

He was nearly in tears.

"Can you mend it?"

"I *could* mend it, if I had a workshop and tools."

She was looking around. "First things first," she said. "We got to have a fire."

"I could burn this," he said bitterly.

"No. Don't do that. Get some wood. *Try* to light a fire, Mal. It's really important."

He looked at the listless little child in her arms, the unhappy dæmon pressed so close against her neck, her eyes half closed; she looked ill and weak.

He put the paddle carefully in the canoe.

"Don't touch that," he said. "If it comes apart altogether, it'll be harder to mend. I'll find summing to burn."

He went with slow, reluctant steps up the slope to the mausoleum, avoiding the still-damp blood, and opened the door. He looked respectfully at the coffin he'd opened the night before and murmured, "Good morning, and sorry again, ladies and gentlemen. I'm only doing this because we really need to."

Another fence post, another coffin lid, another skeleton to apologize to, another fire to build. A few minutes later the saucepan was heating almost the last of their clean water, and he went to search among the heap of fence posts for something to mend the paddle with.

The problem was not finding something to bind it to; it was finding something to bind it with—twine, string, any kind of cord. But there was nothing of that sort anywhere. The best thing he could find was a length of rusty wire.

He dragged it out of the heap of fence posts, hauling it loose from the ones it was stapled to, and began to work on the paddle. The wire was stiff and stubborn, and he couldn't wrap it very tightly, but there it was: it was all he had. And there was enough of it to go around several times, so even if the blade broke away completely, it would still be held in a cage of wire.

His hands were cut and scraped and covered in blood-red rust. He rinsed them in the floodwater and noticed that the canoe wasn't floating anymore, but resting on the grass beneath.

"The water's going down," he said.

"About bloody time," said Alice.

He was impatient to be going, and so was she; they got back in the canoe, settled Alice and the child as comfortably as they could, and pushed off once more onto the flood.

The rest of that day was dull going, under a cold gray sky, but they made a fair distance, by Malcolm's reckoning. And the water was going down, and the land they were passing through was more and more urban; there were houses to left and right, roads and shops, and even some people moving about, wading along the streets.

The paddle felt loose and weak, but he didn't have to push against the current, after all. He used it mainly to steer, and he kept as close in to the bank as he could without danger. He and Alice looked intently at the places they passed, because they were both aware, without saying anything about it, of the state Lyra was in.

"Go down there!" said Alice suddenly, pointing to a street of little shops at right angles to the current. It was a struggle to get the canoe to turn and go back, with every nerve in Malcolm's arms aware of exactly how much strain it was putting on the paddle; but finally he had them safely in the backwater that had been a street, and moving laboriously up along the shopfronts.

"There," said Alice, pointing to a pharmacy.

It was closed and dark, of course, but there was someone moving about inside. Malcolm hoped it wasn't a looter. He brought the canoe up next to the door and tapped on the glass.

"Hold her up so he can see," he said to Alice.

The man inside came to the door and looked out. Not an unfriendly face, Malcolm thought, but anxious and preoccupied.

"We need some medicine!" he shouted, pointing at Lyra, who lolled pale in Alice's arms.

The man peered at her and nodded. He gestured: Come round to the back. An alleyway between his shop and the next led to an open door, and the water inside the shop was just as high as it was outside, up to Malcolm's thighs, in fact, as he found when he stepped out and tied the canoe to a drainpipe. It was so cold it shook his heart.

"You better come," he said to Alice. "You can explain what we need."

He took Lyra while Alice got out, gasping at the shock of the cold. He held on to the child as they made their way into the shop.

"I hope the stuff we need en't on the low shelves," he said.

The man met them inside a little kitchenette.

"What is it?" he said, not unkindly.

"It's our little sister," Malcolm said. "She's ill. We got swept down in the flood and we been trying to look after her. But . . ."

The man pulled back Lyra's blanket to look at her face, and put the back of his fingers against her forehead.

"How old is she?" he said.

"Eight months," said Alice. "We just run out of milk powder, and we got nothing else to give her. And we need more nappies, the throwaway ones. Anything babies need, really. And medicine."

"Where are you going?"

"Since we got swept away in the flood, we en't been able to go back home, which is Oxford," Malcolm explained, "so we're trying to get to Chelsea, where her father lives."

"She's your sister?"

"Yes. She's Ellie, and I'm Richard, and this is Sandra."

"Whereabouts in Chelsea?"

The man seemed twitchy, as if he was trying to listen for something else as well as Malcolm's answer.

"March Road," Alice said before Malcolm could speak. "But can you give us some of the things she needs? We en't got any money to pay. Please. We're ever so worried about her."

The man was about the age of Malcolm's father. He looked as if he might be a father himself.

"Let's go and see what we can find," he said loudly, with a false cheerfulness.

They splashed their way through into the front of the shop, where they found a chaos of floating bottles, tubes, cardboard packets gone soggy.

"I don't know if we'll ever recover from this," he said. "The amount of stock that's ruined . . . Now, first of all, give her a spoon-ful of this."

He reached up to a top shelf and took down a box containing a little bottle of medicine and a spoon.

"What is it?" said Malcolm.

"It'll make her feel better. A spoonful every couple of hours. How's her teeth? She started teething yet?"

"She's got a couple," said Alice. "And I think her gums are sore. Maybe there's more coming."

"Let her chew one of these," said the pharmacist, taking a box of hard biscuits from a shelf just above where the water had reached. "What else was it?"

"Milk powder."

"Oh, yes. Lucky about that too. Here y'are."

"This is a different sort from the one we had. Are they made up the same?"

"They're all made up the same. How d'you heat the water?"

"We make a fire. We got a saucepan. That's how we heat her washing water too."

"Very resourceful. I'm impressed. Anything else?"

"Nappies?"

"Oh, yes. They're on the bottom shelf, so none of these'll do. I'll see if there's any out the back."

Malcolm was pouring some of the medicine into the spoon.

"Can you hold her up?" he said, and then whispered, "There's someone else here. He's gone out to talk to 'em."

"I hope it's nice, else she'll spit it out," said Alice, and then whispered, "I seen her. She's keeping out of sight."

"Come on, Lyra," said Malcolm. "Sit up now. Come on, love. Open your mouth."

He put a drop of the pink liquid on her lips. Lyra woke up and began to complain, and then tasted something strange and smacked her lips.

"Taste nice? Here's another drop," said Malcolm.

Alice was looking intently at the reflections in the glass of a medicine cabinet.

"I can see 'em. He's whispering to her . . . and she's going out," she muttered. "Bastards. We better move off quick."

The shopkeeper came back. "Here you are," he said. "I thought I had a few packets left. Anything else you need?"

"Can I take one of these rolls of adhesive tape?" Malcolm asked.

"You'd be better off with individual bandages, wouldn't you?"

"I need it to mend something."

"Go on, then."

"That's very kind of you, sir. Thank you very much."

"What are *you* going to eat?"

"We got some biscuits and things," Malcolm said, as impatient to be away as Alice was.

"Let me go next door—see if I can find you something from the grocer's—I'm sure he won't mind. You wait here a minute. Tell you what. Go upstairs—get out of the water, warm up a bit."

"Thank you very much, but we got to move on," said Alice.

"Oh, no, keep the little one out of the cold for a while. You all look as if you could do with a rest."

"No, thank you," said Malcolm. "We'll go. Thank you very much for these things. We don't want to wait."

The shopkeeper kept insisting, but they moved out and got back into the canoe, cold and wet as they were, and pushed off straight-away.

"He was trying to keep us there while his wife went for the police," said Alice quietly, watching him over Malcolm's shoulder as he paddled them down to the main stream. "Or the CCD."

As soon as they were clear, Malcolm pulled off the rusty wire and wrapped the roll of adhesive tape as tightly as he could around the paddle. It felt better than the wire, but it had little strength, and it wouldn't last very long; but perhaps they didn't have much further to go. He said so to Alice.

"We'll see," she said.

Over the centuries, the engineers and builders of the Corporation of London had learned to make the outward flow of the river and the inward surge of the tide come together more or less smoothly. All the way upriver as far as Teddington, the water level rose when the tide came in and fell when it went out again, and only the skippers and barge owners whose vessels crowded the water and used the city docks took much notice.

But the flood had changed everything. Twice a day, as the tide came in up the estuary, the great weight of the floodwater leaned its might against the sea and tried to force it back; and until the tide turned and went out again, the two vast masses of contending water roiled and seethed in a wild confusion.

All kinds of boating except the most urgent had ceased for the time being. Some barges and lighters held hard to their moorings, though in many cases they were torn loose and swept up or down the river to slam into the embankments, into the wharves and quays or the piers of the great bridges, or to capsize in the surge, or to be carried out to sea and lost.

A number of bridges were shaken badly. Only Castle Bridge and Westminster Bridge held fast entirely. Black Friars, Battersea, and Southwark collapsed, their debris adding to the churning turmoil as the waters met. In the small powerboat he'd hired, Bud Schlesinger rode the wild water, scouring the chaos all around with his eyes, and trying to calm the fears of the owner.

"There's too much debris in the water!" the man shouted. "It's dangerous! It could smash open the hull!"

"Where's Chelsea?" Schlesinger called back from the bow, where he was leaning out and trying to keep the rain out of his eyes.

"Further on," the owner shouted. "We got to pull in and tie up! This is crazy."

"Not yet. Is Chelsea on the left bank or the right?"

The owner shouted back, "Left!" followed by a string of curses. The boat plunged on. The embankments on both sides, as far as Schlesinger could see, were under several feet of water, and on the right a large submerged park spread out beyond a line of great bare trees, whereas on the left a succession of imposing houses and stately apartment buildings stood silent and deserted.

"Slow down a little," Bud called, and made his way to the cockpit at the stern. "You ever heard of October House?"

"Big white place further down— *What the hell's that fool doing?*"

A powerful boat with a navy-blue-and-ocher hull had surged up close, crowding them on the starboard side. A deckhand with a boat hook leaned out and tried to hit Schlesinger, but he swayed back and let it pass in front of him. The man nearly overbalanced, but held on to the rail and swung the boat hook round in another attempt. Schlesinger drew his pistol and fired above the boat, and by sheer luck hit the boat hook, knocking it out of the man's hand.

"You can't do that!" wailed the owner of Bud's boat, throttling back hard. The bigger boat lunged ahead, but then met some obstruction in the water and reared up suddenly. Bud could see the helmsman wrestling with the wheel, trying to get the vessel to turn to starboard, but clearly there was something impeding the propeller. The engine screamed and the boat lost way, and in a few seconds was wallowing helplessly behind them.

"What the bloody hell!" Bud's helmsman was almost incoherent. "Didn't you see the colors? You know what they were?"

"CCD," said Bud. "We gotta get to October House before they do."

"Insane!"

The man's dog dæmon was crouching beside his legs, shivering. The owner shook his head but pushed the throttle forward a notch. Bud wiped the rain from his eyes and looked all around: in the spray and the confusion there were many shapes on the water, and it was impossible to tell which of them might be a canoe with a boy and a girl and a baby.

Half a mile downstream, Lord Nugent's boat slammed into the landing at the foot of a great lawn leading up to a white building in the classical style. The landing stage was under the surface, of course, and it was only the hull of the boat that made contact with it, and there was nowhere to tie up; but Nugent was over the side in a moment, waist-deep in the freezing water, and wading, trying to hold his balance in the strong current, up towards what looked like a massive boathouse at the left of the lawn, whose front, open to the surging river, glowed with anbaric light. There were sounds from inside that came clearly even over the storm and the rage of the water: hammering, drilling, a turbine-like whine.

Nugent made it, still knee-deep, and grasped the handle of a door on the landward side. He hauled it open and went in. Under the glare of floodlights, no doubt powered by the generator that was thudding just outside the door, half a dozen men were working on a long, slender boat. Nugent couldn't see what they were doing: he had eyes only for the man who was crouching on the foredeck, using a welding torch.

"Asriel!" he called, and hurried forward along the temporary decking towards the boat.

Lord Asriel pushed up the mask that covered his face and stood, astonished.

"Nugent? Is that you? What are you doing here?"

"Is this boat ready to go out on the water?"

"Yes, but—"

"If you want to save your daughter, take it out right now. I'll come with you and explain. Don't waste a second."

As *La Belle Sauvage* floated more and more swiftly down into London, the tide was nearing its height, and the consequences for the little canoe were serious. Slammed this way and that, battered by lurching waves and crosscurrents, she kept her course as well as Malcolm could manage, but every time she twisted on the rough water, he heard a creak, as if part of her framework was giving way. If only they could stop . . .

But they couldn't stop. They couldn't stop anywhere. As if the tide wasn't enough, a wind had begun to blow, and was lashing the water into white-topped waves and whipping off the spray; and the sky above, gray and cold and dull all day, had been invaded by hefty rain-bearing thunderclouds. Malcolm kept turning this way and that to look for a place to put ashore, so as to attend to that horrible creak that he could hear now even above the wind, and he could feel it too, a sickening twist that began as the merest suspicion of structural looseness but soon became bigger with every lurch, every sideways rise and fall.

"Mal—" Alice called.

"I know. Hold on."

They were swept onwards past a great palace set so far back in its garden that he could hardly see it through the rain, past streets of elegant brick houses, past a pretty oratory; and whenever he thought he could see shelter, he dug the paddle deep and tried to turn towards it, but it was hopeless; and now the blade was coming loose again, to make everything worse.

Through the murk ahead, he could just see four huge chimneys on the southern bank, rising from each corner of a great clifflike building. Were they near Chelsea? And if they were, how could he stop?

Alice was holding Lyra tight. He felt a surge of love for them both, of love and of infinite regret that he'd brought them into this; but he couldn't dwell on that because there was a new sound now, piercing the noise of the wind and the battering rain: a siren—an alarm—shrieking behind them, its cry like a seabird tossed and flung this way and that in the buffeting air. Alice was straining to see over his shoulder, clutching Lyra to her chest, hand up to keep the rain out of her eyes—and at the same time Malcolm heard a clangor of bells from directly ahead.

And other sounds came to them on the pummeling wind—the roaring beat of an engine, the creak and howl of great masses of wood being crushed together, human cries. Malcolm could focus on none of them. *La Belle Sauvage* was worrying him to madness—was she breaking apart?

Suddenly there came a massive blow from something behind: a powerboat—Malcolm could hear the engine screaming as the propeller rose out of the water, and hear Alice scream over that, and then feel the thrust and shudder as the propeller plunged into the water again and forced the boat against the little canoe. What were they doing? Alice was shouting—her words were snatched away like a piece of paper—another crash as the navy-blue-and-ocher hull of the powerboat shouldered the canoe sideways in the water, and *La Belle Sauvage* leaned over and shipped a heavy wave before swinging upright again. Malcolm was fighting now with every little fraction of his strength, digging the paddle deep, leaning into the stroke, heaving hard—and nursing the broken thing, which was finally coming apart. He snatched off the useless blade and flung it backwards spinning through the air. Was there a crash of broken glass? A shout of anger?

Impossible to hear because now another powerboat, the higher note of a different engine, screamed in from the right and smashed into the first—Malcolm could see nothing: the lashing rain drenched his eyeballs, and the wild confusion of sound and the lurching, smashing, pitching, plunging movements of the canoe were his only guide.

And then a gunshot—two more—four more from a different gun—a sudden immense shock, and immediately the freezing water began to gush in, and nothing would ever stop it now.

Another smash against the wounded canoe, this time from the right. A powerful deep voice roaring, "Pass her up to me!"

Lord Asriel . . .

Malcolm wiped his right hand across his eyes and saw Alice trying to hold Lyra away from the hands that reached down, and he screamed, "Alice! It's all right! Pass her up!"

One wild look from her, and he nodded as hard as he could— "Pass her up!" again in that harsh, deep shout—and Alice thrust the child up, and Lyra was screaming, and those hands snatched her, thrust her backwards, and then, before Alice could move, seized one of her wrists and hoisted her instantly up too, as if she weighed no more than the baby. Ben, as a little monkey, was clinging to her waist.

The first boat had swung back. Now it smashed into the canoe again, a deathblow, and the brave little boat was broken open like an egg. Both Malcolm and Asta cried out with love.

"Now you, boy!" That huge voice again.

Balancing knee-deep in the surging water, Malcolm swung the rucksack up. It was hard to lift with one hand, and those hands from above pushed it aside. "You—you fool!"

"Take this first!" Malcolm screamed, and Alice was shouting too: "Take it, take it!"

Out of his grasp it sprang upwards and vanished, and then he stood in the sinking canoe with Asta as a snake coiled tightly around his leg, and an iron-hard hand closed around his right arm and swung him up, and then he fell on a wooden deck with a crash that knocked every scrap of air out of his lungs, and he stared down with rain-lashed, tear-filled eyes as the little *Belle Sauvage*, smashed to matchwood, died and was borne away forever.

Nothing then but noise and the plunging, thumping, swinging of the powerboat on the wild water. Malcolm scrambled across to Alice, dragging the rucksack, and they sat clinging together with the child between them, all their dæmons clinging together too, as suddenly the movement stilled, the engine fell silent, and they were inside a great shed with anbaric lights blazing down at them.

Malcolm felt a wave of exhaustion move slowly through him from feet to head.

Asriel was shouting, "What the hell do you think you were playing at?"

Malcolm gathered his strength to sit up and answer, but he had none left. Alice leapt to her feet instead, and stood with fists clenched, facing Lord Asriel, and Ben, her dæmon, bristling with defiance as a wolf, bared his teeth beside her. Her voice was like a whip.

"Playing? You think we were *playing*? This was Mal's idea. He said we'd bring Lyra to you to keep her safe, because by God there was nowhere else she'd be safe. I was against it because I thought it was impossible, but he was stronger than me, and if he says he'll do something, he'll bloody do it. You don't know nothing about him to ask a stupid question like that. *Playing!* You dare even *think* that. If I told you half of what he's done to keep us alive and safe, well, you wouldn't imagine it could be true. You couldn't dream of it. Whatever Mal says, I believe. So take that fucking smile off your face, you."

Malcolm was barely conscious now. He thought he was dreaming. But the expression on Lord Asriel's face, warm with amusement and admiration for Alice, was too real to be imagined. He dragged himself to his feet and said hoarsely, "Scholastic sanctuary. We tried to get her to Jordan College, but the flood was too strong, and anyway, I don't know the words. The Latin words. So we thought you might . . ."

And he held out with trembling fingers the little white card that he'd found in the canoe.

Lyra was crying passionately. Once again Malcolm tried to hold himself steady, but it was too hard altogether. Just before he fainted, he heard someone say, "The boy's bleeding—he's been shot. . . ."

When he came to, it was in a different space, small, hot, close to the drumming of a gyropter engine, lit by the glow of an instrument panel. His left arm was ablaze with pain. Where had that come from?

Someone squeezed his right hand. It was Alice.

"Where's Lyra?" he managed to say.

She pointed to the floor. Lyra lay wrapped up as tightly as a mummy, fast asleep, and Pan lay coiled around her neck as a little green snake.

Asta was lying, cat-shaped, on Malcolm's lap. He tried to stroke her with his left hand, but that made his arm throb with even more pain. She stood up and rubbed her face against his.

"Where are we?" he whispered.

"In a gyropter. He's flying it."

"Where are we going?"

"He didn't say."

"Where's the rucksack?"

"Behind your legs."

He felt for it with his right hand: there it was, safe. He felt his left arm delicately, and found a rough bandage covering the forearm.

"What happened?" he said.

"You got shot," said Alice.

The gyropter was shaking and swaying, but Alice was calm enough, so Malcolm decided not to be anxious. The engine was so loud and so close that it was difficult to hear each other anyway. He leaned back in the hard seat and fell asleep.

Alice adjusted the way he was lying so he wouldn't wake up with a stiff neck. Over the thudding of the engine, she heard Asriel shout something and thought she heard her name. She leaned forward and shouted back, "What? I can't hear you."

There was another man in the copilot's seat, some sort of servant. He twisted around and handed her earphones, and showed her how to put them on and bring the microphone round in front of her mouth. Suddenly Lord Asriel's voice was loud and clear.

"Listen carefully, and don't interrupt. I'm going away, and I won't be back for some time. I want to find the child safe when I come back, and the best way to ensure that is to keep yourself and Malcolm quiet and inconspicuous. You understand what I mean?"

"You think I'm stupid?"

"No, I think you're young. Go back to the Trout. I know you work there; I saw you. Go back there and take up your life again. Tell no one about any of this. Oh, you can talk to Malcolm, of course, but not a word to anyone else except the Master of Jordan College. He's a good man; you can trust him. But there are all kinds of dangers ready to pounce when the flood goes down."

"What, the CCD, you mean? Why do they want her?"

"I haven't got time to explain. But they'll be watching you, and they'll be watching Malcolm, so stay away from her for a while. I'd take her with me into the far north, where the dangers are open and obvious, except for one thing."

"What?"

"She seems to have found some good guardians already. She must be lucky."

He said no more. Alice took off the earphones. She bent down to touch Lyra's forehead, but the child was fast asleep, with no fever. Greyhound Ben licked Pantalaimon's emerald serpent head, and Alice took Malcolm's right hand and closed her eyes.

And almost at once, it seemed, they were descending. Malcolm felt a lurch in his stomach and clenched his muscles against it; but it only lasted a few moments, and then the aircraft settled on the ground. The engine noise changed, becoming quieter, and then stopped altogether. Malcolm's ears were ringing, but he did hear the hammering of rain against the body of the gyropter, and heard Lord Asriel's voice above it: "Thorold, stay here and guard the machine. I'll be ten minutes."

Then he turned and said over his shoulder, "Get out and follow me. Bring the child, and bring your bloody rucksack."

Alice found a door on her side and scooped up Lyra before scrambling out. Malcolm hauled the rucksack along and got out the same side, into the bitter wind and the teeming rain.

"This way," said Lord Asriel, and hurried off.

A flash of lightning showed Malcolm a great domed building, walls of stone, towers, and treetops.

"Is this . . . ," said Alice.

"Oxford, yes. This is Radcliffe Square, I think—"

Lord Asriel was waiting at the entrance to a narrow lane lit by a flickering gaslamp. The rain made every surface shiny. His black hair glinted like stone.

He set off down the lane, and after a hundred yards or so, he took a key from his pocket and opened a door in the wall on the right.

They followed him into a large garden, overlooked by buildings on two sides. In one of them, large Gothic windows were lit, showing shelves of ancient books. Lord Asriel made straight for a corner of the garden under a high stone wall and went along a narrow passage that was lit, like the lane outside, by a flickering yellow light on the wall.

"Let me take the child," he said.

Alice handed her over carefully. Lord Asriel's dæmon, the powerful snow leopard, wanted to see her, and Lord Asriel crouched down to let her put her face next to the sleeping child. Malcolm shifted the rucksack awkwardly, and an idea came to him. He'd never managed to give Lyra the little toy he'd made, but perhaps . . .

"Is this Jordan College?" he said.

"As you suggested. Come on. We must be here and gone for this to work."

He stopped by a large door set between two elegant bay windows, and knocked loudly. Malcolm, ignoring the awful pain in his left arm, rummaged at the bottom of the rucksack for the alethiometer in its black velvet cloth. The cloth fell open as he brought it out, and the gold glittered in the dim light.

"What's that?" said Lord Asriel.

"It's a present for her," said Malcolm, and thrust it in among Lyra's blankets.

They heard the sound of a key turning and bolts sliding back, and as thunder crashed overhead, the door opened to show a distinguished-looking man holding a lamp. He peered out at them in astonishment.

"Asriel? Can that be you?" he said. "Come inside, quickly."

"Put your lamp down, Master. On the table—that'll do."

"What in the world—"

When the Master turned back, Lord Asriel put the child in his arms before he could protest.

"*Secundum legem de refugio scholasticorum, protectionem tegimentumque huius collegii pro filia mea Lyra nomine reposco,*" Asriel said. "Look after her."

"Scholastic sanctuary? For this child?"

"For my daughter, Lyra, as I said."

"She's not a scholar!"

"You'll have to make her into one, then, won't you?"

"And what about these two?"

Asriel turned to look at Malcolm and Alice, sodden, shivering, filthy, exhausted, bloody.

"Treasure them," he said.

Then he left.

It was no good; Malcolm couldn't stand up any longer. Alice caught him and laid him on the Turkish carpet. The Master shut the door. In the sudden silence, Lyra began to cry.

Now strike your sails yee jolly Mariners,
For we be come into a quiet rode,
Where we must land some of our passengers,
And light this weary vessel of her lode.
Here she a while may make her safe abode,
Till she repaired have her tackles spent,
And wants supplied. And then againe abroad
On the long voyage whereto she is bent:
Well may she speede and fairely finish her intent.

EDMUND SPENSER, *The Faerie Queene*, I XII 42

To be continued . . .

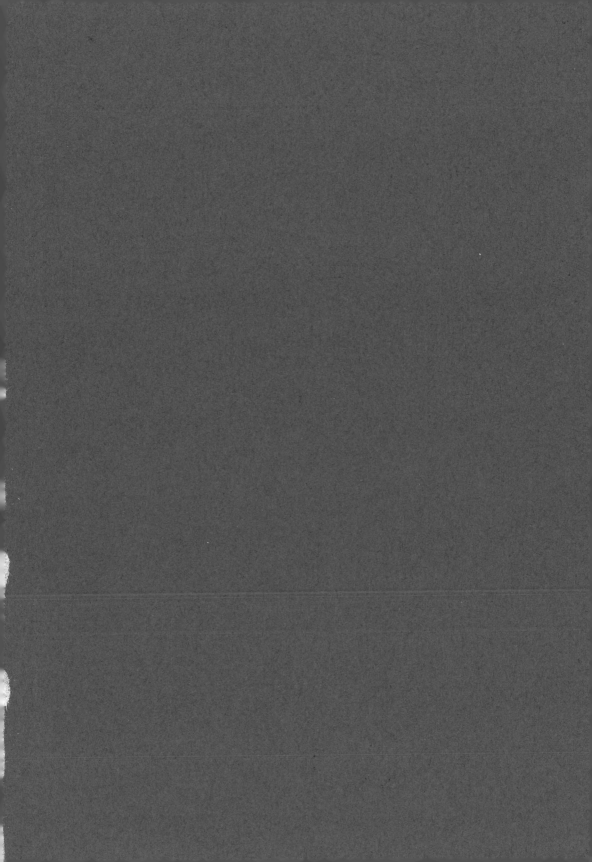